Odin's Island

JANNE TELLER was born to Austrian and Danish parents in Denmark, but since 1988 has lived all over the world. These days she splits her time between Milan, Paris and Copenhagen. *Odin's Island* was her first novel, and has been translated into five languages. Her second novel, *Nothing*, written for young adults, was awarded the Danish Cultural Ministry Prize for best children's/youth book of 2001. Teller has received numerous literary grants and awards over the years and her controversial books have repeatedly sparked heated debate in Denmark.

ANNE BORN won the *Independent* Foreign Fiction Prize in 2006 for her translation of *Out Stealing Horses* by Per Petterson. She was also shortlisted for the Impac prize, Dublin, for her translation of *An Altered Light* by Jens Christian Grøndahl. She lives in South Devon and Oxford.

ODIN'S ISLAND

Janne Teller

Translated by Anne Born

ATLANTIC BOOKS
LONDON

First published in Denmark by Forlaget Centrum,
Denmark, in 1999 as *Odins Ø*.

First published in Great Britain as a Paperback Original in 2006
by Atlantic Books, an imprint of Grove Atlantic Ltd.

1 3 5 7 9 8 6 4 2

A CIP catalogue record for this book is available from the British Library.

ISBN 10 1 84354 348 6
ISBN 13 978 1 84354 348 0

Design by Lindsay Nash
Typeset by Avon DataSet Ltd, Bidford on Avon, Warwickshire
Printed in Great Britain by
Clays Ltd, St Ives plc

Atlantic Books
An imprint of Grove Atlantic Ltd.
Ormond House
26–27 Boswell Street
London wc1n 3jz

Contents

GINNUNGAGAP

First there was nothing
and this nothing was a nothingness
a chasm where nothing was chaos
and chaos was nothing

For this is how we know Ginnungagap

THE DAY ODIN arrived in Smith's Town was a cold one. The earth was covered in snow and the sun shone through a faint mist. On one side of him a group of children were skating on a frozen pond, and in a paddock opposite three shaggy ponies huddled together to keep warm. In front of him, down the narrow road almost blotted out by the snow, he could just discern a small clump of thatched cottages with smoke spiralling from their chimneys. Otherwise nothing at all except field after field as far as the eye could see.

Odin glanced at his own two horses, standing beside him. Or maybe standing wasn't the right word, for while one of them was certainly standing erect with his weight spread equally on all four solid legs, the other leaned perilously to the left to avoid putting weight on her right foreleg, which dangled helplessly in the air. It was a sad sight, such a strong horse with a broken leg and her head hanging down mournfully. Odin heaved a deep sigh; what was he going to do? Again he surveyed the scene around him, but apart from the children there was not a soul to be seen.

'Ah well, there's no doubt at all that we shan't be going any further today,' he said to the horses and began to unharness them from the small green sledge. He wondered whether Balthazar, who still had four serviceable legs, could pull the sledge on his own. Not that Odin thought for a moment of leaving Rignarole where she was. Out of the question. But he had to go and look for help. Odin unhitched the traces and freed the lame horse. But how was he to avoid Balthazar pulling on his side of the shaft and sending them straight into the ditch? Odin soon realized he wouldn't get far like that.

It was at this moment that the skaters caught sight of the stranger standing in the road with his two horses and a sledge as if he had materialized out of the icy blue air. Couple after couple came to a halt until all the children had assembled along the lakeshore from where they gazed at the stranded man. There were twelve children from about three to ten years old. To start with, they stared at the unusual sight in total silence. Then, as if responding to a secret sign, they all began to chatter at once.

'His horse is almost falling down,' said one, whose name was Ejner.

'Those horses do look funny. I bet they can't run nearly as fast as Rufus with those heavy legs of theirs,' said another, called Lauge.

'Do you think he's dangerous?' asked a small boy, starting to cry.

'I've never seen a man with such a long beard before,' a girl said, stepping back a little way.

'And what a weird coat.'

'He won't be going anywhere with that horse, that's for sure!'

'I wonder where he comes from?' murmured a girl called Ida-Anna, scratching her head thoughtfully. She seemed to be the eldest, and as if to demonstrate her position as leader she straightened her back and declared in a firm voice: 'We must do something.'

'We must do something!' echoed the other children in one voice, looking at each other as if not quite sure what should happen next. Then they all turned to look at Ida-Anna, waiting for her to decide the fate of the stranger and his two horses.

'Two of us must run home for help, two others go up for a closer look at them, and the rest wait here.'

There was a slight ripple of dissatisfaction, but no one said anything, and most of the children nodded with a seriousness demanded by the situation.

'Good,' went on Ida-Anna. 'Lauge and Troels, you run home. Ask the Blacksmith and Uncle Eskild to come at once. Ingolf, you come with me. And Ejner, look after the others.' Well pleased with her own resolution, Ida-Anna took her little brother Ingolf's hand, and without a trace of hesitation she set off towards the stranger and the two horses.

While all this was going on Odin had had an idea. He had unfastened the trace from the sledge on Balthazar's near side and was now attaching it to a piece of trace from Rigmarole's harness, so both sides of the sledge would take the same load even if only one horse was pulling. But the leather had grown stiff in the hard frost, and Odin struggled to join the two pieces. He heaved and tugged until the sweat began to run down his forehead and blur his eyesight, but the obstinate knot would not give by as much as a millimetre. Rigmarole watched her master's efforts with big sorrowful eyes as she struggled to keep her balance on her three functioning legs. So Balthazar was the first to catch sight of the two children who approached the sleigh. He turned his head to see them better, and his movement made Odin look up.

'Well, well,' he mumbled, without stopping what he was doing.

Ida-Anna and Ingolf stopped ten metres from the sleigh. Although she didn't want to admit it, Ida-Anna was ready to turn on her heel and run if anything unexpected should happen. But nothing did. The stranger merely went on tying the reins together in big untidy knots, whistling a strange melody all the while, and the horses stood quite still. The children moved closer cautiously, one step at a time, and not until they were just a few metres from the stranger did they notice how small he was; not much bigger than they were. The horses, which at a distance had seemed so huge, were not much taller than the ponies in the field opposite. Yet the stranger's horses looked more powerful than any others Ida-Anna had ever seen. Their legs were as muscular as the Blacksmith's, their backs as wide as her mother's dining table, and their coats as thick and bristling as her own hair. The strangest thing of all, though, was their colour. Both horses were yellow with black manes and tails. But the yellow was more like sunlight than the colour yellow, and the black was more like the darkness of night than the colour black. Ida-Anna shook her head; never before had she seen the like.

Odin paid no heed to the children but continued to work on the harness, and Ida-Anna and Ingolf took another step forward. If Ida-Anna stretched out her hand now she could reach Rigmarole, who looked suspicious and did not quite know what to make of the situation. She was a good-natured horse, and in spite of her unfortunate condition she raised her head and gave a friendly little snort. This made Ida-Anna forget her fear, and she held out her hand, as the Blacksmith had taught her, palm up and flat. She need not have been afraid. The horse sniffed cautiously at her hand and blew out until her breath tickled Ida-Anna's hand so that she could not help laughing aloud.

'Ah well, that's all right then, you've found some friends, have you.' Odin straightened up and patted his horse's neck. Then he looked at the children. Both were warmly clad from top to toe, only their red-cheeked faces were visible. With grey-blue eyes, freckled snub noses and reddish blonde fringes peeping out under their grey caps, the children looked very alike. The girl was just a few centimetres taller than the boy, though, and she gave an unmistakable impression of being the one in charge. Odin addressed her with the courtesy he felt circumstances required. 'How do you do?' He gave a deep bow and almost brushed the snow with his forehead.

'How do you do,' mumbled Ida-Anna, and because she didn't know what to say to a stranger, and because it would be extremely rude to say nothing at all, she directed a few comforting noises at the horse with the broken leg.

Odin wiped his brow with his sleeve.

'I beg your pardon, Miss,' he said, pulling his long white beard. 'But to tell the truth, we have strayed off course a little and lost our way. If I may be so bold, would you be in a position to tell me where in the world I and my two horses find ourselves?'

Ida-Anna laughed, suddenly overwhelmed by courage.

'Don't you know you're in Smith's Town, the most important

village east of Post Office Town?' Not until then had Ida-Anna noticed that the stranger had only one eye. Where the other eye had been, or where it should have been, the eyelid was tightly closed over its hollow space. Ida-Anna took a closer look at the stranger. He was old, older than anyone Ida-Anna had ever known. His hair was long and white, and his beard was even longer and still whiter, and the skin of his face was dark and full of wrinkles and furrows, as if he had been very close to the sun for a really long time. He wore a long coat made of something that looked like sheepskin, and his clumsy boots also looked as if they had once belonged to a sheep. He certainly was a remarkable man. However, Ida-Anna's information didn't seem to help him at all.

The little old man merely furrowed his already immensely wrinkled brow and asked: 'I wonder if you would be kind enough to tell me the precise position of the stars around us. You see, my horse has broken her leg, and I am on the horns of an exceptionally troubling dilemma.' Odin added this last sentence because he felt he was asking the kind girl for too much, and he did not want to seem either pressing or impolite.

At this point the conversation could have landed in difficulties, since Ida-Anna had no idea of either stars or positions or horses with broken legs. But luckily in the meantime Lauge and Troels had run as fast as they could back to the village and gathered the grown-ups, and now the Blacksmith and Uncle Eskild were coming in all haste with a delegation consisting of the entire population of Smith's Town – not counting Oldmother Rikke-Marie, who was old enough to think the world should come to her and not the other way around.

The Blacksmith was an impressive man, at least a head taller and a good few centimetres broader than anyone else in Smith's Town, and when he stopped a couple of metres in front of Odin, all the other villagers also came to a halt abruptly.

'Hmm, hmm,' rumbled the Blacksmith, trying to assess the situation. With demonstrative calm which had nothing to do with his actual feelings, he removed a ferociously smoking pipe from his mouth and cleared his throat again. 'Hmm, hmm, not wanting to seem impolite, but your horse there has a broken leg!' he declared loudly, pointing at Rigmarole with the stem of his pipe. Then he looked at his fellow villagers, and when they all nodded affirmatively, he went on: 'Everyone knows, if I may be so bold, that the people of Smith's Town pride themselves, and not without reason if I may say so, in being very hospitable folk, but who are you?'

'My name is Odin,' said Odin, bowing low. This did not seem to make much impression on the villagers, and he felt bound to explain further. 'I have travelled a long way, and I still have far to go. But I lost my way in a meteor storm. Rigmarole broke her leg, and well, here we are.'

The Blacksmith, who knew very well that there were things in this world he had no knowledge of, but who did not wish to reveal this ignorance to the other villagers, took no notice of Odin's mention of a meteor storm, and later in the day when someone else came to wonder about it, the Blacksmith insisted that 'meteor storm' was merely another term for a particularly violent snowstorm. For the present he chose to concentrate on the problem of the horse, for no one knew more about horses than the Blacksmith of Smith's Town.

'I don't want to be rude, but a horse with a broken leg is, all things considered, the same as no horse at all,' he said solemnly.

'Yes,' nodded Odin, 'I am on the horns of an exceptionally troublesome dilemma. You see, to tell the truth, I am not a little pressed for time. And now I will have to wait until Rigmarole's ill-fated leg is quite healed.' Odin looked anxiously at his horse.

'I don't want to seem impolite, but I know what I'm talking about. The best thing you can do for this one is to put him down.' Again the Blacksmith pointed at Rigmarole, who collapsed to the ground in sheer terror.

'There, there! There, there!' exclaimed Odin, laying a hand on the mare's neck.

'Yes, better put an end to his suffering once and for all,' said the Blacksmith consolingly.

'No, no, that is out of the question!' Odin tugged at his beard. How would he get anywhere with only one horse? 'Surely there is some learned person in these parts or not far away who can deal with Rigmarole's leg?'

Now the Blacksmith was lost for words; he was well aware of the feelings a man can cherish for his horse, but he also knew there was no doctor in Smith's Town, and that the doctor in Post Office Town, who could sometimes work miracles, would never go near a horse and would refuse to do so until his dying day. No, it would never do to even think of that. For the first time in anyone's memory, including his own, the Blacksmith didn't know what to say. And while the Blacksmith searched for the best way of saying nothing, Mother Marie – who was mother to Ida-Anna and Ingolf – decided it was time someone did something or other. Mother Marie was getting cold, and she had a plump duck on the fire which would certainly be badly burned unless she took it off very soon.

'While you men are considering what's to be done with the

poor wretched creature, it's up to someone else to invite our guest into the warm and pour him a glass of Yuletide brew. When all's said and done, it is Christmas time, let's not forget,' said Mother Marie, and all the villagers nodded emphatically to affirm that the people of Smith's Town would be only too glad to invite the stranger for a glass of Yuletide brew. It was not for nothing that Smith's Town was renowned far and wide for hospitality.

Mother Marie didn't wait for an answer, but resolutely took Odin's arm and set off down the road to the village. Ida-Anna's mother was a robust lady, with a round stomach and two strong long legs, and rather than walking along beside her Odin seemed to hang on her arm with the toes of his boots hovering just above the snow.

Alarmed at the prospect of being left alone with the man who thought the best thing was to kill her – and, moreover, thought she was a he – Rigmarole now began to move her legs about so fast that it looked as if she possessed eight legs, of which only one was useless. A billow of snow rose into the air and made the villagers step back. Amazingly, the mare lifted herself up from the ground and flew – later the villagers would swear to their neighbours in Post Office Town that when they said flew they meant flew – through the air to the sledge, where she let herself slide down on to the wide thickly upholstered seat. As soon as his mate was sitting comfortably, Balthazar leaned forward, dug his hooves deep down into the snow and exerted all his strength. His muscles rippled under the golden coat, the blood in the veins in his head and down his legs stood out. The recalcitrant knots tautened with a crack, and the sleigh moved slowly along the road after Odin.

From the head of the cavalcade Mother Marie and Odin

could not see what was going on. But the rest of the villagers were dumbfounded. Never before had they seen a horse rise up above the ground. And never before had a single one of them, not even the Blacksmith, who otherwise knew everything worth knowing about horses, seen one horse pulled in a sledge by another. The residents of Smith's Town rubbed their eyes to reassure themselves they were not dreaming. Then they turned their gaze on the Blacksmith. But he uttered not a word, and as long as he made no comment on the matter, no one else dared to. In a silence never before experienced in Smith's Town, the villagers and their children walked through the snow behind Mother Marie and the little old man and the horse in the sledge being drawn along by the other horse.

It wasn't until they reached the first rows of houses in the village that the Blacksmith opened his mouth, and then he contented himself with whispering a word or two into Uncle Eskild's ear. Luckily Uncle Eskild's hearing left a good deal to be desired, so the Blacksmith was obliged to repeat his words five times, and the fifth time he spoke so loudly that the Master Baker, who was walking just beside Uncle Eskild, could not avoid hearing what was said.

'He must have come from the Continent.'

The Master Baker immediately repeated this astonishing statement to people round him, who repeated it to those behind, until the words reached the children and were sent back up the line, and soon everyone in Smith's Town knew what the Blacksmith had said: *The stranger had come from the Continent*. This was real news, for the last time anyone had come from the Continent had been when Oldmother Rikke-Marie's great-great-grandmother was a child, and no one else could remember so far back.

But you couldn't rely on what the grown-ups said just like that, so the children crowded around Ida-Anna, who had dropped back in the procession. Ida-Anna had been unusually quiet ever since she had spoken to the stranger; in fact she hadn't uttered a single word. While patting the stranger's horse, she had discovered something remarkable: there were no tracks in the snow from the runners, either in front of or behind the sledge, nor had the horses' hooves made any marks. Ida-Anna had been pondering this curious thing all the way back to the village, and now she knew why. She whispered to the other children that she didn't want to talk there, where the grown-ups could hear her. But later in the afternoon, at the precise time when the sheep were herded in for the night, all the children were to meet her in Uncle Joseph's barn. Then she would tell them what she had discovered.

The procession had reached the centre of Smith's Town, an oval area around a small duck pond, which was frozen over and covered with snow except for a watery hole at one end. Facing the duck pond were eight houses, all built of large blocks of stone with crooked shutters at the windows and roofs made of seaweed that reached right down to the doors. Close to the duck pond, a few bare trees stuck out of the snowdrifts. Mother Marie's house lay north of the duck pond and just behind the house was a stable, which Odin was invited to make use of. The Blacksmith, Uncle Eskild and eight other men from the village willingly helped Odin to carry Rigmarole from the sledge and into the stable. The mare was laid as comfortably as possible on a thick bed of straw, and Balthazar was tethered at her side. Ida-Anna fetched some hay and soon both horses were munching contentedly.

All the people of Smith's Town, to a man, had crowded and

elbowed their way inside the stable to get as close as possible to the stranger from the Continent. But Odin took no notice of them. Whistling a quiet tune, as if he was alone, he bent down and cautiously ran his hand along his unfortunate mare's leg; it was broken in not just one but two places. Ida-Anna fetched some of her mother's linen, which Odin tore into long narrow strips and one by one wound around Rigmarole's leg. It took Odin a long time to bandage his mare, but the villagers kept swarming around him to look on. None of them said a word except the Blacksmith, who at regular intervals uttered a few approving noises to reassure everyone that the Blacksmith of Smith's Town knew perfectly well what should be done for a horse's broken leg, even though formerly and up to this very afternoon he had maintained there was nothing to be done. After a while Rigmarole's leg was totally enveloped in Mother Marie's linen, and Odin patted her and straightened up; that would have to do for now.

At that moment Mother Marie pushed through the crowd. 'Now the horses have been waited upon, it's time the man had his share!' she declared firmly, taking hold of Odin's arm.

As no one, not even the Blacksmith – who would really have liked to continue in conversation with the stranger about horses and their ailments and other things dear to his heart – could gainsay Ida-Anna's mother, Odin quickly vanished inside her house. The villagers glanced at each other. Some took a step forward, others one back, but it was not long before curiosity won over good manners and they all swarmed into the house after Mother Marie and the stranger from the Continent.

Mother Marie felt honoured to be the one the stranger visited before anyone else in Smith's Town. However, she found it only right and proper, for Mother Marie had lost her husband to the sea when the children were still quite small, and since then she had worked very hard and today owned more sheep, goats and chickens than anyone else in the village.

Although it was only mid-afternoon, night was already falling, and Mother Marie had lit five small candles to make sure the stranger from the Continent would be fully able to appreciate the riches and neatness of her home. A blazing fire was burning on the hearth and the scent of roast duck and strong Yuletide brew filtered from the kitchen around the rest of the house. Mother Marie led Odin to the biggest and best easy chair in the living room, poured him a large glass of Yuletide brew and urged him to drink. No sooner had Odin sat down, and without so much as grasping the glass, he fell into a deep sleep.

The numerous villagers who had been lucky enough to cram into Mother Marie's house were not a little disappointed and, although they wouldn't quite admit it, also slightly offended because the stranger from the Continent had now abruptly deserted the waking life. They were bursting with a whole list of questions about life and customs on the Continent, and now they had to be content with observing the stranger's outward appearance.

As it was Mother Marie's home, she was in charge. The sturdy woman glanced at the roasting duck, dried her greasy hands on her apron and pushed her way through the villagers in her living room to the easy chair holding the sleeping Odin. There she leaned down until she was so close to his face that she could feel the warmth of his breath. The stranger from the Continent was past his best age. His skin was rough, almost leathery, his face wrinkled and furrowed, and both his long hair and his beard were as white as white could be. But when you disregarded his small stature, his swarthy complexion and the missing left eye, he didn't seem so very different from the inhabitants of Smith's Town. Mother Marie was a bit disappointed. Perhaps the few unusual features were not even unusual but quite normal for the inhabitants of the Continent. In any case, Mother Marie didn't want to be the one who was amazed at something that must be perfectly normal to anyone who had been around a bit. When she had gazed to her satisfaction she stepped back to let the others draw near, and after all the villagers had satisfied their curiosity she politely asked them to leave so that the stranger from the Continent could sleep in peace.

*

Hardly had the last of the Smith's Town folk left Mother Marie's house before the sheep came trundling past. Ida-Anna pulled a thick sweater over her head, threw a scarf around her neck and ran across the village to Uncle Joseph's barn. She pulled open the heavy door a few centimetres, squeezed her way in and saw that all the other children had already arrived. Uncle Joseph's barn was big and dark and smelled of old hay and something indefinable, like a mixture of molasses, bird droppings and musty bread. The ceiling seemed to arch as loftily above them as the sky, the wind whistled through the numerous cracks in the walls, and the mice squeaked and rustled along the crossbeams. A narrow crack of twilight edged itself in through a window in the roof, but was far too feeble to chase away the dimness. The children were all too aware that ghosts haunted the barn at full moon, and normally none of them dared to approach it, but that was the very reason for Ida-Anna choosing to meet there.

Ida-Anna ignored the faint protests and led her friends over to the innermost part of the huge space. There the straw bales formed a natural semicircle, and Ida-Anna urged the others to sit down, as she pulled a bale into the centre and climbed on to it.

'Something really important has happened here today,' she said in a hoarse, solemn whisper, and the younger children at once crept closer to the older ones. 'A man has come to Smith's Town from the outside world, from somewhere other than Post Office Town!' Ida-Anna allowed her eyes to roam enquiringly over the faces before her to make sure that the importance of this event was properly understood. 'The man says his name is Odin.' She lowered her voice, and a small girl began to cry. 'Ssh!' hissed Ida-Anna, with a touch of irritation, and Bodil lifted her little sister on to her lap. 'He says his name is Odin,' Ida-Anna repeated. 'But Odin is not his real name.' Again Ida-Anna inspected the faces in the semi-darkness. 'You must all swear not to breathe a word of what I am going to tell you, or I won't tell you anything at all,' she said.

'Out with it, then!' Ejner broke out impatiently, making a face.

'Swear!' insisted Ida-Anna, pointing to the first child in the circle. 'Swear by the soul of Oldmother Rikke-Marie's great-great-grandmother. Raise your right hand in the air and swear: *Never, never ever may I breathe a word to a soul. Never never ever, or the serpent will gobble me whole!*'

Troels stood up, raised his right hand and swore the oath in a whisper. Then, one after another, the other children stood, raised their hands and swore.

'Come on now, get on with it!' Ejner nagged at her. He was

only six months younger than Ida-Anna and hated her always taking the decisions.

'Quiet!' Ida-Anna ordered and waited until all of them had sat down again. 'It's Christmas Eve tonight.'

'Yes! Yes!'

'But what's that got to do with the stranger?' asked Lauge, exchanging impatient glances with Ejner.

'We all know that Santa Claus brings us presents on Christmas Eve,' Ida-Anna went on, without taking any notice of the boys. 'And we know too that Santa Claus is an old man with white hair and a white beard, and that on Christmas Eve he drives across the sky in his sledge.'

Slowly what she was suggesting started to dawn on the children, and several of them stood up with shining eyes.

'And today, only an hour or two before Santa Claus was due to arrive at Smith's Town a stranger turns up. He has had an accident, one of his horses has a broken leg, so he had to seek help. It's clear as glass: the stranger must be Santa Claus!'

All the children began to dance and jump around, shouting at each other, and in their sheer excitement they forgot to keep quiet. They shouted and screamed and it took Ida-Anna a long time to quieten them down.

'One at a time!' she barked. 'One at a time!'

'But if the stranger is Santa Claus, why does he say his name is Odin?' objected Ejner.

'Because Odin is Santa Claus's secret name, you dimwit!'

'But Santa Claus has reindeer to pull his sledge, and the stranger has horses,' interrupted Lauge.

'That's just something the grown-ups say, so we shouldn't recognize him when he comes,' Ida-Anna snapped back. 'In any case that merely shows you can't rely on grown-ups.'

'But where are the presents?' asked Little Palle anxiously.

'That's quite simple,' said Ida-Anna. 'Santa Claus was on his way to the toy mountain on the Continent to fetch presents when he lost his way in bad weather. His horse broke her leg, and that was that.'

There was a moment's silence, then Ejner piped up:

'That can't be it, because I've already seen the drum I'm getting for Christmas in my father's cupboard,' he said triumphantly.

Ida-Anna hadn't thought of that, but it didn't take her long to find an explanation.

'But that's obvious, the drum is from your parents and not from Santa Claus,' she laughed. 'You see, Santa Claus doesn't come every year. In fact he's never been to Smith's Town and not even to Post Office Town, don't forget. And that's because it's so hard to find the way here. He told me that himself when I talked to him.' Ida-Anna looked around her, sure she had won.

Some of the children nodded, others were still sceptical. But when Ida-Anna told them about the lack of any marks of runners and horses' hooves in the snow, there could no longer be any doubt: Santa Claus had come to Smith's Town!

'But,' Ida-Anna went on, 'Santa Claus's horse won't be able to walk a step for a long, long time. And Santa Claus himself said that he can't go anywhere without that horse. So if we don't find out how the broken leg can be fixed, we won't get any presents from Santa. And not just this year, but next year and the year after that too. If the worst comes to the worst, if Santa Claus's horse is killed, as the Blacksmith said, there will be no more Christmas ever.'

'Oh, no!' yelled the children in horror.

'So you see,' said Ida-Anna, rather full of herself, 'we must do all we can to help Santa Claus's horse!'

'But what can we do? We don't know anything about horses and broken legs. And you heard yourself what the Blacksmith said,' protested Ejner.

'You're right there, for once,' said Ida-Anna almost kindly. 'But while I'm finding out what we can do, we must in any case keep an eye on the horse, so the Blacksmith doesn't put it down.'

'Let's take turns to keep watch over the stable,' suggested Bodil.

'Yes. And if anyone comes we'll blow Lauge's whistle,' added Ingolf.

Now the children worked out a plan and agreed to keep watch over the stable night and day, and to meet in the barn every day, when the sheep had been brought in for the night. Troels would take first watch, because his father worked at the post office in Post Office Town and came home late, and so Troels's family had their Christmas dinner later than everyone else in Smith's Town. As soon as the children had settled the details they made tracks, glad to get away from the murky barn, but before Ida-Anna let them go she made them swear Oldmother Rikke-Marie's great-great-grandmother's oath once more.

'Never, never ever may I breathe a word to a soul. Never never ever, or the serpent will gobble me whole!'

*

Odin was woken up by the steaming vapours of hot food and a strong brew unfamiliar to him. Mother Marie stood at the door;

it was time for the stranger from the Continent to get up and get ready so that Christmas dinner could be served. She showed Odin upstairs to a small room on the first floor furnished with a narrow bed, a table, a chair and a cupboard. A pleasant crackling came from the fireplace in the corner, and a pottery bowl with water and soap was at the disposal of the guest.

'Dinner will be served in a moment, so please don't forget to come down as soon as you are ready,' said Mother Marie, leaving the room.

When Odin entered the living room a few minutes later he found the other guests already assembled. Mother Marie introduced Odin to them one by one. There was the Blacksmith and Uncle Eskild, whom he already knew, Ida-Anna and Ingolf of course, with Aunt Maren, who was Mother Marie's sister as well as being Uncle Eskild's wife. Then there was Oldmother Rikke-Marie, the oldest living person in Smith's Town and mother of the Blacksmith. The Blacksmith's wife sat beside her husband, but she was small and shy and never uttered a word, and as so often happens, her presence was unintentionally overlooked. Odin bowed and said he was very honoured to make the acquaintance of every one of them.

Then Mother Marie said the meal was ready and asked everyone to take their seats. When the Blacksmith had carved the birds and Mother Marie had handed around the vegetables and preserves, everyone was soon munching away, too busy to talk. Odin was exceedingly hungry and set to ravenously, heartily washing the food down with Yuletide brew as if it was water. He was so preoccupied with eating that he didn't notice the stolen glances the others cast at him. What Odin could not know was that while he had been asleep and the children had been listening to Ida-Anna in Uncle Joseph's barn, the grown-ups had hurried to the smithy to decide how to deal with the somewhat unexpected visit of the stranger from the Continent. After lengthy deliberations, not to mention a fair amount of heated discussion, the villagers came to the unanimous conclusion that the only way of showing their friendliness and hospitality would be to treat the stranger just as if he was one of themselves. Accordingly the Blacksmith had insisted that no one must show the slightest surprise if their visitor said or did anything odd, because that would make him feel like a stranger – as well, of course, as revealing the villagers' ignorance of the ways of the wider world.

Odin went on eating for a long, long time, and as the villagers considered it would be wrong to disturb a man in the middle of a meal, the Blacksmith was obliged to rein in his impatience. At long last, when there was no more food on the table and only a pile of cleanly picked bones on Odin's plate, the stranger from the Continent wiped his hands and leaned back in his chair. The conversation could begin.

'Ahem, h'm,' the Blacksmith cleared his throat, trying to gather his thoughts as he filled and lit his pipe. 'Ahem, h'm. I don't want to seem impolite, Mr Odin, not for the world would I be that, but I can't help wondering what you are going to do about that horse of yours there, h'm, h'm, what with her broken leg and all.' The Blacksmith nodded in the direction of Mother Marie's stable.

'I am certainly on the horns of an extremely serious dilemma,' said Odin, twining his long white beard around his fingers. 'An extremely serious dilemma indeed.' He contemplated the situation for a moment. 'I gather there is no one to be found in this district who knows how to set a horse's broken leg bone?'

'No,' said the Blacksmith. 'Without wishing to be rude, I'm afraid that neither in Smith's Town nor Post Office Town or any place between them will you find anyone who can deal with a horse's leg once it is broken.' It was always best to tell the truth, but it was Christmas Eve and the Blacksmith thought it would be the wrong thing to discourage a guest on such a special evening. After all, what did they know about the methods people on the Continent used to treat their horses? After a short pause the Blacksmith patted Odin comfortingly on the shoulder and added: 'Without seeming impolite, you would probably do better to go back to the Continent to seek someone or other to see to that job.'

'The Continent?'

'Yes, where you came from.'

'Oh. Oh, yes, Valhalla.' Odin gesticulated vaguely to hide what he had just discovered: in the meteor storm he had not only become disorientated but had also lost any idea at all of the position of his own home.

'Naturally, Valhalla.' The Blacksmith nodded eagerly. 'Valhalla, naturally.' He laughed heartily at his own foolishness; obviously Valhalla must be an important town on the Continent.

'And you are in a hurry, aren't you?' asked the Blacksmith, chiefly to keep the conversation going while he tried to find something better to say.

'I was on my way to issue a warning of some ill tidings.' Only then did Odin realize he had also forgotten to whom and, worse, what the bad tidings he brought were, and he tugged anxiously at his beard.

Oh, a postman, thought the Blacksmith and suddenly understood the full extent of the stranger's misfortune. No way could the people be without either the postman in Smith's Town or the one in Post Office Town either on working days or holidays or any other time of the year. The Blacksmith hastened to reassure Odin that everything possible would be done to help him. Indeed, as early as the next day the Blacksmith would summon all the people of Smith's Town as well as all the people of Post Office Town, and ask them to rack their brains to find the fastest and best possible way for Mr Odin to be able to get back to the Continent without further delay.

The rest of the evening passed like any other Christmas Eve in Mother Marie's house. Everyone except Oldmother Rikke-Marie joined in singing carols, the children were allowed to taste the goodies hidden under the table, and the Blacksmith puffed away at his pipe, while Mother Marie read the beautiful old story aloud from the Bible, about when the Son of God was born. And finally, last of all, the presents were given out, and there was something for everyone. As it would have been very ungracious not to have a present for the stranger from the Continent, Mother Marie had asked the Blacksmith to bring along a horseshoe from the smithy.

'This will bring you all the luck you need,' said she, passing the horseshoe to Odin.

'Indeed, in all truth, there is no misfortune that a piece of good luck cannot remedy,' replied Odin, thanking Mother Marie warmly, while twisting and turning the horseshoe in his hands. It was an unusual horseshoe: carved from wood, it had a flint edge nailed to the inside. Odin tucked it in his breast pocket and then apologized for not having any presents for his hosts. 'As soon as Rigmarole's leg has been put right I shall bring you the things you desire most of all.'

Ida-Anna winked at Father Christmas to let him know she

understood his predicament and wouldn't hold any grudge against him over the delay.

It was late, the evening was over, and everyone rose. Oldmother Rikke-Marie, who was delighted at last to have met someone who was as old as she was, had stared at Odin the whole evening without uttering a word. Now, after countless glasses of Yuletide brew and after all the others had apparently said what they had to say, she laid a hand on Odin's arm and asked him in a squeaky whisper whether he had ever come across a reddish-blond man called Richard. This man, Richard the Red, who was Oldmother Rikke-Marie's very own father – but that was a story far too long and personal to be told on Christmas Eve – had left the island many years ago, even before she had come into the world, and had never come back.

'No, no, unfortunately, I don't think so,' replied Odin slowly, and twisted his beard with the worrying realization that he could no longer remember who he had met or heard about before he arrived at Smith's Town the selfsame afternoon. A sorrowful shadow spread over Oldmother Rikke-Marie's face, and Odin thought no more about his own situation, but went on kindly: 'From now on I shall be more than happy to keep a good look-out for him wherever I find myself.'

'If I wasn't so old and stiff I would go with you myself,' said the old woman, smiling her toothless smile, as if, after all, she was not so very dissatisfied with the state of things and her own body.

'When Rigmarole's leg is quite better, we'll go out to search for your family,' promised Odin, squeezing Oldmother Rikke-Marie's hand in farewell.

*

Next morning, just as he had promised, the Blacksmith called all the people of Smith's Town, not forgetting everyone from Post Office Town too, to a meeting at the smithy. The forge was large and normally housed a number of horses and carts, and yet this morning it felt quite cramped. All and sundry had an opinion to express on the matter of the stranger from the Continent, and the clamour was deafening. But as soon as the Blacksmith appeared, silence fell.

The Blacksmith took his stand with his legs slightly apart. 'Hmm, hmm.' He removed his pipe from his mouth. 'Good, good. Well, I think I'd better begin at the beginning.'

Odin had entered the smithy behind the Blacksmith and now stood beside a large heap of grey stones and a pile of rounded logs. On the wall hung a few horseshoes made of wood with flint edges, exactly like the one Mother Marie had given him the evening before. Apart from this Odin was unable to see anything else because of the Blacksmith's broad back.

'I have called you all here today, I have called everyone in Smith's Town, as well as all the people of Post Office Town, to my smithy here because there is something to be done which is more of an honour than any other honour that any of us could have had the honour to undertake on this most holy Christmas Day.' The Blacksmith let his gaze take in all his spectators. 'As you all know, yesterday a man arrived in Smith's Town from somewhere other than Post Office Town!'

The villagers started up with a mumbling and a whispering and grew quite noisy as they pushed and elbowed each other and trod on their own and others' toes trying to catch a glimpse of the strange little man from the Continent, who stood there hidden behind the Blacksmith.

'This man, Mr Odin, if I may be so bold...' Here the

Blacksmith turned and in a single sweeping moment lifted Odin up and stood him on the worktop so everyone could see him.

A hush fell over the gathering.

'This man has travelled a long way to deliver a most important message. But he was caught in a particularly violent snowstorm, and one of his horses broke a leg.' To avoid forgetting anything the Blacksmith pulled a scrap of paper from his pocket, on which he had written down everything he wanted to say; now he had come to the more complicated part of his speech. 'On behalf of the people of Smith's Town as well as those from Post Office Town, I have invited Mr Odin to stay in Smith's Town as long as he likes. However, Mr Odin's assignment demands great haste, so he is obliged to see to this very special task without delay. Therefore, and I am sure you will all agree with me on this, it is of the greatest importance that Mr Odin's horse's leg is cured as soon as possible.' The Blacksmith sent a sharp glance around the villagers as if to warn them from thinking, let alone mentioning, that hitherto and as late as yesterday he had always maintained that there was no way to heal a horse's broken leg. 'Now, because the sad fact is that no one from Smith's Town to Post Office Town and back again can cure this horse's leg, the only course of action possible is for Mr Odin to go to the Continent to fetch the Veterinarius to see to it.' The Blacksmith raised his voice and repeated the foreign word: 'The Veterinarius!' He was well aware that not one of his listeners knew this grand word. He had only discovered it himself far into the night as he leafed through a tattered old dictionary that had been left in the attic in Oldmother Rikke-Marie's great-great-great-grandfather's time. By making use of this grand word the Blacksmith hoped to regain his reputation as the most knowledgeable man in Smith's Town despite the brief misunderstanding over the case of the broken leg of Mr Odin's horse.

'As we all very well know, no one has left this island since Oldmother Rikke-Marie's mother was young. And hitherto and up to yesterday no one has come here since the Battle of the Foreigners, which took place even before the time when Oldmother Rikke-Marie's great-great-grandmother was young. And, as we all also very well know, the cliffs make it impossible to land or launch from our shores, even if anyone should wish to do so, which no one from Smith's Town to Post Office Town and back again has done for more years than anyone here could count. Therefore – and because Mr Odin for obvious reasons cannot use his good horses – we must all put our wits together to find some way in which Mr Odin can travel back to the Continent.'

The Blacksmith slowly and carefully folded up his scrap of paper and put it back in his pocket. Silence reigned in the smithy. It was as if the Blacksmith had said all there was to say: the stranger must go to the Continent and back again, but he could not do so. Every child knew that. But the way in which the Blacksmith had expressed it – the villagers found that awe-inspiring. They all knew that the Blacksmith's speech had been made solely in honour of the stranger to demonstrate the good-will and eagerness to be of service that characterized not only the people of Smith's Town, but also the people of Post Office Town. So impressively had the Blacksmith spoken that when his words had been fully assimilated, the villagers clapped enthusiastically and repeated selected phrases from the speech.

'We must all put our wits together!' shouted the Master Baker.

'Cannot use his good horses!' yelled Long Laust from Post Office Town, jumping up and down.

'Must go back to the Continent!' shouted another.

'Has to fetch the Veterinarius!' rumbled Uncle Eskild to emphasize that he knew exactly what the Blacksmith meant, even though he hadn't the slightest notion of what it was.

'The Veterinarius! The Veterinarius!' came in a chorus from all corners of the smithy, as if the villagers thought that the mere force of their voices could call forth this miracle, whose nature they were still unsure of.

After a while the Blacksmith raised his hand and the hubbub died down.

'Not wanting to seem impolite, but solely considering the urgency, the sooner a solution is found the better. And in any case the solution must be found not a moment later than early tomorrow morning, so that Mr Odin will definitely arrive at the Continent not a moment later than tomorrow evening, so that he will be back here in Smith's Town with the Veterinarius not a moment later than the day after tomorrow.'

There was a significant silence. It seemed as if all the villagers breathed at one and the same time. Only a faint crackling from the fire in the forge could be heard. This time the Blacksmith had gone too far, everyone knew that. It was just not possible to find a solution, so it was still more impossible to find one by early tomorrow morning. But the villagers also knew that the Blacksmith himself knew this perfectly well, so what was he playing at? The villagers looked at each other questioningly, and gradually, one by one, they understood. Had there ever lived such a phenomenal Blacksmith anywhere, they wondered. Slowly smiles spread over their faces; in no way could they help the stranger from the Continent, but as long as the stranger believed they could, and as long as he believed they were all doing their very best to help him, he would wait patiently and think they were very helpful and obliging people. And one fine day, when the stranger realized he would never be able to return to the Continent, he would be so accustomed to life on the island and the people of Smith's Town, that he would no longer have the slightest desire to leave.

'Hooray for the Blacksmith!' someone shouted, and all the others joined in. 'Hooray! Hooray!'

The Blacksmith enjoyed his applause for a minute or two before he cut them off.

'Work is calling,' he said.

'Work is calling! Work is calling!' sounded from all sides of the smithy, and the villagers hurried out to demonstrate their goodwill and keenness to serve the stranger from the Continent.

'How can I ever thank you?' asked Odin, who was still standing on the table.

'No need. No need at all,' replied the Blacksmith, still pleased with himself. 'The people of Smith's Town, as well as the people of Post Office Town, always want to do everything possible to help a man carry out his work.'

Odin smiled and said that although they had not known each other long, he and the Blacksmith seemed like old friends. The Blacksmith laughed heartily at this, well satisfied, convinced as he was that his strategy was already bearing its first fruits, and it wouldn't be long before the stranger from the Continent would want to settle down in Smith's Town himself. The two men exchanged a firm handshake. Then the Blacksmith lifted Odin down from the table, picked up a piece of wood and started to work on it with a sharp knife, while Odin went over to Mother Marie's stable to see to his horses.

Balthazar stood there munching hay, and Rigmarole lay quietly on her right side with the unfortunate leg resting on the straw.

'We'd better do something about that leg so you don't make it worse before I get hold of the Veterinarius,' Odin chatted as he looked around for something that could be used as a splint.

Ida-Anna, who had followed Odin into the stable, picked up an old broomstick and passed it to him without a word. She was in a bad mood. All the children had heard their parents praising the Blacksmith for his marvellous speech, and they no longer believed what Ida-Anna had told them the day before in Uncle Joseph's barn. Placing a guard over the stable had been called off; the other children had lost interest in the stranger and played with their Christmas presents instead.

Ida-Anna was grooming Balthazar vigorously with some pieces of straw, and slowly, as his coat grew more and more shiny, she cheered up. What did she care if they made fun of her? What did she care that they didn't believe her? This would give her the chance to have Santa Claus all to herself. Ida-Anna worked forward slowly until she was standing right beside Odin, who was making Rigmarole comfortable. Well, now she had the chance to tell Santa Claus how much she wanted her very own horse for Christmas. But first she must remember to swear she would not reveal Santa Claus's real name to any of the grown-ups. Ida-Anna raised her right hand in the air.

'*Never, never ever may I breathe a word to a soul. Never never ever or the serpent will gobble me whole!*' she said sincerely.

They certainly have some funny habits in this place, thought Odin. As he wanted to behave in a correct and polite fashion – he had said 'Happy Christmas' when the villagers did and had joined in the carol-singing even though he didn't know the words – he raised his right hand and repeated Oldmother Rikke-Marie's great-great-grandmother's oath. Ida-Anna laughed. There, hadn't she been right all along? But just as she was about to tell Santa Claus her wish, her mother appeared at the stable door to say that lunch was ready.

The same evening the Blacksmith paid another visit to Mother Marie in company with Oldmother Rikke-Marie, who had decided that now and then, when the world didn't come to you, it wasn't a bad idea to come to the world.

'Hmm, hm,' coughed the Blacksmith, chewing at his pipe. 'Hmm, hm, Mr Odin, not wanting to seem rude, but I am really extremely glad to be able to declare that everything is ready for your journey.' The Blacksmith straightened his back to emphasize that he was totally in charge of the situation. 'If nothing unexpected happens, Mr Odin, you should be able to set out safely early tomorrow morning, at the very first sign of daybreak.'

Odin thanked the Blacksmith and said he would always be grateful to the people of Smith's Town, not forgetting the people of Post Office Town. He thought he would ask what arrangements had been made, but as the Blacksmith did not volunteer to describe the details, Odin did not want to show such lack of tact as to ask about anything so unimportant. In any case, Oldmother Rikke-Marie now took the opportunity to tell the rest of her story, and without any preliminaries she began where she had left off the night before.

'It was a cold and windy September morning.' Everyone turned their heads to look at the old lady, although she seemed to speak solely to Odin. 'Richard the Red went to see my mother and said the time had come. He kissed her farewell, assured her of his eternal love and promised to return very soon. He thought he had discovered a navigable channel between the cliffs and would prove it was possible to sail to the Continent and back again. No one knows if he ever did get there, but it is certain that he never came back. It was not until after he had gone that my mother revealed that she was expecting what would one day be me.' The old lady leaned back in her chair and at once fell asleep, quite overwhelmed by her own story.

Mother Marie rose to her feet. It was time for them all to go to bed. It was already far into the night and Mr Odin had a long journey in front of him. She nodded at the Blacksmith, who once more assured the stranger from the Continent that he could enjoy a peaceful sleep and there was no doubt at all that he would reach the Continent before night fell the next day.

*

Now it so happened that during that night a harder freeze than any in living memory struck Smith's Town and Post Office Town. As early as December it had been colder than any other winter Oldmother Rikke-Marie had experienced. But never had it been so cold as that second night the stranger from the Continent spent in Smith's Town. When Odin rose, long before dawn, not only had the water in the earthenware jug on the table frozen hard, but the ice on the inside of the shutters was so thick you couldn't see out at all.

At breakfast everyone had on thick woollen jumpers, scarves and mittens even though they sat right beside the hearth. Mother Marie insisted on Mr Odin borrowing a scarf that had once belonged to her late husband; otherwise he would not be able to keep warm on his journey. Since she did not know when the Blacksmith had in mind to reveal to the stranger that he would not leave that day, and to show her genuine goodwill, Mother Marie had made a huge lunch-pack for Odin, which she also insisted he should accept. Ingolf had soon finished his breakfast and gone out to play, but Ida-Anna stayed at the table, impatient for her mother to leave the room. Just a few moments were all she needed. It wouldn't even take half a minute to tell Santa Claus what she wanted. Her mother had at last gone out to the kitchen to fetch more hot water, and Ida-Anna leaned forward and coughed gently, as she had learned from the Blacksmith, when Long Laust from Post Office Town burst in without knocking.

'The sea has frozen over, the sea has frozen over! The stranger can walk to the Continent today. The sea has frozen over!' yelled Long Laust, breathless with excitement and the long run from Post Office Town to Smith's Town.

Long Laust was not as young as he had been, but his mind remained as if paused in childhood. He had yelled 'the sea has frozen over' more than a dozen times, jumping up and down in sheer excitement, before Long Laust realized that the Blacksmith was not present. And it was not until Mother Marie had set a steaming cup of soup in front of him, while discreetly pulling him by the arm, did he see that maybe he shouldn't have told the stranger about the frozen sea before the Blacksmith had given him permission.

But it was too late now. After hearing Long Laust's words

Odin had risen at once, picked up his lunch-pack and thanked Ida-Anna and her mother for their hospitality. Daylight was close at hand and it was time he was on his way. With the lucky horseshoe snug in his breast pocket Odin pulled on his heavy overcoat and went outside. He had already arranged for Ida-Anna to look after Balthazar and Rigmarole while he was away and now all he had to do was bid farewell to the horses.

On his way out of the stable Odin ran into the Blacksmith. He seized the big man's hand and shook it warmly. 'A thousand, thousand thanks,' he said, bowing. 'What fantastic people they are, the residents of Smith's Town as well as those of Post Office Town. I could never thank you all enough!'

'No need, no need at all,' replied the Blacksmith jovially. He hadn't yet heard the news of the frozen sea and gaily waved farewell to the stranger from the Continent, who set off down the road to Post Office Town and the coast.

Odin walked briskly westwards and reached Post Office Town in less than twenty minutes. People were standing at their doors, and waved to the stranger from the Continent, who waved back and called 'Thanks for your help' all the way through the village, which consisted of not much more than a cluster of houses, a shop and, in the very middle, a very small but very well-kept post office. It took only a couple of minutes for Odin to arrive at the coast and the end of the island, where the sea stretched out before him – or rather, where the sea stretched out behind a line of colossal cliffs that totally concealed the horizon.

Odin put one foot on to the frozen water, then the other. The ice creaked and cracked, but it held. Cautiously he took another step or two; the thought of falling through the ice down into the dark water was not alluring. But the ice seemed firm enough, and soon Odin was striding out at a brisk pace without worrying about anything other than getting to the Continent as soon as possible to find the Veterinarius for Rigmarole.

To start with, the towering cliffs sheltered him, but as soon as Odin reached the open sea, a stiff north-westerly struck him right in the face. He wound Mother Marie's late husband's scarf more tightly around his neck and leaned into the wind, but his headway was considerably slowed and several times he had to sit down on the ice to avoid being blown backwards by the gusts. The air was so cold that Odin's breath soon turned into ice, even before it left his mouth, and it was not long before his lips were as stiff and blue as the threatening cliffs behind him. His hair and beard, that had already been covered with frost at Post Office Town, soon became icicles. Now and then the ice grumbled and complained beneath his feet and each time Odin came to an abrupt halt and held his breath; it was certainly no pleasure trip, but to turn around without first getting hold of the Veterinarius was out of the question.

'He who dares may be overcome, but he who does not dare, has already been overcome,' mumbled Odin to himself, patting the horseshoe in his breast pocket.

Shortly after Odin had passed the cliffs he had been able to glimpse a faint outline of the land which the people of Smith's Town called the Continent, and he had not thought it would be difficult to walk there. But he was very wrong. He paced on for hour after hour without ceasing – and he ate his picnic and drank the water until that too froze hard – without slackening his pace. Yet he seemed to get no nearer to the land.

Well into the afternoon it began to snow, and Odin was now frozen to the very marrow of his bones. He could barely move and each single step seemed to demand the last remnants of his strength. He was no longer sure if he could make it to the coastline, which was now hidden behind the densely falling snow. But long after darkness had fallen, and long after the snowfall had become a snowstorm, Odin, almost without being conscious of it, had in fact set foot on the Continent.

NIFLHEIM AND MUSPELHEIM

Niflheim lay north of nothing
Muspelheim was south

The fog-bound world of Niflheim
kept Ilvergelmer hidden
From her womb sprang Elivagar
gave mother rivers life

Elivagar gushed into nothing
twelve steaming streams turned into snow
till Nothing nothing other was
than fog and ice and arctic mist

The flaming realm of Muspelheim
spat sparks and glowing embers
Surtur's sword fierce swished in feud
winter die and summer live

Ginnungagap was cold and not
but Surtur gained his victory
Fire melted ice and banished frost
and rime grew most outrageous now

And so was born the monster Ymer

IT WAS JUST after eight o'clock. Sigbrit Holland drove north along the snow-covered coastal road. She was tired and in an odd kind of mood. Although it was a holiday she had gone into the bank to finish her six-monthly report on the movements of the dollar. But she had worked slowly and mechanically and without her normal enthusiasm. She had completed the report, but wasn't satisfied with it. Now it was late and she knew her husband would be annoyed that she was not at home preparing for their guests.

A violent gust of wind struck the car and Sigbrit Holland was hard put to prevent it from skidding into the ditch. She drove as fast as she could but the world in front of the windscreen was shrouded in a grey mass of thick snow and darkness, through which her headlights made little impression. The road was as slippery as ice and she made slow progress. It seemed the blizzard had frightened others from venturing out, as she met neither cars nor pedestrians. Sigbrit glanced at the clock on the instrument panel and when the road straightened out soon after Hverv Harbour she defied the weather and picked up speed.

Suddenly something was there in front of her. Sigbrit slammed on the brakes, swung the car hard to the left and miraculously managed to avoid hitting the silhouette that had appeared in the middle of the road. The car slid around in the snow and when it finally stopped it was with its nose pointing south in the wrong lane. She closed her eyes and took a deep breath. She drummed her fingers nervously on the wheel. She had driven too fast, she knew that, and she had not been concentrating. But what was this person thinking of, walking in the middle of the road at this time and in such weather? Luckily there was no traffic. For a brief moment she considered driving on, but whoever was out there, he surely did not deserve to die of cold. She started the car again and drove in to the side of the road.

Sigbrit wrapped her coat tightly around her and climbed out of the car. The snowflakes whirled into her eyes, and after a few seconds she could see nothing. She wiped her face with her gloved hands, but still couldn't see more than a metre or two in front of her.

'Hallo. Hallo, are you hurt?' she called and again wiped the snow from her eyes. There was no answer. She took another step or two forward and called again. No answer came out of the swirling snow. She walked further along the road, but there was no sign at all of another living soul nearby. Maybe she had been mistaken, or maybe it had just been an animal that was by now far away. Or perhaps fatigue and the snow had caused her to see things. Sigbrit called out once more, then gave up and turned around. She had almost reached her car when she literally stumbled over him.

'Sorry!' she exclaimed, seizing the man's shoulder just before he lost his balance.

How tiny he was, she thought, probably not much more than one metre tall, clearly slight beneath the many layers of clothing and covered with snow and ice from top to toe. It was a marvel that he could still remain on his feet.

'I didn't hit you, did I?' she asked with all the friendliness she could muster.

The little man made no reply, but merely stared at her with – yes, now she saw it – only one eye. His complexion was dark, an immigrant from the south, she guessed. Sigbrit Holland bit her lip in irritation. Why should this have to happen on this precise evening?

'Where are you heading for?' she went on, but there was still no response from the little old man. She tried a different language: 'Do you speak South Nordic?'

The little old man only went on staring at her, and apparently had no intention at all of replying.

Odin had every intention of replying. He wanted to tell the kind woman, that he himself – quite apart from some coldness in his marrow and bones – was perfectly all right, but that Rigmarole was in quite a bad way and he needed to find the Veterinarius very promptly. He wondered if the woman, if it wasn't too much trouble, would be so kind as to tell him, more or less precisely, where was the best place to look for him? But Odin couldn't open his mouth. No matter how he tried, his lips would not part; the frost had sealed them.

Sigbrit glanced at her watch; if she hurried, she wouldn't be too late. 'If you tell me where you are going I can drive you there,' she said, forcing a smile, as she impatiently brushed some long dark locks of hair away from her face.

The kind woman seemed to be in a hurry. She had offered to help him, yet it seemed as if she was already somewhere else. Odin thought he really ought to let her go, but it was impossible for him to say so. He tried to lift a hand to point to his mouth, but his arms were also locked fast by the ice that encased his whole body. Suddenly the woman seemed to understand his situation completely. She nodded and pointed to a very strange-looking vehicle, and Odin would have been more than happy to follow her directions, but while they had been standing still he had lost the last remnants of movement; his feet were frozen fast to the ground.

Sigbrit weighed up the situation. She wished she could jump into her car and drive off and forget about all this, but no matter how busy she was she couldn't just leave the little old man here in this predicament. She looked at her watch, then at the numbed figure before her, and with unusual decisiveness she bent down, pulled Odin free of the ice and carried him over to the car, where she placed him across the back seat. Then she got into the driving seat, started the car and drove back southwards towards the town.

When they reached the hospital the ice had melted sufficiently for Odin to be able to move his limbs. He still could not talk, but at least he could crawl out of the car unaided. Sigbrit led him into a yellow brick building and a sudden flood of light. They walked along a narrow corridor where doctors and nurses rushed around without heeding them. Sigbrit bit her lip in irritation – she must have chosen the wrong entrance – but after a few minutes she succeeded in stopping a porter who pointed out the way to the casualty department. She and Odin walked along more corridors, and finally reached a large waiting-room.

Most of the people in the room certainly didn't look the picture of health, and Odin shuddered in disquiet. He wasn't quite sure what he was going to do here, but the kind woman pointed to a chair, and as he didn't seem to have any choice, he sat down. He had better stay on good terms with her if she was going to help him find the Veterinarius for Rigmarole.

A nurse came over to them and asked what was wrong. She looked enquiringly at Odin, but it was Sigbrit Holland who answered.

'I almost knocked this man down on the road,' she said quickly. 'And he looked as if he was about to freeze to death, so I thought I'd better bring him along to you.'

'What is his name?' asked the nurse.

'I don't know.' Sigbrit shook her head briefly. 'I don't know whether he doesn't understand South Nordic, or whether he has been out in the cold so long he has lost the power of speech.'

Odin succeeded in nodding agreement with her, but only Sigbrit saw this, for the nurse had already turned to another patient who had just been brought in. The patient was bleeding profusely from some deep cuts to the face and chest and was on a stretcher. Odin didn't care for this place at all.

Shortly afterwards the nurse returned to ask more questions, which Sigbrit answered with rising impatience, while Odin kept an anxious eye on the bleeding patient. No, she didn't know whether he had a health service number or other identification. The bleeding patient was carried down the corridor and out of sight. Sigbrit gave her own name and, slightly unwillingly, her telephone number and address. Then the nurse indicated to Odin that he should accompany her. Odin rose, and the melting ice dripped from him. Where he had been sitting, there was a small pool, and each step left a new puddle on the floor. Sigbrit couldn't help smiling.

'I'll have to go now,' she said, 'but they will look after everything.'

'Thank you,' replied Odin happily. Now at last he understood why the woman had brought him here. He asked when he could expect the Veterinarius. But his voice made no sound.

Sigbrit saw the little old man's mouth open and close like a fish gasping for air. She looked at her watch and hesitated; she was at a loss. They would take care of him here, she said to herself, and hadn't she done more than enough already? In any case, she really couldn't stay; her husband had banged down the receiver before she had had a chance to explain the situation to him.

'You mustn't worry. They will do all they can for you,' she

said, and on a sudden impulse she wrote her phone number on a scrap of paper and put it in Odin's wet hand. 'If you have any problems...'

Odin went off with the nurse along a short corridor and into a consultation room where he was asked to lie down and wait for the doctor. When he was alone he looked at the numbers Sigbrit Holland had given him. He speculated over their meaning. Was it perhaps a kind of code that they used on the Continent, or did the figures give the directions to or the position of the Veterinarius Odin would be able to make use of if they were unable to bring him here? He decided to learn them by heart: five hundred and forty-two, six hundred and fourteen, thirty-four. Five hundred and forty-two, six hundred and fourteen, thirty-four. Five hundred and forty-two, six hundred... Odin slipped into a deep sleep.

*

Next morning Odin woke up without any recollection of how he had come to this place. The walls were bare and white and there were no curtains at the windows. But the room was warm, he lay on a comfortable mattress in a large bed, and if he hadn't been in such a hurry he would really have liked to lie there much longer. But as things stood, Odin thought he had better get up and dress.

At first he couldn't find his clothes. Someone or other must have undressed him and stuffed him into this overlarge garment of thin white material, which would do him no good out on the ice. Odin began to search the room, and after a while he found his things, dry and neatly folded, in a cupboard in the wall. He must remember to thank the kind folk who had seen to that. Next to the door there was a small room where he had a wash after he discovered a metal spout from which water came pouring out when he turned a knob. Odin still felt coldness in marrow and bone and enjoyed letting the hot water run down him. But he had things to do and ought not to spoil himself.

Odin was fully dressed and ready to go when a lady in white uniform came into the room.

'I see we are up,' said the uniformed lady. 'It's excellent to see you're feeling better. But you will have to stay in bed until Dr Martinussen has time to see you.'

'I am sorry, I am in some haste, and it would not be good to wait any longer,' said Odin. It was already broad daylight, and considering the long journey ahead it would not be a good thing to postpone his and Veterinarius Martinussen's departure.

'No, you can't go yet,' the uniformed lady went on calmly but firmly. 'First we have to make sure that everything is as it should be. After that you can go. That's not so hard to understand, is it?'

Odin would not give way, and the nurse, who was starting to get impatient, asked him quite sharply to get back into bed and answer one or two questions.

'You see, there are regulations for that kind of thing. We need some information, so be good and get back into bed again and tell me your name.'

Oh, now Odin understood; why hadn't she said that before? The nurse had seated herself on the only chair in the room, so Odin scrambled into bed with the aid of a stool. The uniformed lady did not seem to be so kind after all, and Odin wasn't sure what good such information would do, but if it was Veterinarius Martinussen's ruling he was quite happy to comply. Odin leaned back against the pillows.

'Your name?' asked the nurse.

'Odin,' said Odin.

'Odin, Odin what?'

'Odin. Just Odin.'

'But is Odin your given name or your surname?'

Odin didn't know anything about given names or surnames, so he merely repeated his name again.

'Odin. Odin. Odin.'

And this time the lady seemed to understand. She wrote 'Odin' twice, once in each of two different spaces on the form in her lap.

'And your identity number?'

Odin knew quite well this was some part of Veterinarius Martinussen's regulations, but as he didn't know what the nurse was talking about, he just looked at her without replying.

'The identity number?' she repeated. 'Or perhaps a driving licence or some other form of ID?'

'If it isn't too much trouble, I wonder if you would be so kind as to explain a little more precisely,' said Odin twisting his beard around his fingers.

'Identification!' exclaimed the nurse with undisguised irritation.

Odin shook his head. He had no idea what to say; he needed to get hold of Veterinarius Martinussen, but to do that he had to answer every possible kind of question to which he didn't know the answer.

The nurse gave a deep sigh and closed her eyes, then opened them again and glanced almost tolerantly at Odin.

'Let's try something different,' she said, appearing calm. 'Where do you live?'

'You see,' said Odin slowly, tugging at his beard as he

puzzled over how best to explain. 'It is really very unfortunate, but I am afraid I am unable for the moment to give you any exact position for my home.' Odin wasn't sure if it would help his situation if he told the uniformed lady that he could not remember it. In order to be as obliging as possible – and taking into consideration Veterinarius Martinussen's regulations – he went on: 'It is probably reasonably accurate to say it is more or less a couple of weeks' journey north of the Pole Star.'

'Now just give me the full address,' the nurse ordered him in a sharp tone. Her lips narrowed into a slit, and a deep furrow appeared on her forehead.

Odin tugged at his beard and didn't reply. First, he had no idea what an address was, and next, he had to admit that he was no longer quite so happy about the white-clad lady's curiosity.

'If you cannot give me an address, then at least tell me where you were born? Or which country you come from?' said the nurse, becoming exasperated.

Now Odin had had enough. 'You must truly pardon me, but I honestly have no idea what purpose all these questions can afford. Regulations or no regulations, I am in very great haste and so have no time whatsoever for all this, and I am absolutely sure and certain that Veterinarius Martinussen will understand. So please be so kind as to excuse me, but if you are unable to fetch Veterinarius Martinussen now, I had better go out and search for him myself.' Odin rolled around and was on his way out of bed again, but the white-uniformed lady looked so furious that in order not to seem rude he added: 'You see, I am on the horns of an extremely troubling dilemma. A day or two ago I flew into a meteor storm, and Rigmarole broke her leg. I was forced to land my sleigh on an island not so far from here, where the people of Smith's Town, as well as the people of Post Office Town, were kind enough to rack their brains, until the sea froze over and I was able to walk to the Continent to fetch the Veterinarius. I thank you for all you have done, but I really am obliged to leave.'

At last Odin had succeeded in making clear his need for haste to the white-uniformed lady.

'Wait here, I'll be back in a moment,' she shouted and dashed out of the room.

At this point a few moments more or less would make no difference, and Odin sincerely wanted to show his goodwill and deep respect for Continental traditions and regulations. Mumbling, he climbed back into bed and lay down; he was ready to greet Veterinarius Martinussen.

After less than a minute the white-uniformed lady came back with a black-haired man also in white.

'Thank you, a thousand thanks for your help. Many, many thanks,' said Odin to the nurse, greatly cheered, and bowed as gracefully as he could from his prone position.

As the patient seemed completely harmless Dr Martinussen winked briefly at the nurse, indicating her presence was no longer necessary.

'Now, sir,' he said to Odin, 'just tell me what the problem is?'

'Oh, I am truly uplifted to have finally found you, for I am on the horns of an extremely troubling dilemma. Rigmarole needs your help as quickly as possible,' said Odin and repeated his story word for word, exactly as he had told it to the nurse. 'So now you will understand how urgent it is,' he concluded his account.

Meanwhile Veterinarius Martinussen had sat down, and he made no sign of wanting to move again immediately.

'If you don't mind, you should put on a warm overcoat, it is very cold out on the ice.' Odin rolled around and was about to get out of bed for the third time when Dr Martinussen asked him to wait a moment.

'My dear sir,' said the doctor, laying a friendly hand on Odin's arm. 'I am afraid you were out in the blizzard too long yesterday. And although you seem to have survived remarkably, I think you will have to stay here for a day or two.'

Odin pulled at his beard anxiously, and Dr Martinussen hastened to add: 'There is no need to worry. It is merely a question of following regulations, purely routine. I will look after everything, and it will certainly not take more than a day or two, three at most.'

A day or two or at most three were more than Odin had expected to spend on the Continent, but if the regulations prescribed that, there really was nothing he could do about it. So he nodded in agreement and began to describe the way to Smith's Town as well as he could remember it, so that Veterinarius Martinussen should be well prepared when they set off.

'No need to worry, sir. Not at all,' Dr Martinussen interrupted Odin's explanation with a big smile. 'Everything will be in order before you know it, you can rely on that,' he said, and rang for the nurse.

*

The next few days were very confusing for Odin. Various people clad in all kinds of white uniforms kept coming to see him and asking the same questions time and time again. Each time precisely the same thing happened: Odin answered all the questions in every particular as well as he could. At some point or another, almost always when he came to the meteor storm or the description of Smith's Town, or to his home in the direction of a week or two's journey north of the Pole Star, or when he get to the point of describing how the people of Smith's Town had been so very kind and racked their brains to work out how he could walk across the sea to the Continent, the white-uniformed ones said he was hallucinating and asked him what he really meant and if he honestly could not remember anything more. In the end he gave up and refused to say another word, and just waited for Veterinarius Martinussen to be finished with his regulations.

The medical experts discussed Odin's case at various meetings. They did not doubt the little old man was disturbed and had developed obsessions from being out too long in the cold and the blizzard, but nor did they doubt that in time he would recover if he was to receive the correct treatment and was kept under strict observation. No, the real problem lay elsewhere: they were unable to establish Odin's identity. They had contacted the police, but no one answering to Odin's description had been reported missing, and no one with the name Odin Odin was registered in the census, which contained the names of the entire population. The woman who had brought the little old man to hospital had no more information on his identity than the doctors and was of no help. Indeed, she was actually becoming a nuisance; she had already phoned four times to ask after him. No matter how many times the nurses explained to her that the little old man was suffering from obsessions and hallucinations, she continued to insist that he had seemed completely clear-headed the evening she had picked him up – although she had to admit he hadn't uttered a word.

The doctors kept on transferring Odin from one unit to another, and each time Sigbrit Holland rang she was obliged to repeat who she was, and why she was asking, merely to find herself confronted with numerous different voices before she finally reached one who was able and willing to inform her about Odin's state of health. Even then they would not tell her any more, because she was not a relative and therefore had no right to be told anything at all. The only reason for her being able to follow Odin on his travels around the hospital was that some of the nurses felt sympathetic towards the little old man.

Sigbrit had no idea why she took so much interest in the case of the old man, who, the hospital informed her, called himself Odin Odin. But it seemed she could not forget him until she was sure he was doing well, and when she discovered on New Year's Day that the doctors had transferred him to the secure section of the National Hospital she felt bound to take action. First she tried without success to convince the nurse that there had been a mistake. But the nurse had no power to alter the decision of a doctor, and no doctor would come to the telephone to discuss a case which caused no actual alarm with someone who was not a member of the patient's family. The only thing Sigbrit achieved was to persuade the nurse to phone the National Hospital and obtain permission for her to visit Odin.

At the National Hospital Sigbrit had to identify herself, fill in a lengthy form and write her signature in a book. A muscular and somewhat scruffy nursing assistant took her through two locked doors and down a bare corridor to Room 13, which Odin shared with three other patients. Luckily the other patients, with the exception of a very thin and rather bald man who sat absolutely motionless on a chair in the corner, were in the over-crowded television room which Sigbrit had passed in the corridor.

There was an unpleasant reek of old sweat and disinfectant in the room, and for a brief moment Sigbrit regretted she had come. But she pulled herself together, drew up a chair beside Odin's bed and sat down. She spoke softly to the little old man, who was lying on top of the duvet with his eye closed.

'Odin. Odin, it's Sigbrit.'

Odin opened his eye and sat up. 'Sigbrit Holland, five hundred and forty-two, six hundred and fourteen, thirty-four. Good morning and welcome,' he said, bowing politely.

Sigbrit shook his hand. Then she asked him how he was feeling.

'I? I am really well and better than ever. But Rigmarole, that is another matter, I fear.' Odin twisted his beard around his fingers and wrinkled his brow anxiously at the thought of his horse.

'Rigmarole?'

'Do you not remember? Rigmarole is the one of my two horses who had the misfortune to break her leg, and now we cannot go further before Veterinarius Martinussen has been good enough to set the unfortunate leg.'

Sigbrit raised her eyebrows. 'Veterinarius Martinussen?' she asked, for the first time ready to admit to herself that the doctors might be right.

'Yes, the one you brought me to,' insisted Odin. 'As soon as Veterinarius Martinussen has finished with the regulations, he will go back with me to Smith's Town and Rigmarole. But truly I do not understand what is keeping him so long.'

Sigbrit drummed her fingers on the edge of her chair. 'Smith's Town?' she said tentatively. 'Where is Smith's Town?'

'Smith's Town is the most important village east of Post Office Town.'

Sigbrit shook her head, and her fingers danced faster; she had never heard of either of the villages.

'On the island, about a day's walk across the sea,' maintained Odin.

Sigbrit shook her head again. She knew for certain that the only island in the Strait was Ur Island, and there were no towns there called either Smith's Town or Post Office Town. 'Are you sure you did not come here to the Queendom of South Norseland from North Norseland?' she asked.

'North Norseland?' Odin repeated, pulling at his beard thoughtfully. 'Is that part of the Continent?'

'Not entirely,' said Sigbrit. 'It is the land that lies on the other side of the Straits, north-east of South Norseland.'

Odin chewed over this piece of information for a moment, but no, he was sure that the people of Smith's Town had never mentioned any place called North Norseland. But it was also true they had not mentioned that the Continent was called South Norseland either. With one hand Odin smoothed his already perfectly smooth beard.

There was something odd about this story. Sigbrit was convinced Odin was telling the truth, at least the truth as he knew it, but at the same time she knew that the island he spoke of did not exist.

'You said your horse had broken a leg. As far as I know it is very difficult to heal a horse's leg. Would you by any chance be able to tell me where the break is?' she asked, to test Odin's mental powers in another way.

Odin's face lit up; finally here was someone who was interested in Rigmarole, and he started on a long and detailed description of where he had found the two fractures in his unfortunate mare's leg, adding finally that Ida-Anna was looking after Rigmarole, yes, and also Balthazar, his other horse, while he himself was on the Continent finding the Veterinarius. Next he went on to describe Smith's Town, as well as Post Office Town, and all the people he knew there: the Blacksmith and Oldmother Rikke-Marie and the Baker and Mother Marie, the mother of Ida-Anna and Ingolf, and Uncle Eskild, whose hearing left a lot to be desired, and Long Laust from Post Office Town, who had been the first one to tell him the sea was frozen over.

Although it sounded strange, it made enough sense not to be pure fantasy, thought Sigbrit. And it might well be true that Odin had walked all day through the blizzard when she met him, he had been so frozen. She glanced at her watch and rose hastily.

'Now listen,' she said, a little nervously. 'I have to leave now. But don't worry, I will do what I can to untangle things. I'll be back in a day or two.'

The very thin, very bald man who had been sitting quite still during the whole of Sigbrit's conversation with Odin, now leapt to his feet and shouted, 'I have a horse too! I have a horse too!' Then he slid down on to the floor and began to sob wildly as he hammered the brown linoleum with his clenched fists. Two male nurses came running, and while one took a firm hold on the distraught patient, the other gave him an injection of something that must have been fairly effective, since it immediately reduced his weeping to quiet sniffling.

Sigbrit shuddered; she couldn't leave the little old man languishing in this madhouse.

When the doors had slammed behind his guest, Odin went into the television room, where most of the other patients were deeply immersed in a football match. For a few minutes Odin too gazed at the rectangular screen, on which twenty-two diminutive men in short trousers chases around after a small ball that they kicked away from themselves as soon as they succeeded in getting close to it. This in itself was quite remarkable, Odin thought, yet still more remarkable was that the twenty-two men ran around on green grass in clear sunny weather. He looked around but none of his fellow patients looked as if they found the scene surprising, and after pondering the phenomenon for a while Odin couldn't help asking: 'Where is all the snow?'

A huge man with a gigantic head, who was at least half as tall again as Odin, turned around in his chair and stared angrily at the little old man. 'What do you mean, *where is all the snow?*' growled the man. His name was Gunnar, and not only was Gunnar's head a great deal larger than the Blacksmith's, he was also both very much broader and a great deal taller than anyone else who had ever set foot in the secure section for the mentally ill at the National Hospital. Gunnar was fond of sport – that was why nothing else was ever watched in the television room. Something which Gunnar did not care for was being disturbed in the middle of a game of football. Only a new arrival could be ignorant of that.

A nervous silence spread around the television room.

'A couple of days ago I arrived in a truly terrifying blizzard, and look at that, there is no snow.' Odin pointed at the screen without noticing the big man's scowl.

Gunnar turned his giant's head and glanced in the direction of Odin's finger. 'It's Brazil, isn't it, you great fool!' he roared.

'Now, now,' Odin said amiably. 'There's no need to shout. I may be old but I am not deaf.'

Tension rose in the television room, and several of the patients crept out, while others were not going to miss being entertained by the new arrival's boldness.

'You're new here, aren't you?' Gunnar rose from his chair with a sly grin. Odin also rose, as he thought that would be the polite thing to do. Gunnar's smile vanished immediately; a little wimp like this wouldn't offer the feeblest resistance.

With slow strides Gunnar started to walk towards the window where Odin stood. Eager as he was to show goodwill and deep respect for the people of the Continent and their customs, Odin also took a step forward, trying to hold his right arm to his side in exactly the same manner as the man opposite him. What Odin could not know was that Gunnar, besides once having been an excellent blacksmith, had also been a fine football player who had won many victories for the home side. One day, when Gunnar threw himself at a ball, his head had cannoned into another player's, and ever since he had been unfailingly convinced that his head was a football which he was obliged to carry with him wherever he went.

When Gunnar saw Odin holding his hand to his side in the same way as he did himself, he blinked once or twice and then burst into hearty laughter, slapping himself on the thigh with his free left hand.

'Ha, ha,' chuckled Gunnar. 'I might have known it. Sorry about that.' He clapped Odin on the shoulder in all friendliness, but with strength enough to send the little old man several metres into the room.

'You've certainly had a good one on the old dial, haven't you?' Gunnar had stopped laughing and was pointing at Odin's missing left eye. He put out his hand. 'Gunnar, Gunnar the Head,' he introduced himself proudly and gave Odin's hand a squeeze that made the little old man yelp with pain.

Gunnar the Head sat down again and lifted Odin on to his broad lap. The other patients stared at them transfixed.

'What you gawping at? Ain't you seen a man meet an old mate before? Shut your traps and let us watch the rest of the match in peace.' Gunnar the Head put an arm around Odin to make sure his friend was sitting comfortably.

*

Sigbrit visited Odin again the following week, but she had no good news to bring him. She had phoned and written to the doctors at the National Hospital, and when that yielded no result she had contacted the Chief Executive, and when he was unable to help her she had consulted a lawyer – but all to no avail. The doctors were within their rights: an individual who posed a danger to his own or others' lives and welfare could be sectioned by the correct authorities for as long as was considered necessary. Sigbrit didn't think Odin was a danger to anyone, but the doctors maintained that he had already put his own life in danger, and since he still did not seem to have the slightest idea of who or where he was he would most probably do so again.

Sigbrit gave up on the authorities and instead started to search for Odin's relations; by taking responsibility for his welfare a relative would have the right to get the little old man released. She could find no one, however, either in South Norseland or the other Nordic countries, who had the surname of Odin. Even the Immigration Department had never heard of the name.

In the meantime the police began to take a certain interest in Odin's case. Their assumption was that Odin was an illegal immigrant who had dreamed up a fantastic fairy tale about meteor storms, horses with broken legs, strange beings and non-existent islands merely to gain asylum in South Norseland. The Queendom of South Norseland was well known for its tolerance of foreigners from every corner of the world, but with increasing unemployment and rising numbers of immigrants this famed tolerance had considerably faded. There is no doubt that if the police had been able to trace Odin's origins to a country south of the South Norseland border they would promptly have sent him back there on a single ticket. But the police had no more success in their search for Odin's forebears than Sigbrit Holland, and taking into account the cuts in their budget and the subsequent loss of staff it was quickly decided to put the case on hold for the time being.

Sigbrit had to acknowledge her own failure. There was only one resource left to her: she could go to the press. She pushed aside her work – and her bad conscience – for a few hours and wrote a brief article on Odin. She explained how he had turned up on an apparently unknown island on the twenty-fourth of December, how on the twenty-sixth he had walked over the sea to South Norseland (she noted the place where she had met him and his appearance), and she wrote how the authorities had refused to release him from hospital. After some consideration she added Odin's own account of his home somewhere in the direction of a week or two's journey north of the Pole Star, about the unspecified warning he carried, and his encounter with a meteor storm, in which his mare Rigmarole had broken her leg – which perhaps was a key to something she had not yet understood. Sigbrit sent the article to a national newspaper, but some days passed without it being printed. She called the editor only to be informed that they could not print such twaddle; this was a serious newspaper. Sigbrit was on the point of saying that Odin's story was just as serious as any other story in the paper, it was a case of the rights of the individual in South Norseland, but the editor had already put the receiver down. Next she tried one or two other papers and television channels, all with the same result: no one was interested in Odin's story.

'This can't be right!' exclaimed Sigbrit, with rare anger, to her husband; Odin was in effect being locked up for an indefinite period with no possibility of appeal.

'What are you getting so excited about?' smiled Fridtjof. 'The poor chap is old and senile. He has no family. One day you'll find he invented the whole story merely to get a spot of attention and human contact.' Fridtjof went into the kitchen and came back with a glass of red wine. 'Here, drink this. You need to calm down a bit.' He handed the glass to Sigbrit.

'What d'you mean, I need to calm down? I can't just allow this to happen to someone I know.' She drummed the fingers of her right hand hard against her thigh.

'But you barely know him! Stop this now, you've just been led up the garden path.' Fridtjof laughed and drank from the glass Sigbrit had refused.

'How can you say that? You haven't even met him. Come with me one day, then you'll see what I mean.' She didn't voice the tinge of doubt that was gnawing at her.

'Sigbrit, for God's sake! I don't want to waste my time on that kind of thing, and nor should you. When will you realize that you can't be responsible for every single nutcase you come across?'

'Odin is no nutcase!' Sigbrit shouted angrily. She ran upstairs and slammed the bedroom door behind her. She leaned her back against the door and drew deep breaths. She could still hear Fridtjof laughing.

Next day Sigbrit visited Odin in her lunchbreak. She had had an idea. 'It's the internet,' she said. 'I have access to it through the bank where I work. If I put your case on the 'net, we might find someone who can get you out of hospital.'

'It is not because I want to complain at the service here on the Continent,' said Odin, scratching at his beard. 'But it's true I am in great haste, so if you would remind Veterinarius Martinussen that Rigmarole and her unfortunate leg is waiting, and that it would be best if he could hurry up a little with the regulations, I would really be extremely grateful to you.'

'Of course,' Sigbrit replied a little hesitantly, before going on in a firmer voice. 'Do you know if any of your friends have access to the internet?'

'The internet, the internet,' repeated Odin, trying to look as if he really had heard of it before.

'Yes, the computer network that reaches all over the world.'

Odin twisted and tugged his beard as he considered which particular net for which kind of fish could reach from Smith's Town across the sea to the Continent and on to the rest of the world.

'No, I don't think so, unfortunately,' he said at last, shaking his head. 'No, all things considered, and taking account of the cliffs, I don't think it would be possible.'

Sigbrit sighed.

'I don't know what else we can do. Unless you get out of here you can't show the Veterinarius the way to your horse.

And I can't do it because I don't know where Smith's Town is. So let us have a try, anyway.' She bit her lip. 'Look, if only I could find one person who knows Smith's Town or Post Office Town or just the island itself, it would confirm your story and the doctors would have to let you go.'

As Sigbrit did not want to discourage Odin she didn't tell him about the police enquiries. There was no point in him knowing that, as things were, he would – even if he escaped from hospital – immediately and until his identity was established, be taken into custody by the police.

As soon as Sigbrit was back at the bank she switched on the computer, logged on to the internet and typed in Odin's story. A few minutes later it was on its way out into the world.

*

At first the internet seemed to be yet another blind alley. Sigbrit Holland arrived at work early next morning and quickly skimmed through the numerous answers. There were scores of them, some morally enlightening, some about self-help groups for missing persons, some were racist, others religious and others obscene. But not one contained so much as a straw to clutch at. Towards the end of the morning Sigbrit received two phone calls. The first was from a nurse at the National Hospital who asked whether she had anything to do with what was going on.

'What is going on...?' Sigbrit did not understand.

'There is a crowd outside the windows, they have banners with all kinds of things on them: *"Free Christ"*, *"Jesus Christ has come again"*, and *"Odin, hold out, we know who you are – we have come to save Our Lord"*. And then they are singing hymns and that sort of thing. There's a god-awful racket!' The nurse's voice shook with anger.

'No, I'm sorry, I don't know anything about that. I really have no idea what it can be about.' A smile slowly spread over Sigbrit's face. Maybe it wasn't so crazy after all. 'No, I have no idea what can have caused it.' Sigbrit was about to ring off but at the last moment she added: 'Listen, you'd better be careful, maybe they're right!'

She rang off and laughed quietly; now surely the press would be interested in Odin. For safety's sake Sigbrit seized the phone again and dialled the number of the national television channel. Without giving her name she suggested they should go to the National Hospital.

A moment later her phone rang again.

'You must talk to Ambrosius,' said a hoarse man's voice.

'Ambrosius who?'

'Ambrosius the Fisherman.'

'And what can Ambrosius the Fisherman tell me?'

The voice hesitated, then continued quietly, 'He knows the island.'

Sigbrit straightened her back and seized a pencil. 'Where can I find him?'

'A fishing boat alongside Firø Canal. Green and orange.'

'But at which end of the canal?'

'She is called the *Rikke-Marie*. You can't miss her.'

'And you, who are you?' asked Sigbrit, but the receiver had been put down.

Ambrosius the Fisherman. It couldn't do any harm. Her lunchbreak was due in a few minutes, so why not try?

At precisely half past twelve Sigbrit Holland put on her coat and left the large office building. Firø was a tiny island in the midst of a wilderness of canals, which were connected to the capital of South Norseland, Fredenshvile, by one single bridge. Sigbrit walked briskly, but the sleet was slashing down and in spite of her umbrella her clothes and hair were quickly soaked. She crossed the bridge and then walked northwards beside the first canal. She walked slowly now, carefully inspecting all the boats. There were houseboats, sailing boats, fishing boats, rowing boats and all kinds of Heath Robinson models, but not a single one that resembled a green and orange fishing boat. At the end she turned on her heel, trudging back through the slush and then following the southern section of the canal. She walked as close to the quay as possible in order not to overlook anything, but there was no boat that matched the description she had been given.

She drew near the other end of the canal where the water took a turn to the right and joined wider waterways. Here only a few boats remained. Sigbrit stumbled over the uneven cobblestones and stepped into a deep puddle. She swore soundlessly; what a fool to let herself be taken in like that and in such weather.

'Hey, sweetheart, what are you up to?' Two middle-aged men sat on a bench with full and empty beer bottles spread around them, apparently completely indifferent to the downpour.

She might just as well ask them.

'*Rikke-Marie*? Ah yes, isn't that Ambrosius the Fisherman's?' one of the men mumbled. He pointed to the bend in the canal. As soon as Sigbrit had rounded the corner, behind a big white motorboat she could see an old wooden fishing boat. It was pretty battered, but without doubt green and orange. A nameplate on the bow was inscribed in neatly hand-written letters '*Rikke-Marie*'. The boat was fourteen to fifteen metres long, and a large part of the deck was covered by a wheelhouse that looked as if at some point the owner had built it on to make a more comfortable residence. There was no bell on the quay to ring but having come so far she didn't intend to give up.

'Hallo!' she tried calling. 'Hallo-o, is there anyone at home?'

No one answered and Sigbrit called out once more. She hesitated for a moment, glanced at her watch and then jumped resolutely over the rail and down on to the deck. The door was on the port side of the wheelhouse at the stern of the boat. She knocked hard three times. A few seconds passed, then a hoarse voice uttered: 'Come in!'

Sigbrit opened the door and entered a narrow but shipshape, cosy space. Two houseplants hung from a hook in the ceiling, the windows were framed in white canvas curtains, and here and there candles in port wine glasses filled with sand threw a warm light. A row of well-polished instruments, unfamiliar to Sigbrit, filled the rear wall.

'See, see,' said a man's voice behind her, 'what fine guests we have today, Ambrosius.'

Sigbrit spun round.

The man had unruly reddish-blond hair and a trim beard with just a hint of grey. His face was broad and weatherbeaten, his eyes deep grey-blue and at the moment screwed up into a teasing smile. He didn't get up, but even sitting down he was impressively large.

'I am sorry to burst in on you unannounced like this,' Sigbrit apologized nervously. 'But I have a rather strange problem, and someone whose name I did not catch rang and said Ambrosius the Fisherman could help me.'

The man waited.

'Ambrosius?' asked Sigbrit tentatively, casting her eyes around the wheelhouse without seeing anyone else.

'Speak out, speak out, Lady Fair. We are here to listen. But first sit down and get comfortable. Make yourself at home and pour some coffee from the jug over there. There are cups in the small cupboard, indeed right in front of your fairy-tale eyes.' The Fisherman pointed to a cupboard hanging on the walls above a narrow kitchen table.

Sigbrit poured herself a mug of steaming coffee, took off her wet coat and sat down in the corner of a narrow wooden bench.

'Now you can talk.' Ambrosius the Fisherman leaned back and looked at her expectantly.

He wasn't young, but nor was he as old as Sigbrit had imagined. She drummed her fingers, pulled herself together and started on her story.

'I don't know how to explain this. I don't know where to begin or where to stop. It's a pretty strange story.' Sigbrit gulped a mouthful of coffee, put down her cup and then told Ambrosius the Fisherman how she had come across Odin one evening over a month ago, how the authorities had sectioned the little old man, how he couldn't persuade them to discharge him, and finally the hardest part, Odin's explanation. 'I know it must be hard to believe but I am convinced he is telling the truth, at least, the truth as he knows it.' She sighed and shook her head. 'If only I hadn't driven him to hospital that first night, but instead had taken him home with me. As it is, it's my fault that he is locked up, and it's my fault that his horse hasn't received any treatment yet.'

Ambrosius the Fisherman had listened to Sigbrit Holland in

silence, calmly smoking his pipe and now and then lifting his mug to his mouth.

'Although it's a crazy situation it is not completely mad,' was all he said.

'I was told you know the island?' Sigbrit tried after a moment's silence.

'People say so many things.' The Fisherman glanced enquiringly into her eyes. 'Listen here.' He suddenly grew serious. 'What we are going to tell you now, we have never before mentioned to anyone. The fact is that if we had told anyone about it they would not have believed us, or else the few who would have known we were telling the truth would have made sure we remained silent. Don't ask us why. That's just the way it is.' The Fisherman glanced around the wheelhouse, then leaned forward and went on in a hoarse whisper: 'The island does exist!'

'What?'

'Yes.' Ambrosius the Fisherman nodded and straightened himself again.

'And you know it?'

'Shh.' He fidgeted nervously on the bench. 'Know it and don't know it. We know it is there, if that's what you mean.'

'I don't understand...' Sigbrit shook her head.

'As true as our name is Ambrosius, as true as we are a fisherman, and as true as we have ploughed the Strait more thoroughly than anyone else in this country – that island exists!' He hesitated a moment. 'The island exists, but at the same time it doesn't exist.' He placed his cup in the saucer with a violence that made the contents spill.

'I don't understand...' Sigbrit repeated.

'Lady Fair, Lady Fair! How many times must we tell you? The

island exists, but it doesn't exist.' The Fisherman sounded irritated. 'It doesn't exist in this world, that's what we're saying.'

'I'm sorry.' Sigbrit bit her underlip and a faint blush coloured her cheeks.

'Now, now. No need for tears, Lady Fair. Maybe it isn't so simple, after all. Listen here, no matter what you are going to hear, you didn't get it from us.'

'No, no. Of course not. I won't say anything to anyone,' Sigbrit said softly.

'Swear you will not tell.'

Sigbrit couldn't help smiling, but the Fisherman's face remained stern.

'I swear.' Sigbrit suddenly felt gripped by the situation and went on in a serious voice: 'I swear in the name of Odin and by all I hold dear that I will never ever tell anyone that you have told me what you are now about to say.'

'Good.' Ambrosius the Fisherman pulled at his pipe, and sweet blue tobacco smoke wafted around the wheelhouse. 'In the end there is not much we can tell.' He took his pipe out of his mouth and lowered his voice. 'As we said, the island does exist, and it does not. It is located in the middle of the Strait, precisely midway between South Norseland and North Norseland, just off Hverv Harbour. Where it does not exist is in people's heads and in official records.'

Sigbrit Holland understood less than ever and was almost regretting she had come. The Fisherman seemed even more disturbed than the doctors accused Odin of being; only think, she had been about to take him seriously.

'In the place we are talking about there is a line of high cliffs.' Ambrosius the Fisherman caught sight of Sigbrit's sceptical expression and continued angrily: 'All the men of the sea know them, they are even noted on the navigation charts. Indeed, it is a fact that no one out in the Strait can fail to catch sight of them.'

Sigbrit lowered her eyes.

'The rock formations rise up from the seabed, sharp and treacherous. It's sheer suicide to go anywhere near them.' The Fisherman hesitated a moment before going on. 'When you are navigating the Strait you sail either to the east or the west around the cliffs, and you always see precisely the same series of rocky cliffs. One after the other, precisely the same. Or rather, that is what you think you see.' Again the Fisherman hesitated. 'What you really see are two different series, an ellipse of symmetric formations.' He looked Sigbrit Holland straight in the eye.

'And the island lies in between?' she guessed.

'In between them, there lies the island.'

There was silence for a few seconds in the wheelhouse, then Sigbrit asked: 'But why is it such a secret?'

Ambrosius the Fisherman rose and went over to the port-hole. He looked out for a while, then closed the curtains and turned back to his guest. 'We don't know,' he said. 'We really don't know. We have pondered over it for many years, and we still do not know.'

'But planes?' asked Sigbrit. 'Although no boats can approach it, you must be able to see it from the air?'

The Fisherman looked at her as if he wasn't sure whether to reply or not. Finally he said in a hushed voice: 'There is a yellowish grey mist over the cliffs. Always, whether the sun shines or it is pouring with rain. And the planes don't go there. They don't fly over the island and they don't go anywhere near it.'

'But why not?'

'We don't know,' sighed the Fisherman. 'They just don't.'

He rested his hands on the worn mahogany table and leaned forward, until Sigbrit could feel his warm breath on her face. *'Name the island, and all Hell will break out,'* he whispered, straightened up and went on in a normal voice. 'That's what the men of the sea say. Some think the island is the devil's fireplace. If it is mentioned, it wakes the devil, and war and misfortune will follow. Others think the island is paradise, but that it will vanish if you talk about it.'

'And you believe that?'

'Well, what do we know? We are only an ignorant fisherman, and all this is a cock and bull story, like those the men of the sea spend their evenings dreaming up when they are far from home and there are no women around.' Ambrosius the Fisherman's eyes twinkled roguishly. 'All we know for certain is that the island must not be mentioned, and that's good enough for me.'

Sigbrit drank the rest of her coffee. 'So you think Odin might have come from the island between the cliffs?' she asked.

'It might be, and then again it might not. How should we know?' Obviously Ambrosius the Fisherman felt he had said more than enough.

'What good is it to me, what you have told me, if I can't talk about it to anyone, and if you don't believe Odin can have come from the island?'

'Firstly we didn't say the little old man did not come from the island, only that we cannot know that. Secondly, we didn't say you cannot talk about it to anyone, only that all Hell may break out if you do, and that regardless of what happens, you must never tell anyone you heard the story from us.'

Sigbrit considered the situation; the story she had just heard did not seem to have clarified it at all.

'What shall I do now?' she asked.

Ambrosius the Fisherman stroked his forehead wearily and sat down.

'What do they teach you young folks at school these days? Obviously not to use your wits. We have to tell you everything. Everything!' He hesitated, as if weighing something up, then leaned forward and looked sharply at Sigbrit. 'If we tell you now what to do you must promise us to bring the little old man here.' He laid a hand on Sigbrit's arm. 'We cannot tell you why, but we would very much like to meet him.'

Sigbrit nodded.

'Ring the Ministry of Justice. Ask to speak to the Minister.'

'I would never be allowed to get through to him!' Sigbrit had not expected such a silly idea.

'Hang on, Lady Fair. You are far too impatient. Don't young people learn how to behave at all nowadays?'

Sigbrit reddened, but the Fisherman did not seem to be as cross as his words suggested. 'Now listen, if they block you, just say you know about the island without a name, and that the Minister would be very annoyed if he knew they had refused you. If they continue to cause problems, threaten them with the press. There's nothing a politician fears more than journalists. Do you understand?'

'But I still don't know anything whatsoever about the island.'

'That's of no consequence. You only need to *say* you do, and that you intend to make it public knowledge if the Minister does not guarantee that the little old man is immediately set free, with permission to stay in South Norseland just so long as he wishes or needs to.'

'What if that doesn't work?'

'Believe me, it will.'

Sigbrit bit her lip; she didn't much like the idea of phoning the Minister. She glanced at the clock on the wall and jumped to her feet. It was two o'clock already; she would be late back at the bank.

There was a shadowy movement at the far end of the wheel-house, and a faint cough. Sigbrit could not see anyone, but someone was certainly there.

'If I'd known we were not alone...' she began.

'No need to be alarmed.' Ambrosius the Fisherman indicated the corner where the shadow had moved. 'Der Fremdling. He has no voice.'

Sigbrit felt like saying something, expressing her sympathy or introducing herself, but his voice did not encourage her. Instead she thanked the Fisherman for the information and promised to let him know what happened next. Then she left the wheelhouse, climbed on to the quay side and ran the whole way back to the bank.

She was very late, but she was glad to get away from the green and orange fishing boat. She felt unsure of herself, without knowing why. Perhaps it was the strange story of the island, or perhaps it was Der Fremdling; the mere thought of the gaunt dark figure sent cold shivers down her back. And yet there was something else too.

Sigbrit walked into the bank, took the lift to the third floor and tried to ignore the disapproving faces of her colleagues as they watched her walk through the office right over to her own desk.

*

'We shall overcome. We shall overcome...' roared the crowds.

'It's all right, you can come out now, it's quite safe. They're only singing,' called Gunnar the Head from the window, waving to Odin. But the little old man did not move.

It had started early in the morning. They had sauntered along, one after another, or in small groups of two or three or four, and gradually they had grown into a sizeable congregation of a couple of hundred people. To start with, while it was still dark, they had arrived carrying lighted candles and torches; later they had strident banners and umbrellas against the sleet. They massed in the car park in front of the psychiatric unit and sang hymns and called upon Our Lord, and some of the women passed round coffee and cakes. At first there were no obvious leaders and if it had not been for the writing on the banners, the constant yelling of battle cries and the appalling weather, the demonstration could have been taken for an office outing. From time to time an individual daringly stepped forward and shouted out a few words before retreating into the safety of the crowd. Then, at mid-morning, a young man with spectacles pushed resolutely between the demonstrators with an empty beer crate in his hand. The man in glasses turned the crate upside down and climbed on to it with solemn earnestness. He looked around him, but few had noticed him.

'Our Lord has come back to us!' yelled the man dramatically, blinking vigorously.

Several demonstrators turned their heads and looked at him.

'The Day of Judgement nears. You, who are without faith, are afraid. But do not let the unbelievers repeat Pilate's crime. Do not let the South Norseland authorities confine and crucify our reborn Christ, the Mighty One. We must force them to free the Son of God!'

The bespectacled man had spoken well. His words had moved people, and an elderly gentleman shook a clenched fist in the air.

'Free Christ!' he yelled.

'Liberate the reborn Christ' chimed in a frail woman from her wheelchair.

'Give us Odin! Give us Odin!' screamed the man in glasses, raising his arms above his head, and soon all the other Pious chorused: 'Give us Odin! Give us Odin!'

At this point Odin took fright and retreated along the corridor, where he found shelter under a table. Regardless of how many times nurses and doctors assured him he would come to no harm, Odin refused to come out. The only time he moved his huddled body was when Gunnar the Head had some lunch delivered to him. No, Odin had not much faith in human beings carrying lit torches in broad daylight, who shouted his name so loudly. How truthful the doctors had been when they told him the world outside the unit was a dangerous place it was best to avoid; there were indeed good reasons for the doors to the Continent outside to be double-locked.

In mid-afternoon, between two showers, the man in spectacles led some of the Pious forward in an attempt to force entry to the hospital and liberate the reborn Christ. A minor episode ensued, security was intensified and the Pious were forced back. The security guards had shown their superiority and neither the bespectacled man nor anyone else dared to move forward again. Towards evening most of the Pious went home; cold, tired and hungry. Only a small core of the most fervent stayed in the car park to prevent the Son of God being moved under cover of darkness to a different hospital.

*

The same evening there were pictures on the news bulletins showing the Pious praying, waving their banners and battling with the security guards.

'The demonstrators, who call themselves Born Anew Christians' – the camera zoomed in on the man in spectacles, who was exhorting the other Pious from his empty beer crate – 'maintain that an elderly man who was admitted to the National Hospital, is the Reborn Christ. The so-called Born Anew Christians believe the elderly man has come to warn of an impending doomsday and a thousand-year Kingdom of Peace on Earth, and they are insisting that the hospital should release him immediately.' The newsreader could not hold back a smile. 'The elderly man, Mr Odin Odin, is considered by the medical experts to be seriously ill. He is said to be suffering from delusions and has been in hospital since...'

Fridtjof switched off the television.

'Look what a hullabaloo you have caused!' he said, pushing his plate away angrily.

Sigbrit shrugged her shoulders and made no reply. The right-hand corner of her mouth crinkled into a little smile; there was no longer any need to call the Minister of Justice.

*

The news came to an end, and in an apartment in central Fredenshvile – not far from the hospital where Odin had at last emerged from his refuge – the young law student Ezra switched off the television and went into the dining room where his parents were listening to his little brother Ezekiel reciting verses from the Torah.

It was the night before the Sabbath, and his mother had already lit the candles and put bread on the table. Ezekiel's dark blond ringlets were long and feminine and often fell over the sacred text, but he simply brushed them aside without once breaking off his reading of the holy word, which he knew by heart though he still read his way through as prescribed. Yes, Ezekiel was a good Jew and his parents' pride and joy; but Ezra had never studied the Torah and the other sacred texts, nor was he well versed in the daily and weekly prayers and sacred rituals.

Ezekiel turned a page reverently and only broke the rhythm of his reading to draw breath. How Ezra hated him! No, they could just wait and see what he, Ezra, would achieve in this world one day, while Ezekiel would show himself to be the nonentity he was.

With a deep sigh Ezekiel ended his devout recitation and carefully closed the book in his hands. Ezra regarded his pious expression with scorn – a little brother whose vacant eyes and lack of basic talents had been taken almost for divinity – and his thoughts reverted to the news item he had just seen. An idea was dawning on him.

YMER AND AUDHUMLA

Four streams of milk to monster Ymer flowed
Cow Audhumla was his sister born

Well fed, brute Ymer lost to sleep
his armpits salty sweat begat
Rimturser's son and daughter
while one leg with the other bred
Trudgelmer, six-faced giant
who in his turn brought forth the one
to father future giants
  but evil is this Bergelmer
  no good will he let live

Audhumla hungry licked the ice
And Bure god was born
He had a son, the good brave Borr
but giants set upon both

  Alas, here starts
  the endless fray of world ascendancy

THE NEWS COVERAGE of Odin's story produced an instant reaction: the numbers of demonstrators in front of the National Hospital more than tripled. Indeed, as Saturday wore on the demonstration grew so big there was no longer any room for cars in the car park and the police were obliged to step in to control the chaotic situation on the street as well as ensuring the staff could get in and out of the buildings. During the afternoon the doctors deliberated whether to move Odin to a provincial hospital, but gave up the idea because the risk of an attack on the ambulance – which would put the case on the front pages – was too great. Odin stayed where he was.

This, perhaps, was a mistake. On Sunday morning Fredenshvile awoke to heavy, constant rain. The city was enveloped in grey-black clouds and even when night finally receded about half past nine, no real daylight broke through. Everything was wet – streets, houses, trees and people. Screen wipers operated at top speed and even then motorists could hardly see the asphalt, cyclists were soaked after a few minutes in the saddle, and lively streams rushed alongside the kerbs and formed bigger and bigger lakes above the drains, which couldn't cope. It was one of those days when both cats and mice stayed indoors. But not the Pious. If just a few stayed away, they were soon replaced by enthusiastic new arrivals. Hundreds and hundreds more gathered in front of the hospital clad in raingear and Wellington boots in every shade. Some brought the usual equipment; candles and torches went out, but the banners fluttered defiantly in the rain.

Late in the morning, when the crowd had grown so huge there was not a centimetre of space left in the car park, the young man in spectacles climbed on to his empty beer crate. He raised his hand and a hush spread over the crowd.

'The new millennium approaches,' he proclaimed to the wet faithful. 'God is testing us! God is testing our faith before Judgement Day! We must not be overcome, we must not give up. Let the storm fall on your bare heads. Let the awls of the Almighty drive into your naked souls!' He tore off his raincoat and with dramatic violence flung it down in a puddle to the right of the crate.

A devout mumble rose from the crowd.

'Show the Lord you do not waver!' The bespectacled man disdainfully shrugged off an umbrella an elderly lady was trying to hold over his head. With both hands he took off his glasses and stowed them away in a red case that vanished into his breast pocket. Then he turned up his face to the heavens and let the water pour into his passionately blinking eyes and wide-open mouth. He uttered a long ecstatic howl, and he later explained to the other Pious that in that very moment his true identity was revealed to him: he was no other than Simon Peter II.

Many of the Born Anew Christians followed the example of their self-proclaimed leader and soon stood soaked to the skin, while a few folded their hands and begged the Lord for forgiveness; it was too cold.

A small group of nine men in black hats, with dancing ringlets and large umbrellas, now approached the National Hospital. At the head of the train, half a pace in front of his father, the young Ezekiel walked along wearing a devout expression, while his brother Ezra brought up the rear with a humbler mien. The nine black-hatted men did not stop when they reached the car park, but without hesitation squeezed past the other Pious right up to the blue police barrier at the hospital entrance. Simon Peter II's voice was clearly audible above the human mass, but the black-hatted men took no notice of him. Instead they edged and shoved to both sides until they had created enough space for a round woven carpet which Ezekiel's father slowly and carefully unrolled on the wet asphalt. The umbrellas shot up to shield the carpet from the rain. Then Ezekiel solemnly bent down, took off his shoes and stockings and walked on to the carpet.

'Speak to us, Ezekiel. Speak to your father, to your six uncles and speak to your brother.' The father laid his hand on his son's shoulder and gave it an encouraging squeeze.

Ezekiel let himself fall to his knees and folded his hands. He closed his eyes, raised his intense face to the clouds of umbrellas and said nothing. Several minutes passed. Ezekiel's father looked around at his brothers, who seemed more and more impatient and less and less devout with each minute that passed. Ezekiel's father smacked his lips nervously but dared not disturb his son's divine concentration. Then suddenly, just as the two eldest uncles blinked at each other in irritation, the desperate expression on Ezekiel's face was replaced by a formidable rapture. Ezekiel opened his eyes and looked at his family as if he did not see them but something quite different in their stead, and when he began to speak his voice was hoarse and strange.

'I have come to Ezekiel to speak through Ezekiel to you, my chosen people. The end of the second millennium of the people who were led astray is near. On the Day of Judgement those shall be saved who have lived according to the word of the first and only faith. Those shall be saved who have revered their Creator and conducted themselves as His true children, the chosen ones.' Ezekiel paused and drew breath with a rasping sound. His father beamed and nodded encouragingly. 'I have sent the Messiah to give you forewarning of the end of the world you know, and to save the chosen few. I have sent the Messiah, the Mighty One, in the figure of a little old man. Praise be to those who defend the Messiah against the unbelievers. Listen to Ezekiel the Righteous. I will speak to you, my chosen people, through him.' Ezekiel closed his eyes and slowly the ecstatic trance passed off. When he opened his eyes again he was his usual self.

Yes, he would certainly speak through Ezekiel, chuckled Ezra to himself. It had taken him two evenings to bore a hole in the wall under the bed of his own room adjoining his little brother's. Ezra's face shone in competition with his father's. What a brother, this Ezekiel; he hadn't forgotten a single word!

Now there was a good deal of pushing and cursing, since the Born Anew Christians did not care for either the behaviour of the Reborn Jews or the behaviour shown by a group of apparently leaderless young Muslim men. In a short space of time this pushing and cursing developed into real fisticuffs, and before the police succeeded in separating the groups, various members of the Pious had been injured and taken to Accident and Emergency, while one or two demonstrators who were unhurt were carted off to the police station charged with disturbance of law and order. The press were on the spot and the police could no longer ignore such events.

On the evening news the Minister of Justice was featured with the National Hospital and the impassioned Pious in the background.

'There's no need for anxiety,' the Minister had to shout to make himself heard. 'The police have complete control of the situation, and tomorrow everything will function normally again here.' He flung out an arm in the direction of the sea of humanity.

'Do you have any idea of the so-called Odin Odin's identity?' asked the journalist as the camera zoomed in on the banners, whose lettering had long since been dissolved by the rain and had run down the white material like dirty tears.

'I certainly reckon that in the course of a day or two the police will be able to inform the government of the identity of the man in question.'

'Does the government have any theories?'

'It is too soon to say anything about that. I have called the Chief of Police and the Director of the Immigration Department to a meeting early tomorrow to have further discussions.'

'And what about the island in the Strait the man maintains he has come from?'

'That is an absurd assertion. Totally absurd!'

'There's a rumour circulating among the fishermen that the island actually does exist, even though no one has ever seen it. Won't the government be investigating the situation?'

'I don't see why we should. South Norse territory is known to all and sundry, and has been so for many years. The very idea is completely absurd.'

The journalist was about to ask another question when the Minister of Justice interrupted him. 'I have no further comment. No comment.' The Minister offered the journalist and all viewing public a slightly forced smile and repeated that he was sorry, but he really had to go. Then he disappeared into the waiting car.

*

Nothing much came of the Justice Minister's meeting with the Chief of Police and the Director for Immigration. None of them possessed any information that could help to identify Odin. The only fact that could be established with any certainty was that no one by the name of Odin Odin was at present seeking asylum in the Queendom, and that put the Director of Immigration out of the picture.

'The little old man's knowledge of the South Norse language indicates that he has been in the country for a good long time,' said the Chief of Police, and described the reports his officers had produced after they had interrogated Odin. 'Still, if he has been here a long time, someone should have recognized his appearance from the media, and no one has reported it.'

'He might be a criminal no one wishes to have their name associated with,' suggested the Minister of Justice.

'Could well be. But in that case his name and description should be in our archives, and they are not.' The Police Chief rubbed the dark circles under his eyes. 'Maybe if we publish a picture of him...'

'You have until this evening,' said the Justice Minister coldly.

'We have already done everything possible: fingerprints, blood tests, teeth, everything. I can only hope that the publicity will yield something.' The Chief of Police raised his voice defensively. 'That will take a couple of days at least.'

'I don't mind what you do, or how you do it. But I must have an answer this evening at the latest!' The Minister of Justice was angry; what an absurd waste of time. 'And one more thing before we part.' He rose to his feet. 'I do not want to see a repetition of that shambles in front of the hospital. Use as many men as necessary to keep the groups apart.' He shook his head. 'The second coming of Christ! The Messiah! The Messenger of Allah!'

When his two guests had left, the Minister of Justice leaned back in his chair and lit a cigar. He rang for his secretary and asked for a cup of coffee. Soon afterwards a young man came in and placed the coffee on the table.

'Thank you,' said the Minister mechanically. And now put me through to the Minister for Ecclesiastical Affairs.'

After a moment the telephone rang.

'I am sorry to worry you, but I think we had better coordinate our statements on this idiotic Odin Odin affair,' began the Minister of Justice.

'Yes, what a story,' replied a female voice at the other end.

'I have told the Chief of Police he must come up with something by this evening. The police should be able to keep the demonstrators quiet until then.'

'With luck – but we must put a stop to the Prophets of Doom before they build up their strength even more.'

'Precisely. So I thought it might be an idea for you to get one of the bishops to repudiate the claim that the man is divine, because that is not only absurd but downright blasphemous.'

'Yes, I'd already thought of that. It may well not stop the worst of the lunatics out there, but it might possibly get some of the more sane demonstrators to go home. It would at least stop the hysteria spreading.' The Minister for Ecclesiastical Affairs paused. 'Yes. The Church must clearly condemn any idea that this man has the slightest connection with Jesus Christ.' She laughed drily.

'What do we do with the Jews and the Muslims?'

'As far as I've gathered there aren't many of them. The Muslims seem to be just a gang of youngsters who are bored, while the Jews consist more or less of a single family who have been on a collision course with their rabbi for a long time. But who knows, might it not help if the Chief Rabbi and one or more of the Mullahs declare themselves opposed to all the mumbo-jumbo?'

'Let's see what happens during the day. If the police uncover the identity of the old man there should be no more reason to worry. If not, it might well be useful if one or two weighty voices from the different faiths made some sensible statements.'

There was a moment's silence.

'And the island?' The Ecclesiastical Affairs Minister hesitated, unsure about whether to pose the question.

'The island!' sniggered the Justice Minister. 'Utter poppycock. It was obviously dreamed up by some sick brain.'

'So you haven't in mind to do anything about that?'

'No, absolutely not! I wouldn't want to give anyone the slightest impression that we take such a ridiculous assertion seriously.'

'No, no, of course not. No, but I will see the faith communities are contacted.'

'Excellent, I'll tell you when you can give them the go-ahead. And thank you for your help.'

The Minister of Justice put down the phone and called his secretary.

'Give me the Prime Minister,' he ordered. This time he was obliged to wait. The Prime Minister was in an important meeting and was not to be disturbed. Finally, after a good hour, the secretary had him on the line.

'Everything is under control,' said the Minister of Justice, and reported on the morning's events.

'Excellent,' said the Prime Minister. Then he continued, as if to himself: 'You know, you would make a capital Foreign Minister.'

The Minister said nothing, but his face lit up. It was no secret that he had always wanted that post.

'Carry on with the good work, and keep me informed on how the affair develops,' said his chief, putting down the receiver.

*

Monday brought nothing but more pious crowds to the National Hospital car park. Tuesday brought Anders Andersen.

Anders Andersen was the blessed leader of the Lambs of the Lord, and Blessed Anders Andersen had long known that the Lord would send his Shepherd to save his lambs before the Day of Judgement and the annihilation of this world. While waiting for that day – and for the diabolical money that the faithful lambs were so fortunate to be allowed to lighten their sinful souls from – the Blessed Anders Andersen had established a fold for the Lambs of the Lord, and a home for himself, in an imposing palace with a gigantic park a little way north of Fredenshvile. In the outbuildings and certain areas of the park the Lambs of the Lord could be assembled, to read the Bible and the hallowed words of Anders Andersen, listen to spiritually inspired music and smoke holy grass, blessed by Anders Andersen himself. From one unpredictable time to another Anders Andersen emerged from the fogs of the interior of the palace to give one of his rare but highly acclaimed sermons.

Exactly as Anders Andersen had prophesied, the Shepherd of the Lord, just as the century was nearing its end, had come to gather the Lambs of the Lord together and prepare them for their journey to the Eternal Pastures of Paradise. The Lambs of the Lord flocked to the car park in front of the National Hospital in order that, for the glory of God, the Shepherd of the Lord, the Mighty One, could perform the sacred ritual – which otherwise was only carried out on Sundays – of shaving their hair, heaping it together and burning it as an offering of wool to the Lord and His Shepherd.

So devout were the Lambs of the Lord that they managed to fight their way through the demonstration and when the Reborn Jews, with the aid of their umbrellas and inborn prior claim, had found their way to the front row too, the Born Anew Christians – despite their numerical superiority – were forced back. Simon Peter II chose to overlook this ignominy and preached on loudly and undaunted from his empty beer crate, while a suffocating smoke rose from the heap of burning hair, and the kneeling Ezekiel the Righteous uttered ecstatic cries from his round carpet. The leaderless angry young Muslims punched the air with their fists in time to sacred slogans, and other groups and sub-groups gathered and dissolved moment by moment. Confusion reigned; the police had their hands full. Several smaller fights broke out among the demonstrators, and at one point the police almost lost control of the situation. Extra officers were mustered, and aided by a heavy downpour the police eventually managed to calm down the Pious.

Meanwhile, inside the walls of the hospital, Gunnar the Head had managed to persuade the terrified Odin to leave his hiding place under the table, and from then on the little old man stuck to his huge-headed friend's side. Odin did not understand a jot of what was going on in the car park, except that in some extraordinary way it had something to do with him.

'You are not to worry,' said Gunnar the Head. 'You and I are one. If anyone touches you, you can be sure he will not live to see his next football match.'

Odin had expected Sigbrit Holland to come in and explain what the noise was all about and to tell him when Veterinarius Martinussen would have finished his regulations. But she did not come. What Odin did not know was that the Justice

Minister had determined that no one was to be allowed to speak to or visit Odin unless they could prove to be related to him. They could not run the risk of fanatics kidnapping or killing the little old man, not to mention the danger of a crafty journalist sneaking in to get a sensational interview.

Tuesday passed, then Wednesday, with nothing new emerging on Odin's identity. A surprisingly mutual agreement came from all the faiths who rejected and denounced every assertion of Odin's divinity. However, their statements had not the slightest effect on the Doomsday Prophets and their followers. The demonstration just grew larger and larger, and the inflamed agitation turned increasingly against the government, which many saw as responsible for the Mighty One's incarceration. It was obviously only a question of time before unrest erupted into violence, so on Thursday morning the Prime Minister summoned the relevant ministers to a crisis meeting.

'What's the latest?' The Prime Minister looked at the Minister of Justice, who fidgeted uneasily on his chair.

'The Chief of Police promised to have unearthed the little old man's identity by Monday evening, but he has still not been able to discover anything. The man is not registered anywhere in this country, nor is he on any central European census list. The police have contacted colleagues all over the world and published enquiries in the press. But up to now every attempt has been in vain.'

'In short, we are no further forward.' The Prime Minister meticulously cracked his right-hand little finger before going on. 'The situation is very serious for us, you should all know that. Even though the whole affair seems risible, it is not only creating considerable disturbance to public law and order, but, and far more important, it gives the opposition the chance of diverting attention from the budget negotiations and instead makes it look as if we do not have the country under control. There will be queries about the immigration laws, and although we might not object to those being tightened, it would not be a good thing if it seemed to be forced on us on account of pressure from the opposition.' The Prime Minister looked around at his colleagues and tugged at his little finger again. 'May I hear your suggestions?'

A moment's silence fell before the Minister for Ecclesiastical Affairs leaned forward. 'I think we are overreacting a little,' she began. 'What are the facts: a little old man turns up out of the blue. The man claims to have come from the heavens to an island in the Strait which no one has ever heard of. He maintains that on the 26th December he walked from this unknown island to South Norseland over the ice on the Strait, which, according to the experts, can scarcely bear the weight of a man. The little old man speaks fluent South Norse, yet no one has been able to identify him, and his name is not on any register. I think we can ignore the question of heavenly descent, the unknown island, and the walk over the water – we'll leave that to the Pious...' Her colleagues laughed. 'And in spite of the man's dark colouring he must either be South Norse, or he has spent a large part of his life in this country; our language is not easy to learn. The fact that he is not listed under the name of Odin Odin does not necessarily mean he is not registered at all. It merely means that his real name is not the one he has given to the authorities. All this hullabaloo can quite easily be boiled down to a case of a disturbed old man, who has invented a bizarre story and taken an imaginary name.'

The Prime Minister smiled with satisfaction. 'Bravo. Bravo!'

he said, and turning to the Minister of Justice went on in a slightly ironical tone. 'Now we only need to find out the man's real name and all our problems are solved.'

'But if no one recognizes the man how can the police prove his real identity?' asked the Minister of Justice.

'Fingerprints, teeth, I don't know! The police have their methods,' snapped the Prime Minister, pulling at his left-hand little finger.

The Justice Minister was about to say that the police had already tried all this, but a single glance at the Prime Minister's face stopped him. The affair would surely have resolved itself in a couple of days, so there was no need to irritate the boss any more just now.

A week went by, and although all available resources were deployed in the search for Odin's identity, nothing was discovered. The Prime Minister was furious. He shouted at the Minister of Justice, who reproached the Chief of Police, who went on to warn the Head of Investigations, who immediately banished two of his officers to the provinces. An example had to be set.

*

Sigbrit Holland was at her wits' end as to what to do.

'Steer clear of it,' insisted her husband, family and friends, and in principle Sigbrit agreed with them. Nevertheless she could not resist calling the National Hospital number repeatedly until they gave her leave to send a brief message to Odin, in which she explained why she was unable to visit him. Any further action on her part seemed to be blocked. There was no longer any point in taking up Ambrosius the Fisherman's suggestion of phoning the Minister of Justice – Odin and the island were already on everyone's lips. She considered going back to the green and orange fishing boat, but she was no longer easy in her mind about the government deflecting the question of the island's existence. Maybe the Fisherman was wrong. Maybe the whole of his story, indeed maybe even Odin's own story, were pure fantasy. Nor was Sigbrit happy at the thought of Der Fremdling. So no matter how much she felt drawn, she put off visiting the fishing boat.

One day after the other passed with demonstrations in front of the National Hospital, solemn denunciations by diverse ecclesiastics, fruitless crisis meetings of the government and uncomfortable questions to the Minister of Justice posed by Members of Parliament and by the press. The police investigators worked around the clock, without any success, and every day one or two more officers were taken off the case and one or two others replaced them. While the authorities argued about who was responsible for the unrest, the size and fervour of the religious demonstrations grew steadily and unstoppably. Early one Wednesday morning a particularly violent confrontation took place between the demonstrators and the police, and as well as the usual bumps and bruises, one officer was so badly hurt that he died before midday. Finally Sigbrit could not restrain herself from taking action any longer.

She excused herself from work with a headache, left the bank and hurried the short distance to Firø and the green and orange fishing boat. The clock above the pharmacy on the street corner showed twenty to five. She had masses of time. If she left again within the hour, she would be home no later than usual.

The boat was still where she had found it the first time. Sigbrit climbed on board and had almost reached the door when it was wrenched open and a wizened head came into view. His sparse grey eyebrows were practically invisible against the parchment-like skin, his eyes were set close together, like hostile stones in their deep sockets, and his mouth cut a straight, almost lipless line in his colourless face. The withered man said not a word, merely stared suspiciously at Sigbrit.

'I beg your pardon,' she said. She hadn't seen his face the last time, but there could be no doubt that it was Der Fremdling. She should not have come. 'I'm sorry,' she said again, shuffling uneasily from foot to foot. 'I must have made a mistake in the darkness and come to the wrong boat.' She turned around and had already reached the rail when she heard Ambrosius the Fisherman's voice.

'Hey, hang on a moment. So it's you, Lady Fair. We thought as much, we recognized the voice. Come along in.'

Sigbrit found herself again in the long narrow wheelhouse, which served both as kitchen and living room. Without asking, Ambrosius the Fisherman poured some coffee into a cracked mug and set it on the table in front of her.

'Well, Lady Fair, what brings you here today?' The Fisherman leaned back and gazed at her expectantly.

In the warmth of the wheelhouse Sigbrit had almost forgotten her errand. Suddenly she felt like a little girl who could not cope with anything by herself but had to run for help the whole time. Although Der Fremdling had crept back into the furthest corner of the wheelhouse, his presence bothered her. He had not uttered a single word and his expression had not changed once since she had arrived. She shuddered.

'That's all right. Just go ahead, Lady Fair,' said Ambrosius, laying a hand on her arm. 'Der Fremdling knows what there is to know about this world. He survived the first Great War, and he survived the second. Then he decided never again to set foot in his fatherland, and he has lived in ours ever since. He has seen what you and we would never see even in nightmares, and he has already heard all there is to hear. His eyes are filled up, his ears are no longer open, and the words he had to say were said light years ago.'

Sigbrit did not know whether to smile at Der Fremdling in acknowledgement of his sufferings, or whether he would consider that an insult. She glanced at the hostile, glassy eyes and turned away quickly. 'It is Odin,' she began, trying to forget the wizened man.

'We have seen the newspapers.'

'They won't let me visit him. I'm not even allowed to talk to him on the telephone, and now it won't help to ring the Minister of Justice because the whole country is talking of nothing but Odin. Yet nothing at all happens, and the government keeps on insisting that it's a case of mistaken identity, and I don't know what to do. They have not even acknowledged the subject of the island!' Surprised at the vehemence of her own outburst, Sigbrit broke off.

'Yes, it is worse than we thought,' said the Fisherman drily.

'What is worse?'

'Earlier we thought they didn't talk about the island because they didn't want to. Now we know they don't talk about it because they know nothing about it.'

'How can you be so sure of that?' Sigbrit raised her eyebrows and her fingers drummed lightly on the edge of the table.

'If it hadn't been so they would have made greater efforts to stop all the chatter about it.'

Sigbrit had not thought of that.

'What shall I do now, then?'

'Lady Fair, you do exactly what you have been doing, taking one step at a time. The ball is out of your hands. It is rolling, but it is out of your hands. You need only wait and see where it lands. Once you know where it has landed it is your turn again.'

Sigbrit nodded and took a mouthful of her coffee, which had grown cold in the meantime.

'Is there really nothing I can do? I can't just sit with my hands in my lap while nothing happens.'

Ambrosius the Fisherman filled and lit his pipe before replying. 'If you really want to do something,' he said slowly, 'I suppose there is one thing: go to the library and study the old maps of the Strait, see if you can find any trace of the island. If we are not mistaken, someone or other somewhere or other must have noted its existence. The island might very well turn up and then vanish again on some old land maps and maritime charts.' He looked meditatively into Sigbrit's eyes. 'It is no easy task, there are hundreds of them to search through. It will be like looking for a needle in a haystack. But, Lady Fair, it is the only thing you can do.'

'Didn't you say I shouldn't mention the island?' Sigbrit fiddled with her hair a touch nervously.

'No, now you're forgetting again. We said you must not say you heard it from us. And we said that the old adage says all Hell will break out if you talk about it. But we have a feeling that Hell has already broken out, so there's no risk to run there. And besides, it is not necessary to talk about the island in order to search for it.'

Sigbrit smiled: she could easily go to the library. At that

moment, without making a sound or giving any sign to the Fisherman or his guest, Der Fremdling rose, left the wheelhouse and closed the door behind him soundlessly. Sigbrit shook herself; it was as if a dank wraith had walked through the place. She nodded towards the closed door. 'Your friend is very quiet.'

'Yes, good company,' rumbled the Fisherman, chewing on his pipe.

Sigbrit lowered her eyes.

'One should speak when one has something to say.' Ambrosius the Fisherman laid a hand over hers on the worn mahogany table.

Sigbrit's hand vanished completely beneath the Fisherman's, and for a moment she studied the veins that ran from the back of the broad, hairy hand into the strong muscular fingers. Then she pulled her hand away abruptly and stood up. 'I must go,' she said quickly.

'See you again soon, Lady Fair,' said Ambrosius the Fisherman calmly.

The very next day Sigbrit visited the library in her lunchbreak. But the Central Library sent her on to the National Library, who sent her to the Maritime Museum, who referred her to the Land Registry Department under the Ministry of Transport, who directed her to their Special Archives. To use the Special Archives she had to obtain an appointment, which would take three days to come through.

'The earliest charts of the Strait?' The middle-aged archivist cautiously ran a hand over his meticulously arranged hair piece. 'Let's see what we can do.' He trotted in among the shelves, and

Sigbrit had almost given up waiting when he turned up again with his arms full of books and unwieldy charts.

The Special Archives were held in a windowless basement. Bulging metal shelves stood in serried ranks from floor to ceiling, glaring neon light came from grubby fluorescent tubes on the ceiling, and the grey concrete floor echoed at every movement. The few scattered readers sat here and there at metal tables leafing through the ancient works, and if they said anything at all to the archivist they did so in a nervous whisper. Sigbrit automatically lowered her voice when she asked where she should sit. The archivist led her to an empty table at the back of the room and gave her a number. He wrote down the same number in a notebook and neatly noted the titles of the works she had received. It took a long time, and when the archivist at length trotted away with his notebook under his arm, Sigbrit's lunchbreak had long since ended. She ought really to leave at once, but allowed herself a hasty glance at the material piled up in front of her.

There were copies of two Dutch periples – the archivist had explained this was the ancient name for the sailing instructions on charts – from the mid-sixteenth century, and from before that date copies of a few rough sketches and charts. The charts were on parchment, which had later been glued on to canvas so as not to fall to pieces. There were charts from right back to the beginning of the fifteenth century, but the oldest ones looked so imprecise that they would be almost useless. The famed Tabula Moderna extrea Ptolemæum, with a map drawn by the monk Donis in 1482, reproduced the South Norse mainland as a peculiar snake, with the large South Norse islands scattered vaguely around it. Neither this nor the next couple of charts showed any sign of a small island ringed by cliffs in the Strait midway between South Norseland and North Norseland. Sigbrit glanced at the next two charts. Most of them were copies of larger works or atlases, but even the copies were several hundred years old, and if the copying was exact it meant nothing to Sigbrit whether she was looking at the original or not. The last chart before her was Cornelis Anthoniszoon's 'Caerte van Oostlant' from 1550. In this, the Continent looked like an oval potato, the large islands were strangely elongated, while the small islands in the Straits were not drawn at all. There was nothing useful here.

Sigbrit sighed and looked at her watch; she was much too late. She quickly stacked the material and delivered it back to the archivist. She would have to borrow the sailing directions on her next visit.

*

The demonstration in front of the hospital had stabilized to a certain extent, the crowds stretching from one end of the hospital area to the other, including the pavement and the street. In addition to the Born Anew Christians, the Reborn Jews, the Lambs of the Lord and the still leaderless young Muslims, there was a new group calling itself Mary's Maidens, who consisted of equal numbers of unmarried women of a certain age and young radicals hungry for action, who were convinced that everything good, including the Son of God, sprang from women, while everything evil sprang from men's bellicosity and brutality. Until this day dawned it was perhaps very fortunate that the police had been ordered to act as a human shield between the groups, who were not allowed to fight each other with any less godly weapons than loud preaching, prayers and song.

Within the walls of the hospital Odin had gradually grown used to the disturbances in the car park, but they increasingly worried his huge-headed friend. Gunnar the Head was not precisely clear over what was going on, but he was in no doubt that sooner or later something unpleasant would happen. Nor was he in any doubt that he and his friend should be far away when this something did occur.

So Gunnar the Head rose early on Saturday morning. He woke Odin; it was time they were going. Odin slipped quietly out of bed, dressed and crept from the room after Gunnar the Head, down the corridor and into the office, where the assistant nurse was asleep on a chair with his head resting on the table. Gunnar the Head had carefully planned their escape and he knew the nurse always took a quick nap before the morning shift, at half past five every morning to be precise. Odin was not quite sure whether it would not be more polite to wake the nurse and ask him to open the doors for them instead of taking his keys and leaving without saying goodbye. But Gunnar the Head convinced him in a whisper that the nurse had expressly asked not to be woken because he never had enough sleep, poor man. With surprising dexterity Gunnar the Head sneaked a set of keys out of the assistant nurse's pocket. Then he and Odin crept back along the corridor, unlocked the first door, then the second, after which Gunnar the Head scrupulously locked both one and the other door behind them. With a smile, the huge-headed man put the keys in his pocket and patted them with satisfaction; so far, so good.

The hospital was silent and the two men went downstairs without meeting anyone. At the foot of the staircase Gunnar the Head put out his hand and stopped Odin. Two security guards were posted at the hospital entrance. They sat, one on either side of the door, chatting sleepily. Gunnar the Head scratched his elbow and thought as fast as he could. But before he hit on anything Odin had walked over to one of the guards.

'Forgive me for interrupting your conversation,' he said, bowing courteously. 'I thought that, if it is not too much inconvenience, you could inform me of the shortest and most direct way to Veterinarius Martinussen?'

'What's that?' the guard dropped his truncheon out of sheer astonishment; how the Hell had Tiny Tim here slunk past them?

'Get out, will yer?' yelled the other guard, getting up from his chair with raised truncheon. Couldn't the Muslims come at a reasonable time like all the other fanatics?

He gave Odin a hefty push out of the door, and Odin's grey hospital gown flapped around his legs, and he was on the point of falling over.

'These fanatics won't stop at anything!' said the guard angrily to his colleague, and at that very moment Gunnar the Head slipped past the security guards' backs. They did not notice him until the huge-headed man was already so far down the street they could only guess where he had come from.

'Unusually disobliging people,' said Odin when they were out of sight, but his huge-headed friend made no reply.

Gunnar the Head was hard put to it to find the best way of getting out of the hospital environs without being seen. It wasn't easy to think clearly with his head under his arm and everything, but he had to manage with what he had. Didn't he recall a path to the park behind the hospital, where he used to play football? Yes, Gunnar the Head scratched his right elbow; if only they could find the way to the park they would be safe. The huge-headed man turned to the right and right again, and luck was with them: there was the park.

It was still dark, and it was hard to see properly under the big trees. Odin stumbled over a fallen branch and stopped for a moment. Gunnar the Head hurried to his friend; they had to get as far away from the hospital as possible before their absence was discovered. Odin's slight stature was not well adapted to flight, and soon Gunnar the Head saw nothing for it but to lift Odin on to his shoulders. This made their progress considerably faster, and it was not long before the park abruptly came to an end and the town was all around them. Now Gunnar the Head realized he had not planned their flight beyond getting away from the hospital area. He scratched his right elbow nervously.

'There is no misfortune that a morsel of good luck cannot remedy,' chirped Odin from his elevated position, with one hand on the horseshoe in his breast pocket.

Because their noses faced east, and because no one direction seemed better than another, they set their course for the horizon, which in the course of a couple of hours would bring the sun or at least daylight with an overcast sky. The road took them as much to the south as the east, but Gunnar the Head saw no cause to worry, as long as his nose pointed in the same direction as his feet.

To begin with they met hardly anyone. A couple of cars went by and a lone cyclist almost fell off when he caught sight of them. By the time Gunnar the Head and Odin drew near the city centre it was almost six o'clock; the bakers' ovens were filled with bread and cakes, newspaper boys and girls were on their way home from work, and workpeople were on their way out. The number of people in the streets grew and grew, and so did Gunnar the Head's anxiety in case anyone recognized Odin and called the police. As they approached a large square, he felt obliged to set Odin on his feet again. 'We want to avoid attracting people's attention,' he said, looking around him anxiously. 'I really must think.' Gunnar the Head sat down on a bench and scratched his right elbow mechanically.

Not far from Odin's feet a pigeon searched for crumbs among the cobblestones. It reminded Odin of something, he could not remember what. He let out a low cackling sound, and the bird raised its head and limped stiffly over to him. That was not quite what Odin was searching for; before the bird reached him it grew frightened and flew into the air. Odin tugged his beard in disappointment. It was high time Veterinarius Martinussen came back with him to Smith's Town, so that Rigmarole's ill-fated leg could be treated and he could travel on with the ill tidings he could not for the moment remember.

'Gunnar the Head,' he said. 'I really must get hold of someone. I must get hold of Sigbrit Holland, five hundred and forty-two, six hundred and fourteen, thirty-four.'

*

Forty-five minutes later, Odin, Gunnar the Head and Sigbrit Holland sat in the wheelhouse of the green and orange fishing boat. It had taken some time to rouse Ambrosius the Fisherman, and he still did not look properly awake. His untidy hair stood up in the air, his eyes blinked sleepily, and he could not hold back a yawn as he put the kettle on the gas stove. His bare torso revealed delicate white skin covered with freckles and reddish blond hair that was darker than the hair of his head, and although he was well covered his body was still firm and muscular. The Fisherman suddenly looked up and caught Sigbrit's eye. A slight flush bloomed in her cheeks.

'I'm sorry we woke you up,' she said quickly. 'But I didn't know where else to take Odin and his friend.'

'No matter, Lady Fair. We are always glad to see you here.' The Fisherman gave her a warm smile. 'Let's have some coffee, so we can talk better.' He lifted the battered kettle off the stove, poured water into the percolator, let it run through and poured four mugs of coffee.

'So you made a dash for it...?' asked the Fisherman and sat down.

'Oh no!' exclaimed Odin. 'My friend Gunnar the Head just unlocked the doors, as he had arranged with the sleeping assistant nurse, and then we walked until we found Sigbrit Holland, and now we are visiting you and your comfortable fishing boat while we wait for Veterinarius Martinussen to complete the regulations, so we can get back to Smith's Town and Rigmarole, for I am in an extremely awkward predicament.'

There was a moment's silence, then Sigbrit said hesitantly: 'I wondered...' She bit her lip. 'I mean, I don't know how much room you have, but I wondered if Odin and his friend could stay with you here for a day or two?' She looked around the cramped wheelhouse and added quickly, 'it is a bit difficult for me to have them at home, because... in any case it would only be until I can make other arrangements. A day or two at most.'

'Lady Fair, Lady Fair. Take it easy.' Ambrosius the Fisherman laid a hand on Sigbrit's arm. 'One thing at a time. We assume no one saw you come on board *Rikke-Marie* this morning?'

Sigbrit shook her head.

'Good. Odin had better stay here. The first place they will look is your home.' The Fisherman turned to Odin again. 'You can stay here as long as you like.'

Odin thanked Ambrosius the Fisherman but then said that even though it might seem rather peremptory, he could not in all truth accept the hospitable invitation unless his friend Gunnar the Head was invited too.

The Fisherman laughed aloud. 'Of course not. We haven't much room here, but we can find a bunk for both you and your friend.'

Sigbrit looked at her watch; it was already ten past nine. 'I'm going to have to go,' she said.

'Where's the fire, Lady Fair? First let us hear what you found in the charts?'

'1550. No luck so far.' Sigbrit opened the door and a gust of cold wind blew into the wheelhouse.

'Not good enough.' The Fisherman ran his hand through his well-trimmed beard. 'We must spur on the horse; you wanted the ball, now you have it. Lady Fair, you had better see to it that you find something, no matter what, just something or other to prove that the island exists. And the sooner the better. It won't be long before they find out where Odin is.'

'Do you play football?' Gunnar the Head broke in delightedly.

'No, not in the way you imagine.' Sigbrit smiled wryly.

'Never mind. I'm no great shakes as a player any more.' Gunnar the Head fell silent and his eyes filled with tears.

Odin was not listening. What Ambrosius the Fisherman had said about the horse running had reminded him of something. 'I should be extremely grateful to you if perchance you could remind Veterinarius Martinussen to make haste with the regulations,' he said, tugging at his beard. 'Truth to tell, I am in great haste.'

'It will all turn out right,' said the Fisherman kindly.

'Yes, everything will be fine,' Sigbrit concurred. Then she closed the door behind her, and Ambrosius the Fisherman showed Odin and Gunnar the Head to their berths.

'Make yourselves at home,' he said, after pulling some blankets and pillows out of a chest.

Odin lay down at once. He was very sleepy, but lay awake a long time feeling the slight rocking of the boat and listening to the plashing of the water along the keel. Thoughts tumbled around in his head; he must remember to remind Gunnar the Head to give the keys back to the nurse at the hospital, and he must find out what was taking Veterinarius Martinussen such a long time, and then there was the strange thing he had forgotten to ask the Fisherman about the: green and orange fishing boat that had exactly the same name as the old woman in Smith's Town. Odin's hand found its way to his breast pocket where the horseshoe lay, and eventually he fell into a deep sleep.

*

Now it happened that the Queen of South Norseland not only was intelligent and had a special interest in history, she had also, in this otherwise so egalitarian a country, received an education both longer and better than that of most other people. Because she had no power but only formal duties, and because she did not need to offer herself for election at shorter or longer intervals, the Queen also had a good deal of free time, and this she used to study various subjects of interest to the country and herself, which often happened to be one and the same thing.

At midday, while Odin still slumbered sweetly under the deck of the green and orange fishing boat, and while Sigbrit Holland hurried from the bank to the Special Archives of the Land Registry, the Queen of South Norseland walked with swift steps through the state apartments of her magnificent home. From time to time she nodded fleetingly to the curtseying maidservants and a little more emphatically to the courtiers she passed on her way, until on the northernmost wall of the northernmost room she reached an almost invisible door. Here she stopped, and after having assured herself that there was no one in the vicinity, she drew a bunch of keys from her handbag. The Queen chose a small, slightly rusty iron key, unlocked the door, took a step forward and closed and locked the door carefully behind her. She looked around her; she had entered a large oval room, filled from floor to ceiling with books, archive cupboards and years of ancient dust.

'I must get someone to clean up in here,' murmured the Queen to herself, but she knew very well that it was her own fault the dust had accumulated so thickly. She allowed no one to enter this private library, which had belonged to her father, her grandfather, her great-grandfather and his father before him and all their ancestors – and now it belonged to her. Here it was that all the private papers of the royal family were kept. Even though the law of the land prescribed that letters and documents, sent or received by the monarchs of the country, belonged to the National Archives, the monarchs' personal letters and papers were always regarded as the reigning monarch's property, unless the addressee decided otherwise. The Queen's forefathers had interpreted this law at their own discretion and from time to time had considered some or other document to be private – always naturally in the best interests of the land. Even though the Queen had never come across any secret that could be decisive for the welfare of her family and the country, she still guarded the library as if the future of South Norseland depended on it.

A dim light shone from a narrow window at the end of the room, and the Queen switched on the electric light to assist her. It was years since she had last been in the library and she was obliged to refresh her memory of its layout. She walked along the crammed shelves; it would be like looking for a needle in a haystack, apart from the fact that she could not even be sure that the needle really existed. Her only clue was that as a small girl of perhaps eight or nine years old, in a conversation between her father and grandfather – quite certainly not intended for her ears – she had heard mention of an unnamed island situated in the Strait precisely between the South Norse Queendom and the North Norse Kingdom. This was why the story of Mr Odin Odin had caught her interest. But where should she begin?

The Queen had no idea which of her forefathers had known about the island. She would have to begin from one end and proceed chronologically. The library had been established at the end of the fifteenth century by King Enevold I, who had collected all the family papers into one place. Although the South Norse monarchy had been established more than a thousand years ago, the oldest find in the library was a weapon from the year 1203, when South Norseland had held the entire northern part of the Great Kingdom. The Queen looked briefly through the oldest objects; there was nothing but some primitive jewels, one or two seals and some coins. She picked up an early South Norse silver coin and weighed it in her hand. She smiled. One of her ancestors must have had the same interest in history as she had herself; the coin ought not to be here, but at the National Museum. With a sigh the Queen put the coin back in the drawer and went on.

It did not take long to go through the material from many of the earliest years, but gradually, as the documentation grew more voluminous, the Queen's work proceeded more slowly. As well as South Norseland, Enevold I had been King of North Norseland and also Long North Norseland, and in a dusty drawer the Queen found a grubby note which described his nomination in 1460 to Duke and Count of the two small states that divided South Norseland from the Great Kingdom. How small the Queendom had become since then. The Queen closed the drawer and the dust rose and made her sneeze. She glanced at her watch; it was six o'clock already. She quickly packed up the papers and let herself out. It had been an interesting afternoon, but so far she had not found one single trace of the unknown island.

*

Sigbrit Holland had been obliged to stay inside too. She had forgotten the time and spent three hours in the Special Archives – and had been reprimanded by her boss – without finding anything of the least use. She had read through one of the Dutch periples and glanced at the other, in which the Strait was loosely described, then she had had to run back to the bank. Now it was past six and she still had hours of work to plough through. She was tired and getting nowhere, but all the same she did not feel like going home. With sudden determination Sigbrit switched off the computer, put on her coat and left the office. She steered clear of the car park behind the bank and instead walked quickly across Firø Bridge to the right along the southern canal to the green and orange fishing boat.

Ambrosius the Fisherman was playing the guitar and singing, and Odin and Gunnar the Head were keeping time with their feet. Der Fremdling sat at the back of the wheel-house with a faraway expression on his face, and it was impossible to say if he appreciated the music or whether it bothered him.

'Welcome, Lady Fair!' exclaimed the Fisherman, and blithely continued his song. Sigbrit, a little awkwardly, took a can of beer out of the crate, as the Fisherman had indicated, opened it and sat down. He sang another couple of songs, then laid his guitar aside. 'No one has said a word about Odin's flight,' he said straight off, stretching out for his pipe in the ashtray. 'It is strange. Either the hospital is covering up for it, or the police are, or the government.' He slowly cleaned his pipe and filled it again before looking up. 'We would certainly like to know who is behind it.'

*

Whoever may have wanted to keep it under wraps was not in luck. Odin's flight was no longer a secret. Early in the evening Odin's skinny bald roommate, Martin, woke from the drugged sleep the nurses had enforced on him when they discovered Odin's exodus. It took Martin only a couple of minutes to realize what it was they did not want him to find out. In a raging fury he smashed a window in the room and shouted to the Pious in the car park that if they hurt a single hair of Odin's head he would personally send them straight back to Hell. It took six male nurses to drag the thin man down from the windowsill and back to bed, where he was once more tied down and helped to fall asleep. The whole incident had only taken five minutes, and as the crowd merely thought the doctors were playing with them to make them withdraw nothing more would have occurred if one of the photographers from the daily press had not been present. Martin's pale naked form in the smashed window appeared in black and white the next day, and hardly had the newspapers arrived on the street before the hospital manager was interrogated by the Commissioner of Police, who was then questioned by the Minister of Justice, who himself had to submit to questioning from Parliament and the press.

For a while it looked as if the Justice Minister would be forced to resign. Instead, after a brief meeting in the Prime Minister's office, the Hospital Manager fired the Head of Security along with two guards who had been on duty when Odin and Gunnar the Head disappeared.

Sigbrit Holland's telephone didn't stop ringing. Doctors, politicians, civil servants in the Ministry of Justice and Ministry of Ecclesiastical Affairs, with one or two pushy journalists, all wanted to know whether she knew of the little old man's hiding place. Sigbrit knew nothing, she laughed, with surprising ease. All the same she felt it best to keep a low profile and refrain from visiting the green and orange fishing boat for a day or two; you never knew whether you were being watched. Not for several days did she return to the Special Archives of the Land Registry.

The Queen took no notice of the latest development in the case of Mr Odin Odin but persevered with her search through the royal archives. She had reached King Enevold IV. Various cupboards overflowed with the personal history of this King. He had ruled South Norseland for almost sixty years, had lost the Thirty Years War and with that – fortunately only temporarily for most of those concerned – a large part of the country. After several wars against the North Norse Kings, Enevold IV was eventually forced to relinquish the South Norse provinces of North Norseland as well as the whole of the Long North North.

'So that was the end of the South Norse empire,' mumbled the Queen to herself. At least it was well documented: Enevold IV's archives held more documents, more letters and more books than any other King's. The Queen had worked for three days and she was only about a tenth of the way through. At that speed it might be years before she found what she was looking for.

The Queen surveyed the work wearily and decided to ignore the bookshelves for the moment and concentrate on the archives. That turned out to be a wise decision. Just the next morning she chanced on a false back in one of the cupboards. It took up the whole width of the cupboard, and she would never have discovered it if she had not dropped a drawer on the floor and seen it was considerably shorter than the cupboard. The Queen pulled out the other drawers, placed them on the floor and ran her fingers along the rear board searching for an opening device. But no matter how much she turned and twisted the cupboard she found nothing. For a moment she considered whether she should summon one of the courtiers to help her. But as she did not wish anyone to suspect what she was searching for, she refrained.

Early next morning the Queen locked herself in the library with a hammer and chisel in her handbag. She went to work at once, and after a few minutes the false panel gave way. The Queen pushed her hand through the dark opening, fumbled around blindly, then struck something hard and pulled it towards her. It was a small dusty book. The cover was of dark-brown leather, and under the dust it was shiny with use. There was no name or title. The Queen opened the book, taking great care not to tear the mouldy pages. It was filled with closely written notes in a strong and distinctive hand that she immediately recognized, and the dates were noted in the margin like a diary. She read a couple of lines but there was no doubt: in her hands she held King Enevold IV's personal diary. The Queen was delighted. She put her hand back in the hole and drew out yet another book, and another and then another. All four small books contained four previously undiscovered diaries. This was better than anything she could have dreamed of. Compared with this treasure the unknown island suddenly seemed completely meaningless. It was unlikely to exist anyway. The Queen put her tools and the four small books into her bag, left the library and carefully locked the door after her. Then she hurried back to her private apartments.

While the Queen began reading through her forebear's diaries, Sigbrit Holland resumed her scrutiny of the maps in the Special Archives of the Land Registry. Seven days had now passed since Odin had disappeared from the hospital, and Sigbrit thought it was safe to venture out again. She gave the excuse of yet another headache – yes, she feared she was start-ing to get migraines – and left the bank at eleven in the morning to spend the whole afternoon in the archive.

In Laurentz Benedicht's *History of the Practice of Navigation* from 1568 she found a mention of Ur Island with a description of the shipping route through the Strait. Then she saw it:

> South of the Island of Ur there is a long series of wicked
> rocky cliffs stretching for four nautical miles which must be
> avoided by rounding both the west and the east points.

'Yes!' exclaimed Sigbrit aloud and the other readers at the
Special Archives turned and stared angrily at her. But her
enthusiasm rapidly waned; what she had found was not really
worth a great deal. Ambrosius the Fisherman had already said
that the rocks were marked on all the charts, even the latest
ones. No, she would have to find the island named explicitly or
drawn on a map, or her discovery would mean nothing.

Next day Sigbrit still had a headache. The research was going
more smoothly now she was accustomed to the Gothic lettering in the books and the strange proportions in the old maps.
The archivist brought her stacks of material but there was no
trace of anything but the rocks, which soon became a regular
detail on all the maps. When she reached 1614 a problem
arose.

The archivist came back to her after a long search of the
shelves. 'I cannot understand it,' he said nervously, straightening his hairpiece carefully. 'There seem to be no maps of the
Straits from 1614 to 1618. But from 1619 I have a number
of new maps to show you.' His hands ran anxiously over his
hairpiece again.

Sigbrit glanced at the new maps, but in spite of the increased
precision in the drawing of the nation's coastlines, there was
no change in the Strait; there was still no trace of any island
south of Ur Island. She kept on working until the Special
Archives closed at five o'clock and she had come to the end of

the century. If the island had been known about much later than the start of the eighteenth century, it would not have been possible to erase its existence from official memory. Unless the knowledge of the island had originated before mapping history, the key to the mystery must lie in the missing years.

Sigbrit went to the desk to return the last stack of maps. The archivist sat on a stool behind the desk with the big old registers spread around him on the floor. He turned a page in one, opened another, went back to the first one, then to a third and a fourth, the tears welling up in the corners of his eyes.

'It is incomprehensible. It is something that cannot happen. As long as I have been archivist in the Land Registry's Archives, nothing like it has ever happened,' he mumbled to himself and ran a hand over his wig so the hairs stood out in all directions. 'And I have never heard that anything like it had happened to any of my predecessors. No, it is quite simply something that cannot happen...'

'Perhaps there was a paper shortage or something like that,' said Sigbrit soothingly.

The archivist turned pale. 'Paper shortage! What a thing to say!' he hissed, scandalized. 'Oh, no, such things can't happen. It is absolutely unthinkable!'

'Could it be that someone or other has taken the maps intentionally?' asked Sigbrit as casually as she could.

The archivist turned paler than pale. 'No, that is really unthinkable!' he burst out tearfully. 'That is something that is totally unimaginable in the Special Archives of the Land Registry. That sort of thing is impossible, quite impossible. Look at this, look at this.' The archivist pulled one of the big black leather-bound volumes up on the desk and opened it.

The book was so old that the pages crumbled at the corners, and the old-fashioned elegant handwriting was almost illegible, but there was no doubt that it contained the titles of the maps and books which the Special Archives had received, with the dates of publication and purchase carefully noted in straight columns.

'See for yourself.' The archivist turned a page or two. 'And now 1612.' He turned another couple of pages. '1613.' Another page, and another. Sweat broke out on his forehead and he began to tremble violently, as if he had a fever.

'Shall I get you a glass of water?' Sigbrit asked, but before the archivist could reply she caught sight of what had caused his distress: in the middle of the vertical columns of titles a large number of lines had been scored through so thoroughly that the paper had almost been torn away. Only one single corner of one single letter was visible. Sigbrit counted eight lines, after that various pages had been torn out of the book right up to the year 1619. She had found what she had been looking for!

*

No one answered. Sigbrit knocked harder. Still no one came. She tried the handle; the door was locked.

'Ambrosius! It's me, Sigbrit,' she called and peered through the windows. She couldn't see anything as the curtains were closed and there was no light. Maybe the police had found them. Sigbrit's heart beat faster. 'Ambrosius!' she called again and hammered on the door with clenched fists. 'Ambrosius! Ambrosius!' Then she suddenly took hold of herself, embarrassed at her own conduct. What was she doing here anyway, when she should have been home long ago? She hurried over the deck and climbed up on to the quay.

'Hi, you there!' a twanging voice came from a bench a little way down the quay. Sigbrit looked the other way, but the woman called again. 'Hi, you, are you looking for Ambrosius?'

Sigbrit turned round.

'Are you looking for Ambrosius?' repeated the woman slowly, as if taking care how she pronounced each word.

'Yes,' Sigbrit replied curtly.

'He went over there.' The woman pointed offhandedly up the street towards a basement bar. 'With the wee small one and the gigantic man.'

'Are you mad?' Sigbrit asked loudly to make herself heard above the music. 'Suppose someone recognizes him?'

Ambrosius the Fisherman rose to his feet without replying and kissed her on the cheek. Then he sat down again and laughed. Sigbrit turned her face away and greeted Odin and Gunnar the Head, then sat down on a chair with her back partly away from the Fisherman. Her fingers drummed on her thigh faster than the orchestra was playing.

'There's no one here who would recognize our friend.' Ambrosius the Fisherman laid a hand on Odin's shoulder. The music had stopped and he could speak in a normal pitch.

What he had said was true. If it had not been for Odin's minimal size and his closed left eye, even Sigbrit would not have known that it was him; his white hair was tucked up inside a shabby American military cap, half of his long white beard had been shorn and instead of his usual loose-fitting clothes he wore a blue jumper and a pair of denims which the Fisherman had borrowed from the son of a friend.

'You look like a child who has pinched Santa Claus's beard!' chuckled Gunnar the Head, almost falling out of his chair.

'Santa Claus or the Risen Christ.' Ambrosius the Fisherman laughed, putting down his beer. 'After all, everyone needs his own faith.'

'There are plenty of people who don't believe in anything at all,' said Sigbrit.

'Well, not believing is a form of belief,' quoted the Fisherman drily, looking hard at Sigbrit. 'And then there's the curious faith in conventions, which makes people swim around like fish in a fantasy aquarium without ever getting near enough the imaginary glass walls to realize they aren't there. Yes, that's really a bit much for my taste.'

Odin wrinkled his forehead and tugged at his beard. 'Fish that can swim straight don't swim in circles,' said he.

'No, I suppose not,' rumbled the Fisherman. 'But there are some fish that are unusual.'

'There is no courage but true courage!' exclaimed Odin, and Gunnar the Head nodded and slapped his friend on the back, proud of his wisdom.

'So the imaginary aquarium becomes a form of religion in itself?' asked Sigbrit, trying to make sense of what the Fisherman had said.

Ambrosius the Fisherman nodded. 'Yes, maybe the imaginary father of the aquarium is a kind of god, the substitute for hope, the scapegoat for misery. But only God promises a better life after this one.' The Fisherman laughed. 'Yes, he has always been one step ahead, Our Lord, hasn't he?'

The music started up again, and the conversation came to a halt. Odin sat deep in thought. He was speculating on this question of belief. In truth he didn't know what faith was, but perhaps it was something like a horse. In that case Ambrosius the Fisherman was right: everyone ought to have their own, or two perhaps. Where would Odin be without Balthazar and Rigmarole?

That brought Odin back to his unfortunate horse, and as soon as the music stopped again he leaned forward and said: 'I really and truly wish Veterinarius Martinussen would hurry up and finish the regulations so we can get back to Smith's Town and Rigmarole.'

Sigbrit and Ambrosius exchanged glances. How could they explain to the little old man that even if Veterinarius Martinussen – or rather some other veterinary surgeon they still had not found – was willing to help him, they could not go across to Smith's Town and the horse. It was already the end of March and the Strait would not freeze over before next winter at best, at worst it might be more than a quarter of a century before the ice would be thick enough to bear the weight of people. And in any case no vet would ever venture with Odin to an island no one knew of.

'You mustn't worry yourself over Veterinarius Martinussen,' said Ambrosius the Fisherman. 'Everything is going to be fine. It may take a bit of time, but it will be all right.'

'Yes,' agreed Sigbrit, 'there's no need to worry.'

Odin felt in his breast pocket for the horseshoe, but it was not there. Then he remembered he had moved it to his trousers pocket when he changed his clothes. Yes, there it was. Odin smiled to himself; it was true that no mishap could not be remedied with a morsel of luck. He must just remind Gunnar the Head to give the key back to the sleeping nurse, and he must remember to ask Ambrosius the Fisherman about the name of the boat, and then he must remember to ask if he could perhaps help Veterinarius Martinussen to complete the regulations. Odin leaned back against the wall, rocking in time to the music, and was soon snoring happily.

Sigbrit then started to tell Ambrosius about her visit to the Special Archives at the Land Registry.

'1614 to 1618. Yes, Lady Fair, we think you are right. That is too remarkable to be a coincidence. What we are searching for could well be found in the missing years. It's not much, but it is something. At least we know now which years we need to look at. It is not so bad in fact, and yet it's not so good either. If the maps are not there, they are not, and we shall have to look elsewhere.' The Fisherman filled his pipe and fell silent. He looked as if he was considering something.

The orchestra packed up their instruments and instead a juke-box began to roar out 1960s' rock. It played half a dozen tracks before people stopped putting in coins.

'We'll go out sailing!' sang out the Fisherman in the sudden silence.

'Sailing?'

'Yes, Lady Fair, sailing. Who knows, perhaps we can find some trace of the island, or perhaps Odin can remember more once we get close to the rocks.'

'When?'

'On Monday.'

'I'm coming too.'

Ambrosius scratched his short beard dubiously. 'You, Lady Fair! Surely you don't mean it?'

'Of course I mean it,' replied Sigbrit, offended; of course she meant it.

'And your husband?'

'What's he got to do with it?'

'That's what we don't know.' Ambrosius the Fisherman laughed quietly.

'I'm coming with you!' Sigbrit insisted.

'Good,' said the Fisherman after a pause. 'But don't forget it can be dangerous out there by the rocks. And the *Rikke-Marie* hasn't been out for several years. We shall give her a thorough overhaul during the weekend, but she is an old lady, you know.'

'Monday,' repeated Sigbrit impatiently.

'I don't like sailing,' mumbled Gunnar the Head to himself.

'There is something I have been thinking about,' said Sigbrit to Ambrosius. 'I hope you don't mind me asking.' She hesitated and went on in a low voice. 'Why did you give up fishing?'

'Ask away, Lady Fair. Answering is another matter, though.'

Sigbrit waited but the Fisherman said no more; she shouldn't have asked.

'It's a short history, and it's a long history,' he said after a long pause. 'But now it is late, and we had better make our way home to bed. The story belongs to the sea, and it can be told at sea. Lady Fair, eight o'clock on Monday.'

Sigbrit nodded, although she suddenly felt unsure whether it really was such a good idea for her to go too. She wondered what excuse she could dream up to give the bank, and how she would explain to Fridtjof that she was going out sailing with Odin and Ambrosius the Fisherman instead of going to work.

They paid for their beer, and Gunnar the Head lifted Odin into his arms and carried him like a child out of the bar and along the quay towards the green and orange fishing boat. Sigbrit waved goodbye and drove north in her car.

*

Over the weekend, while Ambrosius the Fisherman repaired the *Rikke-Marie* and Sigbrit Holland tidied the house and garden with her husband, the Queen studied the four small diaries. Page after page was filled with almost illegible scribbling, and the Queen had to strain her eyes to interpret them. She was so absorbed in the contents that she hardly took a break to eat or rest. Not because there was so much interesting historical detail of the country or similar subjects; no, apart from descriptions of the endless conflict with the North Norse Kingdom and King Enevold IV's strong antipathy to the changing North Norse Kings, the secret diaries were limited to the King's private life. There was love as well and fear of his father, who had died when the King was still only a toddler, his never-failing passion for action, the platonic marriage with his first wife, the constant stream of mistresses, the numerous children and, from the middle of the second diary, on the whole nothing more than the love of his life: '*My heart's dearest,*' as he named the young commoner Drude Estrid. Well, that was before they were married, and the woman subsequently made his life a neverending Hell, thought the Queen as she went on deciphering her ancestor's handwriting.

Towards the end of the second diary the King mentioned he had just had a brilliant idea: he would give the newly discovered island in the Strait to his beloved bride to be, and name it after her – Drude Estrid Island. As he had won the 1611–13 war against North Norseland, King Enevold IV considered he did not need to ask anyone about his right to the minute strip of land in the mid-strait.

The island, said the Queen to herself and immediately

thought of the little old man and his story. With renewed enthusiasm she read on, but there were no more details about the island the King had mentioned. There was a description of a frightful pitched battle in the Straits between the South Norse and the North Norse fleets in which a large proportion of the nation's ships and crews had been lost, not only in the violent confrontations but also on the teeth of some ferocious rocks. The description of the sea battles stopped in the middle of a sentence, next came various crossed-out sections, and the following paragraphs dealt solely with the King's adoration of Drude Estrid, until at long last she said yes, and the wedding preparations could begin. A good many pages were missing from the end of the book, and the Queen opened the third diary. That did not start until several years after the King and Queen Estrid had married, and a quick flip through this volume yielded not a single mention of the island. The Queen returned to the first page, but the book was carefully numbered three in King Enevold IV's hand: no books were missing. What she was searching for must have been on the torn-out pages. The Queen read through the third and fourth diaries carefully, which only confirmed the absence of further mention of the island. She studied the dates; the war against North Norseland, which the King described, was not part of the familiar South Norse history. Despite the hatred nourished for each other by the South Norse King and the young North Norse King, officially there had been peace between the two countries from the signing of the peace treaty in 1613 until North Norseland – without any kind of honourable declaration of war – invaded South Norseland in 1643. How could North Norseland have pushed right through the South Norseland provinces in North Norseland to fight a bloody battle in the Strait without it being recorded in the official annals? It was most extraordinary. History or no, some violent clashes had clearly taken place, and King Enevold IV had never honoured his promise to his beloved. What had forestalled that?

The Queen glanced at the clock on her bedside table. It was past midnight, tomorrow was Monday and she had to get up promptly. With a sigh she laid aside the books and looked at her notes. She had painstakingly copied all references to the island, but there was not much to go on: an unnamed island, some rocks, some ferocious sea battles and a wedding gift that never came to anything. How odd life was, thought the Queen: the ferry she was going to name the next morning was to be called *King Enevold IV*, and the ship, which was to sail between South Norseland and North Norseland, would cross the Strait many times a day, in those very waters where the island – that had once been intended for the King's beloved – by all accounts really did exist.

ODIN, VILE AND VE

Death and torment
struck both Good and Evil
But Bure God the giant Bestla wed
and Odin, Vile, Ve, three sons were born

Spirit, Life and Will their father joined
slain was monster Ymer, ogre worst
his blood flushed forth a vast deluge
and all his kin, but Bergelmer, did drown

Yet, this which seemed the end, was not

'GOD BE WITH you, Enevold the Fourth!' The Queen hurled the champagne bottle at the ship's side, the bottle smashed to smithereens, the spectators clapped, and the shipowner thanked the Queen for her presence and her words. A cold sea fog cloaked the harbour in its damp clutches, the Queen's bright scarlet coat fluttered and she had to hold on to her hat. She glanced up at the sky, but although it was grey and windswept there was no sign of rain. Unless the captain of the royal yacht advised against it, she would carry on with her plans.

The Queen was oblivious to the shipowner's words but walked beside him to the waiting limousine, smiling and nodding at intervals. Then she waved farewell to the freezing spectators and drove off. 'To the royal quay,' she said and asked the chauffeur to get a report on weather conditions from the captain. The reply soon came: cold and windy, but fine providing they did not sail outside the Strait. Half an hour later the royal yacht made its way out of the harbour with its white mainsail roaring in the wind.

The royal yacht cut through the waves at high speed, and it was not long before the captain gave the order for the sails to be lowered. The wind was too strong, the yacht would be more stable with engine power. The Queen stood on the bridge beside the captain with her binoculars glued to her eyes. Almost at once she made out the contours of the rocks and they soon became visible and stood out clearly. As the yacht drew closer the captain slackened speed and steered northwards at the Queen's command.

The Queen studied the formidable grey-black masses rising out of the sea with their jagged points, deep clefts and rugged corners and she wondered whether these might not be the self-same cliffs that King Enevold IV had described in his second diary. Perhaps, but they were too high and dense for anything behind them to be visible. If it had been possible to see anything at all someone or other would have spotted it long ago. The yacht approached the northernmost point of the line of rocky cliffs and the Queen laid her binoculars aside, disappointed. The captain had been right: clearly there was no sign of an island hidden behind the cliffs.

But what was that? For a moment it seemed to the Queen that a strange bulge swelled out of the rank of rocks, though the next moment it returned to its former shape. She asked the captain to turn the yacht round and again raised the binoculars to her eyes. There it was again; for a second it looked as if the midpoint of the rocks bulged out like a ship. Then the moment passed and again there was a straight line of them. The royal yacht turned around on the same spot several more times, and finally the Queen was sure of it: from the very northernmost point it could be seen that the rocks formed an ellipse and not a straight line. But as soon as you moved a metre to the east or a metre to the west, there was only a single line to be seen. Although the strange swelling might be due to an increase in the volume of the rocks, one could not exclude the possibility that a small strip of land was hidden between them. The Queen took up a pencil and paper and began to draw.

By this time the green and orange fishing boat had already been at sea for over an hour. *Rikke-Marie* made her way sedately alongside the coast. The old boat did not hold the warmth too well and the wind sneaked in between cracks in the walls and windowsills, causing Sigbrit to shiver with cold and curse her thin clothes. She had not escaped a heated discussion with her husband over this trip. She had tried to convince him how vital it was to find some trace of the island, but he either would not or could not understand. She couldn't just cry off work like that, it was dishonest, he said. Sigbrit knew he was right, but for some reason did not care. Sometimes there is something you just have to do, she had said. What did it really matter to the bank if she was there or not? Someone else would take over her work, and she had worked hard enough in the past, over weekends and holidays, to have earned a day off now and then. When Fridtjof did not budge, Sigbrit had tried to get him to go with her. He refused to do so, and finally she gave in. Or rather she pretended to. That was why she had joined the green and orange fishing boat in her office clothes.

Sigbrit looked around the wheelhouse: the pot plants, the candles in wine glasses and all the other loose objects had disappeared. Only the curtains were witness to the fact that *Rikke-Marie* did not normally go to sea. Withered and withdrawn, Der Fremdling sat in the darkest corner of the wheelhouse opposite Gunnar the Head, who mumbled constantly to himself, while Odin stood up on the bench, keeping a close watch on the horizon. Ambrosius the Fisherman stood at the wheel, silent and unapproachable. He had been unusually quiet the whole morning. He did not volunteer anything and only replied to questions with one-syllable words. It was as if something weighed on his mind, Sigbrit thought, but she had no idea what it could be.

'There it is, there it is!' Odin jumped up and down and pointed out of the window.

And now they could all see it, a faint line of dark shadows on the north-east horizon.

'I don't like sailing, I don't like sailing at all,' complained Gunnar the Head.

Ambrosius the Fisherman remained silent, merely changing course slightly to the east. The contours of the rocks grew sharper.

'It looks as if the devil is pointing a warning finger at the heavens,' said Sigbrit.

'*Near the island and all Hell breaks out*,' growled the Fisherman through clenched teeth.

'I thought it was "*Name the island and...*"'

'"*Name it*" or "*near it*", what do we know? The men of the sea say so many things. Sometimes they are right, sometimes wrong.' The Fisherman looked at her with a strangely distant expression. 'It's one and one making two, I dare say.'

Sigbrit gazed at the rocks again. She shrugged her shoulders and tried to ignore the knot of fear tightening in her stomach. To distract herself she took up her camera and zoomed in on the rocks. If she could catch just the smallest glimpse of land they would have the proof they needed. She took a couple of shots and then put the camera away; there was nothing to be seen but sea, sky, seagulls and rocks.

'That's no good,' she said, 'we must get closer.'

'Lady Fair, be patient. We are going to get closer.' The Fisherman shook his head. 'It's necessary to take small bites, these waters are pretty treacherous. What you can see isn't a fraction of what there is. The sea is not with us today. We must get over to the other side of the cliffs, then we will have the wind behind us.' The Fisherman steered the boat back and in a semicircle around the southernmost point of the rock formation, on the North Norse side of the Strait. Here the wind quietened and the waves were less wild.

Ambrosius the Fisherman slackened speed. Grasping the wheel firmly with one hand, with the other he unbuttoned his breast pocket and pulled out a plastic pocket containing a piece of paper.

'Here.' He passed it to Sigbrit.

The paper was old and yellowing, and time had nibbled the corners. All it showed was a row of crosses and circles in an odd oblong pattern.

'You see these marks,' Ambrosius the Fisherman pointed to the paper. 'The crosses are the found rocks, the circles probable others.'

'It's a map of the rock formations?' Sigbrit asked in surprise.

'I imagine it's the only one that exists.'

The Fisherman did not relax his watch over the sea beyond his boat's bow.

'In truth it is a pity Veterinarius Martinussen could not come with us today,' Odin remarked, twisting his beard around his fingers.

'Who made it?' asked Sigbrit, ignoring Odin.

Ambrosius the Fisherman hesitated.

'I won't say anything to anyone.'

'Our grandfather started on it, and when he drowned, our father continued.' The Fisherman stretched out his hand and carefully smoothed the plastic pocket. 'The circles and the crosses that stand separately were made by our grandfather. The circles with a cross inside are those our father was able to verify.'

'Is it complete?'

'That we don't know.' Ambrosius the Fisherman rubbed his chin. 'And that's only one of the problems. The other is that we don't know which side of the rock formations are where. So that the chart would not put its owner in any danger, neither the four corners of the world nor the South and North Norse coasts have been inserted. If you don't know it beforehand it is impossible to guess what this paper reveals.'

'But then in reality all it tells us is that the points that are included should be avoided, or rather, they are some of the points that should be avoided, and then only if we have come upon the right side of the island?'

Ambrosius nodded and grabbed his pipe from the shelf. He filled and lit it with one hand without once letting go of the helm.

'It is all we have,' he said hoarsely.

The Fisherman blew out the sweet blue smoke, and the boat picked up speed again. Sigbrit sat down to study the chart. Even though many points were missing there was a remarkable symmetry about the drawing.

'A rock doesn't move regardless of the weather raging around it,' said Odin quietly, tugging at his beard.

Sigbrit nodded slowly, as if a thought had struck her. She turned to the Fisherman. 'Didn't you tell me at one point that the rock formation forms a symmetrical ellipse, and that therefore no one ever discovered that there were two and not one single line of rocks?'

'True enough.'

'So isn't it highly probable that the underwater rocks are also symmetric?' Sigbrit stood up in great excitement.

Ambrosius the Fisherman looked at her with a crooked smile.

'Not bad from such an urban woman. You're a quick learner, Lady Fair,' said he.

Sigbrit turned her back on the Fisherman and looked out of the window. Her cheeks were red and her eyes flashed, partly on account of the Fisherman's patronizing attitude and partly because of her own foolish feeling of pride.

They were nearing the rocks now and the huge masses no longer resembled one single chain of mountains but leapt out of the water like a row of gigantic individuals with sharp teeth and claws. Sigbrit picked up her camera again.

'I still can't see anything but rocks. We must get closer still.'

'It will be pretty rough. Are you all happy about that?' Ambrosius took his eyes off the sea for a moment and looked around at his passengers.

Sigbrit nodded. Odin nodded too. 'I wonder if Veterinarius

Martinussen has gone on ahead and is already in Smith's Town,' he mumbled to himself.

'I don't like sailing. I don't like sailing at all,' groaned Gunnar the Head, rocking forwards and backwards.

Der Fremdling said nothing.

'We'll go a bit further along to find the best place to make our way in. Put on your life-jackets.' The Fisherman pointed to a chest under the table, in which Sigbrit found a child's jacket that fitted Odin, and some larger ones for herself and Der Fremdling. She had to tie two together for Gunnar the Head.

'In the event of a mishap, Lady Fair, get the others out of the wheelhouse and into the lifeboat in double-quick time. Don't think about us.' The Fisherman spoke in a thick, half-choking voice.

He is frightened, thought Sigbrit in wonder. She pulled yet another life-jacket out of the chest and threw it over to him.

'I don't care whether a captain ought to go down with his ship,' she said, when he hesitated. 'Either we all put on life-jackets, or none of us do.'

Ambrosius had found what he was looking for and slackened speed. The waves roared against the rocky walls and they had to shout to make themselves heard.

'Look.' He pointed to a place on the lower half of the map. 'It must be here.'

Sigbrit looked over the Fisherman's shoulder at the small opening in the series of crosses and circles. Then she looked out of the window, and although it was not possible to see past the first rocks, it did resemble a narrow opening. Perhaps it was the entrance.

'I don't like sailing. I don't like sailing at all,' moaned Gunnar the Head, ashen-faced.

Sigbrit Holland looked at Odin, who was still standing up on the bench. His face was so close to the window that his breath misted the glass.

'Let's give it a try,' she said, and changed the film in her camera.

Ambrosius edged the *Rikke-Marie* slowly forward. His eyes were glued to the waves: where the water flowed in circles instead of rolling on, there were underwater rocks. Sigbrit stood beside Odin with her camera in position. It took only a few minutes to come level with the outermost rock. The sea had carved deep into the rock and created a plateau-like hollow into which the waves hammered constantly, and cascades of raging foam rose into the air. The *Rikke-Marie* rolled alarmingly from side to side, and Sigbrit had to hold on to the windowsill to avoid falling.

'I don't like sailing. I don't like sailing at all,' groaned Gunnar the Head, paler with each wave that struck the boat.

The sweat ran down the Fisherman's face in spite of the cold. The green and orange fishing boat passed the first line of rocks, and although the second one seemed a little smaller, the rocks were spread out so unsystematically that navigation was even harder.

'Look over there!' Sigbrit pointed to the north-west and shot a quick series of views of the horizon, where a couple of faint spirals of smoke could be glimpsed above one of the rocks before they melted into air and vanished against the grey sky.

'Smith's Town! Smith's Town!' shouted Odin, hopping up and down, exactly as he had seen Long Laust do when good news came. At the same moment he recalled something he had been meaning to ask Ambrosius the Fisherman about for a long time.

'Family tradition,' answered the Fisherman. '*Rikke-Marie* was the name of our father's boat, and before that *Rikke-Marie* was the name of our grandfather's boat.' He coughed. 'No need to break the tradition.'

'So, then, there's *Rikke-Marie*, and there's Oldmother Rikke-Marie!' Odin wound his beard around his fingers and thought of the promise he had made to the old lady the evening before he left Smith's Town. 'Forgive the liberty, but I wonder if you know a man by the name of Richard the Red?'

Ambrosius turned his head and gave Odin a long wondering look. 'What do you know about Richard the Red?' he asked slowly.

'Richard the Red is in truth the father of Oldmother Rikke-Marie,' said Odin and told the Fisherman how in his youth Richard the Red bade farewell to Oldmother Rikke-Marie's mother before going out to prove he had found the sea route to the Continent and had never returned.

'Well, we never...' mumbled Ambrosius, rubbing his chin thoughtfully.

Suddenly a rock appeared and grew until it filled Sigbrit's viewfinder. She lowered the camera, but it had not been the zoom – they had come too close.

'Look out!' she yelled, but it was too late.

There was a loud crash, the boat shuddered violently, and everyone except the Fisherman tumbled to the floor. The motor stopped, and at once they could hear the roar of the waves.

'I don't like sailing. I don't like sailing at all!' Gunnar the Head rubbed his left shoulder and crawled back to his corner, while

Der Fremdling, without words or gestures and without the least sign of having changed expression, regained his place opposite. Sigbrit picked herself up slowly and then helped Odin to his feet. She looked out of the window. The rock gripped the boat at an angle of about twenty degrees above the surface of the water.

'There's no mishap that a morsel of luck cannot remedy,' said Odin calmly, pressing his hand against the pocket that held the horseshoe.

'Ambrosius, we have to do something,' said Sigbrit, but the Fisherman did not move, his eyes frozen to the rock in front of the boat and his hands clutching the helm so hard that his knuckles were quite white.

'Ambrosius!' Sigbrit grabbed the Fisherman's arm, without raising so much as a wink.

Sigbrit swore quietly; what a moment to go into shock.

'Um, excuse me, but in truth I am afraid blood is running from your brow.' Odin pointed anxiously at Sigbrit's forehead.

She raised her hand and felt the thick fluid; it must have happened when her head struck the windowsill. At once she grew calm. She wiped away most of the blood with the back of her hand, took off her shoes and stockings and fastened a safety line to the ring on her life-jacket.

'Keep your eye on me. If I call for help, get Gunnar the Head to pull me back,' she said to Odin and opened the door.

The deck was wet and slippery. Sigbrit had to push her toes into the cracks between the planks to avoid falling. Icy cold waves were licking over the keel, down the deck and over her feet, and the wind threw itself around among the rocks and seemed to punch her from all sides. She grabbed hold of the rail and clung to it as she crawled rather than walked up the sloping deck. The water hammered at *Rikke-Marie's* hull with a deafening din, and Sigbrit was afraid the boat might give way at any moment. As soon as she climbed high enough to get a view of the damage, she breathed a sigh of relief. As far as she could see, the hole in the keel was not much bigger than a beach ball, and the strange layered rock formation had lifted up the boat so that the opening was above the water. Apart from spray from the waves impacting rocks and fishing boat, no water was entering *Rikke-Marie*. And despite the ferocity of the waves close to the rock, the boat was solidly planted there, not letting the mass of water move her an inch.

'What a boat,' muttered Sigbrit, patting the old green boards as if they were a horse. She slid back down the deck.

'There's no need to worry,' she said. 'It will be hours, maybe days, before *Rikke-Marie* gives way.'

'I don't like sailing. I really don't like sailing at all,' wailed Gunnar the Head.

Ambrosius the Fisherman was still in shock and just gazed in front of him when Sigbrit repeated her words. She shrugged her shoulders, let Odin wash the blood from her face and picked up the camera from the floor. It didn't seem damaged, so she put it under her arm and went out again.

As she ran her eyes along the rocks, Sigbrit could see no gap or cleft that might indicate something was concealed behind it. Again and again she searched along the line of rocks, but it seemed like an impenetrable wall. Disappointment washed over her; they had smashed up the boat and risked their lives, and to what purpose? Perhaps there really was nothing there. Perhaps it was all something that Odin and Ambrosius had dreamed up; delusions, as the doctors would say. She couldn't even see the smoke any more, and maybe that had just been the steam from a ferry on the other side of the rocks. Cold drizzle began to fall. Sigbrit closed her eyes; if only she was back in her office and everything was normal again. How on earth had she ever got herself into this caper? Hadn't she done more than enough by driving Odin to hospital that first evening? The drizzle was turning into a proper downpour, and Sigbrit opened her eyes. She took the remaining exposures in her film of the coast she couldn't see and went inside.

The wheelhouse was warm and smelled of fresh coffee. Ambrosius the Fisherman seemed to have recovered, and somehow or other he had managed to restore the heat.

'We can certainly all do with something strengthening now,' he said and put a bottle of schnapps on the table beside the coffee pot. 'Here.' He passed a faded green handkerchief to Sigbrit. 'Look in the chest under our bunk.' He pointed to the narrow ladder that led down to the interior of the fishing boat. 'You'll find dry clothes there.'

Sigbrit climbed down the ladder, took off her soaking wet things and dressed in some of the Fisherman's clothes after rubbing herself dry. Everything was far too big, but at least it was dry and warm. She climbed back up the ladder and sat down at the table.

Ambrosius put on his wet weather gear and went out to send up a distress rocket. 'We must hope that someone will look up today,' he said on his return.

'There is truly no mishap a morsel of luck cannot remedy,' Odin remarked, patting the horseshoe in his breast pocket.

'Yes, it's only half past eleven,' Sigbrit chimed in. 'There's more than half a day before darkness falls, and surely someone will find us before then. There is quite a lot of traffic out here in the Strait, isn't there?'

Ambrosius did not reply. He merely stared at her with a remote look in his eyes, as if he was thinking of something quite different and had not heard what she said. After a long pause he said in a low voice: 'Lady Fair, you are not at all such an innocent as one might expect from a city lass.' He ran his fingers through his wet hair and then lit his pipe. 'Tell us, what made you choose to spend your life in a bank?'

'Well, you have to do something,' said Sigbrit quickly, and the moment she said it she knew it was true. Someone has to buy and sell foreign currency, or the markets couldn't function, could they? That's what she said to the Fisherman.

'And then what?' he answered. 'Maybe the world wouldn't be so much the poorer for that.'

If they had not been on board a green and orange fishing boat, stranded on a huge rock in roaring waters with the sky cascading down on them, not far from an island whose existence was unacknowledged, and in the company of a little old man with only one eye, a huge man who carried his illusory giant's head under his arm, and a wizened shadow who never uttered a word, Sigbrit would have enlightened Ambrosius the Fisherman on the significance of the instant convertibility of currency, on the curves of demand and supply, macroeconomic imbalances and comparative advantages. But the fact was that they were stranded on a fishing boat in somewhat mixed company, and her explanations suddenly seemed absurd.

Instead she asked, 'You never told me why you stopped fishing?'

'No, that's true, we didn't.'

'And?'

'Lady Fair, have patience!' The Fisherman sounded irritated and Sigbrit did not press him.

Odin looked from one to the other. He did not fully understand the habit some of the Continentals had of getting ill-tempered when there was no cause. On the other hand, how could he know when the Continentals had a reason for being ill-tempered, so he merely mumbled to himself: 'I sincerely hope Veterinarius Martinussen has found a better way of getting to Smith's Town than this one.'

'Don't worry!' exclaimed Sigbrit Holland and Ambrosius the Fisherman with one voice, and the Fisherman went on: 'We'll just have to go back to Fredenshvile to repair *Rikke-Marie* before we can try again. As you can see, it's not so easy to find Richard the Red's sea route, but sooner or later we'll succeed.'

The Fisherman took a pull at his pipe, cleared his throat and began to speak in a whisper. Sigbrit was obliged to lean across the table to hear what he said. 'The bare bones of it is that because of over-fishing the government started to pay the fishermen to stop fishing, and at a certain point we realized that we could earn more by not fishing than by fishing, so we stopped.'

Was that all? Sigbrit got to her feet and cleared the table.

'Have patience, Lady Fair,' said Ambrosius, this time with a friendly smile.

Sigbrit sat down again.

'Some people call it fate, others call it destiny, others again think the Norns have spun their webs across the route. Whatever it is, we have our version. What happened was that we discovered what it looked like – our destiny. So we stopped fishing. It's about two years ago now.' Ambrosius the Fisherman chewed on his pipe and gazed out the window for a while before continuing: 'When our grandfather died we were still only a boy, but we clearly remember the stories he told, about a strange unknown island in dangerous waters, which a single very brave sailor staked his life on to reach. Well, so our grandfather died, and all he left us were his stories – or that was all we believed he had left. After our father's death we found out that our grandfather had also left this little map.' The Fisherman picked up the little plastic pocket that held the yellowing paper and looked at it with a mixture of fear and veneration. 'Some would call it a curse, others a blessing. No matter which, it is our destiny.' He swung the little pocket back and forth between his fingers.

The wheelhouse was silent. Then Sigbrit asked: 'Didn't you say your father died many years ago?'

'He died many years ago but the fisherman who hauled him up in his net never told us what he had found on a cord around our father's neck. Not until after his own death did his daughter send us the map with a letter in which she apologized for the delay and said she had found this odd drawing with our father's name among his things.' Ambrosius smiled sadly. 'Sometimes we have wished that she had kept it.' He ran his fingers through his hair and sighed.

Der Fremdling cackled softly from his corner, and the Fisherman turned his head for a brief moment before addressing Sigbrit again.

'Still, it probably wouldn't have made any difference. Until that chart arrived we had no idea that our grandfather and our father did anything at all other than catching cod and plaice. Not until we held this map in our hand,' again the Fisherman waved the plastic pocket in the air, 'did we know that the brave sailor in our grandfather's stories was none other than himself. We knew that it was not only through coincidence and bad luck that our father and grandfather, experienced seamen as they were, well versed in the ways of the sea, met their end on the same rocks out in the Strait. And we knew that the nameless island, which the men of the sea wove their tales about in the depths of night, when their women were not present, was more than a mere myth. It was at this point that I took on the inheritance that had to be continued – "I" became "we"; we had learned to know our fate.' The Fisherman took a deep pull at his pipe and then ended almost brusquely: 'Oh, well, that was that, and there's no more to be said about it.'

'All the same, you are out here today,' Sigbrit said softly.

'Lady Fair,' Ambrosius sighed. 'On the day you came along with Odin's story we knew one can't win the race against fate – only ask Der Fremdling there.' He nodded towards the withered man in the corner. 'We also knew there was a reason for our having been sent the chart.' A sudden smile appeared on the Fisherman's face. He glanced at Sigbrit. 'At least we know now why our grandfather defied danger, law and custom, and why he left this overstepping of boundaries as his only bequest to his son and later his grandson – and to those generations that would follow.' He turned to Odin. 'To answer your earlier question: yes, we have met Richard the Red. Richard the Red is our grandfather.'

Odin anxiously pulled at his beard, and a deep furrow formed in the wrinkles on his brow.

'I am most deeply sorry,' he said as kindly as he could. He wondered whether the Fisherman's head had been damaged in the meeting of his boat and the rock. 'But that isn't possible, Richard the Red is Oldmother Rikke-Marie's father.'

Ambrosius the Fisherman burst out laughing. 'Don't upset yourself,' he said, patting Odin on the back. 'Richard the Red is both our grandfather and Oldmother Rikke-Marie's father. Yes, in fact, we ourselves are most certainly Oldmother Rikke-Marie's nephew.'

Odin pondered deeply over this situation. 'The ties of blood are inscrutable and yet always recognizable,' he said finally.

'I don't believe in fate,' said Sigbrit quietly.

'Call it something else then. It all comes down to the same thing: genes, inheritance, circumstance, potentiality, calling, chance, indeed, luck even.'

'There is no mishap that a morsel of luck cannot remedy,' said Odin, nodding to himself. 'I wonder whether bad news that is not warned of isn't bad news all the same?'

Silence fell over the wheelhouse for a brief spell, then Sigbrit said: 'There's no such thing as preordained destiny.'

'Call it what you will. Whether the Norns have spun their spells or not, there *is* a predestined line.'

'So nothing is one's own responsibility?'

'The line is there. Whether one chooses to follow it or not is another matter.'

'So, apart from a few circumstances such as environment, time and inherited physical features, everything is up to yourself and coincidence?'

'It looks like that, but it is not so. Or rather, one ought not to let it be so.'

'I don't understand,' said Sigbrit, drumming lightly on the table with her fingers.

'When you are given your biological make-up, your environment, the circumstances of your birth and existence, your destiny is given to you as well.' The Fisherman chewed at his pipe. 'If, within the potentiality that has been given, you stretch yourself to the utmost, the course of your life and with

it the course of your destiny is given as well. Lady Fair, that
destiny is not something that happens to you, destiny is what
you do, the sum of the will and vigour you exert to make use
of your potential.'

They sat in silence. Then Sigbrit said quietly: 'If what you say
is true, it is the island and not the rocks that is your destiny.'

Before the Fisherman could reply, Odin leapt to his feet.
From not far away came a sound like that of a powerful engine.

On the bridge of the royal yacht the Queen lowered her
binoculars and pointed to something green and orange
amongst the rocks. 'It has gone aground,' she said. 'We must
go to the rescue...'

*

In the late afternoon, after Ambrosius the Fisherman and the
captain of the royal yacht had succeeded in getting *Rikke-Marie*
afloat again, an unusual sight could be observed in the Firø
Canal, that of a magnificent gold and white yacht towing a
shabby old green and orange fishing boat through the canal
in pouring rain. After Sigbrit Holland and Ambrosius the
Fisherman had told the Queen their story, the Queen skipped
her tea and went straight to her private library.

Three days passed before she found it. When Sigbrit
Holland's discoveries were placed alongside her own there
could no longer be any doubt that someone had deliberately
removed all proofs of the island's existence. Perhaps King
Enevold IV had done it himself to conceal his humiliation; the
impotence of a King unable to fulfil a promise to his beloved.
From having been a paradise the island must have become a
Hell, a symbol of his failed marriage. And now she knew how

the island and the conflict over it had become such a well-kept secret. The Queen read again the yellowing document she held in her hand, a document that had sealed the fate of the island, an agreement between two Kings. She had found it beneath a further pile of documents under the false bottom of a drawer of a solid old cupboard, with two identical maps that showed the island surrounded by rocks, with an inscription in beautiful gilt lettering: '*Drude Estrid Island*'. Such was the fate of the South Norseland King's brilliant wedding gift, thought the Queen, and the King was never to regain his honour. The Queen almost felt the humiliation as if it had been her own. And at that moment she knew precisely what she had to do.

The first thing the Queen did was to put the yellowing agreement back under the false bottom of the drawer where she had found it. Let four hundred years pass by before anyone finds it again, she whispered to herself, closing up the hiding place as thoroughly as she could. After that the Queen charged her trusted Lord Chamberlain, von Egernret, to take one of Enevold IV's two maps to the Land Registry's Special Archives and discreetly lodge it back there. Then the Queen invited the Prime Minister to tea.

Although it was the middle of spring it was cold, and a bright fire crackled in the grate beside the dark green sofas. The Queen waited until tea was served and the door closed behind the maidservant.

'Prime Minister, I have asked you here today because I would like to discuss the matter of Mr Odin Odin with you,' said the Queen pleasantly.

'Indeed, it is an extremely unfortunate story, Your Majesty.' The Prime Minister took a sideways glance at his watch;

he was fearfully busy and really did not have time for a polite audience with the Queen. 'I can assure Your Majesty that the government has already taken every step necessary to limit the disturbances from the Doomsday Prophets. In a few days the demonstrations will be a thing of the past.' The Prime Minister put down his cup. 'And I have asked the Minister of Justice to assign all the necessary forces into the search for Mr Odin Odin. I am convinced that the little old man will soon be back in hospital, which will prove to the demonstrators that the government had no hand in his disappearance.'

'Prime Minister.' The Queen spoke slowly and distinctly. 'I am not worried about the demonstrations. I have the greatest respect for and faith in the government's efforts in that matter. No, what I want to talk to you about is the question of Mr Odin's origins.'

The Prime Minister's eyebrows shot up in surprise.

'I am afraid this has not yet been ascertained.' He was on the point of cracking his little finger, but thought better of it. 'Your Majesty, it is a highly complicated matter.'

'I realize that, but Prime Minister, I have reason to believe that this whole matter could be much simpler than it looks.'

If only the country had a monarch who would stay within the limits of the job; the Prime Minister sighed imperceptibly.

'Your Majesty, the man suffers hallucinations, he is a danger to himself, and no one has as yet been able to establish his identity.' The Prime Minister had difficulty hiding his impatience. 'I can assure Your Majesty that the government will soon have uncovered all the details of his background story.'

'Prime Minister, it may not be quite so complicated.' The Queen smiled graciously. 'You see, I have good reason to believe that the little old man is not quite as disturbed as the doctors think.'

The Prime Minister raised his eyebrows enquiringly, but the Queen was taking her time. First she nibbled a biscuit and sipped a mouthful of tea and then resumed: 'Permit me to show you something I came across recently when researching in the library.' She calmly handed the Prime Minister King Enevold IV's yellowed map. 'You see, I not only have a good reason to believe that the island that Mr Odin Odin maintains he comes from, does in fact exist, I also have good reason to think that it is this one.'

The Queen had spoken in an extremely gracious manner, but the Prime Minister seemed to be struck dumb. He leaned back in his chair, sat up again, opened and closed his mouth, as if about to say something he was unable to utter. He studied the map, then lowered it and shook his head before picking it up again to study it more closely.

'But how? I don't know of any islands in the Strait south of Ur Island.'

'No, it doesn't seem to be widely known. But, Prime Minister, there it is, as you see.'

'Yes, but...' The Prime Minister cracked his left little finger, stopped and instead picked up his tea cup. 'But Your Majesty, I must say, how can an island exist in the Strait without anyone knowing about it?'

The Queen passed him her drawing.

'The rocks,' she said pleasantly. 'One can neither get to it nor from it. Except, that is, on that one night when the Strait froze over, and the little old man walked over the ice to fetch help for his horse.'

The Prime Minister closed his eyes and swallowed the

saliva that was accumulating in his mouth. He felt a desperate urge to crack the little finger of his right hand, but controlled himself.

'Your Majesty, forgive me, but if this map really tells the truth...' The left-hand side of the Prime Minister's jaw tightened. 'If this map tells the truth, someone must once have known of its existence. In which case surely we would have some knowledge of it today?' He shook his head almost unnoticeably. 'How can it be that no one has previously found a map of or a reference to the island?'

'Yes, it is rather odd,' said the Queen, 'because surely there must be another version of this map somewhere, probably at the Central Library or, who knows, possibly in the Special Archives of the Land Registry.' The Queen sipped her tea. 'Prime Minister, I merely thought it might be a good idea if the government looked into the matter.'

'Naturally, Your Majesty.' The Prime Minister tried in vain to regain his dignity. 'This map, yes... it does considerably alter the situation. And I must naturally thank Your Majesty for the information.'

The Queen nodded kindly, if briefly, and rose to indicate the audience was at an end.

'Prime Minister, now that the government has seen that the map is genuine, it would probably be best if the government and not the Crown conveys the news to the public.'

The door closed behind the Prime Minister, and the Queen sat down. She smiled. Soon Drude Estrid Island would be a part of the South Norse Queendom.

*

'*The government states that information recently received indicates that the island which Mr Odin Odin claims to have come from may well exist. The Minister of Justice has revealed to the press that the government is in possession of a chart of the Strait dating from the seventeenth century, which shows the existence of an island – Drude Estrid Island by name – situated in the Strait between the cliff formations south of Ur Island.*'

'There, you see!' exclaimed Sigbrit Holland, lowering the volume of the radio. 'I was right.'

'I couldn't care less if you had met God in person. You lied to me and you lied to the bank.'

It was the first time Fridtjof and Sigbrit had spoken to each other since she had come home dressed in Ambrosius the Fisherman's clothes, with a big gash on her forehead and a slightly blue left cheek, which in the days that followed turned first purple, then blue again and now was almost greenish yellow.

'I am sorry I had to tell a lie, but it was necessary. Now you must admit I was right – that it was important for us to go out there.'

'Important!' hissed Fridtjof. 'Firstly, this is absolutely nothing more than a bad joke, and even if it should turn out to be true, it is no thanks to you that the government has suddenly rediscovered an old map of the Strait. If you had not got yourself mixed up in this the little old man would still be in hospital receiving the treatment he needs, and Fredenshvile would not have been full of Doomsday Prophets.'

'Just because America was unknown to Europeans before Columbus, it didn't mean America did not exist. Try to picture how American Indians would have been received in Spain before 1492!'

'I don't know what's been going on inside your head. But ever since you met the little old man it's been impossible to talk any sense into you. When will you understand that regardless of his problems, they are no concern of yours?' Sigbrit shook her head, her fingers drumming lightly on the seat of her chair.

'Fridtjof, please will you listen to me. I felt obliged to help Odin find his way home. I almost killed him. He does need my help...'

'Ach, now you're starting again!' Fridtjof stood up. 'Even if that bloody island turns out to exist, even if the ridiculous horse and its broken bones exist, yes, even if the little old man really did walk across a frozen Strait to South Norseland, it's not your problem and never will be. You took the man to hospital, and that was more than enough.' He raised his voice. 'Just leave the rest to others!'

'To whom?' exclaimed Sigbrit.

'To anyone! I couldn't care less. As long as it's not you.'

There was a moment's silence, then Sigbrit stretched out her hand. 'What do you want me to do?'

'What you should have done from the start: leave well alone.'

Sigbrit gazed at her husband in disappointment. She slowly shook her head.

'Sigbrit, please will you stay away from that fishing boat? For your sake and mine?' He took her face between his hands. 'Sigbrit, haven't we been happy together?'

'Ye-e-es,' mumbled Sigbrit, biting her lip.

'Then let's be happy again. Don't think about going to sea any more. I promise never to mention it if you promise me not to go back to the boat and the little old man.'

Sigbrit made no reply.

'Come on, Sigbrit. Then everything will be as it was.' He kissed her cheeks, then her eyes, as if he was trying to stop the tears that never came.

*

Odin's whereabouts could not be kept secret for long.

One Thursday morning – three days after the Prime Minister had visited the Queen, the day after the government had officially acknowledged the existence of Drude Estrid Island, and an hour or two before the Pious and the press found their way to the southernmost canal on Firø – a corpulent man in a navy blue suit turned up at the green and orange fishing boat, closely followed by seven rather slimmer men, all impeccably dressed in white shirts, pale grey suits and dark grey ties.

'Knock, knock,' said one of the impeccably dressed men loudly, when the delegation could not find a bell. 'Knock, knock! Knock, knock!' he repeated somewhat more loudly, and this time the door of the wheelhouse opened a crack, and Der Fremdling's withered face peeped out. The corpulent man in the navy blue suit stepped forward.

'Mr Brams Bramsentorpf, Home Secretary, leader of the Department of Territorial Matters, with this delegation from the government of South Norseland.' He introduced himself with a smile that he felt was a winning one. 'Mr Odin Odin, I presume?'

The door was slammed shut. Mr Brams Bramsentorpf and the seven impeccably clad men gazed into the air and down at the canal and over the newly built houses on the other side of the canal and at the yellow buttercups in the park behind them. They stood thus for a while and looked in every direction except at each other, and not until the door of the wheelhouse was opened again after a few minutes did their eyes meet in a smile of relief.

This time it was Odin's face that came in sight. He stepped out on to the deck and greeted the men on the quay. 'How do you do,' he said. 'Hallo, hallo. I understand you are looking for me, and in truth, here I am.' Odin pointed to his chest and bowed low.

Suddenly Der Fremdling pushed past Odin, climbed up on to the quay and passed just in front of Mr Bramsentorpf and the seven impeccably dressed men without so much as deigning to give them a glance. Mr Bramsentorpf wrinkled his nose in offended surprise, then pulled himself up and again introduced himself and his train.

'This is the delegation of the South Norseland government, which I lead,' he said and with an anxious expression he boarded the gently rocking fishing boat. One after another the seven impeccably dressed men followed him into the wheelhouse, where they crowded on to the benches around the shabby mahogany table. No one but Odin was at home. Ambrosius the Fisherman had gone out shopping for the materials needed to repair the hole in *Rikke-Marie*'s hull, and after the unfortunate voyage Gunnar the Head had emphasized that he didn't like sailing at all and had moved with Der Fremdling into a camper van not far away.

Now Mr Bramsentorpf signalled to the youngest of the seven impeccably dressed men, who immediately whipped a grey notebook out of his briefcase and gave it to his boss. Mr Bramsentorpf opened the book and leafed through it to the page he wanted to use.

'On behalf of the South Norseland government I wish to beg your pardon for the inconvenience that you, Mr Odin Odin, must have suffered in connection with the misunderstanding which led to your lengthy stay at the Central Hospital.' Mr Bramsentorpf spoke in a theatrically nasal tone. 'The people of South Norseland are renowned far and wide for their hospitality, and on behalf of the South Norse government I therefore have the honour of informing Mr Odin Odin that he is welcome to stay in the Queendom of South Norseland as long as he may wish.' Mr Bramsentorpf looked up from his notebook and nodded to Odin to indicate that now it was Odin's turn to speak.

'Thank you, thank you,' said Odin, 'it is truly very kind of you and of the South Norse government together. However, the situation is that recently I met with a meteor storm, Rigmarole broke her leg, and I am obliged to return to Smith's Town as soon as the regulations have been completed.'

Mr Bramsentorpf looked somewhat surprised, but not for nothing was he a high-ranking officer in the service of the South Norse government.

'Exactly, I could not have expressed it more clearly myself,' he said, slightly concerned that his notes had made no mention of this Rigmarole with the broken leg. But since he did not want to give Odin Odin an unfavourable impression of the South Norse government or himself, he ignored that detail and hurried on. 'And that brings me at once to the next point on the day's agenda.' He straightened his tie and seemed to grow a centimetre or two taller. 'There must be no doubt that the South Norse government will do everything in its power to assist Mr Odin Odin to return to his home island, whenever he may wish. As Mr Odin Odin has said, there are just a couple of formalities to be dealt with before he can leave.' Mr Bramsentorpf paused to consult his notes again. 'With regard to the homeward journey I can inform Mr Odin Odin – quite informally of course – that the government has already instituted proceedings, naturally ongoing, to ascertain whether it would be most opportune to build a bridge or establish an air link between South Norseland and Drude Estrid Island.' Mr Bramsentorpf gazed searchingly into Odin's eyes for suitable acknowledgement and gratitude.

Odin was not quite sure what an air link meant, but he pictured a column of sledges flying with passengers behind horses like Rigmarole and Balthazar. That would be the way for him and Veterinarius Martinussen to get to Smith's Town.

'An air link would truly be extremely convenient,' he said, tugging his beard enthusiastically.

'Oh, well, yes, yes.' Mr Bramsentorpf leafed wildly through his notebook; there was no mention anywhere of Mr Odin Odin being consulted on the question of a bridge or an air link. But not for nothing was Mr Bramsentorpf a high-ranking official in the service of the South Norse government, so he continued swiftly: 'The South Norse government will be especially glad to have Mr Odin Odin's opinion on this question, when the decision is to be taken. And Mr Odin Odin, I can assure you that it is the government's intention to appoint a large force of officials to develop the scheme, to ensure that all the formalities are in order.' Mr Bramsentorpf was thinking of international acknowledgement of territorial rights, but his notes did not suggest that Mr Odin Odin should be informed of this. In fact his notes had come to an end, and there were nothing but blank sheets in the rest of the book, so Mr Bramsentorpf rose, shook Odin's hand and left the green and orange fishing boat, closely followed by the seven immaculately clad men.

*

Hasan Al-Basri was a thoughtful man, and he was not at all convinced about all this business of Odin Odin. However, his faith community was fervent in its beliefs and contained numerous loud-voiced elements – in particular young, unemployed, second-generation immigrants, who had found their own way to the demonstration – and the old mullah thought the best way to stifle the smouldering revolt was to take the initiative. After watching the demonstrations on television, Hasan Al-Basri consulted his inner voice and Allah. Through hours of meditation and prayer he reached a conclusion: if there was any significance at all in this Odin Odin figure, the Muslims must not on any account hang back. As sure as his own name was Hasan Al-Basri, Odin was the prophet Jesus, who had come back to earth, sent by Allah to pave the way for the great prophet Mohammed and to herald the ending of the old ways and the beginning of the new.

Being a meticulous man, Hasan Al-Basri sent out scouts all over the town, and thus the Muslim Modernists were the first group of faithful who found their way to the green and orange fishing boat. But it was not long before the others followed. As a result Mr Bramsentorpf and the seven impeccably dressed men had hardly left the *Rikke-Marie* before a fearful din was heard from the quay.

Odin looked out of the window only to jump back as if he

had burned himself; he hoped no one had seen him. He lay down against the wall with a beating heart. When nothing happened he soon crept over to the window again and peeped out beneath the curtain. It was still there, the mob on the quay, but the roaring din had been reduced to a few individual voices, one of which came from a bespectacled man standing on an upturned beer crate. But how had they found him? Odin was sure Gunnar the Head, Ambrosius the Fisherman or Sigbrit Holland had not given away his hiding place. But wait, could it be...? Odin suddenly felt ashamed. That Mr Bramsentorpf was certainly not slow at keeping a promise.

Odin opened the door and stepped out on to the deck: The tumult had broken out again on the quay, so it took a while before anyone became aware of his presence. Not until Odin was right out on the quay did one of the Muslim Modernists catch sight of him.

'The Mighty One is here! He is here!' he yelled, falling to his knees before Odin.

'The Mighty One is here!' the cry resounded all around, and as one the entire gathering of Muslim Modernists, Born Anew Christians, Reborn Jews, the Lambs of the Lord and Mary's Maidens fell to their knees and bent their heads to the dust. Odin looked about him in amazement at the rounded backs. He tugged at his beard; they certainly had some strange customs here on the Continent. He wanted to be very polite and show respect for those officials Mr Bramsentorpf and the South Norse government had sent to help complete the regulations and the formalities. So Odin too kneeled and bent forward until his forehead touched the cold asphalt between his hands. A divine breeze seemed to blow through the Muslim section of the crowd, and Odin raised his head to see whether people had risen to their feet. But as soon as the Pious saw the Mighty One had lifted his head they again buried their noses in the ground, and Odin did likewise. Four times Odin looked up, and four times he lowered his own head. As the officials in front of him kept on raising and lowering their torsos, and since Odin could not stay on his knees all day, he finally stood up.

'Truly it warms my heart to see you have come to my rescue,' he said. 'The unfortunate Rigmarole has brought me here. But there's no mishap that a morsel of luck cannot remedy and in unhappy times people of good faith have to find each other. With your assistance the regulations and formalities will soon be completed, and then that day...' Odin was interrupted by a zealous roar from the gathering, who had risen to their feet and were now hurling flowers and banners into the air. The noise was deafening, and Odin became frightened again. He quickly crept back on board the green and orange fishing boat and locked the door of the wheelhouse behind him.

The Mighty One had spoken. Hasan Al-Basri thanked Allah and his inner voice. He had done the right thing; Odin was theirs! Not only was the Mighty One dark-skinned and clad in a long shalwar kameez-like robe, and not only had the Mighty One prostrated himself four times precisely before the time for midday prayers, but he had also promised to bring them luck – a certain answer from Allah to their prayers that He would send the Messenger to cleanse the world of crosses and slay Dajjal, the anti-Christ. Judgement Day was near! There was great joy among the Muslims.

'I, Simon Peter the Second, a fisherman poor in body and soul, for many years have awaited the second coming of Jesus Christ, and now I tell you: He has come!' Simon Peter II had recovered from the initial defeat, and with a defiant face and passionately blinking eyes he now climbed up on to the empty beer crate again.

'Our Saviour has come!' shouted the Born Anew Christians.

'You have seen the Mighty One with your own eyes. You saw how he looked at me, his chosen disciple, and nodded before he spoke of the good faith, the good and true faith, which is that of the Born Anew Christians.'

Ambrosius the Fisherman, who was sauntering quietly and calmly along the quay with two planks and a shopping bag under his arm, at this moment caught sight of the crowd of pious believers and began to run. He pushed through the first rows of demonstrators and soon could both see and hear Simon Peter II.

'An ill-fated rigmarole has called Jesus Christ here. Man has lost his faith, that is the misfortune. But we shall turn the rigmarole into a blessing, so when the Day of Doom arrives Our Lord can save his children from their sins.'

'Turn the rigmarole into a blessing!' the plea resounded around Ambrosius.

'But Jesus Christ has come to the earth for the second time to save man from his sins.'

'Yes, yes, Jesus Christ has come!'

One woman was so overcome by strong emotion and pressure from the crowd that she fell over. A young man lifted her in his arms and carried her to their leader.

'In truth here is a holy woman,' shouted Simon Peter II delightedly and gave a detailed description of the woman's holiness. Ambrosius did not stay to hear any more. He had pushed his way through the crowd and now reached a gathering of habited and cowled shaven-headed people.

'The Lambs of the Lord will help the Shepherd of the Lord with the Doomsday formalities, and when the time is ripe the Shepherd of the Lord will lead his Lambs to the Eternal Pastures of Paradise.'

Ambrosius laughed and shook his head in disbelief. Then he abruptly stopped laughing. Above the cowled heads he saw a group of men in black hats and dancing ringlets on their way to board *Rikke-Marie*. The Fisherman shoved at the people around him, but the crowd was so closely packed that it was difficult for him to take a single step.

'The century nears its end!'

'Our righteous God will judge the believers and the unbelievers.'

'When the day dawns those who love God will roll like stones and form an avalanche of good against evil.'

'We must spread the gospel of the resurrection of Jesus Christ.'

The Fisherman cursed and sweated and no longer saw anything amusing in the fractured sentences that reached him from all sides. Slowly he squeezed his way through the crush and then he heard the young man speaking on the deck of *Rikke-Marie*.

'Just as Jahveh sent Moses to save the people of Israel from Egyptian slavery, so now he has sent the Mighty One to take us to the Eternal Sabbath.'

Ambrosius the Fisherman pushed and squeezed, the crowd gradually thinned out, and eventually he made his way through the last ranks. Somehow the danger seemed to have evaporated of its own accord. After reading a passage from the Bible where Mica tells of the day when the Lord's law will judge between the tribes and turn swords into ploughshares, spears into vineyard knives, Ezekiel had risen to his feet, and was now leaving the boat, closely followed by his father, his brother and his six uncles.

'This is private property,' said Ambrosius the Fisherman, incensed. 'Private property, understand?'

Ezekiel the Righteous opened his mouth, and a thin stream of spit slid out of it, but he made no reply, nor did his father, his brother and the six uncles. They merely stared at the Fisherman as if wondering what he was thinking.

'Private property!' yelled Ambrosius.

Ezekiel the Righteous's eldest uncle looked at the Fisherman with indescribable contempt. 'To God nothing is private,' he said.

At that moment Odin opened the door of the wheelhouse. He was in great good humour; with all these officials to help Mr Bramsentorpf and Veterinarius Martinussen, the regulations and formalities would very soon be completed.

MIDGARD, ASGARD AND UTGARD

Bergelmer fled o'er the sea of blood
with his spouse gave form to Jotunheim
far away abode of giants
Fortress Utgard
   – all did fear this place

Gods to nothing plunged dead Ymer's corpse
carved from his body earth and sky
Midgard of the flesh was fashioned
home for many men to come
Ymer's eyebrows bent to fence
ensconcing Midgard
   – keep out giants, bloodied ocean swells

Bone made hills, locks made copse
Giants' teeth cut into cliffs
brains as misty clouds were scattered
drained dry skull to heaven's vault
   – See what beauty came of loathsomeness

High above the land of Midgard
deep in the heart of nothing
gods built a home for peace and play
said: 'Asgard be thy name'

   Upon world's creation, gods could rest

It was the last month of spring – the days were long and more often mild than raw – when the South Norse government, through its ambassadors in the relevant capitals, asked the chairman of the Western Bastion, together with the Secretary General of the World Community, to include Drude Estrid Island in the South Norse Queendom in accordance with King Enevold IV's map of 1615. Under normal circumstances this would not have caused any difficulties, as in principle it was a mere formality to add the new square metres to South Norseland. But as the circumstances in this matter turned out not to be completely normal – as is often the case when questions of territoriality are concerned – complications quickly arose.

The Secretary General of the World Community referred the case to a commission, which appointed a committee with the name Committee for Questions Concerning Drude Estrid Island, who after a week or two concluded that it ought to suspend work until the Western Bastion had completed its deliberations on the case and made known its opinion. Meanwhile, the Chairman of the Western Bastion had assigned the case to the Directorate of Jurisdiction, which again had referred it to the Department of Territorial Affairs. Normally it would have rested there in peace until someone or other had ploughed through the mountains of documents, after which – following an initial hearing in a sub-working party consisting of members of the Western Bastion's member countries – it would have been incorporated as a routine matter in all the necessary outlets through the computer system, stating that Drude Estrid Island was an acknowledged part of South Norse territory.

There was in the Department of Territorial Affairs a very tall, very blond young North Norse man, Lennart Torstensson by name. Lennart was a zealous and most ambitious lawyer who had been taken on two months previously and had still not had a chance to demonstrate his particularly outstanding talents to his superior, Mr Hölzern. So the zealous Lennart Torstensson was delighted when by coincidence the case of Drude Estrid Island landed on his very new, more or less bare desk one Friday afternoon. Although it was a quarter to five and most of his colleagues were packing their bags, Lennart sharpened his pencil and settled himself down to read the case, which in its topmost right-hand corner bore a few words in Mr Hölzern's characteristic hexagonal handwriting: '*Please add to South Norse territory as stated in the letter.*'

After Lennart had read through the letter from the South Norse government, and glanced at the attached card for a moment, he spent a long time in thought. Then he rose from his chair and picking up the documents he walked across to the other side of the corridor to the copying room and made three copies: one for his personal briefcase, one for his reserve briefcase as a precaution against loss of the documents, and one to underline and write on in order not to mess up the original, which he placed with care in a transparent plastic folder. Then he resumed his seat, bent over the documents and read through them three more times, whereupon he carefully summarized the case in his notebook. After a good hour and a quarter he felt he had understood all the implications of the case and what should be done about it, which to his great regret was comparatively simple and did not demand particular talent or industry. There was, however, one thing that he could do: he could expand the case just a little by adding one or two specific facts and details to the memo he would write to his boss, when he reported that the case had been given thorough consideration – he could almost hear Mr Hölzern's voice praising him for his superb insight, thoroughness and efficiency.

It was already past six o'clock – but what is time to a man with work to do? – and Lennart took the world atlas from the shelf and opened it at Scandinavia. It took him a while to localize the island as marked on King Enevold IV's somewhat distorted map, but in the end he succeeded.

But what was that? He was dumbfounded. His eyes flashed from the atlas to King Enevold IV's map and back again; the island did not lie absolutely in South Norseland waters, as the letter had indicated. No, Drude Estrid Island stretched out in the Strait midway between the South Norse Queendom and the North Norse Kingdom. Lennart picked up a ruler and measured all the distances very precisely, and with the aid of a pocket calculator he made some complicated calculations. There was no doubt: Drude Estrid Island lay precisely midway between the two countries.

Once more he read the letter from the South Norse government which revealed that the South Norse claim that the island belonged to that country was based on the fact that in 1614 King Enevold IV had declared that the island belonged to the South Norse Crown, and named it after his second wife, Drude Estrid, and that no one at that time or since had made any objection to this.

Lennart chewed the end of his pencil in the uncomfortable realization that he was caught up in something he had been quite unaware of until that moment: where should the loyalty of the international public servant lie? As an official in the service of the Western Bastion he ought not to consider his own nationality but should aim for the benefit of the whole Bastion – whatever that might mean. But as a North Norse citizen it might be considered as markedly disloyal, indeed, almost on a par with treachery, if he did not contrive to see that a demand was made to secure what rightly belonged to his country. He weighed up the situation earnestly for a long time. His immediate career depended on his satisfying his department, which at the moment was equated with Mr Hölzern, and thereby executing the order to declare the island to be South Norse territory. But as you can never know what is going to happen in this world, his long-term career could well depend more on the North Norse authorities' opinion of him. It wasn't easy. One moment Lennart inclined to one conclusion, at the next the other one seemed more expedient. Finally, when his watch showed half past eight, he had to admit that he would not be able to solve his dilemma that evening. He returned the case document to its folder, placed the folder in the top drawer of his desk, put on his jacket, switched off the light and left the office.

Lennart Torstensson cogitated over his dilemma the whole weekend. He did not go out, he did not use the telephone, and he did not eat anything. He was so preoccupied that on Sunday morning he even forgot to call his old mother in the North Norse capital, Godeholm, as was his custom. It was an intolerable weekend, the like of which he hoped never to endure again. Saturday went by without a solution, Sunday followed, but at last, at five o'clock on Monday morning, after another sleepless night, he knew precisely what he was going to do.

'Good morning, good morning,' said Lennart cheerily to the sleepy security guards and cleaning ladies he met at dawn on his way up to his office. He sat down at his desk, humming as he took the folder with the case of Drude Estrid Island from the drawer. '*Morning has broken, you North Norseman,*' he sang. On closer reflection, he had to ask himself whether there could be any real certainty that Drude Estrid Island was the name of the island? No, it was his responsibility, right enough, to see that the matter should be concluded with impartiality. With firm strides he returned to the copying machine and made two fresh copies of the letter from the South Norse government and King Enevold IV's map. He then carefully folded each set and – after having made a discreet note on each of them to prove their origin, should he later find that opportune, but likewise would not identify if it turned out not to be opportune – he placed them in two envelopes. He addressed one to the North Norse Prime Minister, the other to the North Norse King. When he had thus done his civil duty to his satisfaction, he cleaned his fingernails with a shiny silver file, pushed back the cuticles on all ten fingers with the blunt end of the file and then put it back in its leather case, after which the case of Drude Estrid Island returned to its folder and was secreted in the top drawer of the desk. If nothing had happened after a fortnight, he – with a good conscience – would register Drude Estrid Island as part of the Queendom of South Norseland.

If Lennart had only sent the letter to the North Norse Prime Minister, nothing more would have happened, because the North Norse Prime Minister was eager to win South Norse support for employing a North Norse firm to be contracted to build the planned bridge between South Norseland and North Norseland. The small strip of land between the rocks in the middle of the Strait was of no interest to North Norseland, and one good service of course deserves another...

But Lennart had in fact sent the letter to the King of North Norseland. And the King, who did not have much else to spend his time on, found the question of the newly discovered island in the middle of the Strait immensely significant in the light of the numerous wars the two countries had waged against each other, the periodical tendency of South Norseland to get the better of North Norseland, and especially because of the South Norseland King's treacherous murder of the North Norse aristocracy in 1510 in Godeholm. So the King of North Norseland did not nourish particularly kindly feelings for the South Norse Crown and the South Norse people. And bad was only made worse by the fact that South Norseland wanted to name an island halfway into North Norse territory after the bourgeois, less than virtuous second wife of King Enevold IV, against whom North Norseland had fought unusually numerous and loathsome battles. No, if it should be up to the King of North Norseland, South Norseland's arrogance was riding for a fall; he only needed to find one single credible argument to challenge the South Norse claim to this scrap of an island.

However, either King Hermod Skjalm had kept his word better than King Enevold IV, or the North Norse King was not quite as smart at finding hidden documents as the South Norse Queen. One thing was clear anyhow: the North Norse King was obliged to base his case on a vague note in the diary of Regent A. Væddermåne which had puzzled the historians of North Norseland ever since the book was discovered in 1877. On 5 September 1615 A. Væddermåne had noted that a division of soldiers had been sent out to defend an island in the middle of the Strait south of Ur Island, which King Hermod Skjalm intended to name after himself.

A few days later the Secretary General of the World Community and the Chairman of the Western Bastion received a letter from the North Norse government in which North Norseland advised that an island lying in the Strait between the South Norse Queendom and the North Norse Kingdom had been declared North Norse territory under the name of *Hermod Skjalm*.

*

'The day is approaching.' Odin stood on the quay beside a placard announcing '*No Admittance*', which Ambrosius the Fisherman had set up. 'The day when the regulations and formalities are completed is approaching and...'

Uttering a heart-rending howl, one of the Lambs of the Lord hurled himself to the ground at the feet of the Shepherd of the Flock and flung his long, thin, yearning arms around Odin's legs.

'The day approaches! The day approaches!' howled the Lamb of the Lord in exaltation. Terrified, Odin took a step backwards, but the arms around his legs held fast and only his torso moved. Luckily the noise had summoned the Fisherman, who now leapt forward and seized hold of Odin just before the little old man hit the ground. The Fisherman tore Odin away from the exalted Lamb's arms, carried him into the wheelhouse, set him down on the worn mahogany table and closed the door behind them.

Ambrosius scooped his still-glowing pipe out of the ashtray and took one or two pulls before saying anything.

'Odin, there is something you must understand.' The Fisherman spoke slowly. 'It would be better if you kept a little distance from the people out there on the quay. They might do you a mischief.'

'No, no.' Odin stroked his beard; he smiled a warm smile. 'They have only come to help Mr Bramsentorpf and the South Norse government, not to mention Veterinarius Martinussen, to finish the regulations and formalities.' He sighed and admitted something he would in truth have preferred not to have to admit: 'It's just that sometimes they get a trifle energetic.'

The Fisherman laid a hand on Odin's shoulder and looked into the little old man's eye. 'We regret, but you will have to realize that the folk out there,' he nodded in the direction of the quay, 'have *not* come to help you.'

'But Mr Bramsentorpf...'

'Of course we don't know what Mr Bramsentorpf has told you, but those people out there on the quay are sick.' Ambrosius shook his head sadly.

Odin's eye widened, he wound his beard around his fingers; it really was extraordinary that all the officials working for Mr Bramsentorpf and the South Norse government should suffer from the same sickness.

'Fanaticism,' went on the Fisherman, taking his pipe out of his mouth and pointing with the mouthpiece. 'Fanaticism, dear Odin, that's what it is.'

'Fanaticism,' said Odin, puzzled. Maybe that was something serious, like rabies perhaps. If all the officials of Mr Bramsentorpf and the South Norse government also needed the Veterinarius, it was no wonder that the regulations and formalities were taking so long to complete. Very probably Veterinarius Martinussen was a busy man. 'I wonder if they will find a cure one day?' he said, but his words only made the Fisherman lean back his head and laugh heartily.

'Odin, Odin, Odin,' he laughed. 'What a hoot you are. A hundred years ago we could have believed in a cure.' The Fisherman went on laughing. 'Today there's a choice. Science should long ago have made short work of fanaticism, but one thing is certain, not everyone wants to get better. Otherwise Adam and Eve would have undoubtedly found it harder to survive Darwin, Galileo and DNA.'

Odin didn't understand a word of what Ambrosius the Fisherman had said, but he did not want to question him because it might land him in the same boat as those people the Fisherman said did not want to get better. And compared with them Odin did in truth wish he knew better; he was just not absolutely sure what it was he did not know.

'You mustn't worry yourself about it,' Ambrosius broke into Odin's thoughts. 'You can't do anything about people who actively don't want to be cured.'

He pointed at a picture of the North Norse King in the opened newspaper. 'That means much more to you and your horse: now the King of North Norseland is staking a claim to the island too!'

Odin could not quite see the connection between the King of North Norseland and himself, or between the King and Rigmarole, for that matter, not to mention between the King and Veterinarius Martinussen. But if the Fisherman said so...

There was a knock at the door, and before Ambrosius the Fisherman could react, Sigbrit Holland entered the wheelhouse.

'Have you seen it?' she asked without preliminaries. Her eyes travelled around the wheelhouse. It was the first time she had visited the green and orange fishing boat after its mishap on the rocks.

'Come in and sit down, Lady Fair.' Ambrosius threw out his arm with exaggerated courtesy towards the vacant place on the bench beside Odin.

Sigbrit sat down on the edge of the bench without taking off her coat. She felt a cold draught on her neck, and turned her head; Der Fremdling had stepped in behind her but now vanished into the far corner of the wheelhouse. A shadow crossed Sigbrit's face and she drummed her fingers anxiously on the table edge. She turned back to the Fisherman.

'Have they the right?'

'Perhaps, perhaps not. How should we know? Anyway, it doesn't matter who has the right. It all comes to the same thing for Odin.'

'It can take years to smooth out a disagreement like that,' said Sigbrit indignantly.

'Yes, you're right there.' The Fisherman smoked on peacefully.

'So it could take several years before there's an official route to the island.'

'Too true, Lady Fair.' The Fisherman smiled and nodded. He took the pipe from his mouth and grew serious. 'That's precisely why we have begun to search for another way to get Odin and his Veterinarius over there.'

'Truly, that is not a problem,' Odin interrupted briskly. 'Once the regulations and formalities have been completed, we will simply walk back by the same route that I took to get over here.'

'I'm afraid it is not quite so simple,' murmured Sigbrit.

But Odin didn't see any reason for worrying. If the people of Smith's Town had been capable of freezing the sea, surely some of the Continent's inhabitants – if they set their hearts and minds to the task – would be capable of doing it too.

The clock on the wall thrummed out half past six, and Sigbrit jumped to her feet.

'I must go,' she said.

But Ambrosius the Fisherman had risen also, and before she could open the door he seized her arm. 'Why are you always in such a rush, Lady Fair?' he asked with a laugh, but Sigbrit was not sure whether he was teasing or scolding her.

'My husband will be waiting for me at home,' she said, as calmly as she could.

'And?'

'He likes me to get home early so we can spend the evening together.'

'And you? What do you want?'

Sigbrit looked down without replying.

'Aren't you just about old enough to take responsibility for yourself? Isn't it high time you did what you feel like doing?'

'It's not so simple,' objected Sigbrit, avoiding the Fisherman's eyes. 'There are certain demands. When you have committed yourself...'

'Try to listen to yourself,' interrupted the Fisherman. 'Demands! Duties! What demands? What duties? That is what we ask you. Shouldn't it be your duty to work for what you believe in? Surely more is demanded of you than dinner for two with a man who is like a stranger to you?' Ambrosius shouted.

Odin put his hands over his ears, while Der Fremdling did not so much as blink. Sigbrit shook with fury. 'You know nothing about my life,' she screamed and tore herself free. She stormed out of the door and shoved her way through the Pious on the quay.

*

Mr Bramsentorpf and the seven impeccably dressed men had fetched him early in the morning, and after a short drive they had all moved through the air in a strange apparatus whose like Odin had never seen. They were now sitting in a conference room that was almost as large as Uncle Joseph's barn in Smith's Town. It was a sunny day outside and Odin wondered why the inhabitants of the Continent chose to stay indoors in such good weather. Although he could not in truth imagine what it meant to work in what the Continent called an administration, Ambrosius the Fisherman had told him that people who worked in this trade expected to be treated with indisputable respect, so Odin thought it best not to say anything without being asked first, and kept his mouth firmly and obviously shut. At Odin's side, behind a notice carrying the word 'Chairman', sat a slightly hump-backed, frail man wearing round spectacles. Odin recalled having given the man his hand in the vestibule earlier that morning, when the man had said a great deal and bade him welcome to something Odin had not quite understood – the hearing in the Western Bastion concerning the island described as Drude Estrid Island by the South Norse government, and as Hermod Skjalm Island by the North Norse government. This was perhaps the same as what Ambrosius the Fisherman had called 'a little chat about Odin's highly dispiriting dilemma', and which Mr Bramsentorpf had explained was part of the formalities.

The hump-backed man then pressed a red button on a strange metal instrument and began to speak in a high, strained voice that Odin found quite alarming. When he had grown used to the loud, cackling sound, and as he assumed the speech to be part of the regulations and formalities, Odin listened very carefully to every single word. However, there was a problem: no matter how much Odin concentrated, he could not understand a word. He listened and listened, but it was no good. He could only catch a few words here and there, and some quite meaningless numbers and dates. There was nothing about horses, nothing about Veterinarius Martinussen, and nothing about Smith's Town or Post Office Town. The hump-backed man did not even mention the Blacksmith or Oldmother Rikke-Marie, the rocks or the sea that the inhabitants of Smith's Town, not forgetting those of Post Office Town, had caused to freeze over, or anything else Odin recognized. In the end Odin gave up and instead gazed around at the participants in the meeting. They were all listening with intense concentration, with some seeming to take in every single word the hump-backed man said. One would think it was their horse that had broken a leg, thought Odin, quite overwhelmed by the realization of how many inhabitants of the Continent were needed to complete Veterinarius Martinussen's regulations and formalities.

In the end the hump-backed man had no more to say, and the incomprehensible flood of words dried up. Odin was about to get up, when at that moment Mr Bramsentorpf leaned forward and pressed his red button. He started by expressing his regret that this little controversy had arisen between the South Norse Queendom and its northern neighbour, the North Norse Kingdom, with whom South Norseland had so many interests in common and throughout history had enjoyed and still today had such close relations.

'The matter could not be simpler,' said Mr Bramsentorpf and allowed himself the liberty to express his expectation that everything would work itself out as soon as the committee for the investigation of the case of the island named Drude Estrid Island by the South Norse government – here Mr Bramsentorpf ingeniously avoided mentioning the rest of the committee by name – had heard what he, Mr Bramsentorpf, had to say. He then produced a long explanation of why it was obvious that Drude Estrid Island should be regarded as South Norse territory, and included a long list of King Enevold IV's achievements and conquests, as well as the deeds and conquests other South Norse Kings and Queens before and after him had accomplished, yet without naming a single one of their many losses. In conclusion, Mr Bramsentorpf said in an extremely conciliatory tone that with all respect for his North Norse colleague he nevertheless had to express the South Norse government's complete amazement that North Norseland could have arrived at the idea that Drude Estrid Island could be a part of North Norse territory, when it so clearly belonged to the the South Norse Queendom.

Mr Bramsentorpf sat down and almost immediately a man stood up behind a placard bearing the name 'North Norseland'. Apart from the fact that he was a good deal thinner, the man behind the North Norseland sign was the spitting image of Mr Bramsentorpf. What was still more remarkable was that seven men sat around him that Odin thought could have been mistaken for Mr Bramsentorpf's seven impeccably dressed men – if one of them had not been a woman. The North Norse Mr Bramsentorpf then made a speech which to Odin's ears sounded like an exact rendition of the one Mr Bramsentorpf had just made, apart from the fact that it was not concerned with an island named Drude Estrid Island but with one whose name was Hermod Skjalm Island.

When the North Norse Mr Bramsentorpf ended his address

and sat back in his chair looking satisfied, the hump-backed man, to Odin's surprise, turned to him. 'Mr Odin Odin, naturally the Committee of Enquiry for the Western Bastion will not be bound by your reply, but the Committee would nevertheless be interested to hear to what extent you consider yourself to be South Norse or North Norse?'

Everyone in the room looked at Odin. But he had no idea what he was being asked, or how he should reply. He sat for a long while in the belief that the question would then be forgotten, and that if he only waited long enough the meeting would continue with other speakers. However, when the hump-backed man had repeated his question three times, the silence in the room grew unbearable and Odin felt forced to say something. 'Sir,' he began, 'I should be truly happy to reply to your question, but it would lighten the task and make me really obliged to you if someone could give me a more precise explanation of the difference between being South Norse or North Norse.' Odin smoothed his beard and looked apologetically from Mr Bramsentorpf to the somewhat thinner North Norse Mr Bramsentorpf and back again to the hump-backed man. 'You see, sir, I am in truth not yet especially knowledgeable in matters concerning the question of Continental affairs.'

Odin's question confused the chairman, but apart from a brief twitching of his jaw he kept a straight face. 'Perhaps my South Norse or my North Norse colleagues would be kind enough to clarify the position for Mr Odin Odin,' he said curtly, and Mr Bramsentorpf immediately pressed the red button and explained that being North Norse meant that one had North Norse nationality, while being South Norse meant one had South Norse nationality.

'That ought to clarify the matter,' said the chair and again looked enquiringly at Odin. Odin had no notion of what nationality was either, whether it be the South Norse or the North Norse kind, so the chairman added quickly: 'A nation is a country, and a country is a definition of a territory under a management often characterized by the same language, the same culture, the same ethnic origin and the same religion.'

'Apart from the fact that one does not need to have the same religion,' interpolated a delegate.

'One doesn't need to have the same language,' said another, upon which still another nodded energetically and added: 'A nation can consist of more than one culture and more than one ethnic group.'

'Owing to immigration, most nations today contain various ethnic groups,' said a fourth.

'With that in mind,' the chairman broke in slightly impatiently, 'then do the inhabitants of the island consider themselves to be of South Norse or North Norse nationality?'

'You see, in all truth I do not know,' replied Odin with conviction, without having understood one word of the explanation of nationality or being of South Norse or North Norse nationality, but thankful to be able to give the humpbacked man an honest answer.

No one had further questions for Odin, and the discussion on that day's agenda was at an end. Before the chairman closed the meeting he requested that the discussions concerning the case of the island known as Drude Estrid Island by the South Norse authorities, and as Hermod Skjalm Island by the North Norse authorities, should remain confidential until further notice. All the delegates were agreed on this point, and since Odin felt it would be suitable here – with regard to the eventual finalizing of the regulations and formalities – to demonstrate his goodwill, he raised his right hand and announced loud and clear, so everyone could hear: '*Never, never ever may I breathe a word to a soul, otherwise the serpent will gobble me up whole!*'

A painful silence settled over the room. Never before had anyone heard anything like this at a meeting of an investigative committee under the Western Bastion or for that matter any other meeting in the Western Bastion's regime. The delegates looked at each other uncertainly. Mr Bramsentorpf was struck by the thought that this was an excellent opportunity to illustrate Southern Norse knowledge of the islanders' customs and traditions, and he stood up, raised his right hand, and repeated Odin's words in a firm and authoritative voice. As the other delegates were unsure what to do next, they stood up one after the other and swore Oldmother Rikke-Marie's great-great-great grandmother's oath.

After lunch the delegates were going on to discuss other pressing matters, but for Odin the day was at an end. One of the impeccably dressed men was going to take him back to the airport and home, but in the confusion outside the conference room he lost sight of the man. He tugged at a pale grey jacket three times, convinced he had found the right impeccably dressed man, but every time he was mistaken, and after searching for a quarter of an hour he was exhausted and getting quite depressed. At that moment a very tall and very blond young man stepped in front of him.

'Lennart Torstensson, Department of Territorial Affairs,' said the very tall, very blond young man, stretching out his hand to Odin.

'Odin,' said Odin with a low bow as he tried to memorize the man's lengthy name. Then an idea struck him. 'Forgive me, but I am just looking for one of Mr Bramsentorpf's officials and, if you will pardon my asking, perhaps you would be able to help me?'

'With pleasure, with pleasure.' Lennart smiled broadly; what an incredible stroke of luck. He took Odin's arm in a firm grip and led the little old man over to the fire escape. He glanced around to make sure no one had seen them, then opened the door and quickly pulled Odin with him into the staircase leading upwards.

'Mr Odin, it will only take a moment to find Mr Bramsen-torpf's official; in fact we are taking a short cut to him.' Lennart was quite out of breath with excitement and had to wait a few minutes before he could go on. 'Mr Odin, while we are following this short cut there is something very important you might be able to explain to me.' He lowered his voice to a whisper. 'It is also vital in order to solve the whole problem of the island and not least your return to it.' Lennart hesitated as he searched for the correct words, and they took a number of steps before he found them. 'When you left the island, Mr Odin,' he began in a hoarse, tense whisper, 'was there a particular reason for you to go westward to South Norseland and not eastward to North Norseland?'

The inhabitants of the Continent ask some truly remarkable questions, thought Odin, and considered not answering. He realized that would probably seem very impolite, and simultaneously he remembered something Sigbrit Holland had once said: that South Norseland was the Continent, while North Norseland was not.

'The Blacksmith said I would be able to find the Veterinarius for Rigmarole on the Continent,' said Odin, twisting his beard around his fingers, somewhat unsure whether this was the right answer.

It must have been just right, because the very tall, very blond young man's face lit up with fervour.

'Well now, that explains everything,' beamed Lennart, almost dancing with sheer joy; it was clearly a pure coincidence that Mr Odin Odin had landed up in South Norseland instead of North Norseland. Now he had to think fast. To gain time he bent down and pretended to tie up his shoelaces. His fingers fumbled for a long time, first with the laces on the left shoe, then with the ones on the right shoe, but suddenly he straightened his back and gazed into Odin's eyes. 'We have a brilliant Veterinarius in the North Norse Kingdom,' he whispered triumphantly, then checked himself and continued a little less excitedly. 'In fact, and not wanting to boast, we have the most brilliant Veterinarius in North Norseland. I am sure that if you came to North Norseland, that most brilliant Veterinarius would go with you to the island immediately to put your horse's leg right, just like that.' Lennart snapped his fingers and pictured the honours and medals that would be his when Hermod Skjalm Island became part of the North Norse Kingdom.

Odin tugged at his beard in amazement at this news; he had never imagined that other Veterinariuses existed besides Veterinarius Martinussen. 'Excuse me, but this North Norse Veterinarius... would many regulations and formalities be necessary there?' he asked thoughtfully.

'Absolutely not. You only have to say the word, and I will come to fetch you as quickly as possible.' Lennart's eyes gleamed cunningly. 'All I need to know is where you live.'

They had reached the bottom of the stairs, but Lennart kept Odin back while the little old man told him about Sigbrit Holland and Ambrosius the Fisherman and about Gunnar who had lost his huge head in a football match and now carried it under his arm, and about Der Fremdling who never said a word, and about all Mr Bramsentorpf's officials on the quay who suffered from a disease called fanaticism, and about the green and orange fishing boat which had the same name as the old woman in Smith's Town, whose father, Richard the Red – who incidentally was also Ambrosius the Fisherman's grandfather – had once sailed from Smith's Town never to return. It took a long time and quite a few misunderstandings, but in the end the conscientious Lennart Torstensson felt he would be able to find the way to the green and orange fishing boat to collect Mr Odin Odin, and he smiled happily and opened the door.

Straightaway, Odin found himself in a large vestibule and almost at once ran into the right impeccably dressed man. Before he had time to thank the very tall, very blond young man with the long name for his kindness, the impeccably clad man had taken his arm and pulled him through the hall out of the rotating glass door.

A large group of journalists and photographers immediately surrounded Odin. Cameras flashed, there was shouting and screaming.

'Mr Odin Odin, what was decided at the meeting?'

'May we have your comments?'

'Is the island South Norse or North Norse?'

'Mr Odin Odin, would you prefer to belong to South Norseland or North Norseland?'

'If it came to a serious conflict between South Norseland and North Norseland, which side would you be on?'

Odin, who was not yet used to the customs and traditions of the media, believed the journalists had been struck by an illness uncannily like the fanaticism suffered by Mr Bramsen-torpf's officials on the quay beside the *Rikke-Marie*. So even though the right impeccably dressed man pulled at his clothes from inside the car, Odin turned round.

'It is a difficult situation,' he began, and all the journalists immediately fell silent. 'Luckily there is no misfortune that a little bit of luck cannot remedy. Recently Rigmarole suffered a mishap, and she broke her leg. A lot of people, from the Blacksmith in Smith's Town to the Queen of South Norseland and to the very tall, very blond young man with the long name, are working on it together, and the day will soon dawn when the regulations and formalities have been finalized, the leg will be cured, and the unfortunate Rigmarole will be well again and able to take to the skies, and I can convey the bad news. Thus all those people who have shown patience and good faith will soon be released from their travails.'

Odin expected that the sick people in front of him would give their answer, but the journalists were so dumbfounded by his speech that they completely forgot the questions in their notebooks. No one said a word, so Odin thought he could safely submit to the insistent pulling at his clothes. He climbed into the car and sat back in the seat beside the impeccably dressed man.

*

Next morning Simon Peter II received a revelation.

No sooner had the newspapers arrived on the street before the Pious came streaming along to the southernmost canal on Firø, and before midday there were so many that the local inhabitants could hardly go in and out of their own houses.

There was a clear sky, and a young spring sun shed a sharp light as fluffy white clouds hurried along before the wind that chased them. Simon Peter II stood on a rather rackety podium built by his specially chosen fellow disciple.

'*Our Father who art in heaven, hallowed be thy name...*' With folded hands and closed eyes Simon Peter II took the Born Anew Christians through the 'Our Father', paying no heed to the rude gusts of wind the Lord, time after time, blew in their faces. '*For thine is the Kingdom, the power and the glory, for ever and ever, Amen.*' Simon Peter II raised his head and opened his eyes only to shut them again hastily; it was at that moment the revelation came to him.

Simon Peter II's body executed a long and remarkable dance through the air and fell gently down on to the podium, where it stiffened in mid-movement. A couple of the fellow disciples immediately tore off their jackets and rolled them up to support their leader's head. It was an impressive sight: this most excellently pious man lying perfectly still as if he was dead. His fellow disciples were busy pushing back those standing nearest so that as many as possible could see with their own eyes the divine inspiration that had seized their leader.

Overwhelmed by momentary devoutness, the Born Anew Christians hardly dared draw breath, and for some minutes not a sound was heard apart from the rattling of the pennants and sheets of the boats. Then, as abruptly as his senses had left him, Simon Peter II came to and he opened his eyes. He waved away the helping hands and got to his feet. After he had collected himself a little and had polished his greasy spectacles on a checked handkerchief, he raised his hand.

'I Simon Peter the Second, once a fisherman in spirit and body, now the Entrusted Disciple of the Mighty One, have just received a message from the Son of God,' shouted Simon Peter II into the megaphone, and his voice resounded far past the last row of Born Anew Christians and in among the Lambs of the Lord, Reborn Jews, Muslim Modernists and Mary's Maidens, when he described how the Son of God had told him to resume his old tradition of speaking in parables.

'Speak in parables!' shouted the other disciples.

'Speak in parables! Speak in parables!' sang the echo from all the Born Anew Christians.

The Entrusted Disciple waited until the noise died away.

'These parables are told in simple words, but they are not immediately easy for everyone to understand. That is why the Son of God, the Mighty One, has chosen me, Simon Peter the Second, fisherman of body and soul, the Mighty One's humble servant, to be the trusted translator of the parables.' Simon Peter II was carried away by his own words; the tears poured from his passionately blinking eyes and buffeted on his cheeks by the wind until they dried into patches of salt in his thin moustache. 'Yesterday in the Western Bastion's capital city the Mighty One told us about the unfortunate Rigmarole that will be well again when the regulations and formalities are completed,' shouted Simon Peter II, and gave the Born Anew Christians a vivid description of how on Doomsday they would be released from their pain and sufferings, from the unfortunate rigmarole of earthly life, and instead would awaken to blissful redemption in the Kingdom of a Thousand Years. 'Salvation will be ours when we have stood with the Son of God in the battle against the temptations of the Evil One, against the regulations and formalities.' Exhausted with fervour, the sweat broke out on Simon Peter II's brow; he wiped it away with a checked handkerchief, while the Born

Anew Christians took each other's hands and danced and yelled and sang; salvation was in their grasp! Some of the women pushed their way up to the Mighty One's Entrusted Disciple in order to touch him and kiss his feet, while others in sheer ecstasy tore the clothes from their breasts.

The Muslim Modernists had arrived at the quay late and couldn't get even a glimpse of the water in the canal; Hasan Al-Basri was hard put to it to keep them under control. 'There is no God besides Allah, and Muhammad is his prophet,' he intoned, beaming, while the angry young men grumbled sourly because their leader would not let them jostle in front of the Born Anew Christians and get closer to the *Rikke-Marie* and the messenger of Allah. 'The Mighty One has spoken,' continued Hasan Al-Basri. 'Allah's Messenger, Jesus the Prophet, pledges us that when misfortune strikes, when the bone is broken, all must stand together for its healing, and regain blissfulness. Brothers, Allah has heard our prayers. When the backs of Muslims are bowed down in the lost western world, the Muslims of the World must rise and as one straighten their backs in the name of Allah, the only One.'

The Muslim Modernists nodded enthusiastically. 'Allah Akbar. There is no God except Allah, and Muhammad is his Prophet.'

And the others too – the Lambs of the Lord, smoking their holy grass determinedly to be sure of salvation, Mary's Maidens, singing anti-war hymns in order to be saved, and the Reborn Jews, who were born for salvation – were delighted at the words of the Mighty One: salvation was approaching!

But even nearer than salvation was the 10.30 hovercraft from North Norseland to Fredenshvile, filled with blue-clad North Norsemen who certainly did not consider that the Pious beside the Firø Canal were anywhere near salvation, but instead were condemned to a Hell which the True Christians were going to present them with as a foretaste.

Once safely on shore the True Christians immediately ranked themselves in seven straight lines, seven behind seven – the precise number of days it had taken the Lord to create the world – and unrolled their banners, on which were emblazoned in blood-red letters for the whole world and the blasphemous South Norsemen to read: '*Stop the false prophets and stop the false Messiah.*' Then they marched towards the Firø Canal at a brisk pace, as their leader, in time to their marching feet, yelled: 'We, the True Christians, say...' – the sentence ended in a deafening thunder of voices from the blue-clad rows – 'Stop the false prophets!'

'We, the True Christians, say...'

'Stop the false Messiah!'

The rhythmic stamping went right through the hermetically closed windows on the first floor of the bank, and Sigbrit Holland's colleagues crowded together to see what was going on. Sigbrit herself turned up the radio to hear the midday bulletin, which was announcing some shocking news about the island. The din from the street soon drowned out the newsreader's voice, and Sigbrit went over to her colleagues at the window.

'We, the True Christians, say...'

'Stop the false prophets!'

'We, the True Christians, say...'

'Stop the false Messiah!'

There were several dozen, if not more, of the blue-clad North Norsemen. Without giving a thought to the promise she had made herself, her husband and her boss, Sigbrit grabbed her coat, called to a colleague that she had been asked out to an early lunch, and ran out of the office. She pressed the bell for the lift but it was slow in coming, so instead she took the stairs in great leaps, through the vestibule, out of the glass doors and straight into the ranks of marching True Christians.

'We, the True Christians, say...'

'Stop the false prophets!'

'We, the True Christians, say...'

'Stop the false Messiah!'

Sigbrit fought her way through the seven ranks of blue and emerged in the middle of the quay. Cars hooted at her but she ignored them, jumping in and out amongst them, once or twice coming close to getting knocked down by their front fenders. She was soon past the leading troop of blue marchers and had reached the pavement. She puffed and groaned and her heart hammered with fear and from running, but she didn't slacken her speed. Dashing over the Firø Bridge, then to the right along the southern canal, she stumbled on the uneven cobblestones but did not fall. If only she could make it in time, she whispered breathlessly to herself, and if only Ambrosius the Fisherman was there.

Gradually the yelling of the True Christians grew fainter behind her, but now Sigbrit heard the Doomsday Prophets, and it was not long before she caught sight of them.

'Go away, they are coming!' she shouted. 'The North Norsemen are on their way. They will attack you!'

The Pious did not so much as turn their heads, and Sigbrit hadn't time to worry about them. It would be impossible to force her way through the crowd, so she jumped on board a large motorboat, ran across the deck and on over an ancient steel boat, straight across three other smaller boats, then a white motorboat, until she was able to climb on to the green and orange fishing boat.

Sigbrit gripped the handle of the wheelhouse door, but it was locked. 'Ambrosius, open up, it's me!' she yelled, hammering with flattened hands on the door. It was wrenched open and she tumbled into the wheelhouse.

'They're coming to seize Odin,' she stammered, out of breath.

Ambrosius the Fisherman took one glance at her face and started up the engine. Sigbrit ran back on deck and threw off the mooring rope, and just as the green and orange fishing boat slid away from the quay she saw the first blue-uniformed ranks of True Christians reach the Doomsday Prophets.

'We, the True Christians, say...'

'Stop the false prophets!'

'Beloved friends, fellow believers...' Simon Peter II crowed from his rickety podium. 'You must give a humble ear to the Son of God.'

'Blasphemer!' countered the True Christians.

'Brothers in faith, if only we stand together, all the people of the Book,' squeaked Hasan Al-Basri's frail voice, but no one heard him.

'The Day of Judgement nears. God will...'

'Our Lord has sent his Son to cleanse the world from man's warring spirit.'

'Heathens. Stop the false prophets!'

'The Day of Judgement...'

A True Christian fist hammered straight into the pale face of one of the Lambs of the Lord. The man swayed backwards and forwards for a moment, then dropped without a sound to the ground.

'Murder! Murder!' screamed the Blessed Anders Andersen

and the other Lambs of the Lord, who immediately joined the fight against the common enemy. Fists, stones and any other weapons that were to hand flew to right and left.

'Welcome on board, Lady Fair, welcome,' said Ambrosius the Fisherman, after the *Rikke-Marie* had turned out into a wider channel, and there was no longer any danger of the True Christians getting to them.

'I don't like sailing. I don't like sailing at all,' complained Gunnar the Head, rather dazed by events.

'Make friends with strength and courage, meet your enemy face to face!' said Odin, patting his huge-headed friend on the arm.

Sigbrit sat down beside Gunnar the Head and silently regarded the disorderly mix of old and new buildings gliding by alongside the harbour, thinking of what she had just heard on the radio. The green and orange fishing boat turned right into the upper stretch of the Firø Canal and Ambrosius the Fisherman slackened speed.

'What do you think of it all?' she asked, when the Fisherman had moored the *Rikke-Marie* beside a large yacht.

'About the Prophets of Doom or the aeroplanes?' Ambrosius looked at her enquiringly.

'The planes. Yes, actually, both.'

Der Fremdling gave a dry cough and made Sigbrit jump; she hadn't noticed him up to now.

'Can't we do anything?' She mustn't let the withered old man get her down.

'Lady Fair, about the planes or about the Prophets of Doom?'

Sigbrit's face grew dark.

'Ambrosius, not today. I haven't the time. Both, I mean. Or

start with the Prophets of Doom, if you like.' Her voice was sharper than she meant it to be but the Fisherman seemed not to notice.

'There's not much we can do, is there?' He laid a soothing hand on Sigbrit's shoulder. 'If some people have decided to believe that Odin is Christ Come Again, while others think he is not, I suppose there's nothing you or we can do about it.'

Odin looked up. In all truth he did not know who 'Christ Come Again' was, but from the way Mr Bramsentorpf's sick officials talked about him he must be almost as important as Veterinarius Martinussen. He wondered whether Christ Come Again was the most brilliant North Norse Veterinarius the very tall, very blond young man with the long name had told him about. No matter how glad Odin would have been to help the poor fanatics, he could not; he himself needed the Veterinarius. However, he could at least ensure that the misunderstanding was smoothed out.

'I can only say that I am not Christ Come Again,' he said, tugging at his beard.

A ghastly sound broke out in the darkest corner of the wheelhouse. It was Der Fremdling laughing – like a sick seagull, thought Sigbrit and shuddered, while the hollow hiccup kept on and on.

'That won't help in the least, Odin,' said Ambrosius the Fisherman when Der Fremdling's hiccuping eventually died down. 'The Prophets of Doom will just think up any old fairy tale that suits them, and then use your name and presence as a pretext. Speak to them, and in a trice your words will become part of a new dogma, and soon there will be just as many versions of your words as there are people on the quay.' The Fisherman smoked for a few minutes while he observed Odin's anxious face. 'You mustn't worry yourself over these fanatics, Odin. As we said, they are sick people. In a way you are doing them a favour, offering a little entertainment, a good story or two. Try to imagine what the fanatics' lives would have been without your story.'

Naturally Odin could not know anything about that, so he said no more. If what Ambrosius the Fisherman said was true, Odin would be glad to cheer up the fanatics by telling them a lot more about Smith's Town as well as about Post Office Town, not forgetting that, and about the Blacksmith and his smithy, and about Oldmother Rikke-Marie and about Ida-Anna and her little brother, and about Mother Marie, and about the unfortunate Rigmarole and about Balthazar and everything else he could recall. If only he could remember what had happened before Smith's Town... Odin wound his beard round and round, quite lost in thought.

'If we could find a way for Odin to get back to the island, things would definitely calm down out there.' Sigbrit looked out of the window as if she could still see the horde of brawling Pious.

'Perhaps, perhaps not. I suppose it is a first step, but we doubt it would be more than that.' Ambrosius took a pipe from the shelf. 'For Odin's and his horse's sake a way around every obstacle must be found. But at the speed the planes are dropping around our ears it may well take some time.'

'What do you think happened?'

'In the space of a second, a reconnaissance plane vanished without trace over the island. In the space of a second both the first and the second rescue aircraft too. It was sunny, blue sky, only a breath of wind, and yet the coastguards could not find as much as a scrap of the wrecks. And now the Minister of Defence has suspended the operation.' The Fisherman filled and lit his pipe. 'There is no way forward, for us or anyone else. As the seamen say, *near the island and all Hell breaks loose!*

'*Near the island or name it?*' Sigbrit laughed half-heartedly, but when the Fisherman did not move an eyelash, she went on in a serious tone: 'Wait a minute, you said yourself it was all old wives' tales. And if nothing else, you know from your own experience why no one can approach the island by boat. But that still doesn't explain why modern planes should crash.'

'Who said they crashed?'

'If they didn't crash, where did they get to?'

'How should we know?' Ambrosius the Fisherman shrugged his shoulders. 'If they crashed – experienced pilots with the best equipment – why didn't they put out an alarm? And why hasn't a single piece of wreckage been found?'

There was a brief tense silence, then Sigbrit asked: 'What are you going to do then?'

'Nothing,' replied the Fisherman.

'Nothing? How, nothing?'

'Just nothing.'

Sigbrit's fingers drummed impatiently on the table edge.

'Listen here, Lady Fair, at this moment we know nothing, and we cannot do anything apart from continuing our speculations, naturally.' Ambrosius pulled at his pipe and then shook his head. 'There is something odd about this.'

Sigbrit waited, but the Fisherman said no more. His eyes ranged along the boats moored at the quay.

'Have you given up looking for the channel your father took from the island when he left?'

'You saw for yourself what happened when we tried that.'

'Even though we didn't find it the day we were wrecked, that doesn't mean it isn't there.'

'True enough. But how do you intend to find it without getting smashed to matchwood?'

'I don't know. There must be a way. Perhaps with a smaller boat?'

'No, Lady Fair. We have already considered that. You saw the rocks, you saw the seas. There is no way of getting around them unless one knows beforehand precisely which course to follow.'

'The Blacksmith told me in person and in all truth that ever since Oldmother Rikke-Marie's great-great-grandmother's time, no one has come to the island from the Continent,' said Odin, smoothing his beard.

Ambrosius the Fisherman stiffened, then slowly took his pipe from his mouth. 'Say that once more.'

'Ever since Oldmother Rikke-Marie's great-great-grandmother's time no one has come to the island from the Continent,' repeated Odin.

'There we have it!' the Fisherman interrupted him.

Sigbrit raised her eyebrows and looked blank.

'Look, if no one has gone to the island since Oldmother Rikke-Marie's great-great-grandmother's time, it means that before that time, people *did* go to the island.'

'You're right!' exclaimed Sigbrit.

'And regardless of what happened earlier, we would surely be wrong to think that ships didn't sail to the island both to and from it precisely during the period when the maps of the Strait are missing. Ships commanded by captains who may have made detailed notes...'

'And now you are going to search for those notes?' enquired Sigbrit.

Ambrosius the Fisherman carefully balanced his pipe on the edge of the ashtray, then looked at Sigbrit searchingly. He laid his hand over hers and held tight when she tried to pull it away. 'And you, Lady Fair. What are you searching for?' He raised his voice. 'Are you with us or not?'

'What do you mean, with us or not?' she said, biting her lip. 'I know I haven't had much time lately, but...'

'That isn't the question. Lady Fair, are you with us or aren't you? Whose side are you on?'

'Of course I am with you,' she said, but her voice was not convincing. 'I just haven't so much time, and my husband...'

'It is that "just" which says you are *not* with us.'

'That's not the way it is,' protested Sigbrit. She grew angry and pulled her hand away abruptly. 'Why do you think you can decide who is with you and who against? Remember I was the one who found Odin. Without me he would either be dead from the cold or still locked up in the hospital,' she shouted, scarlet in the face. 'What have you ever done to help Odin? You just sit here talking while I do all the work. You have absolutely no right to decide who is with and who against!'

A crooked smile spread over the Fisherman's face.

'OK, OK, OK,' he said, chuckling gently. 'Lady Fair, you are right. We will take this on.'

But Sigbrit was still angry. She didn't know how to react to the Fisherman's mood changes, and what's more her lunch-break had ended long ago.

*

The very next morning, after having assured himself that the police officers stationed on the quay to keep law and order among the demonstrators would also keep an eye on *Rikke-Marie*'s and Odin's safety, Ambrosius the Fisherman went to the Maritime Museum sited at the northern end of the Firø Canal. The Fisherman did not have much faith in the authorities, so he chose to look around the museum on his own rather than ask advice. On the walls of the old timber-framed building hung paintings of the South Norse fleet right back to its establishment in 1491. Some of the glass showcases exhibited sailors' uniforms through the ages; others showed models of the ships as well as miniature reproductions of some of the numerous bloody battles fought out between the South and North Norse fleets. There was no sign of any diaries, descriptions of channels or other personal notes. The receptionist told Ambrosius the Fisherman, when he finally persuaded himself to ask, that to see them he would have to travel all along the coast to the Prince's Castle.

Two hours later Ambrosius walked across the cobblestones leading to the ancient castle, from where ships entering the Inner Sea had been controlled since the earliest history of South Norseland. The museum held not only the notebooks and account books on display – which were interesting if not useful to Ambrosius – but with the aid of equal helpings of courtesy and stubbornness the Fisherman gained permission to visit a small library behind the museum which was filled with old navigation documents and books. The curator pointed past the bookcases, which were tightly crammed together, to one at the far end of the room, and left the Fisherman to his own devices. There was a musty smell of old wood and mouldy paper, and the dust rose in all directions with each step the Fisherman took. The bookcase indicated by the curator held more shelves with account books, and the Fisherman thought it

would take him weeks to go through them all. However he discovered almost at once that there were no account books before
the eighteenth century and those recent ones were not of any
interest. Moreover, most of them were from large cargo ships
which would not have been able to anchor at a small island that
was difficult to access. After the business books came some
shelves holding diaries, log books and personal descriptions of
the channels, left by various captains. The Fisherman opened
one, then another, but they were all too new to be of any help.
He shook his head in frustration; what a waste of time. Then he
caught sight of something in a bookcase to his left: Customs
Books for the Strait. Customs duty had been initiated in 1429,
and although the books only dated back to 1497, that was quite
early enough for Ambrosius the Fisherman.

The first customs books were not specially promising, listing
cargo boats on their way to and from Fredenshvile and the
countries beside the Inner Sea. But after looking through a
series of almost illegible notes, Ambrosius came upon the
island of Ur; a ship coming from Old Norseland would anchor
off Ur Island on its way to Fredenshvile. A little further down
he found Ur Island noted again, and then again. A number of
ships on their way to and from Fredenshvile through the Inner
Sea had anchored off Ur Island. And as Ur Island was not
many miles from Odin's island, it was not impossible that a
ship on its way to Ur Island should have made its way via that
one. Ambrosius the Fisherman ran his finger down the page
and stopped each time Ur Island was mentioned, to look at the
notes beside it. For many entries there was nothing that could
indicate Ur Island's southern neighbour, and the Fisherman
replaced the book and missed out one or two more until he
found one starting at the year 1614. Here too the Fisherman

came upon Ur Island without anything remarkable, leafing on until he came to 11 April 1614. A ship on its way to Ur Island carrying grain was to go on to Fredenshvile with another cargo, and no other stop was mentioned. But there was a strange blot beside Ur Island, resembling something between a big fly stain and a small ink blot. There was a similar mark beside the next entry. The Fisherman read on; the mark was there almost every time Ur Island was mentioned, almost as an extra letter. The book came to an end, and the Fisherman opened the next one. He ran his fingers down the first couple of pages: Ur Island, the mark was still there. He grew excited and skimmed through the notes as fast as he could. The mark followed Ur Island the whole way through the years 1615 and 1616, then in January 1618 it vanished, and Ur Island no longer had an accompanying blot. Ambrosius went back to the earlier entries and followed the mark right back to 11 April 1614. He studied the marks more closely. Most of them resembled ink blots, but a few revealed that there had once been some letters underneath them, perhaps a short placename.

'I'll be scuppered if the old sailors don't turn out to be right!' he said to himself as he packed up his things: '*Name the island and all Hell breaks loose...*'

*

'Now this superstitious nonsense has got to stop!' The Prime Minister tugged hard at his right ring finger, as if he wanted to pull it off. 'It has already gone on far too long, and a territorial conflict between South Norseland and North Norseland is more than enough. A religious confrontation would be far too much.' He was referring to the True Christians, who had declared a Holy

War against the South Norse Born Anew Christians that same morning. The Prime Minister sat in his armchair at the end of the group of sofas in his office, opposite the Minister of Justice, the Minister for Ecclesiastical Affairs and the Minister of Defence. It was late, but in order to meet the demands of the next morning's press it was imperative for him to prepare a plan.

'Unfortunately these North Norse super-Christians have only provoked many more South Norsemen to join the Prophets of Doom,' said the Minister for Ecclesiastical Affairs, concerned. 'And that's not the worst thing. The bishops are furious, I can't keep them calm much longer. They claim the government is responsible for the continuation of this crazy circus.' She fingered her necklace nervously.

'The battle for survival,' chuckled the Minister of Justice.

'Yes, it must be strange for the Established Church to stand there with empty pews Sunday after Sunday while thousands are out in the rain and wind celebrating Christ's Second Coming. That's not easy to explain to the few faithful still left,' remarked the Prime Minister.

'No. But the declaration of a Holy War has really stymied the bishops. Any critical attack on the Born Anew Christians will be seen as if they are taking the part of the North Norse True Christians.' The Justice Minister laughed again, but this time less wholeheartedly, since it was his responsibility to restrain the True Christians from carrying out their declaration of intent, and at the moment this could only be done by keeping them out of South Norseland. Passport control was not what it once was, especially when the police did not possess more than a few names among the True Christians. The rest would easily be able to cross the border.

'A revolt against the government from the Established

Church is the last thing we need,' said the Prime Minister. He was irritated and the left-hand corner of his mouth quivered ominously. 'We need to concentrate on the actual problem.' He paused to crack his left-hand long finger. 'Don't forget, there must be an election no later than next spring, and we must sincerely hope this mess will have been cleared up before then and forgotten about. How do we stop the Prophets of Doom without seeming as if *we* are siding with the North Norsemen?' He pronounced each word slowly and screwed up his mouth scornfully when he came to the last one.

For a moment no one said anything, then the Minister of Justice leaned forward in his deep armchair. 'Some photographs really would be useful,' he said as casually as possible, wilfully ignoring the Defence Minister's resentful expression. 'Because the sooner the island becomes normal in the people's perceptions, the quicker these absurd demonstrations will stop.'

'I am not so sure,' said the Minister for Ecclesiastical Affairs quietly, fingering her necklace.

'It's true.' The Justice Minister rose to his feet and walked up and down the floor. 'As soon as people come to realize that there is nothing more on the island than grassy meadows, beech trees and small hills, like every other little piece of landscape in South Norseland, I am convinced they will quieten down.'

The Prime Minister looked from one to another. 'So perhaps it is time to send another plane out,' he said slowly.

The Minister of Defence turned pale.

'We might try a helicopter this time...' added the Justice Minister with an ironic glint in his eye.

'We do not use helicopters for that kind of thing,' replied the

Defence Minister curtly. 'There is nothing to indicate that helicopters would be better than planes. Before we know what happened to the first three I am not at all happy about sending yet another plane out over that godforsaken place.' He shook his head. 'It is a week since the accident happened, or rather accidents, and the search team has still not found anything. Six experienced pilots, but not a single trace.'

'Is there any reason to consider terrorism?' broke in the Prime Minister.

'Not so far as is known. No one has claimed responsibility for anything at all, and the military planes are kept under strict control. It is not easy to get at them. Of course we can't rule out the possibility of someone or other having manipulated the instruments or engines. Though that is highly improbable.'

'Any other ideas?'

The Minister of Defence hesitated.

'There is a weird superstition linked with the island,' he said at last, looking uncertainly from the Justice Minister to the Prime Minister. 'According to this belief there is something in the airspace above the island that pulls down the aircraft.' He tried to smile but only managed a grimace.

'Dear God! Have all our countrymen gone mad?' The Prime Minister leaned back in his chair and smiled coldly.

'It might look like that, apart from the fact that it is not a new phenomenon. I had my people investigate the matter, and it turns out that ever since the start of flying history, pilots have avoided that area. Apparently many aircraft have disappeared inexplicably over the island without leaving any trace, and without any wreckage ever being found. So today it is an unwritten rule that pilots do not fly into that airspace.'

'You're not serious?'

'Unfortunately, deadly serious.'

'They must have totally lost their marbles.' The Prime Minister's mouth tightened. 'It's as if we had a Bermuda Triangle in the middle of Scandinavia!' He lifted his cup with an exaggerated gesture. 'Skål for the sensible South Norsemen, clearly a unique race!'

The Minister of Justice and the Minister for Ecclesiastical Affairs raised their cups too and smilingly drank the toast with the Prime Minister. The Defence Minister's cup was left standing in its saucer.

The Prime Minister again turned to the Minister of Defence. 'What you are telling me is that we cannot get aerial photographs of the island on account of a laughable old superstition?'

'A superstition that has been convincing enough to keep pilots from flying into the area for decades.'

'But not convincing enough to keep me from asking for one more attempt.'

SOL AND MANI

Nordri, Sudri, Austri, Westri
celestial dome upheld by dwarves
Muspelheim spewed out inferno
stellar nights secured forever

Most splendid sparks gods forged together
sun and moon were born to life
Brother, sister Sol and Mani
doomed to journey each alone
In haste the siblings crossed the sky
Pursued by wolves
  – Skoll and Hate howled 'stop the light'

Near Mani rode Night, Narfi's daughter
Dim carriage drawn by darkest steed of gloom
Hrimfaxe sweated through the night
thus earth was wet with dew and hoar-frost
when Mother Night gave birth to Son of Light

Young Day chased closely brother Sol
Skinfaxe fairer than the fairest
His mane cast far a blazing lustre
No longer could the earth keep sleep

  From now on thus the year went round

Aʟʀᴇᴀᴅʏ ᴛʜᴇ Jᴜɴᴇ sun was high in the bright blue sky; there was not a breath of wind. All signs promised a beautiful day. Alvilda slowly took the plane to the end of the runway and turned its nose to the west.

'Mission 2474, clear for take-off, runway 28,' came the message from the control tower.

'Clear for take-off.'

The aircraft quickly gained speed, Alvilda pushed the joystick forward and the small gulfstream jet rose into the morning light. How she loved the feeling of freedom that seized her every time the wheels left the asphalt and her metal casket defied the laws of gravity and hurled her into a sky filled with fantasies and superstition.

'I haven't found Paradise yet. Nor have I met God,' Alvilda would grin when any of her friends or colleagues attempted high-flown spiritual discussions. Alvilda loved adventure; she had nothing but respect for and trust in modern technology and nothing but scorn for religion and superstition, which she felt amounted to the same thing. She had worked as a reconnaissance pilot for the South Norse Air Force for seven years, but this was far the most exciting mission she had been on: to photograph an island no one had known of until a few weeks ago. Who would have thought it possible in these modern times that one single piece of virgin land could exist, and in this part of the world?

There was something else that had made Alvilda volunteer for the task: the three aircraft that had disappeared over the island, not to mention the two North Norse ones of course. It was as if the old superstition really was true. Who wouldn't rise to that challenge? From what was said about this place it was obvious that ships could not survive an encounter with the rocks surrounding the island. Alvilda was not one to listen to old wives' tales about planes that mysteriously vanished without trace. True enough, tradition and unwritten regulations kept pilots from venturing into a rectangular airspace over the Strait, stretching from the tip of Ur Island a good kilometre to the south and including the strange cloud that always hovered over the rock formations. It was true that one or two unsolved disappearances appeared in the flight books in precisely that airspace, but they had happened many years ago and were not particularly well documented. Apparently no one had tried to fly over the area since the Second World War – that is, until a couple of weeks ago. But 'human error is the cause of most mysteries,' Alvilda laughed, repeating one of her instructor's mantras. She and several of her colleagues had always thought the area was closed off because the government was engaged in some secret development project or other – until this business with Drude Estrid Island began.

'As if the Devil lived among us,' Alvilda had laughed when one of the officers had admitted, a tad apologetically, that they preferred not to take the responsibility of selecting someone for this assignment and so left it to people to volunteer. That had been Alvilda's chance.

Mission 2474 had reached a height of nearly 2,500 metres. Alvilda turned the plane almost 180 degrees and headed northeast. Visibility was perfect and the sun shone from the south-west in through the window and warmed up her left side. They would get superb pictures of the eastern coastline with the sun at their back. Where the western coast was concerned it was up to the photographer's skill to counter the backlight.

Alvilda turned to the co-pilot, a boyish dark-blond man whose slight physique matched his uneasy expression.

'Nervous, Balder?' she teased, slapping his thigh good-humouredly. Balder hadn't been in the air force long and felt he had to demonstrate courage and manliness by undertaking every job others might hesitate over. So when Alvilda noticed the quivering pearls of sweat in his thin moustache she showed no mercy.

'Well, we're in the same boat here. If the captain goes down the crew goes too. That includes you, Valdemar,' she called back to the photographer, a tubby middle-aged man with his photographer's gear spread over the seat beside him.

'Not me, I can swim,' he grinned.

'Now look, pals, I haven't found Paradise between the clouds yet, but maybe we'll manage to find Hell today!' Alvilda went on.

'Yes, better watch out, Balder,' added the photographer. 'The devil isn't too keen on being disturbed on a Saturday.'

The co-pilot shifted in his seat. He tried to look unshaken but his eyes flickered uneasily over the green water underneath them. The photographer kept on.

'Even the old heathens knew that, when they named the days after their gods, all of them except Saturday. Saturday is the Devil's washing day. Just wait and see whether the Evil One doesn't give us a good ducking today!'

Alvilda and Valdemar laughed, and Balder produced a hoarse sound as if to demonstrate that he could see the funny side too.

'There it is!' shouted Alvilda suddenly.

True enough, on the north-eastern horizon they could clearly discern the blackish grey rocks rising from the sea against a light mist, and not long afterwards the rocks took the shape of an ellipse that seemed to hug the yellow-grey fog. Alvilda noted the time, 8.23. It had taken them no more than eight minutes to fly here, and after half an hour's reconnaissance work they would soon have the wheels back on the ground.

They were nearing the fog cloud and Alvilda decided to pass it on the west side. She took the aircraft down to 3,500 metres, then 2,500, 1,000.

'Now's the time for you to earn your living, Valdemar,' she said. 'I'll keep her west of the cloud. You just keep your pact with Satan.' Alvilda grinned happily; how she did love flying.

The photographer had already begun to take pictures of the rocks, which looked quite small and insignificant. It only took a moment to pass over them and then Alvilda turned the plane and flew two more sorties back and forth along the edge of the cloud.

'I'm going to try and go in,' she said. 'Hold tight, are you ready to meet the Devil?'

The photographer laughed and grabbed another camera. Balder didn't speak; he just stared stiffly at the instrument panel. Everything started flickering yellowish grey around them. Alvilda went a little further down, then a little more, but there was still nothing but mist, and before they were able to glimpse anything underneath them they had come out on the other side and saw nothing but water.

'Once more,' said Alvilda and turned the aircraft round again. She took a deep breath and let the plane sink a further 120 metres. The fog embraced them, 100 metres more and the next moment they were out in clear air and a light green landscape with a sparkling lake in its middle leapt into view in an unexpected way.

'My God, that's doesn't look like Hell!' exclaimed Valdemar, clicking away at his camera.

'Look over there,' shouted Balder, pointing at a small huddle of houses and farms on the end point of the island.

'A village! That must be the one the little old man comes from,' said Alvilda.

'Turn round, there's one behind us too,' said the photographer.

Now something very strange happened. Just as Alvilda was turning the aircraft a shudder ran through it. Balder paled, but said nothing. Alvilda tried to gain height again, but it felt as if the plane's nose was suddenly full of lead. No matter how much she tugged and fought with the wheel the nose kept on dipping forward. The plane shook again, then began to shudder violently, as if its sides were being tickled.

'Just take it easy. Mama will soon calm down the ship,' Alvilda exclaimed, although neither of her colleagues had said anything. The photographer went on taking pictures of the village, trying to counter the shaking of the aircraft by raising his body from the seat and pressing his heel in front of him.

'The height meter has failed,' screamed Balder, 'and the speedometer!'

Both her own and the co-pilot's instruments had switched off and Alvilda looked over at the reserve instruments. The hands seemed to have gone mad; they whirled round and round at astounding speed. Alvilda punched one of them with her fist.

'Bloody Hell! What an old bullshit crate. We'd better report in. Call the tower!'

Balder pressed the radio button on his microphone.

'Tower. Mission 2474 calling.' There was no reply and he

tried again. 'Tower, Mission 2474. Do you read?' he shouted. 'Do you read?'

Still no answer. He tried once more. And again. Nothing.

'I think we're in trouble,' he said in a surprisingly calm voice.

'Hell. We've got to do something!' yelled Alvilda. Sweat ran down her forehead, making her left eye smart. 'I can't even tell the speed. But we're going too slow, much too slow.'

The aircraft shook more and more violently.

'Come along now, come on, old friend,' moaned Alvilda, knowing full well they were much too low now to survive a jump.

The photographer had dropped his camera and now held on to his seat with both hands. His eyes were huge with fear.

'Turn left, get her away from the island,' ordered Balder sharply.

'I can't. She won't respond,' replied Alvilda, shaking the controls in a panic. Could she have been wrong, then? No, it couldn't be true, this was merely a technical problem. She pulled the handles towards herself a little, then pushed them forward again and turned the wheel as hard as possible to the left, then to the right. But nothing happened. The plane was nearing the centre of the island, still with its nose pointing down. They were so close to the ground that they could clearly see three small ponies grazing in a field. Then suddenly, just before they reached the silvery sparkling lake, the plane stopped shaking. The radio crackled, the screens flashed once or twice, then showed a clear picture again. Alvilda pushed the controls forward, the motor roared, the nose lifted itself and the aircraft gained height again.

'That was a close one.' Alvilda wiped her brow with her sleeve, then pulled the microphone to her mouth and pressed the radio button. 'Tower. Mission 2474.'

There was no answer, and Alvilda repeated her call.

'Mission 2474, go ahead,' came the voice from the tower clearly.

'Thank God. Some Paradise,' sighed Alvilda with relief. But at that moment Mission 2474 reached the precise centre of the island. A colossal force struck the plane, and the only thing Alvilda was aware of was a breakneck speed that tore everything apart and flung her into the feeling of freedom for ever.

*

'Did you see that?' Ida-Anna pointed up at the sky.

'See what?' Her little brother looked up, but seeing nothing but the grey-blue sky he doggedly resumed his search for worms for Sunday's fishing trip.

'There was a droning sound from a shining thing, then a rushing noise, a big splash from the lake, and now whatever it was has gone.'

Ingolf looked up again. He shaded his eyes from the sun with both hands and gazed at the sky for a long time. Then he looked in the direction of the lake, but apart from one or two vanishing circles the surface was smooth.

'I can't see anything.'

He bent down and went on digging.

'It's true. I saw it as plainly as I see you.'

Ingolf straightened up. 'You're always thinking up stories,' he said sulkily. 'I don't believe you any more. It's just like that time at Christmas, when you said the old man from the Continent was Santa Claus. Did we get any more presents for helping him? He didn't even come back for his three-legged horse.'

'Shut up,' snapped Ida-Anna. 'You don't know anything about anything at all. There was something in the sky just now. And the little old man is Santa Claus. Just you wait and see.'

'You're a liar,' yelled Ingolf, moving away a few steps.

Ida-Anna chased after her brother as he flew across the field with the bucket of worms dancing on his arm.

'Liar! Liar!' Ingolf turned his head without slackening speed.

Ida-Anna followed him a little further, then stopped. She had lost interest in catching him up, and anyway he mustn't see the tears she wiped away crossly.

'It's just about that time,' mumbled Oldmother Rikke-Marie to herself, swaying back and forth in her rocking chair. She sat in the shade under the tall ash tree by the duck pond. She had counted six shooting stars in only twice that number of days on her bent fingers. That could mean only one thing: her time had come. She was not unhappy about it, not even sad. No, she was sincerely looking forward to following in her family's and her forefathers' footsteps to the Cliff of Life, never to return.

The only thing that Oldmother Rikke-Marie did feel sad about was that she might not be in Smith's Town when Mr Odin came back to fetch his horses. She would dearly have liked to have heard with her own ears whether he had discovered anything about her father, Richard the Red, and she would dearly have loved to go for the ride with him in his sleigh that he had promised her. But Oldmother Rikke-Marie was old enough to know that some wishes were meant to remain wishes. Mr Odin could not be expected back before the nights had stolen time from the days, and the sea had become a precarious bridge of ice between the island and the Continent, and it might be many winters before the island froze up during the forty nights it took for the sea to freeze, as her grandmother had said. Oldmother Rikke-Marie had no more winters to wait in; the one now on its way would be her last.

*

'Have the Pious been fighting again?' asked Sigbrit Holland as soon as she had opened the door of the wheelhouse. 'The police are all over the place and they didn't want to let me through.'

'Come and meet Brynhild Sigurdskær,' said Ambrosius the Fisherman, ignoring her question, and only then did Sigbrit notice the woman leaning against the worn mahogany table.

Sigbrit stiffened; the woman was about her own height but there any likeness stopped. Brynhild Sigurdskær was so fair she was almost transparent. She had long, thick, curly hair, her eyes were so light blue they looked almost white, and her skin was so untouched by colour that the abstract pattern of her veins was clearly visible. Her spare body was clad in a long, sleeveless lacy dress as white as her skin. It was impossible to see how old she was, she could be anything between thirty and sixty. She was not beautiful or ugly, merely strikingly different. A couple of hundred years earlier she would have been burned as a witch, thought Sigbrit, shuddering. Almost against her will she stretched out her hand.

'The world is on the brink of madness,' said Brynhild Sigurdskær softly, putting the kettle on.

The transparent woman spoke so quietly that no one would have been able to hear if her words had not seemed to vibrate in the air for a moment. She took four cups out of the cupboard and placed them on the table; she was clearly familiar with the

Rikke-Marie. She glided around as if her feet didn't touch the floor, and it was impossible to distinguish one movement from another.

'Well, no matter what has happened here today that is surely a bit of an exaggeration.' Sigbrit couldn't prevent a touch of sharpness in her words, and for a moment the two women stared into each other's eyes.

'The world is on the brink of madness,' insisted Brynhild in her soft whisper, and went over to the window without waiting for an answer. She looked as if she was pondering. She turned around and glanced at Ambrosius the Fisherman. '*Name it or near it;* you're not telling me much,' she said mildly.

'It's all we have.'

'Then I must make do with that.' Her eyes lit up. 'Leave before the madness spreads. And take your friend with you.' Brynhild nodded towards Odin, who thought that perhaps madness was another word for the disease Ambrosius the Fisherman called fanaticism. 'Nothing will ever be the same again, nothing ever is. This time the world will go mad.' With nothing but a slight swish from her long white dress, Brynhild vanished.

'When the world runs amok, it is no use running away,' said Odin, winding his beard round his fingers.

Sigbrit Holland felt like questioning the Fisherman about the transparent woman, but wasn't sure that was a good idea. Instead she asked what he had discovered.

'A lot and yet not so much,' he replied evasively. He raised a chipped mug and slowly took a mouthful of coffee. 'Something is happening on that island, and this is the key to the whole mystery. The next step depends on Brynhid Sigurdsær.'

Sigbrit turned pale. 'You don't take all that old superstitious nonsense seriously?' She forced herself to laugh.

'Then maybe you can tell us why one plane after the other keeps on disappearing? And why the island vanished from every map and register almost as fast as it was discovered?'

'In tall tales the wise find wisdom,' mumbled Odin.

The Fisherman nodded and took a deep pull at his pipe before he laid it on the edge of the ashtray. 'Lady Fair, let us tell you something else.' He leaned forward and told her about the blots beside Ur Island in the Strait customs books.

'Almost the same time as the missing maps.' Sigbrit was suddenly alert. 'They stopped again in 1618?'

'January 1618. Something must have happened. From one day to another something or someone must have not only stopped people going to the island, but also frightened them into blotting out all trace of it. To such an extent that in the course of one generation the island and the passage into it had been obliterated from folks' memories. There you see it, Lady Fair: *Name the island and all Hell breaks loose.*'

'Or *near it.*' Sigbrit Holland laughed without a hint of irony. She chewed over the Fisherman's story for a few moments. 'If something strange really does go on there on the island, how can Odin calmly sit here at ease with the world?' she asked after a pause.

'Rigmarole broke her leg,' Odin interrupted. 'But I have forgotten what happened before Smith's Town, not forgetting Post Office Town, as well as the ill tidings I'm in a great haste to pass on.' The little old man wound his beard around his fingers. 'Truly that is no small misfortune to happen to someone in the middle of a meteor storm. Luckily there is no misfortune that can't be remedied with a spot of luck.'

Sigbrit could not hold back a smile; sometimes the little old man came out with some odd things.

'And ever since Mother Marie gave me the horseshoe I have met with nothing but luck,' Odin went on, putting his hand on his breast pocket where the horseshoe lay. 'Yes, if only the regulations and formalities would soon be completed, I would reckon myself to be a very lucky man, in all truth.'

'Lucky or not. Strange or not,' said Ambrosius the Fisherman slowly, 'the fact is that it could be a hundred years before the sea freezes over again, planes can't approach the island for unknown reasons, and it is impossible to sail to it unless by some incredible stroke of luck one should come across a detailed chart of the passage. Forget everything about a bridge. Even if the status of the island should be clarified – and that in itself could take years – it would take them at least ten years to build the connection. And we get the feeling that it would not even be possible to build it. Something is going on in that island.'

'But will this something show us the way?' asked Sigbrit. 'How about a helicopter?' But she thought better of that idea at once; why should a helicopter manage any better than a plane? She had another idea. 'The chart!' she exclaimed. 'Of course.' She knocked over her coffee cup in sheer excitement.

'Go on, go on.' The Fisherman mopped up the coffee with a dishcloth.

'You said yourself, a detailed sketch. Remember, King Enevold IV's map is an incredible match with Odin's description of the island. There's no doubt that the cartographer who drew it must have been on the island. And a cartographer could perfectly well have made rough drawings and notes not only of the island but also of the passage leading to it.'

'You've certainly hit on something there.' Ambrosius brightened.

'Yes,' Sigbrit went on. 'That cartographer's scribbles and notes could quite well be in the hands of some great-great grandson or -daughter who hasn't the slightest idea what a treasure they possess.'

Ambrosius the Fisherman laid a hand on Sigbrit's arm and gave it a gentle squeeze. 'You never cease to surprise me, Lady Fair,' he said warmly, meeting her gaze.

Sigbrit smiled, but it rapidly faded as she saw from the clock on the wall that it was a quarter past one. How could she explain that it had taken her three hours to fetch a few documents from the bank on Sunday morning?

'I'll have to go now.' She pulled her arm away from the Fisherman's grasp and stood up.

'You never cease to surprise me, Lady Fair,' the Fisherman said again, but this time Sigbrit couldn't discern any warmth in his voice.

*

Next day Sigbrit sneaked out of the bank early and reached the Special Archives of the Land Registry half an hour before closing time.

The middle-aged archivist was not there. Instead she was greeted by a scruffy young man with longish, greasy hair. The regular archivist had suffered a nervous breakdown, something to do with an old map that had turned up. The scruffy young man grinned fatuously but did not understand when Sigbrit asked for King Enevold IV's map of 1615. He took a long time to find it; he was not used to the registers and shelving systems, and he did not look as if he intended to master them. In the end he found the small map that was framed in glass and bore a label stating: '*Not to be lent to readers*'. He handed it to Sigbrit without bothering to read the label, and did not even note her name.

Sigbrit sat down at one of the metal tables and studied the map. She had already seen it reproduced in the newspapers and was not interested in the details of the light green landscape, the dark brown coastline, the grey rocks or the pale blue sea. She was hunting for a name. But the letters and numbers scattered around all appeared to be statements of positions and distances. The pale blue sea extended to the very edge of the paper, and nowhere was there a cartographer's signature. She took a ruler from her bag, laid it flat on the glass above the map and drew it slowly downwards. She carefully observed each quarter of a millimetre, and not many minutes passed before her doggedness produced results. In the middle of the left side of the map were four minute letters a little separate from the others: T H I T. It was clear they had nothing to do with positions or distances, but on the other hand they did not represent a name. Sigbrit borrowed a magnifying glass from the scruffy young man. The four letters were in an elegant hand, much smaller but clearly the same one that had written '*Drude Estrid Island*'. THIT; that was not a name. Suddenly something struck her. She asked to borrow the records of purchases in King Enevold's time. A royal cartographer would undoubtedly have made many maps and not just the one of the island. She ran her finger down the pages and soon found what she searched for. Then she closed the book and left the Special Archives. If she hurried she could just make it to the green and orange fishing boat.

*

'Thorvald Henrik Innocente Thorvaldsen,' repeated Ambrosius the Fisherman. 'So that's our man.'

Sigbrit Holland nodded.

It was warm, and for once peace and quiet held sway. The sun blazed like brass from a cloud-free sky and the air seemed to stand still. The water lapped gently on the fishing boat's sides, the ducks chattered away happily and now and then a canal boat filled with satisfied tourists chugged past. The police were still banning access to the area, so no Pious could be heard or seen. Instead the local drunks had reoccupied their favourite benches and were laughing at the same old jokes. Odin and Ambrosius the Fisherman sat out on the *Rikke-Marie*'s deck in the shade of the wheelhouse wall. Sigbrit went inside to get a bottle of mineral water and noted Der Fremdling sitting in his usual corner, gazing straight in front of him. Neither Gunnar the Head nor Brynhild Sigurdskær were anywhere to be seen. Sigbrit opened her bottle, went outside again and sat down with her back against the rail.

'Now we just have to find the heirs,' she said to the Fisherman, taking a slurp from her bottle; she was in high spirits.

'Just', exclaimed Ambrosius. He laughed hoarsely. 'You're talking about the state archives, church registers and I don't know what else. It could take months, and we don't have months.'

Sigbrit drummed her fingers lightly on the bottle and looked from the Fisherman to Odin. Suddenly she looked disheartened.

'Time is either won time or lost,' said Odin calmly, winding his beard around his fingers as he considered whether the delay of ill tidings should be reckoned as won or lost time.

The boat rocked gently, and Brynhild Sigurdskær joined them. She wore a different ankle-length white dress.

A wrinkle appeared on Sigbrit's forehead.

'We need all the hands we can muster,' said the Fisherman, taking her hand.

'Yes.' Sigbrit nodded, trying to sound enthusiastic. 'Of course.' She glanced at her watch; half past six, she ought to go. Yet she stayed where she was, and didn't pull her hand away.

Ambrosius the Fisherman regarded her with a strange expression. Their eyes met.

'It will not be easy,' Brynhild whispered huskily, and Sigbrit shuddered. 'It will not be easy to find the heirs, and it will not be easy to get them to give you what you are searching for.'

Sigbrit lowered her eyes. For a second she thought Brynhild had read her thoughts.

'No, but it is still our best bet, isn't it?' she replied, getting up abruptly.

'At this stage it is our only bet!' Ambrosius added drily. 'That is, unless Brynhild has brought us anything?'

Brynhild looked out over the rail down into the black water. It took a long time for her to reply, and even then she did not look up. '*Name the island and all Hell breaks loose; Name the island and all Hell breaks loose.*' She gave a hoarse laugh as if something amused her, then suddenly she straightened up and turned around. 'Neither is right, both are wrong.'

'Wrong?' Ambrosius wrinkled his forehead in surprise.

'The words have no rhythm, no harmony. Whatever they were, they were different.' She laughed again, but this time mirthlessly. 'One or two, I don't know, but the sound was quite different. The long road of change has brought us what we know.' Brynhild twirled around and her white dress stood out.

The Fisherman rubbed his chin. 'What do you think, were there one or two?' he asked when the transparent woman came to rest again.

Brynhild gazed into his eyes. 'Two. There are two. Neither is the right one, but there are two of them.' She took a step backwards as if afraid of her own words. 'There may have been more.'

'More?' exclaimed Ambrosius. 'We should really have listened more intently to the sailors' ramblings in those late night hours when we were one of them. Now we've got to find one willing to talk.' He winked at Sigbrit. 'But it might be a bit easier than finding the descendants of our friend Thorvald Henrik Innocente Thorvaldsen.'

*

'A church! What do they want with a church?' asked the Prime Minister, cracking his right-hand index finger.

'Precisely what the words say,' said the Minister for Ecclesiastical Affairs. 'The Born Anew Christians insist on being acknowledged by the state and getting approval for a church of their own in the capital, and that is just the beginning.' She shook her head, while both the Justice Minister and the Minister for Defence laughed. 'You wouldn't find it so funny if you had had them outside your office all day,' she added.

A waiter brought their meal and for a while the Ministers were occupied with eating. The four of them were at the small Mongolian restaurant not far from Parliament.

'What are you going to tell them?' asked the Justice Minister.

'Even if we were in favour, we cannot possibly allow it.' The Minister for Ecclesiastical Affairs put down her fork. 'Bishop Bentsen is already about to explode. It's no longer only the Prophets of Doom. Believe it or not, a couple of priests in the Established Church have got wind of it and have started to talk about the imminent advent of Judgement Day. Giving the Born Anew Christians a church would be tantamount to pouring petrol on the fire.'

'You'd think they had all lost their senses.' The left side of the Prime Minister's mouth began to twitch. 'If this is what the last year of the millennium does to people, it makes me worry about the final six months we still have to go.' He turned to the Defence Minister. 'And the planes?'

'Still no trace. But the investigation team is –' The Defence Minister's voice died away; obviously the Prime Minister had lost interest.

'What about the North Norse?' enquired the Prime Minister, and again his mouth tightened with cramp. 'It would be hard for me to accept if they get pictures before we do.'

'They have lost one or two planes over the island themselves,' the Minister of Defence pointed out quickly.

'That doesn't mean they won't get there before us,' maintained the Prime Minister, cracking his right thumb.

The Defence Minister had just taken a mouthful and he chewed a long time before replying. 'Can't we suggest a ban on flying over the island until its status is decided?'

'Like cowardly dogs, you mean?' laughed the Justice Minister. 'North Norseland would never go along with that, in any case.'

'Considering your own loss that might be just as well,' said the Prime Minister slowly, liking the idea more and more.

'With a little dexterity our negotiators should be able to turn it into a North Norse suggestion that we can then magnanimously give our approval to.'

'Possibly,' replied the Minister for Justice hesitantly. 'But that still doesn't solve the problem of the Doomsday Prophets.'

There was a brief silence, then he went on. 'How about asking Mr Odin Odin to move to some place or other the public doesn't know about?'

'We-e-ll, I'm not so sure...' said the Prime Minister. 'Removing the man doesn't necessarily solve the problem.'

'No, but it could create enough confusion among the Doomsday Prophets to give us a space, at least for a while. Once the focal point is removed it should be possible to avoid some of the worst confrontations among the groups. It would also take the wind out of the Born Anew Christians' demand for a church.'

'I'm not quite convinced. It could worsen the situation considerably. If we relocate the little old man we might easily turn the demonstrators against the government, and we can't risk that.'

'We don't even know if he will agree to move,' the Minister of Defence interjected. 'As far as I gather, the little old man has a pretty strong will of his own. Just picture him refusing if the government advises him to go into hiding. What a gift for both the press and the Doomsday Prophets.'

'No, we can't run that risk,' said the Prime Minister. 'Not even if we claim to do it for his own safety. Even if he did go along with it, it could all too easily turn against us. We shall have to think of something else.'

Again the Ministers chewed in silence.

'If the time isn't ripe to ask him to go into hiding, what about asking him to stand up and deny that he has anything whatsoever to do with the Resurrection of Jesus Christ or the Messiah or anything like that?' The Minister for Ecclesiastical Affairs energetically twisted her ring round and round.

'Not a bad idea at all,' said the Prime Minister slowly. 'But do you think we can control him?'

'As far as I know, apart from a touch of dementia in his fantastical stories he has never claimed anything more than to have come from a village called Smith's Town on the island, where his horse broke a leg,' said the Minister for Ecclesiastical Affairs, and went on with a broad smile: 'If he himself denied his divinity I could at least silence the bishops.'

'Yes, if we make sure he talks only about the island, nothing can go wrong, can it?' The Minister for Justice liked the idea as well.

'No, and when Mr Odin Odin has demonstrated to the crowds that he is a perfectly ordinary confused little old man from a perfectly normal island, this Simon Peter II will have a hard job keeping up his demand for a church.'

'Not to mention keeping hold of his followers,' added the Justice Minister.

*

'The Blacksmith knows all there is to know about horses, and Oldmother Rikke-Marie has seen everything there is to be seen. If you need anything you only have to ask Mother Marie,' Odin said to the peculiar object pointing at his face. Ambrosius the Fisherman had told him it would ensure all his words would reach all the fanatics and a good many others in danger of being infected. 'Then there is Uncle Joseph's barn full of hay and...'

The journalist fidgeted uneasily. 'I am sure the viewers would like to hear more about life on the island,' he broke in.

There were so many things Odin would like to tell the sick Mr Bramsentorpf and the civil servants, if only he could remember them.

'Yes, I well remember the day I arrived in Smith's Town.' He smiled at the camera at the thought. 'It was cold, the sun shone through a light mist and the ground was covered with snow.'

The journalist nodded encouragingly and discreetly wiped a nervous drop of sweat from his brow with a pale blue hand-kerchief.

'I had been journeying across the sky for days with the ill tidings.'

More sweat broke out on the journalist's brow and he leaned tensely forward searching for a question that could get Odin back on to a safer path. But Odin had already moved on.

'Then we flew into a meteor storm, and the unfortunate Rigmarole broke her leg. It was truly a bit of a misfortune. But luckily there is no misfortune that a little luck cannot remedy. So after a good night's sleep I walked across the sea to the Continent, where in truth so many people have demonstrated such great kindness and strong faith that it can't be long before the regulations and the formalities will be finalized, and the happy day dawns when I can make my way home.'

Odin tried to hit on something else to tell the sick people, but to his great disappointment – and the journalist's great relief – he couldn't think of anything more at that moment.

It was more than enough, however. When Sigbrit Holland hurried away from the bank that afternoon to the green and orange fishing boat, the numbers of pious at the police barrier had more than doubled.

*

'It was no good,' said Sigbrit Holland. 'The childless widower never married again and drowned at the age of thirty-one.'

Sigbrit had been lucky. After two lengthy lunch hours she had only just avoided getting into trouble at the bank. Meanwhile a helpful librarian at the Special Archives had referred her to the government record books in which most of the official royal correspondence and instructions were kept during the period from 1513 right up to 1660. The records also contained a list of prominent people, among which Sigbrit Holland – in the course of a greatly extended lunchbreak – found the names and personal details of the cartographers.

Ambrosius the Fisherman chewed the stem of his pipe. 'So our friend Thorvald Henrik Innocente Thorvaldsen was not a lucky guess. Well, at least it took you only eight days and not eight months.'

'Maybe there's something we still don't know...' Sigbrit was not ready to give up so easily.

'And will never find out,' the Fisherman interrupted her. 'No, Lady Fair, you had better face the fact that whatever rough drafts and notes about King Enevold IV's maps may have existed, they have either long since turned to dust or they are kept in the private royal library. And unless you are the Queen that private library is as good as dust.'

'But there must have been others besides the cartographer – assistants and traders. Perhaps the captain made some notes?'

'Lady Fair, we have already been down that road. It was a good idea but it led nowhere. Let's try another tack.'

'Back to, *Name the island and all Hell breaks...*' Sigbrit laughed.

'Laugh away, Lady Fair. Something is happening on that island, and we're probably going to find out what.'

At that moment the door opened and Brynhild Sigurdskær entered the wheelhouse. The transparent woman greeted Sigbrit warmly and sat down beside Ambrosius the Fisherman. Sigbrit tried to appear calm.

'Anyone who can freeze the sea must be able to melt the snow too,' murmured Odin to himself and searched for something more to tell the fanatics next time he was talking to the peculiar object that could reach all of them. 'But a broken bone on a horse is a broken bone, as the Blacksmith would say. At least until Veterinarius Martinussen is finished with the regulations and Mr Bramsentorpf with the formalities.'

The clock on the wall thrummed seven. Sigbrit ought to have been at home long ago, but for once she did not care.

'I'm not going to give up,' she said with sudden determination. 'We have to get Odin back to the island before the situation becomes completely impossible.' She waved her hand in the direction of the Pious behind the police barrier. 'Someone or other on that voyage to Drude Estrid Island in 1614 or whenever it was must have written down their course. Even if I have to go direct to the Queen I am going to find out who it was.'

'You are more than welcome, Lady Fair.' Ambrosius smiled for the first time that evening. 'But how will you find the time to search?' His eyes sparkled teasingly.

'I don't know, but I shall!' said Sigbrit with a conviction that surprised even herself.

'The mermaid tempts the fisherman, the elf girl seduces the hunter and the angel lures the soldier. Going back to listen to the true song is bravery and wisdom,' said Odin, patting the horseshoe in his breast pocket. 'Of course there is no misfortune that a spot of luck cannot remedy.'

Brynhild Sigurdskær, who had sat silent with a gently distant expression on her face, now turned to Ambrosius.

'What did the sailors have to say?' she asked in an almost normal tone.

At first the Fisherman made no reply, but picked up his pipe from the ashtray and smoked in silence for a while. When he finally spoke he looked attentively at the transparent woman as if to study her reaction.

'One tells us there is another saying but he can't remember it. Another says the one we have is wrong, indeed, even both of them, but he can't remember the right one. A third that the proper saying has nothing to do with *Hell* but instead with a *bone smith*, but he really can't remember the words. Then there was one who said that the one of them we have is correct but that he can't remember which, and that there is yet another one that has something to do with *Kings*, but that was all he would say.' The Fisherman shrugged his shoulders. 'Those were the ones who were willing to talk.'

'The Blacksmith of Smith's Town is the only one there is, including, not forgetting, Post Office Town,' said Odin, tugging his beard.

Brynhild Sigurdskær coughed and rose to fetch some water. On her way her hand stroked the Fisherman's shoulder.

Sigbrit looked the other way. Her fingers drummed rapidly on the edge of the table.

'A *bone smith*,' said Brynhild Sigurdskær, as if tasting the words. '*Kings*.' She hesitated. 'There are three, if not more. The two you have heard of are not the two there are.'

Ambrosius waited, but Brynhild said no more, and for a long

while there was silence in the wheelhouse. Then the clock struck the half hour, and Sigbrit leapt to her feet. Brynhild rose as well.

'Stay for the bonfire,' said the transparent woman. 'The changing of the hours. The epoch of light that becomes the epoch of darkness.'

'Or perhaps the other way around.' Sigbrit tried to force a smile, but it was not a wholehearted one. She shook her head. 'I can't.'

'Midsummer Night is for the burning of fear,' Brynhild went on. 'They were right in the old times, although they did it in quite the wrong way. Burning witches doesn't so much as scorch fear. They were afraid of the woman who knows but not because of her. They were afraid because they knew well what she saw through the surface froth. They were afraid of the nothingness within them. Today they are more frightened than ever. They are terrified, indeed, where nothingness has grown. How they would love to point to the witch, how they would love to burn her on the fire. Courage is such a simple thing, and yet so demanding. It is easier to burn witches. That is how they forget what Midsummer Night is for: to burn the fear that the endless day has cast light on.' Brynhild Sigurdskær's eyes shone white, but she went on in a gentle, almost inaudible tone: 'And why don't you walk through the embers to the other side?'

Sigbrit turned pale.

'That is enough!' Ambrosius the Fisherman interrupted sharply.

The transparent woman stopped speaking but she continued to stare into Sigbrit's eyes. Sigbrit felt a knot of fear in her stomach, and she suddenly became clammy with cold sweat. Then she grew angry.

'I am not afraid of fire,' she snarled and stared back at Brynhild Sigurdskær. Her cheeks were regaining colour. 'And be sure I shall find the captain of Thorvaldsen's ship, whatever it costs. So you two can go on with your little word game.'

Sigbrit jumped over the rail up on to the quay and ran as fast as she could the whole way back to her car in the park behind the bank. She was very late.

*

That same night – as the bonfires blazed in the South Norse Queendom and the glare of the flames competed with the light of the night – the first in a series of mysterious dreams came to the conscientious Lennart Torstensson.

He twisted and turned. He found himself in a murky dark nothingness that had neither beginning nor end. Then a tree shot up in front of him. It grew and grew, far into a misty blue sky that widened itself as the tree grew. Lennart again looked ahead and now the trunk of the tree was so big it was like a wall filling his whole field of vision. He was horrified, and when a long heavy branch seized him around the waist and lifted him up he was completely paralysed with terror. Soon he was so high that he stopped fighting against the branch and instead clung to it. Higher and higher the branch lifted Lennart until he was higher in the sky then he had ever imagined possible. When they reached the crown that stretched out boundlessly in every direction, the branch set him down abruptly in a fork close to the trunk. The fork was so narrow that he could hardly move.

A sound of flapping wings came from nearby and a lively twittering and trilling started up in several places. Lennart looked around him, but no matter which direction he peered he could see nothing but dark green foliage. The flapping wings came nearer and the lively twittering grew noisier and more insistent and at last started to sound like human words. He could distinguish one but it meant nothing: *Ginnungagap*. Other syllables merged into a still stranger babble which he could not make anything of. It was as if the birds were trying to tell him something. But Lennart understood nothing of their song and nor was he sure he really wanted to understand it. He felt afraid of the birds and despite his fear of falling he twisted round and grasped the branch above his head, looking for another branch to place his feet on. There it was. He allowed his body to slide out of the fork, but his foothold vanished, and the branch he was clasping tightly turned to nothing in his hands, and he fell.

Lennart Torstensson screamed. He opened his eyes. He lay on the floor with his head halfway under his own bed. Slowly he got to his feet. He had not hurt himself in the fall, but he was still shaking with fear. He clutched his head – what a peculiar dream!

But he didn't have time to think about that now. It was already eight o'clock and at nine there was a meeting of the Investigating Committee of the Western Bastion to discuss the case of the island the South Norse government had designated Drude Estrid Island and the North Norse government Hermod Skjalm Island. He was to have all the background documents ready for Herr Hölzern before the start of the meeting.

At the Investigating Committee meeting the South Norse delegation generously ceded to the North Norse demand that no one should be allowed to set foot on or fly over the island before its formal status had been clarified. But further than that nothing budged. None of the delegations were willing to listen to the arguments of their counterparts, and both parties merely continued to repeat their own standpoints and emphasized that they had received unalterable instructions from their governments to maintain these. The chairman could do nothing but request the two parties to subject their standpoints to further consideration before the next meeting, which was fixed for a week later.

'The situation had not been fully developed,' said Herr Hölzern, and Lennart noted these words of wisdom in his notebook beside the other important sentences he needed to remember to make use of when he himself became a great man.

The delegates were about to pack up and leave the room when the North Norse delegation asked for another word.

'Concerning equitable procedure in this case, the government of North Norseland desires to put forward the request that Mr Odin Odin should no longer reside in South Norseland. It is highly inequitable and can in the worst case lead to bias in the matter, should an inhabitant from the North Norseland island, Hermod Skjalm Island, take up residence in a country that maintains falsely that the island is a part of its sovereign territory.' The North Norseland delegates drew a deep breath. 'In order to show goodwill, and out of respect for its South Norse neighbour, the North Norse government is prepared to make a compromise whereby Mr Odin Odin spends half his time in each country.' With a significant expression the North Norse delegate here made a long pause. 'However, since Mr Odin Odin has stayed for six months in South Norseland, the North Norse government finds it both just and right that for the coming six months, that is to say with and from the

1st July this year, Mr Odin Odin takes up residence in North Norseland.'

The South Norse delegation was outraged. Mr Bramsentorpf hammered on the table with his fist and shouted that the North Norse delegation was utterly out of its senses; Mr Odin Odin had himself already made a measured choice of where he preferred to stay, and this happened be South Norseland.

It took quite a while for the hump-backed chairman to re-establish quiet, and he soon found to his chagrin that he could do no more than conclude that at this point everyone who came from the disputed island would have to be considered either South or North Norse regardless of which country this person resided in, and also place the subject at the top of the agenda for the next meeting of the Investigating Committee. Considering that the North Norse proposal – which he diplomatically called the 'demand' – was not completely unreasonable, he encouraged the South Norse delegation to consider the matter seriously.

Lennart smiled to himself. The North Norse delegation had expressed its demand in much the same words as he had used in his latest anonymous letter to the North Norse government. Naturally South Norseland would never give way. It would only increase the esteem in which Lennart Torstensson would be held when soon – and quite alone – he would escort Mr Odin Odin to North Norseland.

YGGDRASIL

Father Tree, Yggdrasil the ash
tree of time, of everything and each
took root in foggy swamps of Niflheim
A second one in Udgard's soil
And yet one more in Asgard's grew

Ever green, so tall he rose that topmost bough
laid earth and moon both far below
In his crown an eagle perched
between the eyes Vedrfolnir falcon sat
*   — he saw it all*
and gods now knew where happened what

But in Niflheim the dragon Nidhug hid
gnawing roots of Father Tree
Suirrel Ratatosk told the eagle what Nidhug did
back down along the trunk went he

*   Keep an eye on Father Tree*
*   the end of gods, bode soon, wither he*

'No, no and no!' The Prime Minister gave his right-hand middle finger a vicious tug. Under no circumstances will I hand him over to the North Norse.'

'Well, maybe, but it might be a help to us.' The Minister of

Justice paced nervously back and forth in front of the Prime Minister's desk. 'And it might calm down the doomsday prophets.'

The Prime Minister shrugged his shoulders scornfully. 'I'm not so sure about that. If you consider their Holy War with the North Norse True Christians, if Mr Odin Odin took a little hop over to the other side of the Strait it might have pretty far-reaching consequences.' He shook his head. 'And think what the voters would say: a feeble government that gives in to the demands of our adversaries just like that. No, the situation is bad enough as it is.' The Prime Minister laughed coldly. 'If only they knew,' he nodded in the direction of the Kingdom of the North Norse to the east, 'how glad I'd be to get rid of him...'

The Justice Minister stopped in mid-stride. He had a last try. 'Maybe we could get him to go somewhere else. Somewhere he would be neither in the Queendom, nor in the Kingdom of the North Norse.'

The Prime Minister shook his head.

There was a tap at the door and the Prime Minister's secretary stuck her head around it.

'Didn't I say I was not to be disturbed?' snapped the Prime Minister.

'I'm sorry... but, er, I thought this was something you should know about at once.' The secretary gabbled so fast that she stumbled over her words. 'They have occupied Our Saviour's Church.'

'Who are *they*?'

'It was announced on the news just now. The Born Anew Christians...' The secretary made her exit hastily and closed the door quietly behind her.

The Prime Minister looked at the Minister of Justice in

alarm. He rose from his chair, walked slowly to the window and looked out. He cracked the fingers of his left hand one by one. After finishing all five, and without turning round, he asked wearily: 'What do we do now?'

Closing his eyes the Minister of Justice gave a sigh of relief. He joined the Prime Minister at the window.

'There are various ways and means,' he said slowly. 'For instance, the little old man could go away on holiday.'

'On holiday?' repeated the Prime Minister, amazed.

'Making an informal suggestion for him to take a holiday in no way contradicts our official statement that Mr Odin Odin should naturally stay on in the Queendom. He will of course keep his present address while he is away.'

'And how are you going to convince Mr Odin Odin to agree to the suggestion without arousing suspicion?'

'As I say, there are ways and there are means, and I have mine. You can trust me. I promise the little old man will go off on his trip, and it will be impossible to trace that back to the government.' The Justice Minister smiled. 'And naturally I shall make sure he doesn't take his holiday in the North Norse Kingdom.'

So it came about that on a bright warm morning in early July Mr Brams Bramsentorpf turned up at the green and orange fishing boat, on his own and without the seven impeccably dressed men. This time Mr Bramsentorpf did not stay on the quay but climbed straight on board where he almost stumbled over Ambrosius the Fisherman repairing a loose plank on the decking.

'Um, um,' rumbled Mr Bramsentorpf apologetically and gave the Fisherman to understand that he wanted to speak to Mr Odin Odin, strictly alone.

'Well, Mr Odin, how goes it?' Mr Bramsentorpf adopted a jovial tone to create a suitable atmosphere of mutual confidence and trust.

'I am in the very best of health, thank you,' said Odin. 'And even better now you have come.' Odin was very happy to see Mr Bramsentorpf as he had heard nothing about the air connection, not to speak of the regulations and formalities, since the meeting with the group of Continentals. So as soon as he considered it proper to bring up the subject – after they had discussed the wind and the sunshine and the blue sky for a while – he asked Mr Bramsentorpf how it was all getting on.

'Ah, yes, the formalities, Mr Odin, the formalities,' repeated Mr Bramsentorpf, throwing out a hand in a way that made it quite clear that, just for the moment, it was best not to talk about the regulations and the formalities and everything concerned with them, and not to mention the air connection.

Just then Odin recalled something he had temporarily forgotten, and he gave Mr Bramsentorpf an encouraging smile.

'Well then, Mr Bramsentorpf, in that case I am truly more than pleased to be able to tell you that you need worry no more about the regulations and formalities because the very tall, very blond young man with the long name will shortly come to fetch me and take me to North Norseland, where they have the most brilliant Veterinarius who can go back to Smith's Town with me, and put Rigmarole's leg to rights, just like that.' Odin clicked his fingers exactly as he had seen Lennart Torstensson do.

At this Mr Bramsentorpf's face turned bright red with fury; this time they really had gone too far!

'Mr Odin Odin,' he began. 'I shall speak to you as a friend and not as a high-ranking civil servant in the service of the

government of South Norseland. As a friend,' Mr Bramsentorpf lowered his voice to an intimate whisper, 'it is my duty to
tell you that the North Norse people are not to be trusted.'

Odin twisted his beard between his fingers: in truth
Continental affairs were not easy to understand.

'No,' said Mr Bramsentorpf loudly, shaking his head theatrically. 'It is one of the unhappy facts of life, but Mr Odin, you
had better get this into your head and the sooner the better:
Never rely on a North Norseman.'

'But the very tall, very blond young man with the long name
said that the North Norse King...'

'Least of all the North Norse King, Mr Odin!' exclaimed Mr
Bramsentorpf with exaggerated horror. 'No, no, the North
Norse Kingdom is no country to have dealings with.' Mr
Bramsentorpf was well satisfied with the way the conversation
was going, although it had been problematic to begin with.
'It is a question of history,' he went on in a confidential tone,
'terrible wars, so many deaths...' Then Mr Bramsentorpf
described in graphic detail the frightful sufferings undergone
by the Queendom of South Norseland through the past four or
five hundred years at the hands of their brutal northern neighbours, and when at last there was nothing left to say on that
subject he leaned forward and whispered hoarsely: 'And now
the North Norse government intends to kidnap you!'

Odin's eye grew round with fear. He was not exactly sure
what 'kidnap' meant, but from the way Mr Bramsentorpf
uttered the word he knew it must be something one would certainly not wish to experience.

'I can see that you understand perfectly the seriousness of
the situation,' said Mr Bramsentorpf, and to be quite certain
that the little old man would be in no doubt, he played out his

triumph. 'And if the North Norsemen succeed in kidnapping you, not only will the completion of the regulations but also the establishing of the air connection be seriously delayed. Yes, I would almost go so far as to say *very* seriously delayed.'

Now Odin understood the full extent of the disaster Mr Bramsentorpf was talking about, and the rest was easy enough.

'A very long and very delightful holiday. One could even go so far as to say, the longer the better,' Mr Bramsentorpf concluded his lengthy explanation of how Odin could best avoid being kidnapped by the North Norse government. 'But, Mr Odin, nothing is so dire that it has no benefits whatsoever, and I can almost certainly guarantee that when you return from your holiday the regulations and formalities will have been completed, so you and, er, your Veterinarius will be able to go back to Smith's Town at once.'

Then Mr Bramsentorpf said goodbye, after wishing Odin a really long and delightful holiday, and left the green and orange fishing boat with a smug expression despite the sweat that streamed down his legs and back and made his skin itch violently under his navy blue suit. The Minister of Justice would be more than satisfied, grinned Mr Bramsentorpf to himself, and when the Minister was more than satisfied...

*

Bishop Bentsen was a patient man, but he was also a man of honour. When the Born Anew Christians had occupied the Church of Our Saviour for five days with no intervention on the part of the authorities – the government wanted at any price to avoid more unrest – Bishop Bensen's honour was at risk. He summoned the Episcopal Council to a crisis meeting, and the ten bishops of the South Norse Established Church quickly agreed that the cup was full; enough was enough! Within ten minutes the Council had decided unanimously that the Established Church would no longer be silent witnesses to the spread of false prophecies concerning the Second Coming of Christ and the First Advent of the Apocalypse. The Episcopal Council would go to the press to criticize the failure of the government to intercede, and it would initiate demonstrations against the Doomsday Prophets.

However, as well as being a patient man and a man of honour, Bishop Bentsen was a wise man. He was well aware that counter-action could be seen by certain groups in the community as tantamount to siding with the North Norse True Christians, and to side with the North Norse in the present climate would be tantamount to treason. No, in order to solve the real problem, Mr Odin Odin would have to disappear – at least for a time. As the upright man he was, Bishop Bentsen decided to give the little old man a chance.

So it happened, only a minute or two after Mr Bramsentorpf had left the green and orange fishing boat, that a certain Vicar Valentino showed the policemen on guard his driving licence and the letter from Bishop Bentsen and was allowed to cross the police barrier. Vicar Valentino was an agile man with black hair, black eyes and black eyebrows – at one time a southern European street boy, now a South Norse priest and Bishop Bentsen's right-hand man. He walked with brisk firm steps along the quay, pushed up his well-pressed trousers and climbed unhesitatingly on board the *Rikke-Marie*.

One hour later Vicar Valentino left the green and orange fishing boat after suggesting to Signor Odino in no uncertain words that he should go as soon as possible on a very long and very delightful holiday, in which event Bishop Bentsen – an exceptionally holy and exceptionally important man – would owe Signor Odino a favour, which Signor Odino seemed to have expressed a desire for, of helping to finalize the regulations and formalities and establish the much-needed air connection.

'Blessed are the pure in heart, for they shall see God,' said Vicar Valentino solemnly, giving Odin his hand in farewell.

*

Meanwhile Sigbrit Holland had made it, if not precisely into the presence of the Queen, then as close as she could get to her: the Lord Chamberlain, von Egernret. By feigning to call from the Ministry of Justice for some information to strengthen the Queendom's negotiating position in the dispute over Drude Estrid Island, she asked for the name of the captain who in 1614 or 1615 had taken the cartographer Thorvald Henrik Innocente Thorvaldsen to the island by boat. And luck was with her. The Lord Chamberlain was a pompous, vain gentleman who never tired of demonstrating his high status and privileged access to vitally important restricted information.

Within the hour the Lord Chamberlain called back, having failed to check Sigbrit's number, to her great relief.

'The vessel was a yacht with the name *Freia II*,' said the Lord Chamberlain haughtily. 'But for reasons completely outside court control, the captain's name is no longer to be found in the registers.'

'Isn't it?' Sigbrit tried to sound surprised, and the Lord Chamberlain dropped his supercilious air immediately.

'Yes, it is indeed most unfortunate,' he said almost apologetically. 'But I can assure you that something like this is extremely rare at court, and personally I have never come across anything like it. However, I can guarantee that the names of all the other captains employed by the King are clearly inscribed beside their ships. Only this one, the captain of *Freia II*, is missing.' The Lord Chamberlain gave a nervous cough. 'But I can assure you that of course I shall personally see to it that the information required will be made available, and in double-quick time. It is merely that I am extremely busy, and therefore am bound to ask whether the matter could wait until tomorrow morning?'

'Well –' Sigbrit sounded a touch impatient, then she went on in a forebearing tone – 'naturally the Ministry of Justice would not wish to interrupt the work of the Court, so if that is the only way, tomorrow morning would have to suffice.'

Next morning she got the name: Captain Hans Adelstensfostre. The Lord Chamberlain had been obliged to contact the Court of the Lower Lands to get hold of the name.

'Apparently Captain Adelstensfostre and *Freia II* undertook a good deal of work for the Lower Lands. Confidentially, madam,' now the Lord Chamberlain was positively ingratiating, 'there is something odd about all this. I do not mean with regard to the Lower Lands, no, by no means, but concerning Captain Hans Adelstenfostre himself.' The Lord Chamberlain's voice dropped to almost a whisper. 'The captain seems to have vanished from every record, not only those of South Norseland, only a year or two after the trip to Drude Estrid Island. He must have jumped ship. Possibly there had been a scandal. Perhaps something to do with a lady.' The Lord Chamberlain sounded quite animated at the idea.

Sigbrit grinned to herself, but aloud she said that might very well be. Then she thanked the Lord Chamberlain for the useful information and hung up.

There were still two hours until lunchtime, but Sigbrit couldn't wait. 'I have a doctor's appointment,' she told her boss casually, trying to ignore his reproachful glance.

'Ambrosius and Odin are out. I don't know when they'll be back.' Brynhild Sigurdskær gave her a friendly smile. 'Some coffee?'

Sigbrit Holland didn't want to be alone with the transparent woman, but she couldn't go back to the bank just yet, so she sat down. Also there was something she wanted to ask Brynhild Sigurdskær.

'Where I live,' the transparent woman repeated the question slowly. 'What an interesting thought.' Her face opened out into a surprised smile. 'I don't think I can give you an answer,' she went on thoughtfully. 'Or perhaps, yes, the answer is everywhere. I live everywhere.' She spoke lightheartedly, though her expression was serious.

'Sorry, I didn't express myself clearly.' Sigbrit tried to sound more friendly. 'I just wondered whether you have a home or...?'

'Oh, I understood that perfectly. When I say I live everywhere, I mean I live everywhere I am. Just at present *Rikke-Marie* is my home. Perhaps my home will be somewhere else tomorrow, and the following week in a completely different place. My home is myself.' Brynhild laughed softly. 'And my backpack, of course. That's it.'

The two women gazed at each other in silence for a moment. Then Brynhild reversed the question.

'And you? Where do you live?' She pronounced the word

'live' as if this was the first time she used it in this context.

Suddenly Sigbrit felt awkward. The right answer would be in a house north of Fredenshvile. But was it the truth? Did she live there? Or was it merely a place she stayed in? She looked down at the rings in the old mahogany table. There was something disquieting about Brynhild Sigurdskær. Instead of answering the question Sigbrit put another question herself. 'Don't you work or... I mean, what do you live on?'

The puzzled smile returned to Brynhild's face.

'You ask very strange questions,' she said, 'but I think I know what you mean. I just don't know how to explain it...' She gazed in front of her as if remembering something sad. 'Today I'm living on the scent of the earth in rain,' she said softly. 'Tomorrow I may live on the crackling of the leaves under the roe-deer's hooves or on the sun's reflection in purple cherries.'

'But what about money?' exclaimed Sigbrit, at once regretting her words. 'Don't you have to earn your keep? Something for the basic necessities?' She felt indignant without knowing why. She lowered her voice. 'I'm sorry, I don't understand, surely you have to eat?'

Brynhild Sigurdskær looked confused.

'You don't have to earn much to eat. I work when I need to.' Then as if she had suddenly cottoned on to what Sigbrit Holland was hinting at, she laughed gently. 'I work when I'm hungry, when I need a new winter coat or when my shoes need new soles. I can do all kinds of things, I make a bit of everything: I tell fortunes, and I know old sayings people have forgotten. When that isn't enough I clean fish at factories, sell bread in bakeries, do cleaning, drive trucks and sometimes, sometimes I go to bed with rich men.'

She noticed the amazed look on Sigbrit's face.

'It all comes to one and the same thing, doesn't it? And that last thing is the quickest. Then I live again.'

Sigbrit looked at her watch and stood up. 'Sorry, I'm late.' That wasn't true, but she suddenly needed to be alone.

Sigbrit strode quickly along the quay. She was upset without knowing why. The transparent woman selling her body now and then was not so unusual, after all. No, it was the way she had talked about it, so casually, comparing it with every other little job, as if it was something everyone did. Sigbrit thought of her own situation. She too slept with a man she did not love, or rather, no longer loved. But wasn't that different? They were married, she earned her own money, she knew Fridtjof well, and though she was not quite sure whether she had ever really loved him, she liked him. But then, who said Brynhild Sigurdskær did not like the men she went to bed with? Sigbrit's own job: did it really matter to her? Could Brynhild be right, that to survive you may need to sell parts of yourself? But that you just have to restrict such occasions as much as possible?

Sigbrit came to the end of the quay and turned left for Firø Bridge.

'Hey, Lady Fair, where are you off to?' A firm hand clamped her shoulder.

'Ambrosius.' Sigbrit stopped. Odin was there too. 'I didn't see you at all.'

'No, you didn't. Where are you going in such a rush?'

Sigbrit told them about Captain Hans Adelstensfostre, but Ambrosius the Fisherman didn't seem to be listening. Before she had even finished he interrupted her.

'There are three,' he said.

'Three what?'

'Three sayings!' said the Fisherman enthusiastically.

'And how do they go then?' Sigbrit tried to sound interested.

'It's not so simple. The first one still runs like: *Name the island and all Hell breaks loose*. The second is something about a smith; the closest we could get was: *Near the island with only one blacksmith*. And the third is to do with *Kings and subjects*.'

'Well, that's a lot of help,' mumbled Sigbrit.

'Can't you see, the mention of "*Kings and subjects*" might well explain why the island slipped out of memory. And "*the black-smith*" might refer to a predecessor to the present Blacksmith in Smith's Town that Odin has told us about.'

A pair of sparrows who had been pecking up crumbs from the pavement suddenly took fright and flew up.

'When the birds of wisdom take their leave you are bound to get lost,' said Odin quietly, watching the birds.

'Ah, Lord, Son of God, blessed be this moment,' yelled a voice suddenly, and the Entrusted Disciple ran across the road taking no notice of the hooting traffic. He threw himself at Odin's feet. 'Ah, Thou Mighty One, my Saviour and Redeemer, let the Day come. Ah, let it come. The day when the regulations and formalities are completed and the unfortunate rigmarole of earthly life is transformed into bliss,' he sobbed.

'Forbearance is in all truth a heavy burden,' answered Odin, amazed but deeply moved over the sobbing man's good wishes for his horse's cure. 'Howsoever, one should never forget that although the long-suffering man has further to go than the less long-suffering man, none the less the first one will reach the goal before the other.'

A small crowd was quickly gathering around them, and Ambrosius thought it best for him and Odin to leave, so while Sigbrit vanished across the bridge, the Fisherman set off with the little old man, who would otherwise have liked to continue this very promising conversation about the regulations and formalities and Rigmarole who would soon be healed.

*

Simon Peter II was in high spirits; that very evening the Born Anew Christians celebrated the seventh day of the occupation of Our Saviour's Church. The occupation had originally been intended as a peaceful reminder to the government that the Born Anew Christians felt things were serious. However, the occupation was so successful, and the ensuing recruitment of new believers so fruitful that Simon Peter II had decided to prolong the action. The streets around the church were lined with stalls equipped with supplies guaranteed to save lost souls, and the Entrusted Disciple encouraged the Pious to do their Christian duty and take turns manning the stalls.

While the Born Anew Christians sang and danced in Our Saviour's Church, the atmosphere was a good deal less enthusiastic in Ezekiel the Righteous's parents' apartment. The Reborn Jews had suffered great losses in the Battle for the Island of the Eternal Sabbath that had followed Alvilda's miraculous passing; not only had the eldest of Ezekiel's uncles become so incandescent that he had succumbed to a fatal stroke, and not only had eleven of the remaining thirty-one Reborn Jews suffered more or less serious injuries, but – far more serious – the prophetic son had lost all his top teeth and since then had refused to utter a word.

Of course what no one could know was that the silence of Ezekiel the Righteous had less to do with the loss of his teeth than with the fact that his brother had decided the moment had come. No matter how desperate and lost his little brother looked, Ezra resisted the temptation of compassion and did not go near the hole in the wall. And when twenty-two days had passed, the divinity had left Ezekiel to the extent that Ezra was able to take action. To Ezra's astonishment he was not even halfway through his explanation of Ezekiel's deception before he was interrupted.

'Out! Out!' booed the five remaining uncles, their wives and children, and the widow of the sixth, as well as the handful of unrelated Reborn Jews, and threatened Ezra with clenched fists. Ten minutes later Ezra found himself on the doorstep of his home, or rather the doorstep of his former home. He was not to approach it before he had made peace with Jehovah and the fact that Jehovah and Messiah had chosen Ezra's little brother and not Ezra to be the blessed prophet of the New Time.

'We cannot risk having fostered a Cain at our hearth,' Ezra heard his father hiss, just before the door slammed, and Ezra had no option but to go out into the light South Norseland summer night to search for a bench to sleep on. That night, while the Born Anew Christians celebrated the seven days' occupation of Our Saviour's Church, and while he twisted and turned on a hard bench in freezing cold, Ezra swore revenge on his brother Ezekiel, on his parents, the five remaining uncles, their wives and children and the widow of the sixth, as well as on the handful of unrelated Reborn Jews.

In another part of Fredenshvile, other voices swore revenge not only on the Reborn Jews, but also on the Born Anew Christians, the Lambs of the Lord and every other group that dared to believe in anything other than the only true faith.

Although many an imam in the Muslim world had threatened and condemned Hasan Al-Basri, and some even demanded he should be tried before a shariah court, the angry young Muslims considered him too weak. They wanted action and revenge, not prayers and forgiveness.

'Didn't Muhammad fight for Mecca?' they asked. 'Didn't the Prophet fight for Medina?'

'Yes, where would the Muslims have been if the Prophet had not waged merciless war against the infidels?' yelled a furious political science student and a stunningly beautiful dark woman with flashing eyes to the forty young men she had gathered in one of the university vestibules. It didn't take long for Aisha and the forty angry young men to agree; although they couldn't make up their minds how to do it or what the precise aim would be, there was no doubt that an Islamic revolution was on its way.

*

'The sun will darken. The trees will wither. It will be intensely cold. The heavens will fall and everything will burn. You must be gone before then.' Brynhild Sigurdskær looked at Ambrosius the Fisherman. She seemed agitated.

That reminded Odin of something and he looked up in surprise. He pulled at his beard and struggled once more to remember the words of ill tidings, but it was no good.

'When you cannot remember small things, in truth you cannot recall the big things at all,' he said, then luckily recalled one small thing he had almost forgotten. 'I should very much like to take a holiday', he said. 'In very truth, I would indeed like to take a very long and very delightful holiday.'

It was the ninth day of the occupation of Our Saviour's

Church, and all was peace and calm. Since the Born Anew Christians were based in the church, and the other groups seemed to have dispersed a little, the police barrier had been moved to the church, and there was once again access to the quay and *Rikke-Marie*. Two remaining constables patrolled slowly back and forth, chatted with the locals and their dogs, and enjoyed feeling the sun tanning their faces and their partially bare arms in short-sleeved uniform shirts.

'It's the calm before the storm,' said Brynhild Sigurdskær hoarsely.

Ambrosius the Fisherman looked from the transparent woman to Odin, then he looked out at the two policemen. They wouldn't be much good if anyone was determined to cause mischief.

'We're going,' he said slowly.

'Where?' Sigbrit climbed over the rail and sat down on deck beside Odin.

'That's something we don't know yet.'

'When?'

'Leave at once. Madness is coming.' Brynhild walked up and down the deck restlessly.

'Madness is here already,' said the Fisherman with a touch of irony, then more seriously, 'We'll cast off as soon as we can. It's Wednesday today, Saturday will surely be soon enough. Then there'll be plenty of weekend sailors out creating mayhem on the water, and no one will notice a battered old fishing boat.'

'In truth I should like to go on a very long and very delightful holiday,' said Odin again.

'Your wish shall be granted,' Ambrosius smiled. 'The day after the day after tomorrow.'

Sigbrit shook her head.

'Ambrosius, wait until I have unearthed some more about Captain Hans Adelstensfostre. It won't take long.'

'You haven't found anything up to now, have you, Lady Fair?'

'No, but I shall. I'm still waiting for answers to some of my requests to various European archives.'

'We sail on Saturday. Not a moment later.'

'No need to get cross,' remarked Sigbrit, nettled, then she realized the Fisherman feared that Brynhild was right.

Not a word was spoken for a long while, and the only sound to be heard was the regular cooing of the pigeons and from Our Saviour's Church the repetitive humming of hymns. Sigbrit went into the wheelhouse to fetch a jug of fruit juice. She was aware of Der Fremdling's shadow outlined against the innermost wall, and his presence, which had not worried her for some time, now struck her like a clammy fog. It seemed to be a disease that threatened to seep into her and paralyse her with indifference. She filled up the jug with juice and water, put out four glasses and hurried out again.

Sitting down opposite the Fisherman, she felt the sunshine warm her face, but the lovely evening made little impression on her. 'What a mess everything has turned into,' she said, pouring out the drinks.

'When the icebergs turn you know the ground you are standing on,' said Odin, scratching his beard. 'And, in truth, as the people of Smith's Town, not forgetting the people of Post Office Town, know how to freeze the sea, perchance they also know how to turn icebergs.'

'Sure enough they have overturned one already,' mumbled the Fisherman, taking his pipe out of his mouth. 'It's slipping,' he said, 'and it's slipping fast. No matter where we go we shall have to find a way back to the island sharpish, one that Odin can use.' He looked up at Brynhild Sigurdskær, who continued to move around restlessly. 'What have you found?'

'There's something wrong – with the words, the sentences, the constructions,' she said. 'But something is right too. There are not just three sayings, but at least four, maybe more. It will take time, and until we know the wording of them all, you should not stay here.'

The Fisherman chewed at his pipe stem for a good while without saying anything. Eventually he nodded and said: 'We'll set out, and we'll stay away. But be as quick as you can. We will not be totally safe in any of the places *Rikke-Marie* can get to.'

Sigrid looked from one to the other in astonishment. Then she looked at her watch and rose to her feet. 'Ambrosius, you can't stake everything on a bunch of outmoded kennings,' she said, fingers drumming on the rail. 'I know you think it's a waste of time, but no matter what you say, Captain Hans Adelstensfostre did once know the course to the island. Wait until I know more. It is not only words, it is reality. He is reality.'

Ambrosius the Fisherman shrugged his shoulders. 'We leave on Saturday,' he said tersely.

'We have to find out what became of his legacy!' Sigbrit insisted, her voice shrill with frustration.

'Lady Fair, you have until noon this Saturday.'

*

On that evening's news the Minister for Ecclesiastical Affairs appealed to the Born Anew Christians. If they voluntarily left Our Saviour's Church before noon on Saturday, no charges would be levelled against them and the occupation would have no consequences. If the church was not cleared by then, however, the authorities would find it necessary to liberate the church by force, and the Born Anew Christians would be charged with illegal entry on to the property. The newsreader then went on to other items.

Sigbrit was putting her notes together. She leafed through a few pages to see how far she had reached. She had already called every single public registry in Europe without getting a step closer to Captain Adelstensfostre's records. The court had told her everything known to them; that left only the museums. True enough, Captain Hans Adelstensfostre was not a particularly eminent man, yet he was not just anybody. Maybe one of the maritime museums might know of him.

'I thought we agreed you would give up that nonsense?' Fridtjof glared angrily over Sigbrit's shoulder at the notebook.

Sigbrit turned around; she had been so immersed in her own thoughts that she had forgotten him. 'You saw for yourself all those fanatical Doomsday Prophets in Our Saviour's Church, and there are hordes of others.' She was being defensive. 'We just have to find a way of getting Odin back to the island before any harm comes to him.'

'Come off it. Surely you don't imagine anything you do will have the slightest influence on what's going on? As for your Mr Odin, I don't think anyone would want to touch him. Don't forget we're in South Norseland. People here are far too down-to-earth to believe that rubbish. They are bored, but soon they'll get sick of playing at being fanatics and go home again.'

'To watch football and wallow in beer?'

'Something like that. Anyway those idiots in the church are nothing but a gang of ridiculous fanatics the government would do well to chuck out as soon as possible.'

'Maybe violence isn't the best method.'

'What is then?'

'Maybe they could be convinced they're on the wrong track.'

'And how would you do that?'

'I'm not sure yet. But there's one thing I am sure about; if Odin gets back to the island, everything will be easier to cope with.'

'That's just what the government is working towards.'

'Yes, but it is taking them far too long.'

'That's not your problem!' Fridtjof punched the sofa in exasperation.

'There you go again. What is my problem then?' Sigbrit shouted, red in the face.

'Your marriage, for instance!' Fridtjof looked her straight in the eye.

'I'm sorry,' Sigbrit said quietly, looking down. 'But I just have to stick at this for now.'

'No, you don't! Right now you should be working on your marriage. Because if you don't...'

'If I don't, what?'

'Then there soon won't be a marriage to work on.' Fridtjof had lowered his voice, but there was no doubt he meant what he said. 'You'll have to choose.'

Sigbrit looked at him as if she was seeing him for the first time. She leaned back and said, as calmly as she could: 'It ought not to be a choice.'

'It *is* a choice, and you had better make it pretty soon.'

The following morning Sigbrit did two things: first she called the bank and reported sick; next she rang all the maritime museums in Europe, one after the other, from north to south. Most of them were surprisingly obliging and helpful, no doubt happy that someone was showing an interest in their work. But her efforts didn't reap much reward. None of the museums had any articles, books or other documents that had belonged to a Captain Hans Adelstensfostre. The only place that had heard of him at all was the maritime museum in the Lower Lands, where the yacht *Freia II* appeared on a list of passing ships. In the late afternoon Sigbrit again rang the Lord Chamberlain, but he could only repeat that the court knew nothing about the man's movements after he left the King's service, except that he definitely did *not* end his days in the Royal Navy, or else his demise would have been on record.

It was past five when Sigbrit finally struck lucky. A woman from a small museum in Long North Norseland rang to say she was sorry but she had overlooked something; they actually did hold a small painting, of a cutter with the name *Frigg*, though not the frigate *Freia II*, but that the captain was stated to be Hans Adelstensfostre. Of course, thought Sigbrit, he had been obliged to take up a commission on a different boat.

'And what is the date of the painting?'

'1628,' said the woman.

'You'll never know how happy you've just made me,' exclaimed Sigbrit and thanked the woman for her help before hanging up.

Sigbrit drove straight past the bank, across the bridge to Firø and found a parking place at the start of the southern canal. She locked the car and ran down to the green and orange fishing boat. Ambrosius, up to his elbows in oil, was lubricating *Rikke-Marie's* engine.

Sigbrit told him about the painting.

'Lady Fair, you want us to change our route to the north instead of the south, do you?' he said, straightening up. 'Not only that, you also want us to go rummaging around the archives and libraries searching for a captain you have a feeling might have gone off to North Norseland some time in the seventeenth century. All because of a little painting?'

'Well, at least it's something concrete to go on,' exclaimed Sigbrit, as the Fisherman shook his head. 'It's obvious you think there's more sense in running around searching for mysterious old kennings,' she went on, unable to keep her voice down.

The Fisherman had finished with the engine and slowly and calmly wiped his hands and arms clean. When he was done he put down the rag and moved towards her. He looked her straight in the eye. 'Take it easy, Lady Fair. There are several good reasons for aiming south instead of north. First and foremost, Long North Norseland is too close, we'd run too great a risk of being recognized.'

Sigbrit looked away. She knew he was right, but on the other hand she felt Captain Adelstensfostre was worth the risk. 'I'm sorry,' she said quietly. 'Can't you see how important it is? Captain Hans Adelstensfostre is one of the few people we know who did set foot on the island. And he disappears from the South Norse Queendom just after the island drops out of all the records. I'm certain that isn't merely a coincidence.'

The Fisherman shrugged his shoulders and made no reply. He went over to the other side of *Rikke-Marie* and started to check the lifeboat fittings.

Sigbrit glanced at her watch; it was seven o'clock already. 'I hope you won't need that,' she said, pointing to the lifeboat.

'We'll manage all right.' Ambrosius did not look at her, but concentrated on what he was doing.

'Do you think you'll be away long?'

'Maybe.' Again he shrugged. Then he straightened up and nodded towards Our Saviour's Church. 'It partly depends on our friends over there.'

Sigbrit expected him to say something more but he only bent down again over the lifeboat.

'What is your plan?' she asked.

'Well, with this old lady we can't go fast. We'll cast off on Saturday about noon, when most of the weekend sailors are out, sail up the coast and moor for the night in Sandeleje. On Sunday morning we'll sail as far north as we can get and anchor off one of the small islands. After that, as soon as we have passed the northern tip of the Queendom, we'll turn south towards Long North Norseland and on as far as necessary.' The Fisherman had finished all he needed to do on the lifeboat, and at length turned to Sigbrit. 'Then we must just wait and see what Brynhild finds for us.'

Sigbrit's frustration returned. 'Ambrosius, how can you take that nonsense seriously when you won't follow up real information?' She couldn't help shouting. 'After all the work I have done, you sit here with your hands in your lap waiting for some magical solution to drop from above. Soon you'll be sounding more crazy than the Prophets of Doom!'

'Lady Fair,' said the Fisherman with a genial smile – her anger seemed to amuse him. 'All old sayings originate in something real. And the ones we're pursuing have at least as great a chance of leading us to the inward route to the island as your captain.'

'So now that I have finally found Captain Adelstensfostre, you want me to just forget about him?'

'No, Lady Fair. We aren't telling you to forget Captain

Adelstensfostre. We shall work with Brynhild on the sayings, and you meanwhile go on with your unravelling work here. Then we'll see who discovers what.'

'But I can't get any further than here, that's the whole trouble!' exclaimed Sigbrit. 'We need to go there.'

Ambrosius the Fisherman raised his eyebrows with a smile. 'Then you must go to Long North Norseland,' he said calmly.

'You know very well I can't!'

There was a short silence, then the Fisherman spoke again. 'Lady Fair, the decision is made. *Rikke-Marie* is going south.' His eyes were roguish. 'That's to say, unless you come along.'

'I can't,' murmured Sigbrit.

'All right, then the ship goes south.'

'You're being unreasonable.'

'Perhaps I am, but who said reasonableness was everything?'

*

It was like a python enveloping him, crushing him and slowly forcing the air out of him. Lennart Torstensson tried to push the branch back. He reached out for its head, the huge green crown, but each time he was about to catch hold, it grew another couple of metres away from him. He dug his nails into the branch, fixed his teeth in the rough bark and bit deep into the flesh. But the tree would not budge. Lennart was suffocating; he gave up, let it have its way!

The tree seemed to have been waiting for this. Instead of tightening its grip, the branch loosened it enough for him to breathe freely. The birds started to twitter; the ringing of a thousand thin shrill voices in chorus. He caught a word:

Ginnungagap. And the birds sang: *First there was nothing.* The ringing grew higher and more insistent, and the words ran together into a piercing note until all that was left was that penetrating pealing. It went on and on. Lennart opened his eyes: the telephone!

It was ten o'clock; he had overslept. Herr Hölzern was furious, his secretary said, he was waiting for a note Lennart had promised to finish regarding the negotiations on Drude Estrid Island or Hermod Skjalm Island, or whatever it was called. Was Lennart ill?

Lennart didn't know what to say. He was not ill, but he was dizzy: the world seemed to be swimming around him. And the piercing peal had started again; oh no, it was only the other phone in the secretary's office.

'I think I've got flu,' Lennart stammered, unable to find any other excuse.

'Are you sure you can't come, then? There's quite a shemozzle going on; apparently the South Norse have rejected the North Norse request.'

Suddenly Lennart was wide awake. 'Are you sure?'

'Yes, the fax is in front of me now. We've just received it: the South Norse government regrets that under the present circumstances and so on and so on... finds itself unable to comply with the North Norse request that Mr Odin Odin should take up residence in the North Norse Kingdom from 1st July this year. Such a decision could only be taken by Mr Odin Odin himself, and up to the present he has not expressed any wish to...' the secretary read out.

'Really ill,' croaked Lennart. 'I am seriously ill.'

'You'd better ring for the doctor,' said the secretary sympathetically.

'Yes, I'll do it at once.' Lennart hung up; the moment had come. *His* moment had come.

Now his dream came back to him. There was something frightening about these bizarre dreams, as if they were larger than he was. He was having them several times a week now. He went into the living room, picked up his notebook and wrote down the sentence he had just remembered before he woke up: '*Niflheim lay north of nothing, Muspelheim was south.*' It made no sense.

He had no time to ponder over it now; it was time to act. He took a red folder from a drawer in his desk and looked through the contents. Everything was ready: there was a rail ticket from the capital of the Western Bastion to Fredenshvile, two tickets for the ferry across the Strait from Fredenshvile to the little North Norse port of Lind, and two tickets for the train from Lind to the capital of North Norseland, Godeholm. The folder also contained notes in both South Norse and North Norse currency as well as a long description of the way to the green and orange fishing boat which Lennart had made on the basis of Mr Odin Odin's explanation. He called the ticket office and reserved a seat for Fredenshvile that evening and put away his folder.

Next he took down a small leather suitcase from the top of the wardrobe and looked through its contents. As well as a suit for himself and diverse essential toilet articles, there was a smaller suit with a hat that should fit Mr Odin Odin. When he was sure he had included everything, he ran a bath and lowered himself into it. He rested his head on a cushion of foam and thought through his plan once more. It was watertight: he would arrive at Fredenshvile Central Station on Saturday morning at 10.30, and before the evening he, the heroic Lennart Torstensson, would be in Godeholm with the citizen of Hermod Skjalm Island.

*

While Lennart made the final touches to his preparations, Sigbrit Holland was pushing documents from one side of her desk to the other without getting anywhere, and by the end of the afternoon the pile had grown even taller than it had been in the morning when she arrived. She couldn't concentrate. Tomorrow Ambrosius the Fisherman and Odin would leave, and she would be left behind with a vital clue to Captain Hans Adelstensfostre's movements that was beyond her powers to use.

She glanced around the office and studied the broad backs of her colleagues. The annual bonus depended on the collective earnings of the section, not on the achievements of an individual. Sigbrit knew that very well, and she also knew that some of her colleagues were sending her odd looks because for months she had not done her share. But she could do nothing about that; not even the ominous note from the Director, who wished to see her in his office on Monday at ten o'clock, could get her to focus on dollar fluctuations. Her fingers drummed lightly on the desk; how in the world was she going to persuade Ambrosius the Fisherman to sail to Long North Norseland?

She straightened her back. There was one thing she could do. She rolled her chair close to the computer and logged on to the web. Long North Norseland: what a time it took. Here it came at last: Adelstensfostre, Benjamin Adelstensfostre. Only one name was registered but with luck that would be enough. Sigbrit typed in a search request for other listed

Adelstensfostres in Long North Norseland, and an email to
Benjamin Adelstensfostre to ask him if he knew of any descendants of a Captain Hans Adelstensfostre who had lived at the
beginning of the seventeenth century. She sent off the message
and hoped that Benjamin Adelstensfostre would read his
emails before Saturday morning.

She started; one of her colleagues stood just behind her,
looking at the screen over her shoulder.

'If I were you I'd be a bit careful with that,' he whispered; he
didn't sound unfriendly but she sensed a touch of coolness.

Sigbrit sighed; she looked at the pile of documents before
her. With an effort she picked up the top one, but instead of
reading it she suddenly leaned back and began to laugh: her
country was about to disintegrate and here she sat trying to
create marginal profits on the equalization of exchange rates of
shares that could be completely lost if she did not succeed in
finding the route to the island.

But there was no way round it; she was paid to talk to currency dealers in other countries and attend to the documents
on her desk, not to search for solutions to the country's problems. In any case there was nothing she could do just now but
wait for the reply from Benjamin Adelstensfostre.

It was after seven o'clock and she was almost finished with
the last report of the day when the reply came: there were eight
adult Adelstensfostres in Long North Norseland, and as far as
Benjamin Adelstensfostre was aware, all of them were descendants of Captain Hans Adelstensfostre. Why was she searching
for them?

A long story, impossible to explain here, wrote Sigbrit, but if
anyone travelled to Long North Norseland to seek further details,
would Benjamin Adelstensfostre be willing to meet them?

The answer was affirmative. Sigbrit now had a telephone number and an address; Ambrosius the Fisherman could not get out of this. It was too late to go out to the green and orange fishing boat now, but that didn't matter. There was still masses of time before midday on Saturday.

Early on Saturday morning Sigbrit told her husband that she had to drive into the bank to finish off some work.

For safety's sake she left the car in the bank car park and walked with brisk strides across the bridge to Firø. She turned down the cobbled street beside the southern canal. It was a peaceful morning. The canal flowed silently, the locals had not yet emerged from their houses, and none of the Pious was to be seen. Sigbrit slowed up and sauntered calmly down the middle of the street. She leaned her head back and closed her eyes, enjoying the early sunshine. She had almost reached the bend in the canal when a white van suddenly came rushing towards her. Instinctively she leaped aside, but the vehicle brushed past close by her before she fell to the ground.

She sat up and looked for the van; what kind of crazy driving was that? Apart from some soreness in her right side, where she had landed, no harm was done, and she got to her feet without difficulty. She gazed around – something seemed to be missing. Then she caught sight of the two policemen who normally patrolled the quay. They lay on their stomachs side by side. One of them raised his head and looked around to every side, then they both got slowly to their feet. Suddenly fear gripped Sigbrit, and she looked over at the green and orange fishing boat – or rather in the direction of it. For where *Rikke-Marie* should have been there was now a gaping hole in the line of boats.

She was too late.

Sigbrit kicked a stone, which flew into the water with a splash. She looked at the scrap of paper in her hand: Benjamin Adelstenfostre's address and phone number. Then she looked at the gap in the moored boats again. Immediately she knew what she had to do.

ASK AND EMBLA

Odin, Vile, Ve
along the seashore strolled
ahead of them on the golden sand
stood ash and elm

Their trunks washed white by salty swells
shaping slowly homo sapiens
truly purer than the virgin
  – before transmuting into man

A gift of doubtful blessing
Odin soul and life blew into trees
Vile gave them mind and motion
Ve bestowed the senses five

Ash and Embla
who soon were
soon were more

  Thus, Midgard's silence came to end

'FIRØ BRIDGE,' CALLED the bus driver.

The bus came to a stop, the doors opened and the heroic Lennart Torstensson got out, lugging his small leather suitcase. He strode across the bridge at a brisk pace, then turned without hesitation to the right along the southern canal. He

was in good humour and walked fast, glancing without interest at the boats on the canal, running through his plan again
in his head: as soon as Mr Odin Odin had changed into the
clothes in the suitcase, Lennart would hail a taxi and drive to
the harbour, where they would take the flying boat to North
Norseland. When they arrived at the other side of the Strait
they had only a simple train journey left. With a bit of luck
they would arrive at Godeholm before evening and although it
was Saturday he did not doubt that the Prime Minister, directly after he had been informed of their arrival, would wish to
meet the Hermod Skjalm islander as well as Lennart himself
– the epitome of North Norse courage and wit, national hero,
symbol of –

Lennart was almost swept off his feet. 'Sorry,' he murmured
automatically, but no answer came from the woman who had
rushed past him. She never so much as turned her head, main-
taining her wild dash up the street, her long dark hair flying
out behind her. Odd, thought Lennart, but then his attention
was caught by two policemen yelling frantically into their
mobiles before leaping into a police car and driving off with
siren wailing. Something must have happened; he shrugged
and concentrated again on the canal. Here was the bend, here
the small park with rose bushes, and one, two, three, what? It
wasn't there! He counted the boats again. Instead of a green
and orange fishing boat, number four from the bend, there
was nothing but a gaping, empty mooring place. Could he have
made a mistake? He grabbed the directions out of his pocket.
No, everything matched Mr Odin Odin's thorough description:
the old buildings, the big tree, the statue in the park, yes, even
the white motorboat to the left of the empty mooring. But
what if Mr Odin had not been telling the truth? No, it was

impossible; the little old man had been so keen to get to North Norseland to find the Veterinarius for his horse.

'Hell!' Lennart kicked peevishly at a feeble-looking roadside sapling. He looked around. It was still quite early and the quay was almost deserted. On a bench between the canal and the little park he found a surprisingly sober drunk.

'*Rikke-Marie?*' growled the sober drunk when Lennart had twice repeated his question. 'Well, she was darned well here earlier this morning. Yes, just over there, that's where old Ambrosius the Fisherman keeps her.' The sober alcoholic stood up with some difficulty and pointed at the fourth mooring after the bend in the canal. He rubbed his eyes and went on, annoyed: 'As you can see, God knows she's not there now!' He sat down again with a bump.

'Any idea where they might have gone?' asked Lennart in his clearest North Norse.

The sober alcoholic screwed up his eyes and shook his head blankly, and Lennart had to repeat his question twice more.

'P'ff, who knows,' rumbled the sober alcoholic. 'Maybe they've gone for a little trip in the sunshine,' he chuckled. Then he narrowed his eyes and stared suspiciously at Lennart Torstensson. 'Tell me, you're not one o' them Doomsday Prophets, are you?'

Lennart looked indignantly at the sober alcoholic and turned his back without answering. Since he had nothing better to do, he strolled slowly along the quay to the main street. Then he strolled back again. He did this a couple of times, back and forth, back and forth. When he grew tired of strolling he sat down on a bench not far from the one occupied by the shameless sober drunk. Lennart leaned back and braced himself for a lengthy wait.

It was not long, however, before strange things began to happen. First, three young men who had come walking quietly along beside the canal, set eyes on the empty mooring place, exchanged a few heated words and ran back the way they had come as fast as their legs could carry them, only to reappear a moment later with a crowd of excited people in train. Next came a group of bald men and women dressed in brown robes like monks' habits, smoking something smelling unmistakably like cannabis and singing a hypnotic hymn of which Lennart could not make out a single word – only to burst into horrified shrieks when they caught sight of the obvious gap where the green and orange fishing boat should have been. Lastly, the two policemen who had just left came back and walked about, glaring suspiciously at all and sundry and asking questions here and there, soon backed up by the arrival of four more cars.

Lennart's view from the bench gradually became completely blocked by confused and hysterical people, and when the danger of being crushed grew really threatening, he got to his feet. The quay was now a scene of huge chaos. Desperate figures pushed and pulled in all directions, and those nearest the water were in constant risk of falling in, until a few did fall in and the rest created a counter-move that opened a few inches of space. At that moment Lennart spotted a young bespectacled man climbing up on to the white motorboat and on up the ladder to the sundeck.

The bespectacled man raised one hand and to Lennart's great surprise the noise died down – apart from the terrifying hymn – immediately.

'I, Simon Peter the Second, of body and soul a humble fisherman, have to announce that something frightful has happened,' shouted the bespectacled man. 'We have been struck by a catastrophe, a misfortune.' He raised his voice to a formidable shout. 'The Devil has bruised us!' His hearers paled. 'The Mighty One has vanished!' The bespectacled man pointed accusingly at the deserted mooring, blinking passionately as if he had trouble holding back his tears. Then his eyes brightened, and he looked around at his band. 'The Mighty One has been kidnapped,' he said hoarsely, and raising his voice, he shouted at the top of his lungs: 'The Mighty One, the Son of the Lord, Our Saviour and Redeemer, has been taken away!'

'The Mighty One has been taken away!' echoed the spectators.

'The Mighty One has been taken away by the unbelievers. He has been carried away by the North Norsemen!' The bespectacled man blinked passionately, and his arm pumped up and down.

'Carried away by the North Norsemen!' roared the crowd. 'Carried away by the North Norsemen!'

Lennart did not feel too happy about this turn of events. He fidgeted uneasily and looked around. He could not see the shameless sober drunk, who was the only person able to reveal his North Norse nationality, and calmed down again. But when the Entrusted Disciple and First Apostle began to describe the punishment and pains the Born Anew Christians would inflict on the North Norsemen until they released the Mighty One, it was time for Lennart to make tracks.

The heroic if somewhat shaken Lennart Torstensson started to squeeze his way out of the crowd, clenching his teeth so that a momentary lack of concentration might not cause him to put North Norse words to an apology to those he dug in the side or

whose toes he unavoidably trod on. The crowd began to thin
out and Lennart hurried along the quay as fast as he could
without, he hoped, arousing suspicion. He had not gone far
before the quay was blocked by another group of excited
people, smaller and clearly of Oriental origin, but in quite as
wild a state as the first lot. Lennart pushed his way through into
the back rows.

'Truly, mankind is always lost except the few who believe and
act righteously and encourage each other to find the truth and
encourage each other to endure,' said a frail old, dark-skinned
man. 'Allah tries us, he tries our faith, our patience, our goodness. We must not give way, but hold fast to our faith.' The old
man paused to catch his breath. 'We must not let our human
weakness get the better of us and deal cruelly with our brothers, whom we ought to lead into the true way. We must not let
our hearts fill with hatred, but instead allow them to swell and
blossom with goodness and love for the only One.' The old
man bowed his head as if he had already lost a battle that had
not yet begun; he could not fight the Mullahs in and outside
South Norseland and the angry young men among his own
followers at one and the same time. He went on in a weary
voice: 'Regardless of what has befallen the Mighty One, the
Messenger of Allah, the Prophet Jesus, those who have done
wrong will be punished by Allah and Allah alone. We shall not
allow the wrongdoers to lure us from the path of love and peace
which Allah...'

Lennart could not hear any more, because a small group of
young people beside him were whispering to each other
angrily. One of them, a strikingly beautiful black-eyed woman,
stepped forward. 'We have had enough!' she yelled, glaring
with angrily flashing eyes at the old mullah. 'True believers are

those only who believe in Allah and his Messenger and do not doubt, but fight with their possessions and their life in Allah's way; thus do they follow the truth.' The woman tossed her head and her long hair danced under her hijab. She gazed around the Muslim Modernists, but it was a great sin to rise against an elderly prayer leader, a learned man like Hasan Al-Basri, and no one met her eyes.

'Truly, the genuine Din with Allah is Islam. And those who were given the Scripture, were not in strife with each other until after understanding had come to them – because they envied each other,' said Hasan Al-Basri quietly, breaking the bewildered silence that had followed Aisha's furious outburst.

'The infidels have carried off Allah's Messenger,' continued the furious woman with flashing eyes. 'The infidels know that if they permit the Mighty One to speak he will prove their wrongdoing. They know he will say that Allah is the only one, and that Muhammad his Prophet has laid the only trail to be followed, and that only those who have followed this trail will meet their Creator in the next world.'

'May the old become wise, and the young become old,' sighed Hasan Al-Basri, and closed his eyes to beseech Allah silently for the true peace of soul that comes with the privileged understanding of age – so that the responsibility for the world and the state of things may no longer rest on his shoulders. 'May Allah's will be done.'

'The moment has come when we must take up arms. That is Allah's will!' shouted Aisha, again casting her gaze around, and this time many eyes met hers.

'Indeed, now is the time for action!' shouted her brother Ali.

'Now is the time! Now is the time,' came the reply from the others.

Inertia was on their side; the Muslim Modernists were tired of peace and quiet, and of the repeated humiliations they suffered in the battles around the square closest to the Mighty One. At the same moment as Aisha turned round, gestured in the air and started to walk up the quay, the Muslim Modernists ceased to exist and instead took on the guise of Muslim Militants.

In the meantime Simon Peter II had finished his sermon from the top of *Rikke-Marie's* former white motorboat neighbour, and the Born Anew Christians were now on their way back to Our Saviour's Church to strengthen their guard. Lennart sneaked up a stairway, and not until the last of the Born Anew Christians had passed by did he dare to return to the all-too-empty berth.

Other excited groups came and went, among them a troop of women constantly invoking the Virgin Mary, but Lennart did not feel like listening to any more fanatical nonsense. He sat down on the bench and blocked his ears while he considered his next move; becoming a national hero was no easy matter.

In the course of the day, while Lennart was making huge efforts to become a national hero, two important events took place in Fredenshvile. One was that the police – amply assisted by tear-gas and other more potent weapons – forced the Born Anew Christians to leave Our Saviour's Church. The other was when a small grubby handwritten note, tied firmly to a round stone, was thrown through a window – which luckily happened to be open – and straight into Ezekiel the Righteous's parents' living room.

Where the mother, the father, the five remaining uncles, their wives and children, with the widow of the sixth and a number of various doctors had been ineffective, the grubby note succeeded: Ezekiel the Righteous started to eat again, and Ezekiel the Righteous started to speak.

'Zer ith going to be a thtupenthous war!' lisped Ezekiel the Righteous through the gap in his upper teeth. 'Armagethon will c-c-c-ome. Blooth will flow like a flooth through the thtreetth, and many people will die. C-c-c-ourage and bolthneth will be tethted. That ith Yahve's tetht of hith chothen people.' Ezekiel the Righteous thought of the grim sketch on one side of the grubby note and the words asking Ezekiel the Righteous and the Reborn Jews to release the Messiah, the Mighty One, from his captivity.

The only problem Ezekiel the Righteous had to solve was a question of numbers. Even if he included women and children, he could not count more than forty-seven Reborn Jews, while the Born Anew Christians obviously numbered not only ten but more than a hundred times as many.

'The chothen people were alwayth few,' lisped Ezekiel the Righteous. 'But didn't we win the Theven Days' War all the thame?' With their natural right of birth, the righteousness of their cause and with God on their side the Reborn Jews could not lose.

At this point the prophetic son fainted away – which was taken to be a sure sign of his sanctity – and his father and the five remaining uncles carried him reverently to bed, where the women bathed his brow and dripped honey-water into his half-open mouth. Then, in order not to disturb the prophetic son, all the relatives together with the few non-related Reborn Jews left the parents' apartment. For safety's sake the youngest of the five remaining uncles stayed on the staircase; with the end of the world approaching one could not be too careful.

Perhaps that was not such a bad idea, because the prophetic son's ousted brother had not yet decided whether he would leave it at the stone and the grubby note. To be more precise, Ezra had lost patience. Ezra had lost patience because the attempt to kidnap the little old man had gone wrong – which threatened his position as the intellectual leader of his new comrades – and he was upset because none of his family had come to apologize to him and persuade him to come back home. As he had no immediate means of changing the latter situation, it was all the more important for him to obtain redress for the first without delay.

They called themselves the Avengers, his new comrades, and they were against government, religion, foreigners and a whole lot more that Ezra couldn't quite grasp. He had met one of them early in the morning on the day after he had been thrown out of his home. And because he was freezing cold, and penniless and had nowhere to go, Ezra had gone along with the young brown-clad man with the crew-cut, who was seriously under the influence of something that Ezra found out later was merely good old-fashioned beer and schnapps. Ezra didn't think much of sleeping on the sofa in the damp basement flat, which was always full of people and stank of stale beer, had overflowing ashtrays and generations of dust mites, and most of all he didn't think much of his new friends, who were primitive, ignorant and brutal. But soon he realized that the comrades offered him a unique chance, and had immediately changed his name to Ace; no need to generate ill feeling.

They were all thrilled – the Avengers – and hadn't the slightest suspicion of the real motive driving their new comrade, as Ace (alias Ezra) devised his plan to lure the Reborn Jews to throw themselves into a doomed battle.

*

Ambrosius the Fisherman opened his eyes; a sound had woken him up. The *Rikke-Marie* rocked gently. The Fisherman sat up and listened, but there was nothing to hear except the soft lapping of the water along the boat's keel. He really ought to take a look around. Now all was quiet; no doubt it was only the wind. Ambrosius lay down again, but no sooner had his head touched the pillow than the sound came again: a faint tapping, as if someone was cautiously knocking on wood.

There was no way round it. He sat up and was about to light the wall lamp, when he thought better of it; no need to show he was on the way. He rubbed his eyes to wake himself up, then swung his legs out of the bunk and lowered his feet to the cold planks. The Fisherman wore only a T-shirt, and he fumbled around in the dark before he found his trousers. As quietly as possible he crept up the ladder and fumbled his way through the darkness of the wheelhouse to the nearest window. The clock on the wall strummed half past one just as he pulled a corner of the curtain aside and peered out into the deserted blue summer night. He tried the front window, but nothing was to be seen from there either.

Ambrosius the Fisherman stiffened; the low knocking started up again, and this time right beside him. He peered sideways out of the little window beside the door and saw the dim outline of a single person. If there were no more he should be able... He opened a drawer and drew out a heavy kitchen knife. Raising the knife in one hand, he pushed open the door.

'Oh, it's you.' The Fisherman lowered the knife and took a pace back so that she could enter. He lit the lamp.

Sigbrit Holland dumped her heavy bag on the floor.

'So it was as I thought...' She pointed at the knife in the Fisherman's hand.

'Mm, we left in a bit of a hurry,' he rumbled and put the knife back in the drawer.

'Who were they?'

'No idea. A group of men with crew-cuts in brown clothes in a white goods van. Quite well armed, unless the weapons were sham, of course. They could have been anyone; Doomsday Prophets or their opponents.' He laughed drily and ran his fingers through his untidy hair. 'We didn't think we ought to wait and ask.' Ambrosius looked at Sigbrit's travelling bag. 'Lady Fair,' he said, suddenly gentle. 'Let us show you where you can sleep.'

'Am I still welcome?'

The Fisherman made no reply, picked up the bag and climbed down the ladder to the cabin. He lit a small wall lamp which gave out a faint golden light. Sigbrit looked around her. Apart from the time she had changed her clothes when the *Rikke-Marie* had been stranded on the rocks, it was the first time she had been down here. Here were two bunks, opposite each other, and a small table near one. Above both bunks hung several shelves full of books, otherwise there were one or two cupboards, a chest, a radio and two portholes – that was all.

'Shh, Odin is asleep in there.' Ambrosius pointed to a low door in the end wall. Then he put Sigbrit's bag on the berth behind the small table. It was made up, though no one had slept in it.

Sigbrit wondered who the bunk had been made up for. There was no sign of Brynhild Sigurdskær, but her rucksack lay at the end of the bed.

'I'm sorry I woke you up,' she said.

'You must sleep here tonight. Tomorrow you can change over with Odin, if you wish,' said the Fisherman, not looking at her.

Sigbrit nodded. There was a metre and a half or perhaps two metres between her bed and the Fisherman's, and the sudden proximity made her feel awkward. He did too, she noticed.

'The bathroom and toilet are up forward.' Ambrosius pointed to another low door behind the ladder up to the wheel-house.

Sigbrit pulled her sweater over her head. 'Ambrosius, thank you,' she said quietly.

The Fisherman smiled and rubbed his chin. 'We're the ones to say thank you,' he replied warmly. Then he added almost brusquely, 'Goodnight', and turned his back on her.

Sigbrit found her sponge bag and went into the bathroom. When she came back, Ambrosius was already back under his duvet with closed eyes. She crept over to her bag, searched through her things and found her pyjamas. She changed with her back to the Fisherman and slipped into bed. In spite of her exhaustion she couldn't fall asleep. Thoughts and scraps of sentences whirled around in her head and she kept tossing and turning. She thought about the letter she had sent to the bank, about calling her incredulous parents and about the unpleasant quarrel with her husband. 'If you go now you are not to come back,' he had said. 'I'm sorry,' she had replied, 'but I have to do this.' 'Goodbye then.' Fridtjof had slammed the door behind him, and she had packed her things.

Early next morning, shortly after Sigbrit had at last

managed to fall asleep, and as the sun slowly heralded day, the green and orange fishing boat set a course for Long North Norseland.

*

Benjamin Adelstensfostre was younger than Sigbrit had imagined and perhaps even a year or two younger than herself. He was tall and thin and had big dreamy eyes in a narrow almost feminine face. The dark blond hair that fell to his shoulders was combed back, and every time he moved it flowed over his black silk shirt.

With a gentle almost shy smile, he led the Fisherman and Sigbrit into a room that had to be the living room although it resembled anything but. A piano that stood beside a stereo system and some complicated recording gear took up almost half the room. In the other half was an amazing muddle. Things lay around everywhere: clothes had been flung down amongst piles of books, jotting paper, a violin and a flute, full as well as empty bottles, used glasses and here and there a dirty plate. Benjamin Adelstensfostre made no apology for the mess, merely cleared the sofa of clothes and books to make room for his guests. He sat down in a tattered armchair on the other side of the crammed sofa table. Without asking them first he poured out three glasses of cold elderberry juice. He hummed quietly to himself and smiled shyly, waiting for their explanation. Sigbrit returned his smile, convinced he would not be able to help them. But Benjamin Adelstensfostre soon showed she was quite mistaken.

'Captain Hans Adelstensfostre,' he repeated slowly, after she had asked. 'Yes, we are all his descendants, everyone in Long North Norseland who carries that name.' He spoke with a drawl, but his North Norse was clear and easy to understand. While he spoke he looked Sigbrit straight in the eye almost as if he had forgotten the Fisherman's presence. 'As you know, Captain Adelstensfostre came to Long North Norseland some time around the year 1620. As far as I have discovered, he was a fugitive from something in South Norseland. What that was I have never been able to ascertain. Perhaps he had to escape from some debt, perhaps from a crime or maybe from a woman, who knows?' Benjamin Adelstensfostre shrugged his shoulders and cast down his gaze. Then he met Sigbrit's eyes again. 'But I have the feeling you have come to ask about something different?'

Sigbrit was about to reply when Ambrosius the Fisherman put down his glass on the table with a thump. 'Yes, we are searching for something quite different,' he said abruptly, and explained in unusually chilly tones that they were engaged in historical research of the traffic through the Strait during the seventeenth century and therefore wanted to know whether Captain Hans Adelstensfostre had left any documents or diaries that might contain relevant information.

That was a lie, and Benjamin saw through it; Sigbrit could tell from the brief mocking flash in his eyes. Yet the young man made no sign, and when Ambrosius had finished his explanation he replied in the same lightly drawling, gentle tone as before.

'Unfortunately, I can't be of any use to you.' He took a mouthful of elderberry juice and then addressed himself solely to Sigbrit. 'You see, after Captain Hans Adelstenfostre came to Long North Norseland he fathered a son. That son had eight children, only one of whom was a boy, who was given the name Hans Henrik, after his father. The son, Hans Henrik II, had two sons and a daughter himself, and as was then the custom the daughter was married outside the family, the firstborn son inherited the entire fortune, and the second went out into the world to seek his fortune, which he apparently found in the capital of Long North Norseland, here in Fjordenhavn.' Benjamin leaned back in his chair. 'I'm afraid I and most of the other Adelstensfostres around here are descendants of this second son.'

'Do you know whether anyone descended from the firstborn son is still alive?' Ambrosius the Fisherman made an effort to sound friendly.

'You're not in much luck there,' drawled Benjamin. 'There were two. One of them, Oluf Adelstensfostre, a doctor, died a few years ago. As far as I know his widow, Asta Adelstensfostre, still lives in Kristiansfjord, a town on the west coast, some distance to the north. I doubt whether she will be able to tell you much more. But who knows, maybe her husband left a book or two.'

'And the other one?'

'Yes, there was a brother. I can't recall his name, but wait a moment...' He rose and began to search through some of the piles of books and papers. To their astonishment he found what he was looking for almost at once. Then he sat down on the sofa beside Sigbrit. 'The family tree,' he said, unfolding the document. 'You see, some years ago I got the idea of tying up the threads of my family history. Strange, perhaps, but –' He shrugged his shoulders, obviously indifferent to what his hearers might think. 'Look, here it is.' He pointed to a name. 'Harald Adelstensfostre, a twin. I don't know where he lives. I did once decide to track down all the Adelstenfostres. Maybe I was just curious, maybe I was searching for a family; I lost my parents early in life.' He flung out his arms as if to say that was nothing for them to worry about. 'But I couldn't find this one. He went to sea when young, something about a girl, and no one in the family knew what became of him. Or rather, his brother Oluf wouldn't talk about it. That was a little odd, I remember thinking. Perhaps he just jumped ship in some foreign harbour.' Benjamin paused to look at the family tree. Then it seemed he became aware that he was sitting very close to Sigbrit and stood up with flaming cheeks.

'There was a cousin, Hannelil,' he went on quickly, at last addressing the Fisherman directly. 'Her name is in last year's telephone directory for Fjordenhavn, and no doubt she's still there. You might try her.' He shrugged once more. 'As far as I know, that completes the present Adelstensfostre family now. There are not many of us left.' He turned to Sigbrit again. 'You have another problem. As I was interested in the origin of the name I looked only in the male line. If the books and documents had been left to one of the daughters for a generation you could be faced with a huge if not impossible task.' He smiled and looked down. 'If you stay here in Fjordenhavn for a while, I might be able to help.' He looked up again shyly. 'But no doubt it will be easier to get hold of the facts...' He spoke lightly, as if to emphasize he knew quite well they had not been telling the truth and it was all one to him.

'Thank you,' said Ambrosius coldly and explained briefly that of course they had numerous other captains to search for. Then he stood up.

Sigbrit looked at the Fisherman in surprise. Then a smile

spread over her face and she too rose to her feet.

Benjamin Adelstensfostre went to the door with them. 'Take care, the waters in the Long North Norse skerries are rough.' He looked at Sigbrit. 'Let me know if there's anything I can do,' he said mildly, and closed the door behind him.

*

'*An island is an island until it is no longer an island,*' sang Brynhild Sigurdskær in her hoarse voice, as soon as Ambrosius the Fisherman and Sigbrit Holland entered the wheelhouse. The shabby mahogany tabletop was covered with papers and opened books. The transparent woman picked up one of the books and repeated the adage.

Brynhild had been on board the green and orange fishing boat when Sigbrit woke up the first morning, when they were already far out at sea. She had sailed with Odin and Ambrosius to Sand Havn, where she had left the boat and not returned until early next morning, bearing a large box of books. The sleeping arrangements had been allocated in such a way that Sigbrit and Brynhild shared the first cabin, where the bunks met in a point, while Odin and the Fisherman shared the larger middle cabin.

'Odin, we may have some good news for you,' Sigbrit overheard the transparent woman say.

'It's a bit early to put it like that,' remarked Ambrosius the Fisherman calmly.

'Well, at least it's a start,' Sigbrit told him. 'Now we know that Captain Hans Adelstensfostre ended his days here in Long North Norseland, we know his descendants are here, and tomorrow we'll talk to one of them.'

'There's a cross-reference to a saying that begins with "*Name the island . .*" to which the book's author has never been able to find the ending.' Brynhild spoke as if she had never been interrupted.

'When is that from?' Ambrosius sat down on the bench, filled his pipe and lit it.

'It was first registered at the beginning of the eighteenth century.'

'That's over a hundred years after the island vanished.'

'A hundred years in the people's mind is an adage for the wise,' said Odin quietly.

Brynhild smiled. 'Yes, this one must be counted too.'

'Then we have four,' said the Fisherman. 'Of which only one is complete, the one you just read out: "*An island is an island until it is no longer an island.*"' He laughed drily and rubbed his chin. 'It certainly confirms what we know about the island.'

Sigbrit looked impatiently from one to the other. 'If Captain Adelstensfostre gives us the route to the fairway we shan't need to play with these old sayings any more,' she said.

The Fisherman smoked his pipe in silence, then took it from his mouth. 'We're not so sure about that,' he replied. 'Adelstensfostre or no, we are still far from getting any hint of the way in. And even if by some fantastic stroke of luck we find the course we are looking for, it would still be a good idea to know the forces at play on the island before we approach it.'

Sigbrit pushed back her hair thoughtfully. 'So you think that whatever makes planes disappear could also affect a boat?'

'Why not?'

Sigbrit nodded reluctantly. Then she started to laugh. 'Then how could Captain Hans Adelstensfostre sail both in and out again?'

'There is still one thing we don't know about, Lady Fair,' Ambrosius the Fisherman spoke as if the discussion was at an end, but Sigbrit didn't give in so easily.

'Up to now we know that some few planes have vanished from above the island, to be accurate, six: four South Norse and two North Norse. There could be many reasons for their disappearance.' She threw out her hands. 'Climatic movements or topographical conditions, and so on.'

'Lady Fair, when did you last see a typhoon in the Strait?' Ambrosius shook his head. 'Don't forget, there is more between heaven and earth than you or we know about.'

Sigbrit's fingers began to drum softly on the kitchen table. 'Ambrosius, if there's anything at all in this, it is a physical problem and not a question of supernatural forces.'

'Call it what you like. The fact remains that there are forces at play here that we humble creatures don't understand...'

'At this point in history, yes.'

'Well then,' rumbled the Fisherman, laughing slyly. 'Although humanity has no understanding of a certain power, not to mention a name for or even some recognition of its existence, that doesn't necessarily mean that it doesn't exist.' He paused briefly. 'So even if the strange conditions on the island do have a physical explanation, it's far from certain that we – or any others for that matter – will be able to put a name to it.'

'Yes, well...' began Sigbrit, but Ambrosius had not finished.

'Now if the saying can give us a clue to what's going on, perhaps we can find a way of getting around the phenomenon too, even without being able to fully understand it.'

'So you think the island is another mysterious Bermuda Triangle?'

'Mystery or no, you can certainly imagine something of the kind.'

'Oh, come on,' said Sigbrit dismissively. 'Next you're going to tell me that Odin really *is* Jesus Christ, or the Lord God himself!'

'Modern civilization can only accept what it can weigh, measure and put into words,' broke in Brynhild softly. 'How convenient it is to ignore all that, all the forces, senses and incidents that our brains are too small to hold.' The transparent woman laughed silently.

Sigbrit bit her lip, uncertainly. 'Maybe you're right,' she admitted reluctantly. 'But on the other hand, you could be wrong. Whichever, it doesn't help us, for up to now you haven't found anything more than I have.' She sighed. 'The only thing we do know is that behind a line of rocky cliffs there is a little, inaccessible and nameless island with two villages, a lake, seaweed-thatched houses, fields, a few ponies, some sheep and other animals as well as a number of trees.'

'True, and there is also the Blacksmith, who knows everything worth knowing about horses,' added Odin, happy the conversation had finally touched on something he knew about. 'And Oldmother Rikke-Marie and Mother Marie and Ida-Anna and Ingolf and all the other children and...'

'And Odin's horse with a broken leg,' laughed Ambrosius the Fisherman.

Brynhild Sigurdskær rose. 'Where mermaids meet, sailors fear to go,' she said, whirling around and leaving the wheelhouse with a book in each hand.

*

Hannelil Adelstensfostre was a disappointment; she had never heard of Captain Hans Adelstensfostre, nor did she know there were two lines of the family, of which she belonged to Hans Henrik II's side. And – which was far more important for Sigbrit and Ambrosius the Fisherman – Hannelil Adelstensfostre had neither inherited documents nor books from his parents; they had been modest folk who owned no other books than the Bible. Hannelil could not even help them with Asta Adelstensfostre's telephone number. But no one could reproach her for that since Asta Adelstensfostre did not have a telephone.

The only thing left to them was to set course for Kristiansfjord, a voyage that even in the best of conditions would take at least a week.

Before they left Fjordenhavn Sigbrit visited the local library and borrowed books on everything from climate, topography and geography to more supernatural phenomena such as earth radiation, waterlines, and one or two about the Bermuda Triangle, which Ambrosius the Fisherman wanted to look at: if they were to search for unknown forces, they must at least have some system in their research.

To start with the weather was favourable. The sun broke through the morning mists early and made the air warm and inviting. There was not much wind and the sea was calm. They could sail from early morning until long into the light August evenings and put many sea miles of the beautiful coastal skerries behind them. But after six days of sunshine, with only a day's voyage from Kristiansfjord, the weather changed. The sky became overcast, the wind rose, and in moments the waves were metres high. The green and orange fishing boat was thrown from side to side, and soon the rain came pouring down. Although it was only midday Ambrosius the Fisherman had to set course towards land, and it was not long before *Rikke-Marie* anchored up in a small coastal town where a single quay passed for a harbour.

While the horizon line was invisible, the news bulletin crackled out of the Fisherman's ancient radio and cheerfully advised them that the bad weather would go on for several days, and that the situation in Fredenshvile had deteriorated considerably. Ever since the Born Anew Christians had been driven out of Our Saviour's Church – with something the South Norse government described as limited but inevitable damage, and Simon Peter II, called now a martyr, now a saint, and the injuries to eleven of God's innocent children – the Born Anew Christians had laid siege to the South Norse Parliament, and only a strong police force safeguarded the members going in and out. The Born Anew Christians still insisted on being allotted a church, and also demanded that the South Norse government break off diplomatic relations with the Long North Norse government until the false True Christians had returned Mr Odin Odin. The news ended with a promise of rain and more rain, and Ambrosius the Fisherman switched off the radio.

'When madness spreads, it spreads rapidly,' said Brynhild Sigurdskær. 'Before the curtain falls, the South Norse Queendom will burn.'

To Odin's ears that sounded like something he had heard before, but he couldn't quite place it. It also sounded a little like something that first Mr Bramsentorpf and later Vicar Valentino had talked about. The little old man twisted his beard around his fingers and asked quietly: 'I wonder if various ill tidings in all truth, and when all's said and done, can mean one and the same thing?' But before anyone could reply, Odin had fallen asleep, overwhelmed by the magnitude of his own idea.

'Madness or no,' said Sigbrit softly so as not to wake Odin, 'might it perhaps calm down the troubled waters a bit if we sent them a telegram saying that Odin is fine and is neither in the hands of the South Norse government nor the North Norse True Christians or anyone else at all?'

'However much we want to do it, we can't,' rumbled Ambrosius, glancing out the window at the merciless rain. 'Firstly, no one would believe us. And if anyone did, it would certainly make a bad situation worse, for then those believers would start to search for us. And we really don't want to lose all the time that would take, because most of our work lies ahead and not behind us.'

This brought them back to the books, and while for three days the heavens poured down their largesse, Sigbrit, Ambrosius and Brynhild read one book after another, and Odin tried to read his forgotten thoughts about what had come before Smith's Town and the meteor storm. On the fourth day – after a large group of True Christians had again succeeded in reaching Fredenshvile and attacking the Born Anew Christians – the skies finally brightened. Drenching rain became drizzle and then stopped, and before evening they were able to sit out on deck. The time had come to plan their next step.

Sigbrit had not found anything worth noting. She had concentrated on the climate of the Strait, its geology and –topography, but there had been nothing of interest. As they already knew, there were no volcanoes in the Strait, no cosmic lines crossed each other, so there was no potential for earthquake, and no tornadoes or cyclones had ever been observed. There remained autumn storms which at times could reach hurricane force, and winters cold enough to be pretty testing. None of these phenomena were exceptional in the Strait and thus on the island, but struck both South Norseland and North Norseland in equal proportions. Moreover, none of the disappearances of the six planes could be ascribed to either cold or autumn storms, since none of the planes had been exposed to either one or the other.

'That's all I have been able to find,' Sigbrit wound up her report despondently.

Ambrosius the Fisherman was more enthusiastic. 'Evil areas!' he said. 'In the course of the past century and a half there have been apparently inexplicable disappearances of at least forty ships and twenty aeroplanes in the Bermuda Triangle. In all these cases the experts have had to write off normal explanations such as tropical storms, typhoons, underwater volcanoes and earthquakes, flood-waves and that kind of thing. They have come to the conclusion that this is a place where from time to time unknown forces are at work, a so-called evil area.' The Fisherman leaned back and smoked his pipe, contemplating the blue sky.

After a few minutes Sigbrit Holland tried to coax him to continue: 'And?' But Ambrosius merely rose and went into the wheelhouse, emerging again soon afterwards with a globe in his hand.

'One of the theories is that there are twelve evil areas in different sites around the world,' he said, putting the globe down on the deck. 'Apart from the Bermuda Triangle, there are the North and South Poles, and the Devil's Sea south of Japan, where a number of vanishings have been registered.' The Fisherman drew four small crosses on the globe. 'The evil areas are apparently precisely 72 degrees from each other. Let us see,' he slowly revolved the globe, 'then in the southern hemisphere, along the thirtieth latitude there should be one just east of the southern tip of Africa, at least thirty-five degrees east of Greenwich, and one in the Atlantic near the coast of Brazil, another in the central Pacific, one from here slightly north of New Zealand and a last one in the Indian Ocean off the west coast of Australia.' Ambrosius marked the last of the southern crosses.

'What about the northern hemisphere?' Sigbrit asked impatiently.

'Well, besides the Bermuda Triangle and the Devil's Sea there should be one in the Pacific north of Hawaii.' The Fisherman put in yet another cross. 'And then we have one in the Mediterranean near the west coast of North Africa, and then there must be a last one, here... in the middle of Afghanistan.'

'Nothing in the Northern Lands?' Sigbrit broke in.

'Nope, doesn't look like it.' The Fisherman scratched behind his ear with the blunt end of his pencil. He sighed. 'So we'll probably have to give up the idea of the evil areas once and for all.' He sounded disappointed, then brightened up a little. 'And yet, that doesn't mean that whatever might happen in some of the evil areas can't also happen on the island.'

Sigbrit was about to protest, but held her tongue; she hadn't anything better to suggest herself. Instead she stood up and was on her way into the wheelhouse when Brynhild Sigurdskær began to speak.

'*When Kings... subjects keep silent,*' said the transparent woman almost inaudibly.

'What's that?'

'*An island is an island until it is no longer an island.*'

'You have told us that before.'

'A horse is a horse with eight legs until it breaks one and is a horse with three, which has no resemblance to any horse until Veterinarius Martinussen has completed the regulations and the horse is a horse with eight legs again,' Odin chattered to himself.

Brynhild took up a book from her lap. It had once been bound in leather but was reduced to shreds of something indefinable. 'They are in the same book.' Her bluish-white eyes shone. 'They are quite close to each other. I overlooked that the first time, because I was only searching for sayings that mentioned an island.' She laughed quietly. 'Then I remembered what the sailors had said.'

'Oh well, that could mean just anything,' remarked Sigbrit from the doorway.

'And it could be part of what we are hunting for,' Ambrosius interjected.

Brynhild rose and gazed out over the sea at the low evening sun. 'The Kings must have done something that consigned the island to oblivion,' she said softly.

'Such as? Why? How?' Sigbrit vanished into the wheelhouse.

'If we consider the vanished maps, the Kings we are talking about can only have been King Enevold IV of the South Norse and King Hermod Skjalm of the North Norse,' said Ambrosius when Sigbrit appeared again with a glass of water in her hand. 'We know the two of them were almost constantly at war.'

'That is true. And the North Norse government's claims to the island are confirmed by the fact that in 1615 King Hermod Skjalm sent a division of soldiers to defend the island against South Norseland.' Sigbrit's interest had been aroused.

'They must have gone to war about the island,' guessed the Fisherman.

Sigbrit shook her head. 'It doesn't make sense. How could a war between South Norseland and North Norseland have been forgotten? All the other wars in the Norse territories are very well documented.'

'One can only know what one knows there is to know,' said Odin, and thought of everything he did not at present know that he lacked knowledge of.

Sigbrit nodded. 'Yes, there might well have been other wars,' she said thoughtfully.

'Possibly a war in which they used such terrible weapons that later on the parties to it agreed that no one must ever hear about them again,' suggested Ambrosius.

'An early atomic bomb?' laughed Sigbrit. 'With the technology available to them then you couldn't expect much more than a cannon or a moat.'

'One can imagine other things,' rumbled the Fisherman, sending the blue smoke from his pipe into the light breeze.

'In any case, the weapons or systems or whatever it was, would have no significance for us today. For since then both your grandfather and Odin have succeeded in leaving the island without problems.'

'Absolutely right, Lady Fair,' said the Fisherman with a crooked smile. 'All the same, it would be significant for us if a war had been so terrible, so unmentionable or so distressing that the two warring monarchs agreed that no one must ever find out about it. The only way they could be sure the struggle for the island would remain unknown to posterity would be to assure themselves that no one knew of the island's existence. And the only way to achieve that would be to remove those who knew the island or to make the penalty for mentioning it so severe that no one would ever dare to name it.' The Fisherman seized Sigbrit's wrist. 'Lady Fair, as likely as not, you have here the explanation of why your Captain Hans Adelstensfostre was obliged to cut and run from the South Norse Queendom.' He gave her arm a squeeze and said quietly: 'Maybe it will turn out that among the captain's things there is something, a book, a document or a drawing that discloses the existence of our little island!'

Sigbrit's cheeks reddened, and she snatched her arm out of the Fisherman's grasp just a little too quickly. She rose and went forward to the bows of the green and orange fishing boat. For a moment she regarded the rolling dark green waves, then looked over at the rocks guarding the mouth of the ford and was reminded of the cliffs that surrounded the island.

'*An island is an island until it is no longer an island. When Kings... subjects keep silent*,' she muttered, screwing up her eyes against the low evening sun. She turned to Brynhild. 'How do these two kennings hang together with the other two: "*Name the island and all Hell breaks loose*" and "*Near the island...?*"'

'That we don't yet know,' replied the transparent woman and opened her book again.

By next afternoon the green and orange fishing boat had arrived in Kristiansfjord. Brynhild and Odin remained on board while Sigbrit and Ambrosius went into the town. First they had to find Asta Adelstensfostre's address, before they could seek her out.

Asta Adelstensfostre lived in a whitewashed house on the outskirts of Kristiansfjord. She was a middle-aged woman, heavily built, with a melancholy smile that bore witness to having lived through tragedies. She had five children and a dead husband, and she showed photographs of them all to her unexpected guests.

'Captain Hans Adelstensfostre.' She slowly repeated the name. 'I'm not quite sure. You see, Adelstensfostre was my husband's name...' She sounded apologetic. 'It may well be. It may very well be, as there aren't many Adelstensfostres in the country. But I don't know, I really don't know.' She seemed embarrassed, began to wring her hands and smooth down her flowered dress. 'You see, my husband didn't inherit anything from his parents. They were poor... well, it's a long story. The long and the short of it is that there is nothing here.' She threw out her hands apologetically.

'Never mind. It's kind of you to be willing to talk to us,' said the Fisherman, putting a hand on her shoulder.

A child's cry came from the garden, and Asta Adelstensfostre excused herself and went to see what was going on. When she came back she was more composed. 'Once there was a brother.' She spoke dreamily and traces of a romantic smile spread over her face and for a moment made her look like a young girl. 'Harald.'

Ambrosius the Fisherman winked at Sigbrit; he wanted to hear the woman's own story without revealing what they knew already.

'My husband's brother, Harald Adelstensfostre, they were twins. He went to sea.' Asta suddenly looked sad. 'I don't know what became of him. We never heard from him again.' She rose and walked nervously up and down the room, wringing her hands. 'He must be dead.' Her eyes brimmed. 'Or perhaps he is alive. Nobody knows, at least I don't.' A tear ran down her cheek and she wiped it away with a corner of her apron, embarrassed. 'Life doesn't always turn out as you had expected,' she said quickly, turning her back on her guests.

Sigbrit coughed. 'We've already taken up too much of your time,' she said. 'It was good of you to talk to us.'

The woman turned to them again and smiled nervously.

'Just one last question, if I may –' Sigbrit Holland hesitated. 'You wouldn't by any chance know whether the parents left Harald any old papers or books?'

'No,' Asta Adelstensfostre shook her head. 'No, there was nothing – and yet everything *was* left to Harald. It's hard to explain.' Again she smoothed out an invisible fold in her dress. 'There were many reasons – well – there wasn't much, the cottage and perhaps just a few things. Oluf had done well, we never lacked for anything.' Asta Adelstensfostre looked uneasy, but she went on without any encouragement. 'I don't know if he was ever given it, Harald. I mean the cottage and every-thing. Once the parents were buried and Oluf had heard the will read, there was nothing more for him to do. The lawyer would have had to find Harald, and that can't have been easy. After the funeral we went home and never heard any more about it.' Her eyes filled with tears again.

'Then that must mean that the lawyer did find Harald Adelstensfostre,' said Sigbrit slowly. She stretched out her hand. 'We won't disturb you any longer. But thank you so much for the help.'

'Just one more thing,' said Ambrosius the Fisherman, when they were already on the doorstep. 'Where was this cottage?'

'Grinde Island,' replied the woman. She smiled shyly as if remembering something personal. 'It's a good seven days' sail north in a small boat.'

*

'The action of the South Norse government is totally unaccept-able,' said the North Norse delegate at the meeting of the Investigating Committee dealing with the island described as Drude Estrid Island by the South Norse government, Hermod Skjalm Island by the North Norse government. 'The North Norse government is convinced that Mr Odin Odin did not dis-appear voluntarily!' His voice quivered with indignation. 'The North Norse government is in no doubt that against his own will and best interests Mr Odin Odin has been forced into secret hiding by the South Norse government.' The North Norse delegate had to pause to catch his breath. 'My govern-ment has required me to say that it is out of the question for us to accept the South Norse government's action. From today's date and until Mr Odin Odin is transferred to North Norse ter-ritory, the government of the Kingdom of the North Norse refuses to continue negotiations regarding the territorial status of Hermod Skjalm Island!' The North Norse delegate snorted as he gathered up his papers and rose to his feet. There was no reason to wait for the South Norse delegate's answer, since the latter had most unreasonably already stated that the South Norse government had no idea of Mr Odin Odin's whereabouts except the fact that he had gone on holiday. As if the North Norse would fall for that!

Closely followed by seven junior diplomats, the North Norse delegate strolled demonstratively out of the meeting room and left an astounded Mr Bramsentorpf and seven equally astound-ed impeccably dressed men, a frustrated, stooping chairman, a desperate Herr Hölzern and twenty-seven dumbfounded rep-resentatives of the other members of the Western Bastion, together with a satisfied, smiling, very tall and very blond young man, the once again heroic Lennart Torstensson.

Lennart had quickly recovered from his sudden setback over *Rikke-Marie*'s deserted mooring. The same evening he had returned to the capital of the Western Bastion and without delay had written another letter to the North Norse government. He had taken great pains to write the letter in South Norse to create the illusion that he was a South Norse civil servant, whose sudden pang of conscience had brought him to let the North Norse government know what the South Norse government was doing in the matter of the island, named Drude Estrid Island by the South Norse government, and Hermod Skjalm Island by the North Norse government.

The refusal of the North Norse government to continue negotiations would certainly not persuade the South Norse government to hand over Mr Odin Odin to North Norseland. However, this halt in proceedings gave Lennart time to rearrange matters to his own satisfaction. Thus the shameful behaviour of the South Norse government would in the end increase the magnificence of the deed he was about to perform. Indeed, there could be no doubt that when he arrived in Godeholm with the little old man, the North Norse government would be overwhelmed with admiration and gratitude, and this gratitude would quite definitely result in medals and honours and women, who would swoon adoringly at his feet.

That night the birds sang a song to Lennart about a cow created out of the vapour from the meeting in the void between endless cold and roaring flames. The cow sent her milk flowing in torrential streams to a giant created out of the same vapour as herself. When he awoke, the newly restored Lennart Torstensson wrote down the words of the song in his notebook: '*Alas, here starts the endless fray of world ascendancy*'.

The strange dream bewildered him. It could not be quite normal to dream such things: a cow by the name of Audhumla and a giant called Ymer. He pondered long over what it could mean, then he resolutely picked up his notebook, placed it in a sandwich tin and put it in the fridge; no one, not even a burglar, would ever find Lennart's dreams notebook. For the present he had no time to worry himself over such trifles; he had evolved a new and extremely daring plan.

*

The following Saturday afternoon a totally unremarkable man could be seen walking past Fredenshvile City Hall, waiting for the lights to change to green, then crossing the road and continuing down the pedestrian street towards the Court House. It was a warm day and the special feeling of last chances that sunny days in late August always gave northerners had enticed old and young out on to the streets.

The totally unremarkable man hugged the pavement close to the shops. His shoulders were stooping and he held his right arm bent across his chest as if protecting the rectangular parcel he carried in a white plastic bag. This demanded both concentration and skill to avoid colliding with the lively crowds moving in all directions, and the unremarkable man sweated with the effort. He turned off down a side street, but that proved to be a move out of the frying pan into the fire, because he ran straight into an excited procession of demonstrators. A banner proclaimed: 'Born Anew Christians against the heathen North Norse'; others stated: 'They took the Mighty One and they will pay for it', while the demonstrators uttered various battlecries.

When he reached the square in front of the Court House the totally unremarkable man stopped and looked around him. It was a large square and full of people, but no one seemed to notice him. Nonchalantly, he entered the telephone booth just outside the Court House. The door was half open, and for a moment it seemed to bother him that there was no door to close behind him. He glared suspiciously through the glass façade as if afraid someone was watching him. Then, suddenly resolute, he picked up the receiver.

The totally unremarkable man held the receiver to his ear with his left hand so it seemed as if he was talking to someone, while with his right hand he carefully drew the end of the rectangular packet out of the white plastic bag. He glanced at his watch and then pressed a small button on the packet, slipped it back in the plastic bag and placed that at his feet. Then he replaced the receiver and casually cleaned one of his thumbnails, again looking around him. No one seemed to have noticed him, and he slid unnoticed out of the telephone booth and walked back up the pedestrian street as fast as he could without breaking into a run. Even without running, the totally unremarkable man was already a long way away when two girls entered the telephone booth in front of the Court House a few minutes later.

The girls were laughing and dancing around in their light dresses as if they wanted to offer themselves up to the summer. 'Tell him we're waiting for him here. That's the easiest way,' said one.

The other girl laughed and picked up the receiver. She dialled a number, and her friend moved closer in order to listen. The telephone rang twice before an answer came.

'Hi,' said a boy, but instead of an answer there was a click, the line was interrupted and he did not hear the sound of breaking glass and a girl's scream, soon to be accompanied by many others.

BIFROST

Gods were bravely guarding Midgard
giants threatened woman, man

Fenris wolf grew huge as tree
Midgard's serpent filled the ocean
Surtur's fire nigh voracious
Dragon Nidhug bit through roots
  – what then were gods to do?

Water, air and kindling fire
woven close to bond of hues
Asgard, Midgard, long the way
now spanned in less than many days

Across bridge Bifrost gods they thundered
At foot of Yggdrasil to hold their council
'Giants nearing, grave the peril
gods must fight or evil reigns'

Trusty weapons they did wield
flawless hammer forged for Thor
Tyr's single hand held sword that hit
Frey and Freya trusted love be it
Heimdal said: keen eye protects
while Balder merely justice pledged
kingly Odin took the word

wisdom is what we most need

To halt Voluspa's omen is no simple deed

'*L*ET ODIN COME *back?*' The Prime Minister repeated the words, incredulous. 'Is that all it says?'

'That's it. There were thousands of them.' The Minister of Justice referred to the minute white slips like confetti that had scattered after the bomb went off. 'They were all printed in the same font, all on the same paper, cut into exactly the same size, and all with the same text. Except that...' The Minister hesitated.

'Except that?'

'Except that some of them were in North Norse instead of South Norse.'

The left-hand corner of the Prime Minister's mouth twitched with cramp. 'Indeed!' he said, raising his coffee cup. 'Who do you think did it?'

'One of two,' the Minister of Justice said a touch nervously. 'Either the perpetrator is North Norse or he wants it to seem he's North Norse.'

'Evidently.' The Prime Minister cracked his left thumb twice, precisely. 'How many flakes of confetti are we talking about?'

'I'm not quite sure, but sixteen or seventeen. The police are still searching for more.'

'Sixteen or seventeen out of several thousand. It sounds more like a mistake than an efficiently conducted strategy.'

They sat in the well-polished leather chairs in the Prime Minister's library. The walls were furnished with bookshelves filled from floor to ceiling with unread books, and the dark parquet floor was partially covered with two thick red carpets. A small, shiny mahogany table held coffee cups and brandy glasses and a set of chessmen was laid out between the Ministers. If they had been playing it would resemble any other Sunday afternoon. But they were not playing.

'Two dead, eight wounded. Not as many as have died in the faith groups' clashes,' remarked the Minister of Justice drily.

'That's scant comfort.' Suddenly the Prime Minister looked tired. 'To be honest, I couldn't care less how many fanatics kill each other, but when they start murdering innocent passers-by, we have a problem. There's to be an election in the spring, and this is just what the opposition will cash in on.'

'It's nightmarish.' The Minister of Justice picked up his glass.

'Surely this must be enough!' exclaimed the Prime Minister and leapt out of his chair, so that the Minister of Justice's brandy went down the wrong way. 'How are the police getting on?'

'Not too well, unfortunately,' coughed the Minister of Justice. 'The confetti is the best clue. In all probability it was made by one and the same person. "*Let Odin come back!*"' The Minister of Justice coughed again and then took another gulp of the golden-brown liquid. 'There wasn't enough left to give any indication of how the materials for the bomb could have been bought. Apart from the shreds of confetti those are the only things they have to go on; I mean, who would put a telephone bomb in front of the Court House on a Saturday afternoon, when you can be sure there's nothing going on inside it?'

'It might be pure chance.' Pondering, the Prime Minister walked up and down the red carpet.

'It might be. And yet I don't think anything's left to chance when you are making a bomb of that size.' The Minister of Justice scratched the bridge of his nose nervously. 'No, the timing probably does mean something. But what, that is the question?'

'What about witnesses?'

'Plenty. You know how the Court House Square hums with young folks as soon as the weather's fine. The police have talked to a good few, but none of them seemed to have spotted anything out of the ordinary. The phone booths were busy that afternoon. There's nothing odd about people going in and out of them, nothing to catch anyone's eye. Apart from the fact that some person left a package filled with plastic explosive. A few seconds were all he needed.'

'He?'

'Or she, of course.' The Minister of Justice laughed mirthlessly. 'Long live women's lib!' He raised his coffee cup as if to toast something, then put it back in the saucer without drinking. 'No, but seriously, I've been speculating all night over who could have dreamed up anything so absurd. Naturally one's inclined to point the finger at one of the Doomsday groups, but that just doesn't seem likely.'

'Why not?' The Prime Minister sat down again.

'The confetti notes don't demand anything except to let Odin come back. Any of the faith groups would have seized the opportunity to preach their message of doom as well. As things are, none of them gain anything whatsoever from the bomb: none of the other groups were in the vicinity, nor any government representatives, and the positioning of the bomb made it just as likely to have hit one of their own followers as one of their opponents. The Born Anew Christians are out to win more followers, and they know well enough that terrorism never arouses sympathy in the Queendom of the South Norse. The Reborn Jews would have tried to hit the Born Anew Christians and so on. The Avengers would have tried to hit one or other of the Doomsday Prophets, or maybe the government, and under no circumstances would they have asked to have Odin back. That also goes for the North Norse True Christians. And even if the Born Anew Christians were demonstrating in the area where the bomb exploded, it would have been much easier to hit them in front of the Parliament House, where they spent most of the day.' The Minister of Justice paused to drink the dregs of his brandy. 'No, only if someone had a particular reason to think that some specific person would use that very phone booth at precisely that time, would any of the Doomsday groups have been involved, which is so unlikely that I think we can exclude it. Even if the aim with the bomb was to hit one specific person, it would not have succeeded. The two girls who were in the booth when the bomb went off were fourteen-year-old schoolgirls with no affinity whatsoever with a religious community.'

'If you're right, there is no likely group other than the new fanatical nationalists, either our own or the North Norse ones.' The Prime Minister's mouth twitched again. 'As for the small language error, that was probably from a North Norseman,' he added, pushing the white chessmen across the board into the black ones, so that several of them fell over. 'They will go on,' he nodded crossly to the east, 'accusing us of hiding the little old man here in South Norseland. As if we would dream of such a thing.' Again his mouth tensed up. 'The way the North Norse negotiators are taking things in this affair is totally unacceptable.'

'Yes, and even if the disappearance of the false Messiah does suit the North Norse so-called True Christians, there are certainly many other nationalistic North Norse people who believe that the islander should rightfully be in North Norseland now.' The Minister of Justice sighed. 'It matches all too well the numerous threatening letters we have been sent in North Norse demanding Mr Odin Odin's release.'

'So maybe it wasn't such a brilliant idea to make the little old man disappear,' the Prime Minister said, vexed.

'It did give us a brief window...' the Minister of Justice began, fidgeting restlessly.

'A bit too large a bloody window!' exclaimed the Prime Minister, flicking another chessman on to the floor. 'It didn't take more than a day or two before they besieged Parliament instead of Firø. And now this.' He flung out his hands expressively. 'Now it's gone too far! I won't stand for it!' He stood up again and took one or two impatient turns across the floor. 'To let off a time bomb in South Norseland in this day and age.' He shook his head angrily. Then his rage seemed to evaporate and he slumped in his chair, exhausted. 'What are we coming to?'

They sat in silence for a moment until the Prime Minister pointed at the wrecked chessboard. 'We might just as well play and leave speculation to the police,' he said. 'I assume you've seen to it that this matter receives the highest priority?'

'Naturally,' the Minister of Justice hastened to assure him.

'Good.' The Prime Minister leaned forward and began to return the white chessmen to the board.

They had not been playing long when there was a knock on the door and the Prime Minister's daughter entered the library. There was an urgent call for the Minister of Justice: the Chief of Police. The Minister was only away for a few minutes, but when he returned he was ashen-faced.

'The Born Anew Christians,' he said in a hoarse, shaking voice and sat down slowly. 'They admit responsibility. The call came through to the police twenty minutes ago.' He closed his eyes for a moment as if trying to picture to himself what might follow. 'There goes my theory.'

'Couldn't it have been a fake call?'

'The police chief said it sounded genuine enough, but of course they are investigating.' He coughed heavily. 'You could say that if someone is willing to take responsibility for such a crime they are also willing to commit it.'

'So you think we can expect more of the kind?'

'Let's hope not. But that call changes everything.'

'Yes, but for the worse or the better?'

*

The fearless Lennart Torstensson had not intended to harm anyone. It was just that he had no idea of how else to get his message across.

He had sent countless anonymous letters to both the Queen of South Norseland and the South Norse government, but to no effect whatever: Mr Odin remained hidden. So he had been obliged to think out a new plan to get the South Norse people to talk, and a bomb was the nearest and most natural solution. Lennart really hadn't intended to kill anyone, and he was – truth to tell – not a little shocked at what had happened. At the same time it was strangely liberating, as if an invisible barrier inside him had been broken down, and he could do whatever it took to attain his goal.

Hadn't every historical figure been bound to take legendary decisions? Legendary decisions that turned into legendary action which had legendary consequences? And hadn't they been willing to pay the price, whatever that might be, to attain their goal? Yes, it was precisely that which separated the legendary from the great, and still more from the mediocre, this readiness to pay the price, to run the risk and walk through fire. Just look at Gustav Vasa, at Hermod Skjalm, at Napoleon, at Caesar – why, you need only to read the Old Testament; the Lord himself had allowed his creations, not to mention his Son, to pay. And he, too, the soon-to-be-legendary Lennart Torstensson, was willing to pay the price, any price.

It was morning, and Lennart was getting up. In his dream the birds had sung of three gods walking along a beach. There were two trees on the beach, an ash and an elm, and out of them the gods created man and woman. And what more had the birds told; *truly purer than the virgin – before transmuting into man*. Most extraordinary! Lennart was still not quite sure what to think of his bizarre dreams, but on closer consideration, something peculiar had probably characterized all legendary figures, and therefore the dreams simply confirmed that Lennart had been born to perform great deeds. With this realization, in the course of one moment, the strange dreams stopped plaguing him.

Lennart noted what the birds had sung for him in his dream, then had a bath and dressed in his suit. It was past ten o'clock, but he was in no hurry. For he had known for a long time that his future did not depend on Herr Hölzern and the job at the Department of Territorial Affairs in the Western Bastion Directorate of Legal Affairs. Not only had the negotiations regarding the island, described by the South Norse government as Drude Estrid Island, and by the North Norse government as Hermod Skjalm Island, come to a standstill, they had also been taken out of the hands of both himself and Herr Hölzern and were now under the authority of the head of the Directorate; the matter had become political, as Herr Hölzern had put it resignedly. Moreover, the whole affair of the island had convinced Lennart that he could no longer take the responsibility of wasting his talents and himself in a minor post in a complicated hierarchy. No, legendary labours were calling, and the only reason for him not to immediately leave his post was that '*timing is all*', as Herr Hölzern had said, at a time when Lennart still held some respect for him.

Lennart had learned what anonymous letters could be used for, and now he had discovered how effective explosives could be. In the case of Hermod Skjalm Island there was no doubt that he was well on the way to becoming a legend. Wasn't he the one who had lit the touchpaper of the whole feud between the South Norse Queendom and North Norse Kingdom by getting the North Norse to make demands regarding the island? Wasn't it he who had made the North Norse insist that Mr Odin Odin should be moved to the North Norse and thus made the South Norse hide the little old man? Was it not he who had made the North Norse government break off negotiations with the South Norse? And was it not he who, with the aid of a telephone bomb, would soon set Mr Odin Odin free again?

Yes, indeed, Lennart knew everything – well, perhaps apart from one single thing: what his next step was to be. And, naturally, he did not know why the Born Anew Christians had taken responsibility for a bomb which he had planted.

*

Another thing Lennart could not know was that Ezra (alias Ace) had been born to great things also; and taking responsibility for the telephone bomb in the name of the Born Anew Christians was the smartest thing Ace (alias Ezra) had come up with so far.

The first thing that happened was that Simon Peter II, in police interrogations, in speeches to his followers and in interviews with the press, angrily denied that the Born Anew Christians should have had anything at all to do with the Court House bomb, and the police soon had to admit that Simon Peter II, with most of the Born Anew Christians, was on his way through the streets to Parliament at the time the bomb was put in place. The Entrusted Disciple naturally did not doubt that the whole thing had been organized by the North Norse false True Christians: first they had set the bomb in a – luckily erroneous – attempt at targeting the Born Anew Christians' demonstration; and next, when the bomb did not hit its target, the false True Christians tried to push responsibility for the wicked act on to the Born Anew Christians in order to destroy their good name and reputation. His followers agreed with him, as did many a less faithful South Norseman; this time the North Norsemen had gone too far!

Simon Peter II moved the siege from the South Norse Parliament to the North Norse embassy in Fredenshvile, and the number of Born Anew Christians immediately doubled. At the same time the quantity and brutality of violent attacks on chance North Norsemen in the South Norse Queendom increased considerably.

Ace had hit on more than even he realized: for the Reborn Jews had no doubt that the telephone bomb had been intended for them, since Ezekiel the Righteous, the father and the five remaining uncles had walked past the Court House shortly before the bomb went off. Not only that, it was clearly a crafty trick of the Born Anew Christians to set off a bomb that would get rid of the prophetic son and at the same time – by demanding the release of the Mighty One – try to remove any suspicion that they themselves were keeping him prisoner.

'We must double our effortth to find and thet free the Mighty One,' lisped Ezekiel the Righteous. 'We muth attack the foe's flank again and again, tho hith woundth are tho deep that he collaptheth.' The prophetic son bowed his head, there was nothing more to say.

This time Ace did not need to light the fuse.

*

At 9.20 a.m. yesterday morning a bomb exploded outside the North Norse embassy in Fredenshvile. One person was killed and thirty-three injured, thirteen seriously. The bomb had been placed at the foot of a tree in the embassy drive. Apart from a North Norse messenger who was slightly hurt, the deceased and all the wounded Doomsday group members belonged to the Born Anew Christians demonstrating outside the embassy. It is not yet known whether the bomb was aimed at the embassy or the demonstrators. The leader of the Born Anew Christians, Simon Peter II, has declared that the bomb was yet another cowardly and godless attempt by the North Norse True Christians to hit the Born Anew Christians.

The police do not have many clues to work on; however, they state that initial investigations indicate that the bomb was not similar to the one that went off in front of the Court

*House last week. However, the police do not exclude the
possibility of a connection between both incidents.*

*Later in the morning, two unwitting North Norse
tourists, on their way into the North Norse consulate, were
seized and brutally beaten up by the crowd. The two North
Norse wounded both remain in hospital in a critical
condition.*

*The South Norse Prime Minister has called for calm and
advised the South Norse people to refrain from any kind of
violence, either towards those of other faiths or towards their
North Norse brethren. Likewise, the North Norse Foreign
Minister has encouraged all North Norsemen not on urgent
business to leave the Queendom of the South Norse and in
particular to stay away from Fredenshvile until the situation
is under control.*

Sigbrit Holland lowered the newspaper, and silence fell over
the wheelhouse. Then Brynhild Sigurdskær broke the silence.

'War,' she said softly. 'War the waves sing and war it will be!'

'Do you know that, or do you just think you know it?' Sigbrit
asked with ill-concealed irritation in her voice.

'Comes to the same thing,' interjected Ambrosius the
Fisherman gently.

'There can't be a war between the South Norse and the North
Norse just because of a little island no one knew about until a
few months ago. That's utterly mad!'

'All wars are mad.' The transparent woman stared challeng-
ingly at Sigbrit but spoke in her usual soft voice. 'Madness
generates power.' She laughed softly. 'Territories can make war,
ethnic groups can make war, cultures can make war, beliefs can
make war. This time vanity will make war on vanity.'

It was nearly evening. They had just moored up in an almost non-existent harbour town, which consisted of a single row of red wooden houses and a small grocer's shop. They could have reached as far as Karlsund to take in provisions before continuing on to Grinde Island, but Ambrosius the Fisherman had decided that the risk of staying the night in a larger place was too great. To Sigbrit's surprise she had found a *Long Norse Times* in the little shop – a national Long North Norse newspaper – that was only one day old.

Sigbrit pushed the paper aside and stood up. For a moment she glanced out of the window at the dark waters. There was a fresh breeze and the waves were high even here in the harbour. The green and orange fishing boat rocked from side to side, and the mooring ropes strained at their leashes, which seemed at breaking point. She turned to the others. 'We've got to do something!' she said.

'When believers wish to do battle, ideas are no weapons,' said Brynhild gently.

'You can't mean that!' Sigbrit's voice was shrill. 'You know as well as I do that all this is happening because of Odin. We are a part of it, and we are bound to do something to stop it.'

'Truly, one should not fight unless it's unavoidable,' remarked Odin, winding his beard around his fingers while wondering where he could have heard about the war Brynhild was talking of. 'I wonder if I told Mr Bramsentorpf's sick servant...'

'No, Odin. That's no good. You've seen what happens as soon as you talk to the fanatics.' Ambrosius smiled at the little old man. 'Think no more about it. Our Lady Fair didn't mean it like that.' The Fisherman winked at Sigbrit.

'But we must do something,' she insisted.

'The problem is, we can't do much. It is not our business.'

'What do you mean, *not our business*. You're talking like my husband, my ex-husband.'

The Fisherman smiled placidly and put sugar and milk in his coffee. 'We've got more important things to think about. Don't forget someone has to find the way back to the island for Odin. And that someone happens to be us.'

'We can't just sit here doing nothing while people at home are getting killed.' Sigbrit turned red and her fingers drummed agitatedly on the wheelhouse wall.

'Sometimes it's our business, sometimes it isn't.' The Fisherman stirred his coffee with the end of a fork. 'The art is to know when it's one and when it's the other.'

'You may well be right. But I don't like it, all the same.'

'Do you think we like it?' The Fisherman put down his fork and lifted his cup. He tasted his coffee. 'Try to picture what would happen if we went home now. We would be sending Odin right into the pandemonium and putting his life in danger. Well, you could go off alone but what would you do then? Beg the demonstrators not to kill each other? Or beg them to stop being fanatics? Or tell them they are wrong?' Ambrosius took yet another mouthful of coffee. 'To be frank, Lady Fair, there's really nothing either of us can do.'

'That's not true. I could organize counter-demonstrations. Demand a law be brought in to ban any kind of public offence.'

'In other words, you want the government to forbid illegal activity?' The Fisherman spoke with real sympathy, as if he regretted contradicting her. 'Even though demonstrations are allowed, violence is not. And public incitement to violence is banned as well.'

'Maybe, but we should take a stand. I don't think the greater part of the South Norse population would go along with what's happening.' Sigbrit brushed the hair away from her face crossly. Ambrosius gave her a long look before he replied.

'We're afraid we're not so sure of that,' he said quietly.

'Even if a great proportion of the population is involved I could tell them, couldn't I, that Odin is a perfectly ordinary man from a perfectly ordinary island, whose horse broke her leg, and that now he has to search for a vet and a way of getting back home.'

'So how will you explain to them that no one knew of the existence of this perfectly ordinary island until a couple of months ago? And how will you explain that no one is able to get there? That one aeroplane after another vanishes over the island?' The Fisherman shook his head. 'Unless we can explain what's going on in the island everything else we can say is only fuel to the flames.'

'We could at least try.'

The Fisherman looked at Sigbrit wonderingly. 'Lady Fair, you have changed a lot since we first met.'

Sigbrit laughed. 'No, I haven't,' she said, giving the table leg a tap with her foot. 'I have only just begun to know who I really am!'

The Fisherman rose and went across to her. 'There are many things we would like to say, but this is not the right time.' He glanced briefly at Brynhild.

Sigbrit blushed and looked away. 'It's never the right time, is it?' she murmured.

'It will come.' The Fisherman sat down again, then went on as if nothing had happened: 'Now let us finish off what we started. We need you here. Regardless of what you might possibly be able to do back in South Norseland, it is nothing compared with what you can achieve here. Regardless of what you could do at home, someone else could do it in your place. What you can help us with here can't be done by anyone else. We need to find a way back to the island, and we need to find it soon!'

Sigbrit gazed at the Fisherman for a moment, then looked over at Odin.

'Right,' she said finally and sat down. 'Then we had better get a move on. Time is running out.'

'Time runs with the speed of the individual,' Brynhild interjected. 'A hundred years is a hundred years is a hundred years. But a hundred years is ten years is one year for someone in a hurry.'

'I don't care,' snapped Sigbrit. 'You can work at your tempo, I shall work at mine. If we don't find out something soon, we might just as well leave off searching altogether.'

'Does that mean that Veterinarius Martinussen will not get the regulations finished?' Odin asked, pulling worriedly at his beard.

'Not quite,' chuckled the Fisherman. 'But Odin, you had better resign yourself to the fact that we may find a different Veterinarius than Veterinarius Martinussen.'

'Truly I shall be very grateful if there could be one with fewer regulations,' mumbled Odin. 'This Martinussen has rather too many for my liking.'

'Now I have it!' Brynhild broke in excitedly.

'What do you have?'

'*Name the island and all Hell will break loose*', she said, then repeated the words slowly, enunciating each single syllable. '*Name the island and all Hell will break loose.*'

'That's come to be fairly obvious, hasn't it?' said Sigbrit.

Brynhild got to her feet and without replying climbed down the ladder to the interior of the *Rikke-Marie*.

'*Name the island and all Hell will break loose*,' mumbled Ambrosius the Fisherman, looking at Sigbrit. 'Yes, that is certainly obvious. All the same, you never know what it can lead to.'

As if she had heard his words, at that moment Brynhild came up the ladder with a book in her hand. She opened it at a marked place. '*Only a bone smith can break iron loose.*'

'See?' Ambrosius turned to Sigbrit.

'What does that mean, then?' she asked, rather more interested than she liked to let on.

'I'm not sure about that yet,' said Brynhild gently. 'It certainly has a reference to a *burning Hell*.'

'And the words?' asked the Fisherman. 'Are you sure about them?'

'*Only a bone smith can break iron loose*,' read Brynhild, again emphasizing every syllable. 'No, that's what the book says, but it's not like that.' She thought about it for a moment. '*Near the island*... will give the reply that is the answer,' she said quietly, closing the book with a slap.

It took only a couple of hours to get to Karlsund the next day. Sigbrit set off at once through the harbour and down the narrow streets with low well-kept white terraced houses on both sides, and soon arrived at the town's well-stocked grocer's shop. The sun shone palely from an almost blue sky, though it was already the middle of September and so far north that even the finest weather was a fairly cool affair. Sigbrit shivered, even inside the shop there was a bitter chill. The old weather-beaten grocer stood behind the counter. He punctiliously noted down each item Sigbrit ordered. When she had finished she folded up her list and asked the location of Grinde Island.

'Grinde Island?' The grocer was astonished. 'You can't get there.' He shook his head, obviously shocked that anyone should so much as contemplate it. 'It's impossible. No one has been there for over four years. No, no one has been there for over four years.'

'Why not?' asked Sigbrit in surprise. 'It says in the tourist brochure that there are ferries to the island in the summer, and people go out there to see the old lighthouse.'

'Oh yes, that was how it used to be. That was in the old days – not now.' The grocer shook his head. 'No, it's not like that any more.'

'Why, what happened?'

'Oh, that's a long story. Yes, a very long story.' Looking worried, the grocer went on shaking his head. 'It's a sad tale too. A very sad tale.'

Sigbrit Holland weighed up the situation; if Asta Adelstens-fostre was right and they did have to get to Grinde Island it would have to be in spite of what went on there.

'Anyway, why do you want to go there?' the grocer broke into her thoughts. 'What in the world do you want on Grinde Island?'

If she was going to get anything useful out of him it would have to be a plausible explanation.

'Actually, we are looking for a Harald Adelstensfostre,' she said hesitantly.

'Well, I never... Harald Adelstensfostre. No, I never... Harald Adelstensfostre. Well then, I had better... yes, I suppose I had better.'

The doorbell sounded and a middle-aged woman entered the

shop. The grocer was obliged to serve the woman, who wanted butter, milk, half a dozen eggs, coffee, whey cheese and dried meat – and of course a chat about wind and weather and the latest news in town. It took ages, but at length the goods were wrapped and paid for, and Sigbrit was alone with the weather-beaten man again.

'Where were we? Now, where were we?' The grocer closed the door behind his customer and trotted behind the counter again. 'Ah yes, Harald Adelstensfostre.' He raised his hands in the air as if to pray for the gods' permission to utter the name. 'Harald Adelstensfostre.' Suddenly his eyes lit up with suspicion. 'You're not a relative or such? A relative of Harald Adelstensfostre?'

'No, no. Not at all. I am a friend of an old friend of his who has asked me to give him an important message when I was in these parts,' Sigbrit quickly invented.

'Harald Adelstensfostre doesn't have any friends. He has no friends at all, Harald Adelstensfostre,' said the grocer. He didn't seem to trust her.

'He did have once. I know that.' Sigbrit Holland held her breath, and she was lucky.

'That may be. Now you say it. He did have friends once, Harald Adelstensfostre. Yes, once Harald Adelstensfostre did have some friends.'

'It's important for me to find him,' Sigbrit went on. She was getting impatient.

'Oh, yes, oh yes.' The grocer turned round and shuffled to the back of the shop where he vanished through a door which Sigbrit guessed led into his home. Her irritation increased. Either the man was extremely slow-witted or he had nothing whatsoever to tell her and merely wanted to chat. She waited for a minute or two, then five, then ten, and was on the point of leaving when the grocer at last came back with a small glass frame in his hands. He placed the frame on the counter in front of Sigbrit. It held an ancient, yellowing photograph of a school class of ten-year-olds with a tight-lipped teacher in charge.

'You see, he was at school with my little Ingeborg,' said the grocer. 'Yes, Harald Adelstensfostre was in the same class as my Ingeborg.' He pointed to a little girl with blonde plaits. 'That is the last picture ever taken of my Ingeborg. The following year she took to her bed with a serious lung infection, and never recovered.' There were tears in his eyes and he was so overwhelmed that he quite forgot to repeat himself.

Sigbrit swore soundlessly; how could she get away without seeming too rude? Just then the grocer pulled himself together and pointed at a small fair-haired boy.

'That is Harald,' he said, blowing his nose on a grubby handkerchief. 'Yes, that's Harald Adelstensfostre just there.'

Sigbrit studied the boy's face; he was blond like most of the children in the picture, with a narrow face and a merry smile with one tooth missing. But what can you tell of a future man in the face of a ten-year-old boy surrounded by his classmates and his teacher? Sigbrit's eye fell on something strange. Just beside the boy Harald sat another boy, the image of him. She picked up the photo to study it more closely. There was no doubt; one boy was an exact replica of the other.

'Who is he?'

'Yes, we'll come to that. We'll come to that,' nodded the grocer, as if well satisfied with her question. 'This is where it all started. Just here is where it starts. That one there,' the grocer pointed to the boy beside Harald. 'That one is Oluf, Oluf

Adelstensfostre. Yes, they were twins. Twins they were, Oluf and Harald Adelstensfostre. They were as alike as two peas they looked so much like each other, those two, yes, alike as two peas they were.' The grocer coughed violently and had to pause before he could speak again. 'They were twins both in soul and body, they were. Not only were they as like as two peas, they behaved as if they were one. They were always together. Yes, always together. And they always did the same thing, precisely the same, they did. What one did the other did too. And what the other one did, the first one did the same. If Harald was going out fishing Oluf had to go fishing as well. And if Oluf was going to swim you could count on it, Harald swam too. Yes, whenever you saw Harald, you were bound to see Oluf too, and if you saw Oluf, you were bound to see Harald.'

'Yes...' Sigbrit had understood, but the grocer was not to be hurried.

'When Harald did well at something, Oluf mastered it as well, and what Oluf could not do Harald failed at too. They gained the same marks at school, they had equal strength, and one never outran the other in a race.' The grocer had another bout of coughing. 'That was how they were, always together, always one and the same. That was how they were, Harald and Oluf Adelstensfostre, always like one and the same and always together. Yes, up to one day, and no one really knew why, and when they found out about it, it was already too late, and there was nothing anyone could do about it. No, when they got to know about it, it was already too late to do anything.'

'What happened?' Sigbrit tried, but the grocer ignored her with an irritated wrinkle of his brow.

'Too late. Far too late. The damage was already done.' The

grocer mused for a moment. 'Yes, the damage was already done then.' He pointed to a girl with pigtails. 'Asta, she was called. Yes, it was Asta they both fell in love with. Harald as well as Oluf Adelstensfostre fell head over heels in love with Asta. With hindsight it's easy to say we should have predicted that, both of them falling in love with the same girl. Yes, it should have been easy to predict, and yet no one had ever given it a thought. Least of all Harald and Oluf themselves. Yes, least of all the twins themselves. It was here it all went wrong.' The grocer coughed so hard he couldn't stop himself doubling up, but he waved Sigbrit away when she stepped nearer to help him. 'Yes, then was the time it went wrong,' he said hoarsely when he had regained his breath. 'They must have been about fifteen or sixteen then. Yes, perhaps fifteen or sixteen years old. At first it went well enough. Both of them were in love. Harald picked berries for Asta, and Oluf picked berries for Asta. Oluf wrote Asta little poems, and Harald wrote little poems for Asta. They ran errands for her together, together they carried her shopping bag when it was too heavy for her. Yes, whatever they could find to do for her, they did together. No, those were happy days, there was no predicting what the end would be. No, that was true enough.' The grocer shook his head. 'There was no predicting the end of bliss. You see, at that time, yes, even today the young people have to travel to a larger town for their studies. Yes, they have to go into town to study. And so off they went, Harald and Oluf, just after their seventeenth birthday. Yes, just after their seventeenth birthday they went off, those two. They were starting out on years of study, Harald and Oluf, they were bright boys, you see. Yes, they were bright ones, and everyone thought they would soon forget their passion for Asta, as soon as they were settled in town. There everyone was mistaken, everyone who thought that passion for Asta would be forgotten. For that wasn't what happened. No, that didn't happen.'

The doorbell tinkled again and another customer came into the shop. It took some time before the grocer finished serving her and could turn to Sigbrit again, but this time she felt no urge to leave.

'See, to start with they only came home on holiday in the summer,' the grocer went on. 'The journey was costly so they only came home every summer, Oluf and Harald. Yes, Harald and Oluf always travelled together, and when the boat came in the two of them went straight home, put down their bags, greeted their parents and then hurried over to Asta. Yes, as fast as they could they went over to Asta. Faithful boys, they were. No, you can't call them anything but very faithful.' The grocer looked at the clock on the wall. It was getting near closing time and he still had to clear up and do his accounts. 'Well, to cut a long story short,' he went on quickly. 'Yes, to cut a long story short, the boys began to come home several times a year, and they started to come separately, one without the other.' In his haste the grocer forgot himself. 'At first Oluf came home alone for a week in October, then Harald came alone for Christmas, and then Oluf came again for Easter, and then Harald came for Whitsun. And that went on until there was nearly always one of them at home. Of course their parents were horrified, what with their studies, but there was nothing they could do. And poor Asta, who for the first year or two had enjoyed having two bags of berries or two bouquets each time the other girls had only one, now she was at sixes and sevens. For you see, even poor Asta couldn't tell one from the other. No, poor Asta couldn't even do that, tell one from the other. That's to say, except when they were together, for then they had a rule, Harald would always walk on Oluf's right side, Oluf always on Harald's left. But when one was without the other; no, even Asta couldn't see the difference. So poor Asta was in love but didn't know who with.'

The grocer coughed and choked and had to fetch a glass of water before he could go on. 'Maybe she was in love with both of them, who knows? Yes, who can know whether she was really in love with them both? And had it been up to them, who knows whether they could have worked that out? Yes, the three of them might perhaps have found some way of living with the situation. Naturally it was not up to them. No, it was not up to them, but to the custom. At that time it was customary, as it still is on the whole, that a man shall have but one wife, and a woman shall have but one husband.' For a moment the grocer gazed thoughtfully in front of him, as if he was weighing up the reason behind that custom, which had obviously brought about a tragedy. 'Then something happened,' he went on slowly. 'No one knows exactly what it was that happened, but the whole thing happened during a single summer. Yes, it happened in one and the same summer. Asta promised to marry Oluf, and they were married at once, and then Oluf passed his exams while Harald got nothing and went off to sea. It's hard to know what really happened, but Asta gave Oluf her promise, and they were married at once. And he became a doctor, did Oluf, with brilliant exam results and everything, while Harald went to sea, and no one saw him again. Or rather, no one saw Harald again for many, many years. Some fishermen or other men of the sea who put in to harbour here now and again would say they had seen Harald Adelstensfostre in some or other port. Yes, sometimes one or another of them would tell of having seen Harald, but always far away and in places whose names are impossible to say. Then one winter the father died, and Harald came home as quickly as he had disappeared. Yes, the twins' father died, and home came Harald. Harald moved into the cottage on Grinde Island and looked after his mother who lay ill and wouldn't see anyone else. No, Harald wouldn't see anyone but his sick mother, who soon enough died too, and then Harald went to sea again, even before the funeral had taken place. Yes, even before their mother had been laid to rest, Harald was far out at sea again.'

The grocer scratched his neck as if straining to remember what happened next. 'Well,' he went on after a while. 'Then it turned out that only Oluf and Asta had attended the funeral. And Oluf found out after the funeral that nothing was left to him, because the parents had left everything to Harald. Yes, all they had owned, which was nothing much more than the little cottage, the parents gave to Harald, while Oluf had nothing. He probably had enough, did Oluf, although no one can say what happened at that time. Anyway, Oluf went home, and no one here saw him after that, although it's a good many years ago now. But no one could find Harald Adelstensfostre, who should have had the cottage and everything, until one day when he turned up again out of the blue, which seemed to have become his habit. Yes, and when he turned up he moved straight into the cottage again and wouldn't see anyone then either. Now no one could have anything against that in itself, except that it was a bit odd. No, no one could really object to a man keeping himself to himself like that. Although that was not quite all, because Harald Adelstensfostre seemed to have got tired of people out there at sea, or wherever he had been. Yes, he had grown sick and tired of people, so much so that he would not have anyone on the island, and then he started to chase them away. There were not many families living over there on Grinde Island and those who were did not do him, Harald Adelstensfostre, any harm. It was the tourists, those he chased off with stones and big sticks and they say a great sword he was supposed to have brought home from distant parts. Rumour has it that it all began because someone came to talk to him about his brother – whether that was just a rumour I can't tell. No, but they do say that someone went to talk to him about his brother. And see, Harald Adelstensfostre didn't like that one bit, so he started chasing folk away. The tourists were easily frightened, and soon the last family moved away, for without tourists there was nothing for them to live off on Grinde Island. Then the ferry stopped running, and no one goes to Grinde Island any more. Well, only the supply boat once a month, which has brought the same order to Harald Adelstensfostre ever since he came home, and it is paid for in good salt fish. Still, they never see anything of Harald. Yes, the payment is always in the best salted fish that is found north of Kristiansfjord, but never a glimpse of Harald Adelstensfostre does the skipper get.'

The grocer coughed and glanced at the clock on the wall. It was long past closing time and already uncomfortably close to dinner time and he hadn't made up the till yet. 'The long and the short of it', he said quickly, 'is that no one goes to Grinde Island any more. No, no one can have the pleasure of setting foot over there, for they say he is dangerous, and you never know what might happen. So no one goes to Grinde Island, and I doubt very much whether anyone will ever do so.' The grocer shook his head. 'I can only warn you not to venture there, in earnest I must. No one has anything to do with the place.'

Although the supply boat has just called there, and it will be a month before it goes again, it would be a better idea to send a message from Harald Adelstensfostre's friend via the skipper, so Harald can find it with his supplies. Yes, the best thing would be to send a message with the supply boat's skipper.'

Sigbrit thanked him for his advice and tried to look as if she intended to follow it. At least she knew now that he was still alive.

'No, there's nothing to go to Grinde Island for, that there's not,' repeated the grocer, closing and locking the door after her.

*

Grinde Island rose out of the water like a grey-green wind-battered hill. Ambrosius the Fisherman easily found the narrow wooden jetty on the south side which had once been part of a busy ferry port. Sigbrit made the ropes fast as well as she could around the half-rotten posts, then straightened up and looked around her. Nothing to be seen but stones, moss, scattered clumps of short grass and here and there a few low trees; not a particularly inviting place to live.

Brynhild Sigurdskær had not come with them. Without further explanation she had said she had errands in Karlsund, and would join them again when they returned. Then she had gone ashore with her backpack. Sigbrid couldn't help wondering whether she was afraid of something. She looked at the inhospitable island again; perhaps there was good reason to fear.

Ambrosius and Odin came ashore to join Sigbrit, and together they made their way cautiously over the rotting planks on to the island, where they followed a narrow, half overgrown track up the hillock. They had learned that the Adelstensfostres' cottage was on the western side of the island not far from the lighthouse, and as soon as they reached the top of the slope they caught sight of it. The cottage was built of large blocks of granite and stood in a small well-kept garden. They quickened their pace, but long before they came within earshot the door opened and a powerfully built man with a straggly beard came rushing towards them brandishing a gilded sword and uttering a string of furious words they couldn't understand. They were in no doubt that this was Harald Adelstensfostre. Nor was there any doubt that he thought this meeting had already lasted too long.

Not waiting to see whether the hermit would really make use of his sword, they ran as fast as their legs would carry them – Ambrosius the Fisherman carrying Odin – back down the slope.

It was not until they had reached the rotting jetty that Harald Adelstensfostre relinquished his pursuit. He then stayed at the end of the jetty to make sure they did not try to come ashore again.

'Truly, they don't give you a very hearty welcome on this island,' said Odin, twisting his beard around his fingers in wonderment.

'We certainly don't seem very welcome.' The Fisherman was still out of breath from the rapid retreat. He walked over to the helm.

'But surely we're not going to let him scare us off?' Sigbrit sat down on the bench and looked enquiringly at the Fisherman; now they had at last reached the island they could not give up that easily.

'It would probably be better to come back another time and

see if he is in a mellower mood.' Ambrosius screwed up his eyes. 'Lady Fair, it's up to you, Captain Adelstensfostre is your department.'

Sigbrit looked out of the window. The hermit was still at the end of the jetty, swinging his gilded sword in the air as if to make it clear they were not to dare come again. Sigbrit felt a knot of fear in her midriff; she had to admit she did not much care for the thought of spending the night close to that threatening figure.

'A man who harms no one today will not harm anyone tomorrow,' remarked Odin. He was keeping an eye on the hermit too.

Sigbrit nodded slowly, then turned to the Fisherman. 'We'll stay!' she exclaimed with sudden conviction.

'Stay we shall, then, Lady Fair.' Ambrosius sat down, cleaned, filled and lit his pipe and made himself comfortable in every possible way. 'While we are waiting for a better mood out there, of course there is plenty here to get on with.' He took down a book from the shelf and opened a notebook.

They waited in the wheelhouse for some hours to see if anything happened. All that changed was that at one point Harald Adelstensfostre withdrew a few metres uphill and sat himself on a rock. Apparently he did not object to the boat mooring alongside the jetty, but as soon as they so much as opened the door of the wheelhouse he stood up and swung the sword over his head. Not until well into the evening, when dusk had obscured the view from the island of the green and orange fishing boat did the hermit leave his vantage point after a final threatening swing of his sword.

Sigbrit watched the hermit's silhouette slowly disappearing into the deepening darkness.

'Maybe we should try to follow him,' she suggested.

'No,' said Ambrosius. 'It's too early. We are obviously not welcome, and if we provoke him there's a risk he'll chase us right away. As things are, we can at least stay moored to the jetty. And who knows, he may grow accustomed to us in a day or two.'

After dinner they buried themselves in the books again, but the green and orange fishing boat rocked so much in its exposed anchorage that for the first time on the trip Sigbrit felt seasick. She went out on deck and breathed in the cool evening air. Five minutes later Ambrosius joined her. The wind was slackening and the sky was perfectly clear, but the greenness of the sea and a chill in the air left no doubt that soon autumn would get the better of every trace of summer.

'Let's hope the hermit won't prove too stubborn,' said the Fisherman. 'We'll soon be getting the first autumn storms, and we ought to be a good distance further south before then.'

'Mmm,' murmured Sigbrit absentmindedly, concentrating on letting her stomach rock up and down with the movements of the boat. 'It could be force of gravity,' she quietly remarked a little later.

'Force of gravity?' Ambrosius looked at her enquiringly.

'I knew you'd think that was silly.' Sigbrit couldn't stop herself blushing.

'Take it easy, Lady Fair, we didn't say that.' The Fisherman laid a hand on her arm. 'It might be possible, but you'll have to explain.'

'Even the *"near it"* phrase would make sense...' She gave an embarrassed laugh, suddenly aware how close he was. She took half a step backwards and tried to gather her thoughts. 'I saw in the book I'm reading that the force of gravity is different in different parts of the world. For instance, it is weaker on a mountain top than in low-lying regions, and it's weaker near the poles than near the equator.'

'Yes, but the island is certainly not a mountain or a pole,' protested Ambrosius mildly.

'I know that. But seeing that the forces with which the masses attract each other, and thus the forces that create gravity, depend on the density of the masses, one could imagine that the island was formed of something or other that had a different density than the surrounding sea and land. I don't know if that makes any sense...'

'Both yes and no. It probably does,' said the Fisherman uncertainly, scratching his neck. 'Force of gravity,' he mumbled. 'Well, why not?'

'And if gravity was the reason for the aeroplanes disappearance it could also explain why no wreckage has been found; the parts were simply drawn towards the island and remained there.' Sigbrit's eyes shone with enthusiasm.

'Ye-e-s, that might well be so,' said the Fisherman slowly. 'It's just not that easy to *know*.'

'No,' began Sigbrit, then her expression brightened. 'How is Odin?' She went into the wheelhouse and found the little old man by the window, gazing up at the starry sky.

'Odin,' she began. 'Tell me, are there any birds on the island?'

Odin considered the question. It had been wintertime when he was in Smith's Town, and in all truth there had not been many animals at all. But yes, the villagers had set up sheaves for the birds here and there, and he had caught sight of a few small, grey, ruffled-looking birds.

'Yes, there are birds in Smith's Town,' he said, pulling at his beard, trying to recall some quite different birds that had seemed to him to vanish suddenly with what had come before Smith's Town and the meteor storm, not to speak of the ill tidings.

'Birds,' repeated Sigbrit. 'Were those the same birds as the ones you have seen on the Continent?'

'No.' Odin thought hard. Truly, he didn't remember them in any detail, but he did think he could say with reasonable certainty that he had not noticed any of the scruffy grey ones after he arrived on the Continent. 'No, I am afraid I didn't see those birds on the Continent once.' He pulled at his beard. 'But I do truly hope nothing has happened to them?'

'No, no,' Sigbrit assured him. 'Nothing at all. This is amazing.' She almost ran out of the wheelhouse. 'Ambrosius, Ambrosius!' she called. 'Odin has never seen birds like the ones on the island in South Norseland.'

'So?'

'So, that could mean that those species that can fly on the island can't fly here, and vice versa, and that means that the air space over the island could be influenced by a force that is only active there. For instance, a particular kind of gravity.'

Ambrosius smiled. 'Not bad, Lady Fair. Not bad at all.' Without warning he took her face between his hands and kissed her on the forehead.

Sigbrit felt warmth stream through her, but before she could react the Fisherman had let go of her. She stepped back in confusion. 'What about Brynhild Sigurdskær?' she asked huskily.

Ambrosius the Fisherman made no reply, merely turned his back and leaned on the rail.

Sigbrit waited a moment, then she turned on her heel and

went into the wheelhouse. She drew a deep breath or two, gathered up her physics books and carried them outside. She lighted the lamp above the door and opened a book. 'The law of gravity says that every body in the universe is attracted by every other body with a force that is stronger the more massive the bodies are and the closer they are to each other.'

'And?' rumbled the Fisherman without turning round.

'If the density of the island is, for some reason, greater than the density existing outside the island, then ships and planes will be drawn inwards towards the island with no chance of escaping.'

'But Lady Fair,' the Fisherman said, turning around slowly, almost unwillingly. 'Remember that when *Rikke-Marie* crashed on to the rocks that day she was not drawn towards them. It was merely the wind and the waves working together to hurl us there.'

'How can we be so sure of that?'

At that moment the boat suddenly lurched and the Fisherman's shoulder brushed against Sigbrit's.

'Tell us something else,' said Ambrosius gently. 'How do you explain that a particularly forceful vein of gravity developed in one single area?'

Sigbrit detached herself, though not far, just enough to part their shoulders.

'It's quite hard, I don't really know exactly. But yes, in theory it's possible to explain,' she said in some confusion and then pulled herself together. 'If you imagine the earth as a universe in itself.' She opened the book again, leafed through a few pages and found what she was looking for. '*The force of gravity is not a particularly powerful force,*' she read. '*But it possesses two special characteristics: it is effective for long distances, and it always attracts. These characteristics in conjunction can make the force of gravity extremely strong, such as the gravity that keeps the earth in orbit around the sun.*' She paused to look at the Fisherman for affirmation. He nodded. '*But although the force of gravity always attracts, the universe doesn't collapse. So attracting and repulsing forces of a different nature than gravity must be at play.*' She looked up from the book. 'Somewhere else in the book it states that the universe could still go on developing after the creation explosion. So maybe one could imagine that various places in the universe, indeed maybe on the earth itself, could find themselves in various stages of this development, and therefore there is different gravity in different places...' Her voice faltered and they stood for a while in silence.

'It's certainly not easy,' the Fisherman muttered at last. 'We'd probably best concentrate on the sea route.' He cleared his throat. 'We have gone over the old map of the rocks our father and grandfather left us. There is still no indication of the whereabouts of the fairway, but then it struck us that of course our grandfather found the course from the island outwards. So it could be that it was easier to get away from the island than to approach it.'

'That doesn't help us much, seeing we are outside and not inside,' said Sigbrit, suddenly losing her zeal. 'What you say ruins my theory on gravity. Well, Odin's presence actually does that too.' She slid her fingers along the rail. 'Because how could any human being live under two such divergent forces of gravity?'

'It might be possible,' the Fisherman shrugged his shoulders. 'There could be something like differences in height, thin and dense air, high and low gravity. What do we know?'

'No, but if the force of gravity is strong enough to be able to pull down planes, then it must take a very special constitution to be able to live there.' She stopped and looked at the Fisherman meditatively. 'If that's the case it might be difficult for you to go back to the island with Odin,' she said.

'What makes you think we had thought of doing that?'

'It doesn't matter. But I'm right, aren't I?'

Ambrosius crossed to the opposite side of the boat and looked out at the dark hillside. 'We don't know whether that is what we really want,' he said after a while. 'But that's beside the point. We have no choice, because it's what we have to do.'

Sigbrit had followed Ambrosius. She gazed at the sparkling reflections of the stars in the rolling waves, then lowered her eyes to Grinde Island. 'Isn't there any way of changing one's destiny?' she asked quietly, not turning her head.

'No.' Ambrosius the Fisherman slowly shook his head, then added almost inaudibly: 'But it could well be that another destiny awaits you once you've lived through the first.'

Next morning they made another attempt. But the hermit drove them back on board even before they had begun to walk up the slope. He was obviously keeping watch on them from a distance. And it was even more obvious that he was not prepared to let them come near. All they could do was wait, ration their provisions and go on with their search for the forces that prevailed on the island.

They had no more luck in pinpointing physical phenomena than they had with Harald Adelstenfostre. They went over a number of the theories put forward about the Bermuda Triangle, but time after time they were brought up short; the hypotheses did not match what they knew about the island.

Atmospheric pockets or air quakes would also have been meas-
urable outside the limited air space over the island. Flood
surges and underwater earthquakes had never been reported
in the Strait or the surrounding seas. Earth radiation might
perhaps be the explanation of why some people fell ill, but that
had never been claimed as the cause of modern aeroplanes
falling out of the sky. And differences in the speed of time
rotation was not possible, since Ambrosius the Fisherman's
grandfather had been the same age on his arrival in South
Norseland as he had when he left the island. After four days
they were no nearer a physical explanation than they were to
the hermit. On the fifth day, after they had rejected the theory
that the strange happenings were due to the release of
methane-hydrogen gases from the seabed which temporarily
reduced the buoyancy of the water – this could perhaps cause
ships to sink, but would not affect planes – Ambrosius the
Fisherman had had enough.

'Look, either we go out and speak to him, or we'll leave!' he
said, looking out of the window at the weather-ravaged slope.

'We can't just go before we have spoken to him,' protested
Sigbrit. 'He's our only hope.'

'Almost,' murmured the Fisherman. 'We do have the kennings and Brynhild Sigurdskær.'

'Well, no matter how many kennings Brynhild Sigurdskær
has dreamed up, they aren't going to help us if we can't give
them an actual physical explanation.' Sigbrit sounded upset.
'We've either got to find a physical explanation or the fairway,
or, better still, both.'

'Yes, and since at the moment we don't have either, that only
leaves Brynhild Sigurdskær.'

Sigbrit glared at the Fisherman.

'Good, Lady Fair,' he said, unruffled. 'We are willing to make a final attempt, but if that doesn't succeed, *Rikke-Marie* sets course for Karlsund at dawn tomorrow morning. We can't allow ourselves to be caught by winter so far north. *Rikke-Marie* isn't built for that.'

Sigbrit slowly shook her head, pulled on a sweater and followed the Fisherman and Odin out of the door.

It was four o'clock in the afternoon, the light was already fading and the few greenish shades on the island looked greyer than ever. The breakers roared in on to the stony shore, and the wind beat chill against their cheeks. Long before they reached the top of the slope and the hermit had chased them back to the boat with his gilded sword raised high above his head, uttering incomprehensible furious yells, Sigbrit knew she had lost; Ambrosius had been right, they couldn't hang on much longer.

Back in the wheelhouse the Fisherman sat down calmly and filled his pipe. 'Well now, it's no use crying over spilt milk,' he said, lighting up as he watched Sigbrit pacing restlessly up and down. 'It was a good idea,' he went on consolingly. 'It was worth a try. It just didn't work.'

'A defeat is never a defeat before you accept it is a defeat,' said Odin, thoughtfully twisting his beard.

Sigbrit came to an abrupt halt and looked at Odin, then out of the window. The hermit still stood at the end of the jetty with his hands resting on the handle of the sword he had pushed firmly into the ground between his feet. He didn't look particularly welcoming. All the same, he didn't actually seem threatening. So they were not to set foot on shore, no, but he wouldn't drive them away from the jetty. She was reminded of the myth of Kraka, who had to appear before Regnar Lodbrog dressed and yet naked, fasting but after eating, and without company and yet not alone.

Sigbrit turned away from the window and looked again at Odin, then at Ambrosius, and without a word to either she resolutely went out of the wheelhouse, took off her shoes and socks, then her sweater and trousers. Then she jumped head first into the sea.

The water closed around her with an icy shock, and gasping, Sigbrit surfaced with chattering teeth, for a moment unable to feel anything at all. Then her senses returned with painful coldness and she began to swim. She swam along the coast westwards, trying to estimate whether her body would hold out as far as Harald Adelstensfostre's cottage. But Sigbrit had not swum far before she discovered she was not moving to the west, but to the south, away from the island. Now the hermit came running on to the beach, waving his arms in the air and shouting something she couldn't hear. For a second she thought he was shouting to stop her swimming, but his gestures were different from before, and he no longer held his sword. Although she could not understand his words, she suddenly realized what he was trying to tell her; there was a strong undercurrent.

Sigbrit put all her strength into her strokes, but she could not resist the strong current. No matter how hard she swam she was drawn further and further away from the coast.

'Ambrosius!' she shouted, treading water, as she tried to prevent her mouth getting filled with salt water. 'Ambrosius!'

But the green and orange fishing boat was already too far away.

She started to swim again, but she was getting cold and her cramped movements weakened. Metre by metre the current was winning the unequal battle. The waves grew larger and soon it was all she could do to keep her head above water. She looked over her shoulder; there were a few scattered rocks, after that nothing but the open sea.

'Ambrosius!' she screamed again, although she knew he could not hear her. She gritted her teeth, changed from breast-stroke into crawl, then to breaststroke again. Her muscles hurt. She was a good swimmer, but the current was stronger than she was, and the cold was defeating her last strength. She wasn't going to make it. Then a wave lifted her up and she caught sight of a head further in. The hermit was on his way.

Relief washed over her and she relaxed for a moment. Then she was off again, breaststroke, then crawl, then breaststroke again. The current was still pulling her out but the hermit was slowly approaching. He raised his hand and called out some-thing. She couldn't hear what he said but raised her own hand in a wave; she had seen him. Harald Adelstensfostre called again and pointed to something behind her. Sigbrit trod water and turned her head, but too late. At that moment her leg struck something sharp, and before she was able to ward herself off with her hands she was hurled on to the rock head-first.

MIMER'S SOURCE

Far away in Udgard's land
feeding root of Yggdrasil
sacred were the tears of insight
Giant Mimer watched his fountain spring

Odin flew in eagle's guise
tricked the giants in their dwelling
but to Mimer showed his face
deceiving sense, a senseless game

'Let go an eye and lend it me
I then give a sip to thee
One drop of mind is well enough
if you hold to thought and memory'

Ravens two arose from Odin's ears
heard all was clear, then time to act
left eye of god they deftly plucked
pawn in Mimer's hand set firm.

At once, Odin wiser than wisest was

On the first day of October the North Norse Embassy in Fredenshvile burned to the ground. Now the time had come for the roadside trees in the capital to turn yellow, then red and brown before the leaves slowly fell into the gutters, from where they were collected to be used as kindling for the numerous bonfires lit by the Lambs of the Lord here, there and everywhere. The Blessed Anders Andersen was piqued because their sacrificial fires were totally outshone by the sparkling radiance from the North Norse Embassy. The embassy burned all night, and throughout the hours the eastern region of the city was bright as a summer's day. The fire crews could do little more than keep the curious crowds at a safe distance and prevent the fire from spreading to other buildings.

Yes, they had done well; Ace (alias Ezra) was proud of them. The six young men with crew cuts who had lit the fire had even managed to spray-paint the selected message in red letters in the middle of the well-mown lawn behind the embassy: *Hand over the Mighty One to the chosen people*. These words left little doubt as to the identity of the fire-raisers, and to dispel even the slightest hint of misunderstanding, Ace had walked past the embassy during the evening, and behind the hedge – which the six Avengers climbed over later that night – and, following a precisely planned coincidence, he dropped a fountain pen engraved with his brother's name. There was no doubt that the Avengers would soon be ready for the great revolution; anyway, that was what Ace told them. In fact he was fed up to the back teeth with revolutions and couldn't see the point of turning society upside down, but when you have wolves to run your errands you should choose those that howl loudest. As soon as this ridiculous Odin affair had reached its peak, or more precisely, as soon as his insufferable brother had been arrested and charged with arson, he, Ezra would re-emerge on the family scene and save the situation. He would be the family hero; the tenth piece of silver, the lost and found son, and in his honour the fatted calf would be slaughtered.

Precisely as Ace had planned, suspicions fell on the Reborn
Jews even before the fire crews had extinguished the last
ember from the wrecked embassy. What Ace had not planned
was that Ezekiel the Righteous, the father and mother, the
five remaining uncles, their wives and children with the
widow of the sixth and the few non-related Reborn Jews
without a shadow of a doubt could prove, that they had been
gathered together to study the Holy Scripture at the time the
fire broke out. After that, suspicion was immediately directed at Simon Peter II. The Born Anew Christians were, as
Ezekiel the Righteous's eldest uncle was not slow to point
out, the only ones who had a genuine motive for the crime.

The Mighty One's Entrusted Disciple and First Apostle was
furious. But after he had thought things through for a couple of
hours, happily the Lord revealed the truth to him. 'I, Simon
Peter II, fisherman in soul and body, have received a message
from the Lord and his Son, the Mighty One, which suggests to
me that the fire at the North Norse Embassy, like the telephone
bomb a fortnight ago, was lit by the false True Christians in an
attempt to harm the only true believers,' he declared without
hesitation before his followers.

Not lacking in conviction or powers of persuasion, the True
Christians – and with them many a patriotic North Norseman
– immediately declared that without doubt the fire had been
ignited by the Born Anew Christians, who had added insult to
injury by casting the blame on the North Norse. Just as for a
long time it had not been safe to be a North Norseman in the
Queendom of the South Norse, now it was no longer safe for a
South Norseman to be found on North Norse ground. The True
Christians had found an effective means of fighting for God
and righteousness; the South Norse made haste to leave North

Norseland, and before the week was out, the South Norse ambassador to the North Norse capital found his embassy was little more than a smoking pile of rubble.

It was at this point that Mr Brams Bramsentorpf disappeared.

*

'Set Odin free or Bramsentorpf is a dead man.'

'What in the world is this?' An uptight Prime Minister pointed to the letter the Minister of Justice had just laid on his desk. It was written with letters clipped from newspapers and magazines.

'It is a copy...' began the Justice Minister.

'I can see it's a copy!' hissed the Prime Minister with twitching cheeks. 'What I would like to know is who wrote it, where Bramsentorpf has gone and what the police are doing to find him?'

'The police are doing all they can. They have people all over the place. But they haven't yet tracked him down.'

'Not yet! It's five days since he was taken.'

'The police are working at full capacity. They have interviewed colleagues and everyone who was in the vicinity of the Ministry when the abduction took place. No one has seen anything unusual except that one or two of the Doomsday groups were in the area.'

'It's likely that no one would notice anything at all these days when letting off bombs, setting fire to buildings, violent demonstrations and fanatical processions in fancy dress are everyday spectacles.' The Prime Minister suddenly looked washed out. He sat down and carefully cracked his fingers, one after the other until all ten had given way. 'How in the world have things come to this?'

'Yes, it is most regrettable.'

'Regrettable! What do I care about regrets, keep them for the press. It's a catastrophe, that's what it is!' The Prime Minister hammered a fist on the table, making the Minister of Justice jump. 'I have a team of security men constantly around me. Last year I rode around on my bicycle, and now the security chief is talking about bullet-proof cars. We have an election in the spring. Try to imagine how the voters will react to all this.'

The Minister of Justice blinked uneasily; not only was the Foreign Office portfolio well out of his reach, but he could also feel his grasp of his own office growing shaky. He swore soundlessly. If only it had not been for the little old man and... well, no good thinking of that.

'There's one small problem hampering the police work,' he said nervously. 'The North Norse police, yes, how shall I put it... they, er, are not cooperating.'

'What's that supposed to mean, *not cooperating*?' The Prime Minister leapt to his feet and began to stride up and down.

'Officially they say their police are upset because our police have not done enough to find the criminals who set fire to their embassy,' the Minister of Justice put in quickly. 'I have been informed informally that the police are under orders from the highest authority. Apparently the North Norse government still believes we are hiding the little old man in order to gain the right to the island.'

'That's totally absurd.'

The Minister of Justice made no reply, and there was a moment's silence in the Prime Minister's office. Then the Prime Minister flopped down on his chair and exclaimed with a shake of the head: 'Abducting a civil servant on his way home from work. I don't know what things are coming to.' His mouth twitched. 'Why Bramsentorpf of all people?'

'He's leading the delegation in the negotiations for the island.'

'It sounds as if you're taking it for granted that the North Norse so-called True Christians are holding him?'

The Minister of Justice nodded cautiously. 'The error in the text is certainly not one that a South Norseman would make,' he said. 'If a South Norseman wanted to make it look as if it had been written by a North Norseman, he would probably have gone to more trouble to write the whole text in North Norse.'

'You may well be right,' said the Prime Minister almost kindly, but then went on in a sarcastic tone: 'but you'd better explain why the True Christians demand that we hand over Mr Odin Odin when they are the only ones who are not interested in him?'

'Well, they regard him as a false Messiah. And he is the key to the island.'

The Prime Minister pulled at his little finger, but no sound resulted.

'If they are so keen to get hold of him, it makes you wonder why they don't abduct you or me.'

'With the tight security we lay on these days it wouldn't be so easy.' The Minister of Justice massaged the bridge of his nose. 'Poor man, I'm sure he regrets ever setting foot in the Ministry of Justice now.'

'There are others who regret that this Mr Odin Odin ever set foot on South Norse soil!'

The Ministers sat for a moment in silence, then the Justice Minister said quietly: 'It shouldn't take long. The police have marshalled all their resources to join the search for Bramsentorpf.'

'Hmm,' chuckled the Prime Minister. 'They'd better get a move on, then. And we,' he laughed coldly, 'we had better find our little old friend.'

*

Sigbrit rolled over on to her other side and winced slightly. '*In the light of the events of the past few days the South Norse government earnestly requests Mr Odin Odin to return to the Southern Norse Queendom without delay. If this is not possible, he is asked to report immediately to the nearest South Norse embassy to reveal his whereabouts. Bearing in mind the urgency of the matter, the police wish to receive information from any person who may have news of Mr Odin Odin's movements.*' Sigbrit opened her eyes and gazed up at the planks above her bunk, but the words, repeated on the radio every hour all through the day, kept ringing in her head. She thought of Mr Bramsentorpf. They could not go back now, not before they had talked with the hermit.

When Sigbrit had woken up for the first time after her accident, she had been lying on the bench in the wheelhouse with a primitive bandage around her left shin and sharp pains in her head and back. Harald Adelstensfostre was not there, but Ambrosius the Fisherman had told her how the hermit had suddenly opened the wheelhouse door a few hours earlier with her in his arms. Without saying more than the names of the articles he needed to use, the hermit had cleaned and bandaged her wound and immediately afterwards left the green and orange fishing boat without a word to either Odin or the Fisherman.

That had been four days ago. The headache was almost gone and apart from the bruises and some slight backache, Sigbrit had recovered remarkably quickly. Unfortunately that also meant that as soon as the sun rose, *Rikke-Marie* would weigh anchor and set course back to Karlsund. While Sigbrit had been laid up, Ambrosius and Odin had made another couple of attempts at making contact with the hermit, but they were met with the same fierce hostility as before. It was no use wasting more time on him, the Fisherman had said, and refused to listen to Sigbrit's objections; the autumn storms were on the way.

Sigbrit got out of bed slowly. She pulled a thick sweater over her head and crept through the middle cabin, past the sleeping Fisherman and up the ladder to the wheelhouse. Odin slept on the bench in the fore part of the wheelhouse with his face turned up to the open sky – he said it reminded him of something, he just couldn't remember what – and in order not to disturb him, Sigbrit went forward to the bow.

She sat down at the end of the deck and let her feet dangle in the air above the surface of the sea. It was a cold foggy night, the clouds veiled both stars and moon and cast an ominous glimmer over the stillness. A new day would dawn before many hours had passed. Sigbrit searched vainly for an idea that might persuade the Fisherman to wait another few days. She couldn't think of anything they had not already tried, and after a while one of her legs went to sleep, and the raw dampness of the clouds made her shiver. She rose and walked restlessly back and forth over the deck once or twice. Then she gave up and went into the wheelhouse to climb soundlessly down the ladder. She crept past the Fisherman, who slept heavily, and was about to open the door to the forward cabin when she withdrew her hand and turned around. She crept back to the Fisherman's bunk and studied his face.

He looked calm and unworried, and his deep breaths came in regular rhythm. His eyelids lay peacefully over his eyes, the wrinkles on his forehead were smoothed out, and his lips curved in a slight smile. Sigbrit tried to reciprocate the smile. She forced the corners of her mouth upwards, but it was no good, all she achieved was a stiff grimace. What she wanted was a real smile. Ambrosius the Fisherman's smile. She leaned forward, and quite slowly, so as not to wake him, she laid her lips over his. They were soft under the cracked surface, slightly parted and seeming to belong to a world that had nothing to do with her or Odin. In sudden desperation Sigbrit longed to share in the Fisherman's tranquil sleep. She lifted the duvet and crept cautiously into the bunk. The Fisherman shifted and mumbled a few vague sounds without waking up. The bunk was not wide, but when she lay on her side there was just enough room for her. The Fisherman's body was warm, and Sigbrit could feel how his warmth gradually became hers, where their skins met. She rested her head on her arms and studied his features for a long time. He was fast asleep again. Sigbrit ran her fingers very lightly down the Fisherman's face; over his wide brow, the bushy eyebrows, the weatherbeaten cheekbones, his nose and in the midst of the trimmed beard the full, slightly cracked lips that still curved in a contented smile. She leaned forward and again rested her lips on his. This time she let them find their way down into each fold, each single line, and finally she could feel it: his smile in her mouth. She kept her lips against his for as long as she could. Then her neck started to ache, and she raised her head.

'Stay here,' whispered Ambrosius, opening his eyes.

Sigbrit Holland sat up; she was shy. 'I'm frightened,' she said quietly.

'Aren't we all?' The Fisherman put his arm around her back and pulled her down to him. But he held her like a child, not like a woman.

'You just fall asleep and forget everything.'

'No, we don't do that. We sleep to be able to meet what you call *everything*. It's no good without sleep.'

'But South Norseland...'

'Precisely. South Norseland is merely a place where people have gone a bit off course. It's disheartening, but that's how it is.' He ran his hand slowly down her back. 'You can lie awake from now until Christmas and it won't change things the least scrap.'

'I don't believe people are naturally bad,' Sigbrit whispered.

'We're not saying that. People are neither good nor bad. No more than any other living creatures.' Ambrosius sighed. 'It's just that human nature needs to be checked sometimes to stop it running amok. It is neither good nor bad, merely painful.'

'You sound so cynical.' Sigbrit bit her lip thoughtfully. 'I believe some things are right and some are wrong, and that people can choose whether they do one or the other. They can choose not to run amok.'

'We are not cynical, merely realistic.' The Fisherman sighed again. 'Look, you may be right. In that case it only makes things worse, for then people actually choose to act, wrongly or with evil intent or whatever you like to call it.' He gave a little cough. 'Anyhow, good and bad, right and wrong, it's only a question of who uses the words. You can be quite sure that all those Doomsday Prophets killing each other for the first right to believe in Odin, will maintain they are doing a good deed by opposing those they consider infidels. They are convinced they are saving humanity from the torments of Hell.'

Sigbrit shook her head, her face tensing briefly with pain. She thought about what Ambrosius had said. Then she recalled the government's radio appeal. 'Shall we call them?' she asked bluntly.

'No,' Ambrosius replied firmly. 'We don't trust them. Even if we don't tell them where we are they can all too easily track us down. Although the government has no evil design in mind, there are many others out to get Odin.' He stopped for a moment and then said quietly: 'Tomorrow we start the return trip. We'll decide what to do while we sail.'

Sigbrit sat up abruptly, ignoring the pain in her back. 'We can't just go back before we have found anything.'

'Nor can we stay here not finding anything,' replied the Fisherman calmly. 'We've tried everything to get the hermit to talk to us – you have even risked your life – but nothing has helped. He doesn't want to talk to us. There's no more to say. The autumn storms are on the way and we are running out of food and water too.'

'We could buy more provisions in Karlsund and come back here. That wouldn't take more than half a day.'

'Right and wrong.' The Fisherman smiled. 'It is not a question of half a day but of winter that is closing down on us. Neither *Rikke-Marie* nor we ourselves are dressed for the cold up here. As it is, the homeward trip will be more than hard to bear.'

Sigbrit thought of how the hermit had rescued her. 'He can't really be so dangerous,' she said quietly. 'Or he would just have let me drown.'

'Since then he has kept on chasing us away, Lady Fair, you have to admit it. Harald Adelstensfostre doesn't want to talk to us.' The Fisherman paused briefly. 'We weigh anchor tomorrow,' he said quietly. 'No, stay here.' He held her fast as she started to get up. 'Do you think you can sleep now?'

'Maybe.' Sigbrit would have liked the Fisherman to kiss her, but wasn't sure about asking him to. Then something else occurred to her. 'You never answered my question,' she whispered almost inaudibly.

Ambrosius the Fisherman hesitated. 'No, we never answered your question.' He raised himself on his elbow. 'Well,' he nodded. 'Once we did love Brynhild Sigurdskær.'

Sigbrit stiffened, but the Fisherman held her eyes and went on calmly: 'We loved Brynhild Sigurdskær for thirteen long years. Then one day it ended. Brynhild is the daughter of the blue icebergs, the sirens' sister. She longs for the warmth of a strong embrace, but she cannot stand up to it. She burns her lovers to ashes one after another, until the day she meets one stronger than herself. Then she will melt away. It is her fate to suffer what the old women call eternal longing; she will live only as long as what she longs for has the power to annihilate her.'

'What happened?' whispered Sigbrit.

'One day we woke up knowing that Brynhild was not made for us.' In the darkness the Fisherman's eyes searched Sigbrit's face. 'You see, Lady Fair, people are made of different clay. If two are made of the same, love will either destroy you or annihilate you both or melt you into one. If you are not of the same clay, one day you will move on.' He took her face between his hands and looked her straight in the eye. 'Brynhild and we are made of different stuff.'

Sigbrit took a deep breath. 'There is more, isn't there?'

Ambrosius released her face and looked away a moment. 'There was a child,' he said slowly in an altered voice. 'There was a child, and the child died.' He cleared his throat. 'She was called Embla, and she died when she was four. She died because a demonstration turned violent. She and her mother fell and were trampled down. Brynhild tried to protect our daughter, but failed.' The Fisherman sighed. 'Since then Brynhild cannot stand being in a crowd, or where violence is rife.'

'I thought Brynhild was afraid of nothing?'

'When you have nothing more to lose, you are not afraid of anything except being reminded of what you have lost.'

Sigbrit lowered her gaze. 'We did not live together, it wasn't like that,' the Fisherman went on. 'Brynhild wanted a child, not a man, at least not us. Anyway, it was many years ago. We have been just friends for ten years. Friends and parents, together only in our loss.'

Sigbrit said nothing more, but raised her hand and caressed the Fisherman's face. Ambrosius lay back on the pillow and closed his eyes. Sigbrit studied him a moment, then bent over and kissed him lightly on the mouth.

'I have been waiting for you to come,' he whispered and put his arm around her. 'I have waited every night since I first saw you, every night since you came to *Rikke-Marie* in Sand Harbour, and every night since we came here to Grinde Island.'

'Why didn't you say something?'

'Because it was up to you.' He hesitated. 'I have nothing to offer except myself and no future. Only the sharing of a moment.'

'I know that.' Sigbrit kissed the Fisherman again. 'I don't ask for more.'

*

A ray of light crept through the porthole, and Sigbrit opened her eyes. She had hardly slept, but she was alert at once. She listened to Ambrosius's calm breathing and stretched lazily. Then she suddenly sat up; in a few hours they would leave Grinde Island behind them, and they knew no more about the fairway now than when they came. Without waking the Fisherman she crept cautiously out of bed, put on her trousers and sweater and climbed up the ladder to the wheelhouse. She found a pen and a scrap of paper and wrote a brief note. Then she folded the letter and put it in her pocket, grabbed a bottle of schnapps from the Fisherman's larder cupboard and left the *Rikke-Marie*.

The sun had not yet risen, but the misty morning light allowed her to make out the path in front of her, and she reached the top of the hillock in no time. She gazed at the hermit's stone cottage for a moment or two. There was no sign of life, but she slackened her pace and made a point of looking towards the old lighthouse, as if that was what she was making for. When she was close to the garden gate she took the folded note out of her pocket and placed it on the ground with the bottle of schnapps on top of it. She glanced at the cottage and thought she could glimpse a shadow behind the window. Then it was gone. Sigbrit turned around and started to walk slowly back the way she had come. Just then the door of the cottage opened and Harald Adelstensfostre came into view. He looked at Sigbrit briefly, then went to pick up the schnapps and the letter. '*Thank you for saving my life. Oluf is dead. Asta asked me to talk to you.*'

As soon as Harald Adelstensfostre had read the letter he

disappeared into the cottage. Sigbrit hung about for a little, then took a deep breath and began to walk away. As she reached the garden gate the door was flung open again and the hermit rushed out, uttering furious cries. Sigbrit quickly retreated and was just about to turn and flee when she clenched her teeth and dug in her heels; she reminded herself how he had rescued her, and it suddenly struck her why he had known what to do about her injuries. Of course, Asta Adelstensfostre had told them that her husband Oluf was a doctor and, according to the grocer in Karlsund, that meant that Harald Adelstensfostre had studied medicine too. Sigbrit felt suddenly convinced that the hermit would not do her any harm.

Harald Adelstensfostre came to an astonished halt in front of her, then turned on his heel without a word and vanished inside, leaving the door open behind him. Sigbrit decided to regard the open door as an invitation.

The cottage was dark, but surprisingly comfortable and tidy. Along one wall of the room there was a solid oak dining table and four chairs, and at the opposite end stood a shabby but clean sofa with embroidered cushions on it. Harald Adelstensfostre indicated to Sigbrit that she might sit on the sofa. He sat on a chair. For a while there was silence in the room, and Sigbrit drummed her fingers on the green cover; a wave of shyness came over her. Then Harald Adelstensfostre rose abruptly.

'Who?' he asked in a rasping voice, nodding towards her.

'Sigbrit Holland,' she replied, then, pointing to the jetty, explained, 'Ambrosius the Fisherman and Odin.' She held out her hand, first to indicate the taller man, then the smaller.

The hermit pointed to her letter, which lay on the table.

'Oluf is dead. Asta lives in Kristiansfjord,' said Sigbrit slowly,

afraid of saying too much. Although this was not new information, her words still seemed to make a deep impression on
the hermit, who walked pensively back and forth.

'When?' The hermit stopped in mid-stride.

'Two years.' As long as he only used single words, Sigbrit
found it easy enough to understand his Old Norse.

'Children?'

'Five.'

Harald Adelstensfostre sat down again. He remained silent
for a long spell, and when he began to speak it was almost to
himself, as if he had forgotten Sigbrit's presence.

'It so happened once that Oluf Adelstensfostre had the fantastic idea, which his twin brother Harald Adelstensfostre
went along with, either because he did not know better, or
because he believed it would work.' The hermit stared in front
of him as he spoke. 'Oluf Adelstensfostre decided they should
act as one person instead of two. They were two who both
wanted to be in two places at once, so if they sounded as if
they were one and the same, thus one could be in two places
simultaneously. Harald Adelstensfostre agreed and for the
final year at university he studied in his brother's name, while
Oluf Adelstensfostre was at home in Karlsund with Asta.
Harald Adelstensfostre passed all the exams, but the next
thing he heard was that Oluf Adelstensfostre had married
Asta in his own name. Only then did Harald Adelstensfostre
realize that he no longer existed.' The hermit halted his
torrent of words and looked at Sigbrit in some surprise, as if
it suddenly dawned on him that he was not alone. 'Enough!'
he exclaimed and rose to his feet.

Sigbrit stood up too. She wanted to ask him about Captain
Hans Adelstensfostre's books, but the hermit had turned his

back on her to look out of the window. She hesitated a moment, then left the room and closed the door gently behind her.

Ambrosius was still reluctant to postpone their departure, so later that morning Sigbrit walked over the hillock again, and as soon as Harald Adelstensfostre opened the door she put her question to him.

At first he made no reply, merely gazed at her thoughtfully, and she was afraid she had been too hasty. After a while, without warning, the hermit picked up an oil lamp from the chest by the door and signalled to her to follow him. He turned left outside the gate, and without once looking back he walked swiftly down the gravel track to the lighthouse with Sigbrit a few steps behind him. On this side the island came to a sudden end in a cliff, but a narrow, arched wooden bridge took them safely over the savage waves.

Harald Adelstensfostre unlocked the door of the lighthouse. Inside was a dark stairway with a spiral staircase leading upwards. He struck a match and lit the oil lamp, which threw their shadows high up the circular wall. Sigbrit could not see a lot; she had to feel her way upwards step by step. They circled round many times, ascending higher and higher, and at last the hermit came to a halt. Sigbrit caught up with him and saw a low metal door. He drew out a key, and to her surprise, first the lock, and then the door opened soundlessly. Harald took a step back and let Sigbrit enter first.

She screwed up her eyes; the circular room was blindingly light. There were windows the whole way around, and the view over the blue-green sea seemed endless. A row of exotic-looking wood and metal chests was piled beneath the windows, except for one place where instead of chests stood a graceful dark writing desk with a web of decorative carvings. On each side of the desk were two high-backed chairs, also in dark wood. Harald pointed to one of them, and Sigbrit sat down. Then, without hesitation, he picked up a small primitive wooden chest and carried it across the room where he placed it beside the desk. He opened the lid and pulled out a book, then another and one more. He put the books on the table in front of Sigbrit and then took out several more. When the chest was emptied, twelve books lay on the table. Sigbrit picked up the top one. It was a description of sea routes from the Lower Lands, which she had already seen in another version in the Special Archives of the Land Registry. A name was inscribed in an elaborate hand on the first page: '*Captain Hans Adelstensfostre*'. Sigbrit laughed with joy. She picked up the next book. It was a bible, its leaves almost falling apart. The third was a book of astronomy by Tycho Brahe, and another by Copernicus.

'A well-read captain,' murmured Sigbrit, then cried out; the book she had just picked up had a blue cloth binding and was closely written in the same elaborate hand. The first page had been torn out, but she was in no doubt; this was Captain Hans Adelstensfostre's diary. There was another blue book, and further down the pile she found three books of freight lists. There was no map, however, and no sketches. She asked the hermit, but he simply shook his head. There was nothing for it but to go through the books.

Sigbrit opened the first page of the first diary: '*20 March 1612, to Fiordenhaffn...*' – she could read no more. She looked at the sentence for a long time, then gave up and pushed the book over to the hermit. He had obviously read the diary before, for it took him only a moment to interpret the words.

'*To Fiordenhaffn with a cargo of grain. The wind sprang up from the north-west in a violent gale, so we were obliged to lower all sails.*' The hermit read on, but the captain's style and spelling were uneven and a mixture of all the Norse languages, and so progress grew slower and slower.

They continued until late afternoon, when dusk fell and the words could no longer be distinguished. Sigbrit hurried back to the green and orange fishing boat and told Odin and Ambrosius about the contents of the three and a half pages the hermit had managed to interpret. The notes had related solely to a voyage to Fjordenhavn, and the captain's thoughts about wind and weather, and what sales could be made in Fjorden-havn and other ports, but Sigbrit was sure they were on the right track. To her disappointment, Ambrosius did not share her enthusiasm.

'Lady Fair, how many pages did you say there were in each of the diaries?' he asked, opening a can of ham and putting the contents on a chopping board.

'Fifty, maybe sixty.'

'And how many in each freight book?'

'More or less the same.'

'Hm.' The Fisherman carved the ham into thin slices, then he looked up. ''Let's just say there are roughly fifty pages in each of the five books. And it's taken the two of you most of the day to interpret three and a half pages of the first one.' He drained the potatoes and started to peel them. 'At that speed it will take you more than two months to go through the lot.'

'It will speed up when we are used to it, and maybe you and Odin could help.'

'It would still take at least a month, Lady Fair, and you know quite well we should have been off some days ago. We must go south. It's already the middle of October.'

Sigbrit took a cup from the cupboard and poured out the remains of the lukewarm coffee from the thermos. 'Yes, but it needn't take so long. Maybe we'll find something earlier, so we don't need to read through all the books.'

The Fisherman put down his knife and seized her hand. 'Maybe, maybe not. Lady Fair, you must realize that if we stay here another day or two, we can easily risk the weather getting too violent for *Rikke-Marie*, and then we will have to spend the winter here.'

Sigbrit pulled her hand away. 'We've been searching for those books for a month,' she shouted. 'And when at last we do find them, you just say: sorry, we haven't time. The forecast is too chancy.'

The Fisherman picked up his knife again and went on peeling potatoes. 'Lady Fair,' he said gently. 'We have to do the best we can. We really must leave here tomorrow. Winter is about to close in on us, and we heard a disturbing news item on the radio while you were away.' He took out three plates and laid them on the mahogany table. 'Early this afternoon at least three hundred North Norse True Christians crossed the Strait in small boats and launched an attack on the Born Anew Christians in Fredenshvile. There are many dead and wounded.' He shook his head. 'The government has announced that it is considering closing the Strait.'

'They can't do that!' exclaimed Sigbrit. 'There must be loads of ships that need to pass through every day. And what about the countries bordering the Inner Sea?'

'Yes, there must be more than a hundred a day, as well as ferries and sailing boats,' he said quietly. 'No doubt they will start by banning smaller boats, while freighters will still be allowed through.' Ambrosius smiled wryly. 'But we fear old *Rikke-Marie* won't be regarded as a freighter.'

Sigbrit slumped down on the bench. 'So that means...'

'Yes,' the Fisherman interrupted her. 'If we don't get Odin back to the island before traffic in the Strait is limited, it may not be possible for a very long time.'

Sigbrit looked over at Odin, who was dozing at the end of the table. 'It's just a possibility,' she said at last, turning her gaze on the Fisherman again. 'Perhaps we can take the books with us.'

It was a moonless night, the darkness thick and impenetrable, when Sigbrit set off for the cottage for the third time that day. She shivered and walked as fast as she could in the gleam from the yellow torchlight. The damp salt wind was icy on her cheeks, and although she held her jacket tight at the neck, it was little protection against the raw cold. Ambrosius was right: winter was on the way.

Harald Adelstensfostre opened the door as soon as she knocked. He must have seen her light approaching. Without a word of welcome he stepped aside to let her in. The room was lit by two oil lamps on the table with an open book on each side of it. As she drew nearer she could see it was the same diary they had been reading earlier in the day. She turned to look at the hermit.

'It's going to take too long,' she said quietly and told him what the Fisherman had said to her. Then she pointed to the book. 'May we take them with us?'

Harald walked over to the window and looked into the darkness at the invisible sea for a long time. Several minutes passed, then he slowly turned round and it seemed as if something in his face had changed. 'Room?' he said hoarsely, pointing in the direction of the jetty and the green and orange fishing boat.

'Yes,' smiled Sigbrit. 'Yes, there's plenty of room for both you and the books.'

*

'*An island is an island until it is no longer an island. When Kings put their name to paper, subjects keep silent. Name the island and all Hell breaks loose,*' Ambrosius the Fisherman repeated slowly.

Brynhild Sigurdskær nodded. They had found her in the grocer's shop shortly after their arrival at Karlsund, and now they were all sitting in *Rikke-Marie*'s wheelhouse.

'The three of them say the same. The same and yet each says something more.' The transparent woman lowered her voice to a whisper: 'An island that disappears into oblivion, an agreement between Kings and punishment for the transgressor.'

'An agreement between Kings.' Ambrosius put the last bite in his mouth and chewed thoroughly. 'We are getting close, I think,' he said with satisfaction, laying down his fork.

'Not much,' said Sigbrit, starting to clear the table. 'Let's say there was an agreement between Kings, and that it explains why all references to the island have been removed, and why Captain Hans Adelstensfostre had to leave in a hurry. But it still doesn't explain why the planes vanished.' She ran the tap and started to wash up.

Harald Adelstensfostre looked from one to the other, saying nothing. Ambrosius cleared his throat. 'That's true, Lady Fair,' he said, getting up to put on the kettle. 'But it's a start.'

'There is no end without a beginning, but some beginnings come without an end,' said Odin, pulling at his beard.

'There, you see!' said Sigbrit, drying the plates.

'No, Lady Fair, *you* see.' The Fisherman kissed Sigbrit lightly on the brow and put five mugs on the table.

'*Near the island in shoes that can swim,*' said Brynhild. '*Only a bone smith can break iron loose.*' She rose and stood in the middle of the wheelhouse, as if not quite knowing what to do with herself. 'The solution is hidden in the first, and the first hides in the last,' she whispered into the air. She walked over to the window and looked out.

'There must have been some kind of danger on the island, or the Kings would not have made that agreement.' Sigbrit put the plates away in the cupboard and hung up the tea towel.

'If there ever was such an agreement,' Ambrosius added, suddenly vexed.

Brynhild jumped. '*An island is an island until it no longer is an island. When Kings put their name to paper, subjects keep silent. Name the island and all Hell breaks loose,*' she whispered.

Sigbrit looked at the Fisherman in surprise, then laid her hand on the transparent woman's arm. 'I know you're right,' she said warmly and continued with more conviction than she felt. 'And I know we are going to find the solution.' She sat down at the table. 'Perhaps there was an epidemic that only the people on the island managed to survive.' She recalled the aeroplanes. 'No, it must be something else.' She forced herself to laugh and tried to sound optimistic. 'Something that needs shoes, that can swim, and iron that's broken loose.'

'Or else it means something quite different,' said the Fisherman crossly. 'Maybe it's all just nonsense and we'll never find that fairway.'

For a moment Brynhild looked at him in amazement, then glanced across at Sigbrit, and at once her face lit up in a smile. 'It's late,' she said calmly. 'You have demanding days ahead of you.' She looked out of the window into the dark evening.

'And you?' asked Sigbrit.

'I have no more to add. Madness burns, and it is a fire no bridges can cross.' Brynhild laughed. 'There are five kennings. The first three have been clarified, the last two will console you.'

'One and one is sometimes one. But one and the only one that is two, is one too many,' said Odin, twisting his beard around his fingers.

Brynhild opened the door and the damp grey cold poured in. 'Sail with care and know your calling,' she said, looking into Ambrosius's eyes. Then the transparent woman was gone.

A long silence followed her departure. Sigbrit rose and looked out. There was not much to see in the darkness, but here and there the stars were reflected in the water as sparkling rays of light.

'*Near the island in shoes that can swim,*' she tried slowly. '*Only a bone smith can break iron loose.*'

'The Blacksmith of Smith's Town knows all there is to know about horses,' Odin added. 'I would truly like to know whether that Veterinarius is soon going to finish the regulations and Mr Bramsentorpf the formalities.'

The Fisherman nodded, but said nothing.

'If the solution is hidden in the first-named, and the first-named is hiding in the last-named, the solution must have something to do with how one approaches the island.' Sigbrit drummed her fingers on the windowsill.

The Fisherman mumbled something incomprehensible and began to clean his pipe.

'It is not enough to know the fairway,' continued Sigbrit. 'You have been right all the time, some other strange thing is going on.' She stopped for a moment. 'However we are to do it, it's necessary to find out what it was they knew about in King Enevold IV's day.'

Harald Adelstensfostre looked up, and for the first time since they had left Grinde Island, he opened his mouth to speak. 'The books,' he said hoarsely, pointing to the primitive wooden chest he had dragged on board that same morning.

*

Word for word, Sigbrit copied in her legible hand the text that Harald Adelstensfostre read out from the captain's diary. '*A coffin was made for him.*' The hermit closed the book; it was late.

Sigbrit put down her pen and leaned her head back against the chilly wall of the wheelhouse. Her hand ached with the effort of writing, and she felt tired and heavy in every limb. She swallowed the growing lump in her throat.

Ambrosius made all the speed he could to sail *Rikke-Marie* south. Even so they could not cover the same distance each day as when they had set course to the north. The wind was stronger, the waves higher and the days shorter. They had been travelling nine days and had finished the first diary and were well into the second without having found mention of much else but wind and weather and the price of flour, salt, meat and timber and other goods. The next day they would reach Kristiansfjord, Harald Adelstensfostre would leave the boat and let them keep the rest of the second diary, the three freight registers and little hope.

Sigbrit rubbed her wrist. 'Come on, let's just do another page or two before we finish up for today,' she said despondently.

'*Great piles of stone and granite rocks, like cannon balls, large and small, lay on the shore...*' The hermit stopped and pulled the book closer to the lamp. A rare smile lifted the corner of his mouth. '*The war goes on. One King and another cannot possibly sail to the island since the fighting.*' He coughed. '*The island is nothing. Know too much. When the King sets his name to a document, subjects must keep silent. If only the King had not fallen in love with a commoner...*'

'There we have it!' exclaimed Sigbrit.

'So Brynhild Sigurdskær was right; there really was an agreement between King Enevold IV and King Hermod Skjalm.' Ambrosius the Fisherman grinned. 'What has that got to do with King Enevold's feelings for Drude Estrid?'

Sigbrit shook her head. 'I don't know,' she said, wondering. 'Let's read on, maybe it will say something about that.'

But it didn't. In fact there was not much more about anything, for after another three pages the rest were blank.

When Sigbrit and Ambrosius were together in his berth later that evening, she asked him if he thought they would ever find the solution.

'We have to,' said the Fisherman in a low voice.

'But what if we don't?'

'If we don't,' he whispered, 'we'll have to ask ourselves for ever afterwards if we truly wanted to find the solution.'

Sigbrit pursed her lips and nodded. She raised herself on her elbow and asked: 'What about Odin's Veterinarius?'

The Fisherman shook his head. 'One thing at a time, Lady Fair,' he said quietly.

Just before dusk on the following day they glimpsed the rooftops of Kristiansfjord on the horizon. Ambrosius The Fisherman slowed down and when they had rounded a small peninsula and were in calm waters, he switched off the engine. 'We'll drop anchor,' he said. 'Although *Rikke-Marie* is camouflaged it's still too risky to go nearer the harbour.'

They had covered *Rikke-Marie's* name with sand and seaweed so it could not be read, falsified the registration number and painted the orange wheelhouse with red paint. Despite this they still risked being recognized by well-meaning folk who had heard the repeated appeal from the South Norse government. According to the radio news the situation in Fredenshvile was getting worse by the day. Although it might help to get Mr Bramsentorpf released, Ambrosius still considered it would be irresponsible to let Odin show himself in the smouldering capital before they knew how they were going to get him back to the island.

They ate dinner in silence, and as soon as they had finished the Fisherman lowered the dinghy into the water and climbed down the rope ladder. Harald Adelstensfostre gave brief farewell handshakes to Sigbrit and Odin and disappeared over the rail to join the Fisherman.

'I think it is about time the Veterinarius and I went back to Smith's Town and Rigmarole,' said Odin, when they could no longer see the dinghy and its two passengers.

Sigbrit shook her head and took a couple of deep breaths. She turned and went back with Odin to the warmth of the wheelhouse. 'Odin, I feel I must tell you that it may well be a while before we find a Veterinarius for your horse,' she said, and was about to tell him of their other problems when she stopped herself; there was no point in worrying the little old man more than absolutely necessary.

Odin tugged his beard and considered the situation. 'If Veterinarius Martinussen has such difficulty completing the regulations and Mr Bramsentorpf can't finish the formalities, and North Norseland's most brilliant Veterinarius is not in a place it is advisable to visit, perchance there might be another Veterinarius?' He twisted his beard around his fingers. 'Although at the moment I can't quite remember what happened before Smith's Town and the meteor storm, nor what the ill tidings were about, I am sure they should not be delayed much longer.'

Tears suddenly welled up in Sigbrit's eyes, and Odin laid a hand on her arm. 'Now, now,' he said soothingly. 'The ill tidings can't be all that bad. No, I am truly convinced there is no need to weep over them.'

'Odin, finding a Veterinarius is only one of the problems,' exclaimed Sigbrit. 'Another problem is to find one who is willing to go back to the island with you. The biggest problem is that we have still not found a way to get you and your Veterinarius and... Ambrosius the Fisherman across to the island.'

Odin carefully smoothed his beard. He had gradually come to understand that the inhabitants of the Continent, no matter how hard they tried, could not make the sea freeze over so he and the Veterinarius and Ambrosius the Fisherman could walk back to the island the same way he had come, at what seemed a long time back, in a horrific blizzard. What he couldn't see was how it could be so hard to find another way.

'It is wisdom we have great need of,' he said finally and nodded, as if to confirm he agreed with his own words. Then he nodded again and fell fast asleep.

Sigbrit looked at him sadly; indeed, it was true, wisdom was what they needed. Quietly, so as not to wake Odin, she cleared the table and washed up. Then she took the first of the freight books out and started to go through the columns of supplies, dates and prices. She had barely started before she closed the book again. They had found nothing useful in the diaries, and she did not have much faith in the freight books. She yawned, pulled on a jacket and went outside to wait for the Fisherman. The lights of Kristiansfjord seemed to her both near and far, almost like the stars above her. It was a calm evening, *Rikke-Marie* rocked gently, and it was not long before she heard the faint sound of oars striking the water. A moment later Ambrosius came clambering up the rope ladder.

Sigbrit helped him haul the dinghy on board, then sat on the bench in front of the wheelhouse watching the Fisherman silently make the boat fast. When he had done he came and sat beside her.

'We're going to get the better of it,' he said, putting his arm around her. 'In one way or another we'll get the better of it.'

'I'm not so sure any more,' murmured Sigbrit dejectedly. 'We have no Veterinarius for Odin's horse, and we haven't found either the fairway or the mysterious forces ruling on the island. We haven't even any ideas to work on.'

'No, we haven't, but we do still have the last two kennings, and we have the freight books.' Ambrosius the Fisherman tried to kiss her but she drew away.

'You don't even believe that yourself.' She rose and went over to the starboard rail. 'How many months have we worked on this now – six, seven, eight? We've tried everything, with what result? Nothing more than a few stupid kennings about an agreement that means nothing!' She stopped her torrent of words to catch her breath. 'Anyway, what is happening on the island is irrelevant, because we haven't found the fairway, and without that you can't get there, as you can't fly. So we are forced to wait until a bridge is built or some other means of access opens during the next millennium. While we wait, every breed of fanatic is setting out to break up our country, while we are also well on the way to starting up a territorial dispute with our old enemy and neighbour in the north.'

Ambrosius the Fisherman stood up and went over to her. 'Come,' he said, 'Come and look at the moon.' He took her hand and led her aft, away from the glaring lights of the town and into the blue lustre of the moonlight.

Sigbrit Holland shivered; it was cold. She pressed close to the Fisherman and felt the warmth of his body against hers.

'Look at the moon, Lady Fair,' he said. 'Look at it.'

Sigbrit looked up. The moon was not full, but soon would be. Like a promise of something, she thought. She leaned her head back and took a long look at the shining incomplete disk. If she had lived ten thousand years ago or only a thousand or two hundred, what would she have believed the moon to be? A frozen lake in the middle of the void? A group of single stars melted together? The back of the sun? A plate of sparks pulled across the heavens in a carriage drawn by a white horse pursued by wolves? Or would she have seen it as the radiant benevolent face of the God she was born to believe in? She turned to the Fisherman. 'Ambrosius, why do you think human beings need religion?'

The Fisherman stroked her hair abstractedly, looking out over the water. 'Probably it's the desire to have complete faith in the meaning of one's own life,' he said quietly.

Sigbrit considered that. 'Once I read something a writer said in a newspaper; he believed that moral values cannot exist without religion. If he is right, doomsday prophets are merely people who fear a life without morals.' She fell silent for a while, then added: 'Maybe he is wrong. Indeed, he must be wrong, for without religion, to define right and wrong demands much stronger ethics.'

'Lady Fair,' said the Fisherman. 'Try to reverse the question.'

'How can ethical values exist if you never have doubts?' asked Sigbrit questioningly and nodded. 'Yes, if you assume a set of regulations and customs laid down by others and then declare that those who do not conform to those regulations are unbelievers or amoral.'

'Doubt is the virtue of courage, belief is that of hubris,' Odin's voice interposed. He had woken from his sleep in the wheelhouse and soundlessly joined them on deck.

The waves touched the sides of the boat gently, but another sound could also be heard.

'What is it?' Sigbrit stiffened.

They listened in silence for a while. The sound slowly grew clearer, the sound of oars rhythmically cleaving the water. The Fisherman crept across to starboard while Sigbrit pushed Odin into the wheelhouse. She was opening a drawer to get out a knife, when she heard the Fisherman burst out laughing.

It didn't take them long to get the hermit and his little rubber dinghy on board. He ignored their enquiring glances and quietly lifted the boat out of the water, deflated it and folded it up. When he had done that he went into the wheelhouse and sat down beside Odin. Sigbrit set a piece of cake on the table before him and poured some coffee. Then she sat down on the other side of the table. It wasn't until he had eaten the cake and emptied the chipped mug that he began to speak: 'The island,' he said hoarsely.

Sigbrit waited, but Harald Adelstensfostre said no more, so after a few minutes she asked 'Why?'

The hermit hesitated. 'Asta knew about it,' he said, turning to look at Odin and adding quite casually: 'A horse's bone can't be so very different from a human one.'

VALHALLA

A palace to the King of Gods
Valhalla was for Odin raised
Gleaming spears made up the walls
and shields of gold thatched high the roof
five hundred and forty doors gave entry
at once, through each, eight hundred men.

Women fiercest, nine Valkyries
let the lives of men at war
picking from the dead in bravery
Aser's thrust, Vallhalla's happiness

On palace roof Goat Heidrun stood
her heady mead to fighters flowed
Sœrimmer's flesh their stomachs filled
   endless was this gelded hog

Einherier, battling one with one
to death at eve, alive by morn
'Learn fortitude and loyalty
face to face, meet enemy'

   Thus gods prepared for final feud

M R BRAMS BRAMSENTORPF was a courageous man, but
in the face of an ordeal and the prospect of pain his courage

dwindled, until he couldn't stop himself from bursting into tears and before many minutes had passed he had told his guards everything he knew. This, Aisha saw at once, could be boiled down to just two things: first, that Allah's messenger, the Mighty One, was on holiday somewhere unbeknown to the government, and second, that the Mighty One planned to return to the Isle of the Prophet as soon as possible.

The Muslim Militia had prepared the abduction of Mr Bramsentorpf with meticulous care, taking every eventuality into consideration. Or rather they thought they had, for not even in their wildest dreams had they anticipated such a pitiful result. Not only did Mr Bramsentorpf know next to nothing, but the scrap of information he had to give them was worthless. Not only did the South Norse government refuse to exchange the Messenger of Allah in return for Mr Bramsentorpf, in fact the Norse government was not in a position to release him.

Aisha pondered for several days whether to release Mr Bramsentorpf or to get rid of him once and for all. However, because she had no idea what to do with a corpse and she did not know whether the hostage might turn out to be useful at a later time she decided they might as well keep him alive a little longer. When she thought it over, Mr Bramsentorpf had in fact given the Muslim Militia an important piece of information, and when she thought even further, Mr Bramsentorpf had not given that information to anyone else. Therefore Aisha did not need to think much longer before concluding that the best thing the Muslim Militia could do was prepare for the journey to the Isle of the Prophet. Once they had left the Queendom of the South Norse, Mr Bramsentorpf, dead or alive, would no longer stand in their way.

The only thing Aisha, her brother and the thirty-nine other members of the Militia still needed to find out was how they were to get to the Isle of the Prophet, and, naturally, who was responsible for the mysterious threatening letters.

*

Free Odin or Bramsentorpf is a dead man.

Ten such letters had been sent to the government. Each one composed from letters cut from various newspapers and magazines, all written in South Norse, all with one single North Norse word in them, and all sent from Fredenshvile.

What no amount of brain cudgelling could impart to Aisha was that the almost legendary Lennart Torstensson had decided that if the witless hostage takers did not make use of Mr Bramsentorpf's negotiating value, then Lennart wouldn't be slow in doing so. He had even gone so far as to take a train all the way to Fredenshvile to deposit every one of the ten letters in the letterbox single-handed. Yet the expected result had not materialized. All the South Norse government had done was to publish an appeal for Mr Odin Odin to return to South Norseland, as if Lennart would fall for that.

No, he had no intention of waiting any longer to get rid of the 'almost', so he decided he had better hit on something more effective. After scratching his head for a while he realized that he did not actually need the little old man to make the island a North Norse possession; in fact the absence of Mr Odin Odin could be far more useful. This idea was nothing less than brilliant; Lennart would outwit the South Norse by their own methods! The South Norse government would never, either now or later, be able to let Mr Odin reappear without having to give up their claim on the island.

For the first time in several months Lennart stayed on in the office until far into the evening. He worked at the computer for hours and conscientiously looked up every word in his North Norse–South Norse dictionary. It was past eight o'clock and the Commission building had long since emptied of its human contents before he felt satisfied. He printed out six copies of the letter and put five of them in envelopes addressed – with the aid of his secretary's typewriter, since he didn't know how to use the printer for envelopes – to the South Norse Prime Minister, the Queen of South Norseland and the three largest South Norse dailies. The sixth copy of the letter he placed in a plastic folder which he slipped into his briefcase: *Ordnung muss sein*, according to a phrase in his notebook of useful maxims. There must be no sloppiness to undermine a legendary man's legendary actions. Finally he called the station and booked a seat on the train to Fredenshvile that evening.

Lennart switched off the light in his office, put on his coat and closed the door behind him, the next moment only to open the door again, take off his coat and put on the light. He had been on the point of making a fatal mistake; a letter from Herr Odin Odin sent from and franked in Fredenshvile would hardly seem authentic seen through South Norse eyes, since the government had told the public that Mr Odin Odin was not in the South Queendom. Not only would that cause doubt as to the letter's credibility but it would also – which was much worse – allow the South

Norse government to escape from the tight corner they were in.

After pondering a few moments he set about tearing the six identical letters into minute scraps and then walked with firm steps down the corridor to Herr Hölzern's office. He grasped the door handle and with a sigh of relief found the door unlocked. He did not switch on the light to avoid drawing attention from passers-by but fumbled his way across the room to the desk and sat down. He felt around for the computer and hit the power button. He found his way into the system easily; it was no secret that Herr Hölzern was passionately uxurious. The name of Frau Hölzern – Ursula – gave prompt results, and he was immediately logged on to the world wide web, which the computer in his own office was not programmed to do.

Lennart wrote the letter once more, and this time he did not stop at five recipients. Because it was easy and because it would avert any potential attempt at covering up the story, he forwarded the letter to the whole of the South Norse as well as the North Norse press. This internet business was the greatest invention since the steam train, he exulted. The South Norse government and the Queen of South Norseland as well as the assembled South Norse and North Norse press would shortly receive a letter that could not be identified either by handwriting or machine script, paper or envelope. Nor were stamps necessary, which could have revealed the sender. As he forwarded the letter via a small diversion that would erase the sender's address, he was satisfied that no one would know the point of origin of the letter. It was ingenious, and the almost legendary Lennart Torstensson was fast becoming a legend!

*

The South Norse Government has requested the undersigned to return to Fredenshvile as soon as possible. The undersigned will have great pleasure in complying with the South Norse government's appeal, as soon as the South Norse government for ever and for the foreseeable future relinquishes all territorial rights to the island, known to the South Norse government as Drude Estrid Island, to the North Norse government as Hermod Skjalm Island.

Allow me to make use of this opportunity to assure the South Norse government of my humblest esteem and respect.

Yours most faithfully
Odin Odin

'Who in the world has dreamed up this nonsense?' Sigbrit lowered the newspaper.

'Not easy to know,' replied Ambrosius the Fisherman from the helm, thoughtfully chewing his pipe.

It was four days since they had left Kristiansfjord. The sea was quite rough, though the damp cold was less raw here than further north. At the inn in the little fishing port where they had shopped for provisions, Sigbrit had found a national Old Norse newspaper only one day old. She read the article once more, shook her head and laid the paper aside. She nodded to Harald Adelstensfostre, who resumed his interpretation of the freight registers at once.

'*4 May 1614, One load of timber for Fredenshvile...*' he read out slowly.

'Actually, we don't much mind people thinking this little

screed was composed by Odin here,' broke in the Fisherman, nodding towards Odin.

Sigbrit stopped writing in the middle of a word. 'What do you mean?'

'That it probably wouldn't be a bad thing if our government renounced their claim on the island,' said the Fisherman with an inscrutable grin.

'So you'd prefer the island to become North Norse?'

'Absolutely not.' Ambrosius removed the pipe from his mouth and laughed out loud. 'But it wouldn't be so bad if it became independent.'

'Independent. Why should we want that?'

'Independence can only be won by what is dependent,' Odin remarked, winding his beard around his fingers.

'Exactly!' exclaimed Sigbrit. 'All we want is a way back to the island. Why should we be concerned whether it is independent or not?'

'Quite a bit, Lady Fair, quite a lot, in fact.'

Sigbrit gave this some thought. 'Do you honestly think that people would stop fighting over the island if it was declared to be independent?'

'Maybe not the Prophets of Doom, but the others, probably. We may as well start somewhere.' The Fisherman rubbed his chin and gazed out to sea over *Rikke-Marie*'s bows. 'Moreover, there is one small but important detail: independence would allow Veterinarius Adelstensfostre to function as Veterinarius Adelstensfostre.'

Sigbrit smiled; that was true. Without professional proof in his own name the hermit would never under any South Norse or North Norse law be able to practise medicine – not to mention work as a veterinary surgeon.

'Even if the fake document would get the South Norse government to renounce their claim on the island, how would you make the North Norse do the same?'

Ambrosius turned and looked Sigbrit straight in the eye. 'We won't, Lady Fair. *You* will!'

'I?' Sigbrit laughed. Then she realized what the Fisherman had in mind and shook her head. 'No, forget it,' she said. 'That would never work. Instead let's call our government and say the letter was not written by Odin but by some impostor, and that Odin will gladly return to the Queendom of the South Norse if only the government will undertake to transport him over to the island.'

'And how would it do that then, Lady Fair?'

The Fisherman suddenly stiffened. He slackened speed and pointed to starboard. A coastguard boat could be seen in the distance. It was heading straight for them.

'Oh, no,' murmured Sigbrit, staring tensely at the white powerboat coming rapidly nearer. It would be useless to try to escape it.

Soon they could make out three figures on the bridge.

'There is no mishap that a spot of luck cannot remedy,' said Odin calmly, with a hand on the horseshoe in his breast pocket. At that very moment the powerboat passed by without the coastguards casting a glance at the green and orange fishing boat.

Sigbrit breathed out in relief and sat down again.

'I'm afraid we'll need a great deal of luck before we get safely home to the Queendom,' muttered the Fisherman anxiously and resumed their earlier discussion. 'Independence is the only way out of the current impasse for the South Norse and North Norse governments without either of them losing face.

It is the only option they have, unless you want the conflict to go on for years. And whoever wrote that letter,' he pointed to the folded newspaper, 'was right. No one but Odin can demand independence for the island.'

Odin broke in: 'There are also the Blacksmith and Oldmother Rikke-Marie and Mother Marie and Uncle Eskild, whose hearing leaves something to be desired, and the Baker and Ida-Anna and Ingolf and all the children, not forgetting Long Laust from Post Office Town.' He nodded to himself as if something had just occurred to him. 'Then of course they would have to summon up all their strength and courage to freeze the sea and walk to the Continent to talk to Mr Bramsentorpf and his officials, and in truth it is far from certain they would have the time and inclination for that kind of thing.'

Sigbrit smiled. 'No, you may well be right there,' she said to Odin. 'So it seems I had better do the job myself after all.' She turned to Ambrosius. 'Where can I find a computer?'

'A public library, probably?'

'No,' replied Sigbrit. 'Nowhere public. It must be somewhere no one can discover what I'm up to. A place where the letter can't be traced.' She glanced at the hermit and suddenly brightened.

The Fisherman read her thoughts and shook his head. 'There must be someone else,' he muttered.

Odin looked from one to the other. 'In hard times, enemies who can be of help are better friends than friends who cannot help you,' he remarked quietly.

*

The undersigned wishes to inform the North Norse government that the undersigned will never, including at

any future time, near or far, set foot in North Norseland
unless the North Norse government will, for always and in
all time to come, renounce the island known to the North
Norse government as Hermod Skjalm Island, and to the
South Norse government as Drude Estrid Island.

Allow me to take this opportunity of assuring the North
Norse government of my highest esteem and respect.

Yours most faithfully
Odin Odin

In a trice the South Norse Prime Minister was considerably better pleased with the little old man.

'Ha, now we've got the whip end again,' he said, joyously cracking all the fingers of his left hand. 'The little old man will return to South Norseland as soon as we renounce our claim on the island, while he has said nothing about ever intending to go to North Norseland even if the North Norse government relinquishes its demand.'

'Yes,' said the Minister of Defence slowly, clearing his throat. 'There's just the small problem of the public.'

'I'm afraid the public is not one but two problems,' interrupted the Minister for Ecclesiastical Affairs. 'The Prophets of Doom on one side, the rest of the public on the other.'

They were seated on the sofas in the Prime Minister's office. Although it was late, they had only just settled down to their meeting, and were still waiting for the Minister of Justice.

'Unfortunately, all of them have the right to vote,' said the Minister of Defence.

The Prime Minister's left cheek twitched. 'Yes,' he sneered. 'And what is worse, the two groups have gradually come to demand one and the same thing. How many are there left of the *rest of the population* today?'

'Still quite a few.' The Minister for Ecclesiastical Affairs tried to sound optimistic. 'It's true that some of them have jumped on "the-millennium-is-almost-over" nationalistic bandwagon but I am convinced that if the island is declared independent they will turn back to fighting with their neighbours on the football pitch just as in the good old days.'

The Prime Minister pulled at his right middle finger.

'But the Doomsday Prophets,' the Minister for Ecclesiastical Affairs went on, 'the Doomsday Prophets will continue to wage their Holy War no matter what happens to the island's status. Only the coming of the new millennium will put a stop to their zeal.'

'We'll see,' said the Prime Minister, his voice suddenly weary. 'Don't forget, there's always a new millennium on its way.'

The door of the Prime Minister's office opened and the Minister of Justice entered.

'Sorry to be late. It took my people longer than expected to get this finished.' The Minister waved a grey briefcase and took out four documents. He passed one to each of the company, and kept the last set for himself. 'I know very well it sounds absurd,' he threw a nervous glance at the Prime Minister, 'but it's just impossible.'

'Impossible?' The Prime Minister's mouth began to twitch. He looked through the document swiftly, mechanically cracking his right thumb again and again. 'Surely there's a way round this?' he asked, tapping the papers.

'No, we are trapped by our own arguments.' The Minister of Justice fidgeted uneasily. 'We have made an official demand for the territory. We have established through the subtlest legal and historical arguments that Drude Estrid Island belongs and always has belonged to the Queendom of the South Norse. That is to say, in relation to South Norse law the island is just as South Norse as every other of the country's five hundred islands. Neither this nor any other government will summarily be able to declare one piece of the country's territory as independent.'

'But that's a mere formality,' protested the Minister for Ecclesiastical Affairs, playing with her bracelet.

'The formalities you mention are unfortunately the Constitution of the country. As the document indicates,' the Minister of Justice pointed to the documents he held, 'according to the Constitution it is impossible for the island to secede without a referendum. Even if we could get around this claim with a few legal and political subtleties, a new law would be necessary, and you know as well as I that it only needs one third of the Members of Parliament to request a referendum regarding a new law.' The Minister of Justice laughed. 'Add the rightist nationalists to that part of the left that sympathizes with Simon Peter II's revolt against the Established Church and we are far more than a third. With the mood of the country as it is there is nothing to be done; a referendum would be sheer suicide. It is absurd, but we seem to be caught by our own arguments.'

The Prime Minister stood up and walked over to the window. He looked out at the demonstrating Born Anew Christians, who had returned to the square outside Parliament House after the fire at the North Norse embassy. 'Free the Mighty One', read a banner. 'Defend the honour of the South Norse' demanded another in big black letters. 'Punish the North Norse' said a third, hung over a home-made dais, from where the young bespectacled man who called himself Simon Peter II was roaring something that fortunately was inaudible through the double-glazed windows.

'What about the Queen?' the Minister of Ecclesiastical Affairs broke into the Prime Minister's ruminations.

'The Queen?' he asked without turning round.

'Yes, in certain circumstances she can validate a law without there having been a referendum. Or if the situation worsens further, she can surely execute a decree?'

The Minister of Justice looked at his colleague with poorly concealed amusement. 'Before it goes that far we need to have proclaimed a state of emergency and suspended the function of Parliament,' he said in a slightly patronizing tone. 'Although things are in a bad state, we haven't quite come to that yet.'

'That's not the point,' hissed the Prime Minister irritably without taking his eyes off the demonstrators and their banners. 'The Queen is the last one to want to renounce the claim on the island. We're talking about her legacy, you know.' He shook his head and turned abruptly to the Minister of Justice. 'Tell me something else. What has happened in the search for the little old man?'

'It hasn't been as easy as you might think...' The patronizing look was instantly replaced by a servile smile. 'Obviously no one knows where he has gone. His details have been broadcast on radio and television all over the Norselands and the Great Kingdom. But so far the police have not received any useful information.' The Minister rubbed his nose nervously. 'Today I did hear that a fishing boat, which apparently resembled the one Mr Odin Odin was staying on, has been seen once or twice by fishermen along the Long North Norse coast. So far the police have been unable to confirm whether it is the one we are looking for or not.'

'Surely it's not so hard to find a little old fishing boat.' The Prime Minister cracked all the fingers on his left hand crossly, then again looked out over the banners in the square: '*Free the Great Man from North Norseland*'; '*Wage war against the heathen North Norses*'; '*Only traitors will let the North Norse get away with it*'; '*You are not our government if you don't defend us*'; '*Defend the honour of South Norseland*'; '*Free the Mighty One and free Bramsentorpf*'.

'Free the Mighty One!' the crowd began to roar and the double-glazed windows could no longer keep out the angry voices. 'Free the Mighty One!'

The Prime Minister whipped round, his mouth twitching violently. 'Listen here,' he shouted. 'I couldn't care less about that island. I couldn't care less about the little old man. And I don't give a damn for North Norseland! Any more than for this Bramsentorpf! What I do give a damn about are the voters! I'll tell you one thing. We'll suffer a colossal defeat if we so much as attempt to give up our claim on the island.' The Prime Minister paused and then continued with his voice more under control: 'I don't mind how you do it – satellite images, aerial observation from planes, the army, anything – but one thing is certain, I want the little old man home in South Norseland NOW!' He crashed his clenched fist down on the windowsill, overturning one of the pot plants. The Prime Minister did not pick it up, but merely threw a contemptuous glance at the broken blooms and resumed his watch over the demonstrators. He nodded slowly to himself. 'Apart from that there is only one thing we can do.'

Diplomacy being what it is, the South Norse ambassador to

North Norseland was called home immediately amidst carefully prepared publicity. And a few days later the North Norse ambassador left the Queendom of South Norseland with no less hype.

*

'*His Majesty our King will never yield. War is nigh,*' the hermit read out from the margin of the freight ledger.

It had not taken much persuasion to get Benjamin Adelstensfostre to help Sigbrit post the letter on the world wide web, so after only one day in Fjordenhavn she was able to take a train back to the once green and orange fishing boat. She found it again as prearranged in a small fishing port just two days' – or rather two nights' – sail from the southernmost point of Long North Norseland. They had put out at night and anchored in small little-known fjords during the day. The search continued ceaselessly now, and Ambrosius the Fisherman preferred to keep watch at night for rocks and reefs, which after all were marked on the charts, rather than risk having *Rikke-Marie* recognized by the wrong people by day.

'*28 June 1615, Ur Island, brass plates and iron bars. 1 July 1615, Fredenshvile, salted herrings.*' The hermit coughed. '*5 July 1615, I S U with timber.*'

'*I S U,*' repeated Sigbrit slowly. 'What's that?'

'It must be an abbreviation,' remarked Ambrosius from the helm. 'Did you say 1615?'

'Yes, it was the fifth of July 1615.' Sigbrit brightened. 'You're right, it was while the island was known about. Perhaps it is that?'

Ambrosius turned his head. 'But why I S U?' he asked.

'The Island something or other. The Island south of... The Island south of Ur Island, of course!'

The Fisherman nodded. 'Yes, that sounds about right.' He smoked for a while, then removed his pipe. 'So even then the island had no name.'

'No, apart from the names the South Norse and the North Norse Kings wanted to give it.'

Ambrosius rubbed his chin. 'An island could not be known about for long before being given a name,' he said slowly. 'So it must have been discovered just a short time before the Kings started to fight over it.'

'And of course that's why not many people knew about it,' said Sigbrit. 'And still fewer who had ever been there.' Her face broke into a broad smile. 'Perhaps that was why its existence could be completely forgotten.'

'And why Captain Hans Adelstensfostre was in danger,' added Ambrosius drily.

'Wisdom is a dangerous lance,' remarked Odin, suddenly realizing he had probably lost his own lance with the other forgotten things that came before Smith's Town and the meteor storm as well as the ill tidings.

'Yes, Captain Hans Adelstensfostre must have been one of the only captains who ever traded with the island. That's why he had to make himself scarce.'

'I daresay we knew that already, Lady Fair,' sighed the Fisherman.

The misty grey morning light told them dawn was not far off. It was high time they found a sheltered place to moor.

'We believed it, we didn't know it,' insisted Sigbrit. 'Now we also know that it was these freight books that put the captain's life in danger. Not his diaries.'

'He has still not mentioned the way in,' the hermit interjected hoarsely, suddenly resuming his reading. '*18 July 1615, from Fredenshvile with live oxen...*'

Sigbrit bent over her notebook. Maybe at some point or other the captain would describe or just indicate the route he had used to reach the island. Even if it was just a note on the position of the sun, the stars, or the outline of the cliffs, or if it was on the west or east side, it would be a help.

'*16 August 1615. Ur Island, 4 sheep, iron bars and Timber. 18 August 1615, I S U, 2 sheep, timber and wood chips. 19 August 1615, Fredenshvile, salted herring.*' The hermit cleared his throat. '*4 September 1615, Fiordenhaffn, 2 loads of salt and one large consignment lead. 15 September 1615, Ur Island, 2 barrels rye, iron and copper, wool and linen. 17 September 1615, U S I, wool and linen, hemp and barrel wood, load of salt. 20 September...*' This continued in the same vein for a long time, until the hermit found yet another footnote. '*King Hermod Skjalm's ships are in the Strait. Trade with I S U is finished,*' he read.

'When feuds spring up, folk grow poor and fools make fortunes,' said Odin. He felt strangely close to recalling the ill tidings.

Ambrosius the Fisherman slackened speed. He had glimpsed a point that promised shelter. Sigbrit pulled on the Fisherman's big windcheater and went out on deck. The morning mist enfolded her like a cold embrace, and she made haste to drop anchor. As soon as she had assured herself the anchor had taken a firm hold on the seabed, she hurried back to the warmth of the wheelhouse.

In spite of their weariness, they only slept for a few hours. It was necessary to make good use of the daylight as long as it lasted because it made reading considerably easier. They were almost through it and before the day was out they would be finished. A few pages at the end of the book had been torn out, eight were blank. That was it.

'Well, we're not a lot the wiser for all that,' mumbled Ambrosius.

'True, we aren't really,' replied Sigbrit with a thoughtful expression. 'Yet I go on feeling the solution is here somewhere in these books.' She put a hand on the freight ledgers. 'It's just that we don't see it.'

'Lady Fair, you can't have overlooked anything, you went through these accounts with a fine-toothed comb.'

'We are missing something, and I don't know what it is.' Sigbrit laughed a little ruefully and pushed her hair back. She picked up a box of eggs and started to break them into a bowl. 'At least now we're sure of one thing: the freight books don't include any direct description of the fairway.'

There was a moment's silence, then the Fisherman cleared his throat. 'Perhaps we'll have to give it up,' he said quietly.

'Give up?' Sigbrit stared at him in amazement. 'And leave it up to the government?'

The last grey daylight faded into the sea, and the Fisherman lit the lamp above the worn mahogany table. 'No, that's not what we have in mind.' He shook his head as if he wanted to go on but didn't quite know how to put it.

Sigbrit looked out of the window at the fast approaching murk, as she whisked the eggs with a little milk.

'*Near the island in shoes that can swim. Only a bone smith knows how to beat iron loose,*' she murmured. 'The solution is hidden in the former, the former is hidden in the latter.' She turned with the bowl in her hands and met the Fisherman's eye. 'There is a way, and we *are* going to find it,' she declared with conviction.

Ambrosius looked at the hermit, who responded with an almost imperceptible nod.

'There is a way,' said the Fisherman quietly. 'It is a way we have not told you about because we know you won't like it.' He hesitated. 'It is not foolproof, but as everything else has failed, we might as well try it.'

Sigbrit waited.

'Lady Fair, it is not a solution. We will have to take a chance.' His lips touched her hair before he went on almost apologetically. 'Diving.'

'Diving!' Sigbrit put the bowl of eggs down on the table with a thump. 'You must be mad.'

'We haven't found any other way, have we?'

'You'll be dashed to death on the rocks.'

'Maybe, maybe not. If we go right down to the seabed the current will be less strong, and with a bit of luck we can swim around the rocks and in to the island.'

'With a bit of luck! You'll need God's help. How can you even give it a thought?'

Ambrosius reached out for her but Sigbrit pulled away.

'What else can we do?' he asked gently. 'Lady Fair, we have tried every option without finding a single explanation of what is going on. Odin came from the island, our grandfather did too, so it is possible for normal people to live there. If only we can reach the other side of the rocks, everything will be fine.'

'You'll have to wait until next summer, the water is far too cold now.'

'On the contrary. The colder the better. Cold water doesn't

move anything like so much as warm water. The currents are slower in the winter.'

'So you'll freeze to death instead of being torn apart on the rocks.'

'Cold is a slight problem, we know that. But it can be dealt with. It's just a matter of having the right gear. People dive at the poles.'

'You must be stark raving mad!' Sigbrit exclaimed. She turned to the hermit. 'And you'd go along with this?'

Harald Adelstensfostre nodded. Sigbrit looked at Odin.

Odin pulled at his beard, surprised at the sudden question. 'He who can walk on water can walk under water too,' said the little old man.

Sigbrit shook her head. 'You are all completely crazy,' she whispered angrily. 'You will be cut to pieces on the rocks.'

Ambrosius took his pipe from his mouth. 'Lady Fair, what else are we to do? Settle down here in the Old North?'

Sigbrit sat down at the table and buried her face in her hands. She knew for certain it was impossible. Even if Ambrosius chose to tempt fate, Odin still had to return to the island and his horses, and Harald Adelstenfostre had no other life. Suddenly Sigbrit realized that she had not given a thought to what she would do when the others went off. She would have to leave that for another time, right now it was clear what she was appointed to do.

She rose and looked first at Odin, then Harald Adelstensfostre and finally at Ambrosius. 'There is another possibility,' she said. 'And I don't care if you give up, I am going to find it.'

'There is another possibility, we know that,' smiled the Fisherman with his voice full of sad admiration. 'But we haven't found it, and we can't go on looking for it. The government has declared they will close the Strait to private traffic at Christmas, if the country is not at peace before then.' He coughed. 'Lady Fair,' he said feelingly, finding his voice again. 'It is too late now. We shall be back in South Norseland early tomorrow, and in Fredenshvile a few days later. Once we are there we must put all our efforts into preparing for the diving trip to the island so we can get off before they close the Strait.'

Sigbrit looked despairing.

'It is a risk we'll just have to run,' the Fisherman went on, stroking her hair.

Sigbrit met his gaze, then turned to look from Harald Adelstensfostre to Odin before turning back to him. 'How many days have I got?' she asked calmly.

'If the weather lasts,' the Fisherman smiled, shaking his head. 'Four.'

*

Bishop Bentsen was a happy man. To be precise, Bishop Bentsen was a happy man for each one of the thirty-eight days that passed from the expulsion of the Born Anew Christians from Our Saviour's Church, up until two of the leftish opposition parties put a proposal on the agenda of Parliament to the effect that one or more churches be allotted to the Born Anew Christians.

It would take a significantly lesser brain than Bishop Bentsen's to realize that the government would not be able to withstand the pressure much longer. Once the Born Anew Christians had one church they would soon get another and another and then a third, and there was no knowing where that would end. No, Bishop Bentsen was not ready to give way by as much as the tiniest chapel.

Like most of his predecessors, the Bishop believed in the power of prayer. And, like most of his predecessors when it came to earthly affairs, he believed still more in worldly sagacity. So when prayers in this matter turned out to be fruitless, Bishop Bentsen prayed for the Lord's forgiveness and summoned Vicar Valentino.

Thus it happened, shortly afterwards, on a dark, rainy November morning, that Simon Peter II – in the form of an angelically white letter in a gilded Gothic hand – received yet another revelation from the Lord and His Son, the Mighty One.

'At the turn of the millennium,' Simon Peter II intoned into the rain and his megaphone the following day: 'At the turn of the millennium the waters will divide, and I, Simon Peter the Second, the Mighty One's Entrusted Disciple and First Apostle will lead you, the Born Anew Christians, the only true pious ones, to the Isle of Paradise.'

Simon Peter II was ecstatic, as were his followers, and the Entrusted Disciple did not need to pump his arm up and down before the crowd was already roaring: 'The Isle of Paradise! The Isle of Paradise!'

Since Simon Peter II did not regard himself as a fool he had naturally briefly considered the possibility that the angelic letter from the Mighty One was a hoax. But if the sophisticated calligraphy did not totally convince the Entrusted Disciple, the contents did, since the words of the Mighty One tallied so closely with those he himself had declared to his followers not long before. The Entrusted Disciple and First Apostle of the Mighty One begged forgiveness of the Lord for his momentary lapse of faith and immediately called the Born Anew Christians together for an extra divine service on Parliament Square.

Precisely as Bishop Bentsen had foreseen, Simon Peter II was no longer so set on the Born Anew Christians getting a church. According to the Mighty One's message there were no more than seven weeks to Judgement Day and the emigration to the Isle of Paradise, and all their efforts now must be put into the final salvation of damned and miserable souls – and naturally into freeing the Mighty One from his incarceration by the North Norse false True Christians.

Simon Peter II stuck out his arm and pointed to the monumental Parliament building behind him. 'War!' he yelled. 'Our government must declare war against the heathen North Norsemen who so disgracefully kidnapped the Lord's Son, the Mighty One.'

'War!' roared the drenched Born Anew Christians happily. 'War!'

'We shall go to war in the Name of the Lord to free the Mighty One and save him from the treacherous True Christians,' went on Simon Peter II. 'And in the Name of the Lord we shall go to war to save those souls that can still be saved.' He blinked passionately. 'When we walk through the portals to the Island of Paradise, the mighty gardens of the Mighty One, in the generosity of our hearts we will beg the Mighty One to leave the door ajar for those misguided souls who at the last minute realize their love for God and the Mighty One.' Simon Peter II stopped to draw breath, as his eyes filled with the tears of divine bliss and goodness of heart. 'And after we have discovered and freed the Mighty One, in the goodness of our hearts we shall also forgive those we must fight against now, for in the hereafter only God and the Mighty One shall judge sinners and saints.'

'Only God and the Mighty One shall judge sinners and saints!'

The Mighty One's Entrusted Disciple could no longer control his emotions; tears of divine bliss and generosity of heart poured out of his passionately blinking eyes and down his cheeks.

'The world will meet its end, but the Born Anew Christians shall live on the Island of Paradise to aid Almighty God and His Son the Mighty One to create the Thousand Year Reign of Peace on Earth. For as it is written:

> *The dwelling of God is with the sons of man, he will dwell with them and they shall be His people, and God himself will be with them. He will dry all tears from their eyes, and death shall be no more, nor sorrow, nor screams nor suffering shall ever be. For what there was once, shall have vanished.'*

It was also written that:

> *'the throne of God and the Lamb shall stand in the city, and his servants shall worship him, and they shall see his face and bear his name on their brows. There shall be no more night, and they will have no need of lamplight or sunlight, for the Lord God will shine on them, and they shall be Kings for eternity after eternity.'*

The Blessed Anders Andersen, who had for a long while preached that the Lord's Shepherd would save the Lambs of the Lord on the Day of Judgement, thus decreed in the true spirit of the Lord, that the Lambs of the Lord should all have the Lord's name tattooed on their brows, so that it would be easier to distinguish them when the Day dawned. No sooner said than done, and now the Lambs of the Lord proudly displayed the signed brows on which they had hitherto carried their bald pates and grey cowls. The Blessed Anders Andersen prayed and smoked even more sacred grass and sent all the Lambs of God who could be spared out into Fredenshvile to light sacrificial fires and save the lost souls who were still to be saved. And salvation came at a trifling price – they simply paid their fortunes, created in their worldly, sinful lives, into the Blessed Anders Andersen's bank account.

Since Ezekiel the Righteous had neither bishops nor the New Testament to aid him it was lucky he had a brother. A few days after Simon Peter II had proclaimed that at the millennium the Born Anew Christians would make their way between the divided waters to the Island of Paradise, a grubby handwritten note attached to a round stone was sent through the window of Ezekiel the Righteous's parents' apartment with a crash that brought father, mother and Ezekiel the Righteous running in.

> *Travel to the Island of Eternal Sabbath,*
> *leave before the lost ones start.*
> *Hasten like angels through the sky*
> *Hasten away this minute.*
> *I'll be waiting for you.*

The note was signed 'Messiah the Mighty One,' and Ezekiel the Righteous, his father and mother, the five remaining uncles, their wives and children with the widow of the sixth and the few unrelated Reborn Jews did not doubt it was genuine. The Reborn Jews had been aware for a long time that they would soon be going to the Island of the Eternal Sabbath, and naturally had to get there before the Born Anew Christians. There was some discussion about the interpretation of the words '*hasten like angels through the sky*', as the most obvious thing – to use an aeroplane – was not possible. It was the eldest uncle who soon found the solution.

'A helicopter,' he said, and father, mother, the four remaining uncles, their wives and children, the widow of the sixth and the handful of unrelated Reborn Jews nodded and said of course, and that was obvious, and Ezekiel the Righteous at once declared that that was precisely what the Mighty One had in mind.

As the exception is generally the rule, even the most convincing idea becomes less so when money is involved, and the five remaining uncles, their wives and children, with the widow of the sixth and the handful of unrelated Reborn Jews now began to think twice about the necessity of buying a helicopter. Maybe they could manage if they hired one?

What divine inspiration was unable to accomplish, outward and unavoidable circumstances achieved: Now, not only did the police show rather too much interest in Ezekiel the Righteous and the Reborn Jews after the bombing of the North Norse embassy, but the Reborn Jews were increasingly often exposed to violent harassment by the brown-shirted, crew-cut Avengers. They no longer felt safe either inside or outside the four walls of their home, and before long ample sums of money started to pour into Ezekiel the Righteous's money-box.

It was two o'clock in the morning when *Rikke-Marie* chugged slowly through Fredenshvile Harbour into the canals where the afterglow of earlier Christmas candles still sparkled here and there.

'*An island is an island until it is no longer an island. When Kings put their names to paper, subjects keep still. Name the island, and all Hell breaks loose,*' murmured Sigbrit wearily to herself. '*Near the island in shoes that can swim. Only a bone smith knows how to beat out iron.* The answer hides in the former, and the former hides in the latter.'

Ambrosius the Fisherman turned his head and looked at her for a minute. 'Go to bed, Lady Fair,' he said quietly.

Sigbrit nodded but didn't move. The four days were up, going to bed would be admitting defeat. She had been back over all the theories they had rejected, only to reject them one by one again. She had read through her extracts from Captain Hans Adelstensfostre's diaries and freight ledgers once more without finding a trace of the fairway to the island, and had repeated the five kennings to herself one after another without getting an iota closer to the meaning of the last two.

The green and orange fishing boat sailed into the Firø Canal with everyone's nerves on edge in the wheelhouse, although they had no need to worry. Der Fremdling and Gunnar the Head had done what they had been asked to; the two great gates to the disused dock were wide open. Ambrosius switched off the engine, and the fishing boat glided soundlessly into her hideout. The dock was empty and there was no point in attracting attention by using a light; the windows in the roof were not large enough to let in the rays of the moon or the town. When *Rikke-Marie* was safely moored Der Fremdling and Gunnar the Head closed the gates, and shortly afterwards they disappeared into the night. Ambrosius locked and bolted the door behind them.

'Sometimes I can't help thinking that it would have been better for Odin and his horse never to have left the island,' Sigbrit said to the Fisherman, who was shivering after being out in the cold. He put the kettle on. The two of them were alone in the wheelhouse, Odin and Harald Adelstensfostre had gone to bed. Ambrosius nodded slowly.

'If Odin had not come,' Sigbrit continued, 'the Queendom of South Norseland would not have been overrun by all these Prophets of Doom bashing each other up or in open conflict with the Kingdom of North Norseland.'

'Maybe, maybe not,' said Ambrosius, drawing her close. 'But life doesn't consist of "what if" but of "what is". Of course it's possible for many "ifs" to lead to the same "is", but it is certain that no "if" can cancel out what "is".' He smiled and kissed her eyelids. 'And, Lady Fair, what *is*, is you and me.'

'Not for much longer,' murmured Sigbrit.

Ambrosius the Fisherman sat up. 'You're wrong there,' he said sharply and took her face between his hands. 'Whatever *is*, is for always. Anything else is meaningless.'

Sigbrit nodded dejectedly and changed the subject. 'We shall need money for the diving gear,' she said.

'Yes,' smiled the Fisherman. 'We need money, and money is what we don't have.'

'There must be some money from Fridtjof for my part of the house,' exclaimed Sigbrit. 'I don't know exactly how much, but I'll find out when I collect my post tomorrow. Diving gear can't be all that costly, can it?'

'It costs more than you think, Lady Fair.'

Sigbrit yawned.

'Come, let's go to sleep. We'll sort it out tomorrow,' said Ambrosius, but despite her fatigue Sigbrit could not fall asleep.

'What about Bramsentorpf?' she asked after a brief silence.

'That's still up to the government. We can't retract Odin's condition that it must give up its claim to the island before he shows himself. And it would be too dangerous just now to let anyone know he is here in the country.' The Fisherman gave a slight cough. 'There don't seem to have been further threats from the hostage-takers for a while now, and that must mean that either they have done away with Bramsentorpf or they probably won't do so regardless of what happens.'

'And the Prophets of Doom?'

'There's not much we can do about them, except to make sure they don't discover how we get to the island.'

Next morning Sigbrit rose early and left the dock without waking Ambrosius. She quickly covered the short distance to the Firø Bridge and took the bus into town. The capital was unrecogniz-able. In spite of Christmas decorations in the streets and shops and carols blaring from loudspeakers in the pedestrianized streets, Fredenshvile resembled a town under siege. There were banners and posters bearing doomsday prophecies everywhere. On every street corner groups garbed in strange costumes were distributing leaflets and talking persuasively about their cause, or yelling threatening predictions to the lost passers-by. Numerous shops had been closed down, and not been replaced by new ones, and some of the remaining shops had protected their windows by fixing wire fencing or wooden planking in front of them. People hastened by without looking up, and no one, be it child or adult, stopped to look at the goods in the windows or the occasional Christmas display. It seemed as if they feared some-thing terrible was about to happen, although none knew what it would be or how they could prevent it.

Sigbrit went to the central post office and opened the post restante box she had organized as her address while she was away. She crammed all the mail into a large plastic bag and carried it to a café at the next street corner. Finding a table, she sat down and asked for a cup of coffee. She emptied the contents of the bag on to the table and quickly sorted the letters into two piles; official letters in one heap, personal letters in another. She opened two letters at once, her divorce papers and the conveyance document for the house – Fridtjof had bought out her share. She signed both documents without reading them and then calculated the income from the house; it wasn't much. Sigbrit ran through the heap of official letters again and found her latest bank statement. The small savings she had had when she left, together with her latest pay cheque from the bank, had been used up long ago, and the balance was in the red. There was no point in mulling it over; she had only one thing left to sell: her car.

'One two, one two, one two...' Sigbrit heard someone shout in time to the rhythmic beat of hard heels on asphalt, and it was not long before she could see, out of the section of the café window not covered with planking, a group of men in brown with crew-cuts marching in serried ranks with the South Norse flag flying in their midst.

'What's going on out there?' she asked of a man reading his paper at the next table.

'Oh them, they're just the Avengers,' said the man without interest after raising his eyes from the paper for a moment.

'The Avengers?'

'Yes, you must have been away a long time,' the man stated without expecting a reply. 'Ever since all that Doomsday nonsense started, those youngsters out there,' he nodded towards the marching men, 'have run around the streets fighting the Pious.' He laughed sarcastically. 'They are opposed to everything foreign, everything religious and everything modern.'

The man laughed again, a bit louder this time, and pointed with his paper in the direction of Sigbrit. 'Women's liberation as well, ha, ha. They fight pretty savagely sometimes, ha, ha.'

'Why doesn't the government step in?'

'The government doesn't do anything.' The man shrugged his shoulders. 'Or rather, they let the police handle it. Sometimes the police get there in time, sometimes they don't. It's not as if these Prophets of Doom are a lot better themselves.'

'Is nobody at all trying to do anything?'

'Good Lord, yes!' The man roared with laughter, as if he found the situation a huge joke. 'There's even a crowd of daft women who call themselves Mary's Maidens. They trip around the streets singing hymns to peace and tolerance. As if that will help!' The man slapped his thighs with hilarity and then looked at Sigbrit with sudden suspicion. 'Otherwise nothing,' he said curtly, shrugging his shoulders again as if the topic had begun to bore him. He opened his paper and buried his face in it to indicate the conversation was at an end.

Although at first Ace (alias Ezra) had shrunk from the idea, he had not protested when the Avengers had called for stronger action. Even though Ezra was getting into deeper water than he cared for, there was nothing to be done about it. The situation had not come to the point where he could extract himself; his little brother had not fallen into a trap that would reveal his deceit and stupidity, to allow Ezra (alias Ace) to resume his place as saviour of the family honour, their parent's pride and joy, the much missed and most beloved son for whom the fatted calf was to be slaughtered. So Ezra swallowed his disgust and planned a couple of violent offensives which his Avengers carried out with enthusiasm – smashing up shops owned by or employing immigrants, direct attacks on Doomsday groups, crowned by a real crusade against Christmas, which was not a genuine South Norse tradition.

Before Ezra could become the much missed and most beloved son, there was one more task to be carried out, and that was how Sigbrit Holland inadvertently came to witness a grocer's shop being blown to smithereens. In the passage of one instant it seemed as if, with one huge boom, the shop was lifted from the ground floor of the old brick building out on to the street, where burnt fruit and vegetables formed a jumbled mass with scraps of bread, shattered washing powder cartons, blood and body parts belonging to the Oriental grocer, his wife and two unfortunate customers.

'*We will not have Muslim filth on our street*' stated a grubby handwritten note found by the police later in the backroom of the bombed store not far from a handkerchief bearing the initials of Ezekiel the Righteous. This time the police did not hesitate and would have taken young Ezekiel into custody immediately but for the fact he had already gone into hiding.

When the explosion sounded Sigbrit was unaware of all this, and the shock wave knocked her over. Meanwhile the shop burned out on the street, and piercing screams resounded everywhere. The police and ambulance were on the scene almost before she had got to her feet. A rescue worker came over and asked if she needed any help, but she hastily hid her slightly damaged left hand in her coat pocket and assured him she had come to no harm. In the confusion – before the officers taking down the names and addresses of witnesses saw her – she slipped away and blended with the growing crowd of onlookers. She could not risk arousing the authorities' suspicions that Odin was back in South Norseland.

With her bag of mail dangling from her good hand Sigbrit ran at full speed down the pedestrian street without noticing the smashed and boarded-up windows, the ruined Christmas decorations and the row after row of broken Christmas lights. Suddenly a hand seized her by the arm and brought her wild flight to a stop so abruptly she almost fell.

'One ought not to hurry in these sacred times,' hissed a bald middle-aged man with '*The Lambs of the Lord*' tattooed on his brow. 'The Day of Doom will come to us, not vice versa,' he went on, at once smirking and threatening. 'The time has come for prayer and for atonement for sins. You cannot flee from your offences. Once the millennium has come to an end it will be too late.' The man managed to push a leaflet into Sigbrit's bleeding hand before she could tear herself free.

She wiped the blood from her hand on the leaflet, which bore a picture of a white lamb on its front page, threw it into a rubbish bin and went on towards Firø at a calmer pace. She moved almost like a sleepwalker and several times almost collided with someone. She stopped for a moment and leaned against a lamp-post, trying to assemble her thoughts. '*Islamic freedom now!*' she read on the wall in front of her and realized that all the windows in the building were smashed. Sigbrit walked on, shaking her head. Soon she realized the road was barricaded by a police blockade: a huge demonstration was on its way to the Parliament House.

'The waters will divide,' yelled the young bespectacled man leading the troop. 'The waters will divide, and I, Simon Peter the Second, one time fisherman in body and soul, and now the

Entrusted Disciple and First Apostle of the Mighty One, will lead you over the seabed to the Isle of Paradise.'

'The Isle of Paradise! The Isle of Paradise!' roared the crowd so loudly that the air vibrated.

At that moment the mood of the demonstrators changed from ecstatic expectation to terror and panic.

Sigbrit did not wait to find out what was going on, but turned on her heel and broke into a run. She ran as fast as she could – and passed the bank without so much as a cursory glance – back to the pedestrian street where she found a detour leading to the Firø Bridge. She was panting so hard she could barely breathe, but still she ran on right across the bridge.

She no longer had any doubts; since they had not found any other solution, it would have to be diving – and the sooner the better.

*

The legend of the legendary Lennart Torstensson ended even before it began. Or rather it *looked* as if the legend of the legendary Lennart Torstensson was over even before it began.

The disturbing discovery that someone had stolen his idea and in Mr Odin Odin's name had made the same demand of the North Norse government which he himself had made of the South Norse, resulted in Lennart suddenly falling ill. His temperature shot up, his head and limbs began to ache violently and he was overwhelmed over and over again by violent bouts of vomiting. When the attack was at its zenith and his fever went up to 40 degrees, and the no longer legendary Lennart Torstensson had started to fear he would never recover,

the eleventh of the strange dreams came to him and with it the
Idea and an almost instantaneous recovery.

Lennart woke in confusion after the dream and stumbled
into the kitchen for a drink of water and seven dry biscuits. He
pulled his notebook out of the food compartment in the freezer
and went back to bed with the book under his arm. He wrote
down word for word everything the birds had sung to him:
'*Aser's thrust, Valhalla's happiness*'. And then the idea flooded
into his mind. He needed an army, and this army would
become his pride and joy. '*Einherier, battling one with one, to
death at eve, alive by morn.*' What a fabulous idea!

The reason behind Lennart's need of an army was that he –
with one flash of sudden feverish insight – had realized that
his only real enemy was no less than the South Norse government. It dawned on him with sudden striking clarity that of
course the abduction of Mr Brams Bramsentorpf had been
engineered by the South Norse government itself to give the
impression that it was not hiding Mr Odin Odin, and that was
why they had not reacted to his threatening letters; the South
Norse government knew only too well that nothing bad would
happen to Mr Bramsentorpf. The fact that South Norseland
was prepared to resort to such disgraceful tactics could mean
only one thing: that the South Norse government had no intention of releasing Mr Odin Odin, which again could mean only
one thing: that the South Norse government was not in the
least prepared to give up its claim to the island.

As bombs, threatening letters and pressure were clearly
useless as persuasive measures, the only thing remaining to
Lennart was to get hold of an army strong enough to force the
South Norse government to give way. Even before his fever had
completely disappeared he knew exactly where his army would

come from. Among all the Norse lands there was only one person in command of a force powerful enough to frighten the South Norse government: Simon Peter II.

*

'We shall travel in the dolphin's guise, cheat the sea of its prize,' Odin twisted his beard and looked down enthusiastically at his rubber-clad body. In truth, it really was a huge stroke of luck, when Mr Bramsentorpf was unable to offer the air passage on account of his unexpected abduction, and the people of the Continent, even with the combined efforts of the hearts and brains of everyone, could not get the sea to freeze over, that Ambrosius the Fisherman had found the means to walk under the water instead.

It was the last day of November and the diving gear had just arrived. The Fisherman had signed for it, and now they were about to try it. They were to start off early next morning while it was still dark. Depending on the wind direction they could not decide until the last moment whether they should try to approach from the east or west side of the island. Sigbrit was to sail the green and orange fishing boat as close to the rocks as possible, the rest was up to the three men and chance. She was not to wait for them, as that would attract attention. If anything should go wrong at the bottom of the Strait, there would be nothing she could do. A second try was out of the question.

Der Fremdling sat silently in his corner watching the unpacking of the gear with indifference. But Gunnar the Head was struck with awe. 'I've never seen anything like it,' he kept repeating, scratching his right elbow. He pointed at Odin's costume. 'I've never ever seen anything like it.'

Odin opened the wheelhouse door and went out on deck to try to walk in the diving suit. Gunnar the Head followed him slowly. The man with the gigantic head looked very thoughtful and scratched his elbow harder. He had a problem: he really wanted to see his pal walking under water, but nothing would persuade him to accompany Odin the next day. Then he had an idea.

'Don't you think it would be a good thing to try the equipment just to make sure it works,' he said. 'Maybe right here and now.'

Odin pulled at his beard and nodded, then walked straight over to the opening in the rail, took one step into thin air and fell vertically into the water to vanish out of sight.

Gunnar the Head looked down, but there was nothing to be seen in the dark water. Disappointed, he returned to the wheelhouse, where he sat down by the shabby mahogany table and scratched his right elbow dejectedly. 'Not much point in this walking under water,' he said, quite cast down. 'You can't see a thing.'

'Odin!' Ambrosius the Fisherman leapt to his feet and ran out on deck. He tore his sweater over his head, kicked off his shoes and dived into the water head first. It wasn't long before the Fisherman surfaced to draw breath. He shook his head so the water dripped from his hair, and dived down again. Not until he came up for the fourth time, gasping for air, did he have the little old man in his arms. Odin coughed and spat and looked somewhat overcome, but he was able to reach out and grab hold of Harald Adelstensfostre's outstretched hand.

Sigbrit turned up the heating in the wheelhouse and put out some towels.

'I don't like you going under water,' said Gunnar the Head,

looking at Odin rubbing himself dry. 'I don't like it at all when you go under water.'

'It will be all right,' said Ambrosius slowly. 'But you will have to remember to put your mask on.'

Odin smiled. Apart from his chattering teeth he did not seem to have come to any harm. 'What does not work the first time, may well work the next,' he said, squeezing the water out of his beard. But then he started to beat himself on the chest and all over with a flat hand as if he could not get warm. Sigbrit was about to give him another towel when he rushed out on deck.

'The horseshoe! I have lost the horseshoe!' he cried in despair.

Ambrosius and Sigbrit hurried after him to make sure he didn't jump into the icy cold water again. That would not help. The horseshoe would already have buried itself in the mud of the harbour basin's bed and it would be useless to try to find it. To their amazement, only a moment later Odin pointed to something floating in the water near the keel of the green and orange fishing boat.

'There it is!' he yelled, tugging happily at his wet beard so that water poured from it.

True enough; the horseshoe was floating nicely on the black surface.

'Well, we never...' Ambrosius muttered, fetching a landing net, with which he easily lifted the horseshoe out of the water.

Gunnar the Head grabbed the horseshoe and untangled it from the net. He turned it in his hand with a thoughtful face and scratched his right elbow. The shoe reminded him of something he had heard a long time ago, when he was still working as a blacksmith. What was it now? The gigantic-headed man scratched his right elbow for a long time, and just as Odin was approaching him to take care of his precious horseshoe again, it came to him.

'Only a bone smith hammers shoes that can swim,' grinned the gigantic-headed man.

Ragnarok

Leaves fell from ash to earth as loot
Nidhug's teeth made bones of root
Skoll swallowed sun and Hati moon
Fimbul frost came long and cold

Heimdal blew on Galler horn
Einherier, Aser, time for war
the battlefields soon gorged with blood
giants trampled over man
    — no warrior could withstand

Flaming sword of Giant Surtur
torched all dead and all alive
Yggdrasil and Asgard too
lost in flames, what then to do?

Thor hurled the hammer, killing serpent
venom sprang and slew himself
Odin thrust his spear in Fenris
wise god and lance consumed at once

Heaven ruptured, stars turned dim
Midgard drowned beneath the ocean
Triumphant giants plunged with Bifrost
    — not one left to lose or win

     Hear, Ragnarok is known by this

Even though it was only midday it was dark as twilight. Grey-black clouds raced across the sky, and the leafless trees bent before the icy gale that howled against the windows and beat again and again on the castle walls, making the very floors shake.

The Queen glanced thoughtfully into the flames in the cheerfully crackling grate. 'Is there really no other possibility?' she asked, slowly turning to the Prime Minister.

'Unfortunately not, Your Majesty,' replied the Prime Minister solemnly. 'We have tried everything, but the North Norse government will not budge.' The left corner of his mouth tensed, almost as if to hide a smile; a brisk little feud between neighbours was the best way of outstripping a sitting regime before an election.

The Queen looked into the fire again. She was the only person who knew about King Enevold IV's and King Hermod Skjalm's agreement over the island. Without it Drude Estrid's Island rightly belonged to the Queendom of South Norseland, and the Queen would go a long way to maintain that state of affairs. But an armed conflict? South Norseland had not been at war with North Norseland since 1814, when the South Norse lost the Old North to the North Norse Crown. 'To start with, it will be nothing more than a warning, of course,' the Prime Minister interrupted the Queen's train of thought.

The Queen made no reply; the threat of a declaration of war was not far removed from such a declaration itself.

'Mr Prime Minister,' she responded at last. 'Would it not be feasible to resume negotiations and see whether the North Norse Kingdom would come back to its senses?'

'Not as long as the North Norse government continues to accuse us of keeping the little old man hidden in this country,

Your Majesty.' The Prime Minister clasped his hands in order to resist the urge to crack his fingers. 'Everything has been tried, Your Majesty. The North Norse government refuses to listen. It has even come to the point when the North Norse police refuses to help our police to search for Mr Bramsentorpf's abductor, which merely proves that it must be the North Norse government itself that has abducted him.'

Again the Queen took her time before replying. 'The government has completely lost hope of finding Mr Odin Odin?'

'We have done everything possible to find him, but all to no avail,' answered the Prime Minister, silently cursing the Minister of Justice and his rather too bright ideas. 'Mr Odin Odin could not have indicated more clearly that he does not intend to return unless we relinquish our claim on the island, which is not in our power to do – even if we desired it.' He looked straight at the Queen. 'And, Your Majesty, surely we do not want that?'

The Queen looked at the Prime Minister with surprise; she was not sure why the island had suddenly become so vital an issue for him. To her, his reasons were of little importance if they were in agreement that it was a question of the honour of the South Norse and – for her personally – that of King Enevold IV. She shook her head slightly. 'No, Mr Prime Minister, even if it were possible it would not be in the interests of the Queendom of South Norseland to relinquish the claim on Drude Estrid Island.'

The Prime Minister's face brightened. 'Your Majesty, I am glad we are in agreement on this difficult matter.'

'Mr Prime Minister, is there really no other way of resolving the conflict?' the Queen asked again. 'Once we get into the next century and the Prophets of Doom are proved to have been wrong, the situation with the North Norse will probably alter as well.'

'I fear there is a very little likelihood of that,' said the Prime Minister in as prime-ministerial a voice as he could contrive. 'The nationalistic fanaticism will not stop until the situation regarding the island is resolved, and the situation regarding the island cannot be resolved until we have got the better of the fanaticism.' The Prime Minister leaned forward. 'There is another small point. Scaling up the conflict with the North Norse will afford the government the opportunity to implement various measures to deal with the Prophets of Doom which cannot be made use of in peacetime.' His voice had a chill in it. 'Night curfew, a ban on demonstrations, the arrest of suspect elements. Yes,' the Prime Minister laughed, 'in a war situation any number of things can be seen as a threat to national security...'

A brief silence ensued, then the Queen asked: 'Does the government have a majority vote for this escalation of the conflict?'

'Yes, informal discussions have shown there is a clear majority in Parliament in favour of defending the country's honour.' The Prime Minister smiled. He thought of the opinion polls; it was obvious that none of the larger parties dared risk the ire of the voters by resisting a stronger line being taken against North Norseland.

The Queen looked out of the window at the dark sky. Of course the Queendom of South Norseland must defend its honour. She gave an inaudible sigh and then asked in a firm voice: 'How do we go about it?'

'The first thing is to tighten border controls and restrict the entry of the North Norse into South Norseland. We will issue three warnings to the North Norse government, demanding that Mr Bramsentorpf be released before Christmas, and that they must relinquish their claim on Drude Estrid Island.' The left-hand corner of the Prime Minister's mouth twitched. 'Otherwise we shall unilaterally declare Drude Estrid Island to be South Norse territory.' He glanced at the Queen enquiringly. 'If Your Majesty agrees I shall now take the sombre road back to Parliament and ensure the necessary backing for this unfortunate but sadly unavoidable undertaking.'

For a long time the Queen sat in silence, gazing into the fire. She thought about the consequences and costs of a war against the North Norse Kingdom. Then she thought about her forefather, King Enevold IV, and the promise she had sworn to act with honour in his place. After all, it need not necessarily come to war. Most probably the Prime Minister was right, the North Norse would give way when they were confronted with the threat of attack.

'Yes, Mr Prime Minister, I agree,' said the Queen, and rose to her feet.

*

'*Heavens ruptured, the stars grew dim.*' The revived legendary Lennart Torstensson woke up with a cry. He was quaking with fear and clammy with cold sweat. '*Torched all dead and all alive, Yggdrasil and Asgard too, lost in flames, then what to do?*' Like a warning of something on its way, it was as if he had dreamed of that end of the world that all the Prophets of Doom had prophesied: Armageddon, the Apocalypse, Judgement Day. Yes, what was it the birds had sung for him: '*Leaves fell from ash to earth as loot, Nidhug's teeth made bones of root... Fimbul frost comes long and cold... Hear, Ragnarok is known by this.*'

'*Hear, Ragnarok is known by this*'! Suddenly Lennart came to life and leapt out of bed. He made a beeline for the kitchen and snatched his notebook out of the fridge. He leafed through the cold pages, reading a snatch here and there, then went back to the first page. '*For this is how we know Ginnungagap*'. Yes, this was precisely what he needed. He danced round in circles. '*In the beginning was Ginnungagap, in the end comes Ragnarok*'; it was perfect. He couldn't have found anything better himself!

Lennart, giddy, plumped down in an armchair. Just think, those strange dreams were the key to his final victory. It had been right in front of his nose all the time, staring him in the face. '*Odin thrust his spear in Fenris, wise god and lance consumed at once.*' There was no doubt about it. The dreams would prove invincible, Lennart Torstensson was invincible, and invincible strength would soon be his. Once again medals and honours flowed past his inner eye as he imagined how as a general at the head of his army of former Born Anew Christians he would liberate Mr Odin Odin and take him back to North Norseland.

Lennart did not go to work that day. In fact he would never go to work again. Instead he went down to the beach, found thirteen medium-sized flat stones – one should always keep one in reserve – and carried them home to his apartment. Then he went to a bookshop and bought two books on rock-engraving and runes. It took him three days to read both books from end to end, but by then he knew everything he needed to know.

At the local hardware store he bought a solid hammer and a set of twelve different sized chisels, and once home again he set to work. There was no time to waste. As the Prophets of Doom proclaimed: the end was nigh.

And the end was nigh.

At least that was what Ezekiel the Righteous's eldest uncle concluded from the incessant icy winter gales raging in Fredenshvile, as well as from the newspapers he brought to his prophetic nephew in the Second World War bunker.

The police still suspected – wrongly – that Ezekiel the Righteous was responsible for the bomb in the Muslim grocery store in his own street, as well as – rightly – for the bomb in front of the North Norse embassy only a few days before the arson. Sooner or later the police would undoubtedly find out where the prophetic son was hiding. And although it might be later rather than sooner, since many policemen were not too well disposed towards the North Norse and their ambassador nor to the modest Muslim grocery shops now in the country, it might also be sooner, as the police were not too well disposed towards the Reborn Jews either. That was why the eldest uncle decided it was high time to open the money box.

Ezekiel the Righteous was not particularly well acquainted with such a worldly subject as mathematics, so it was his father and the five remaining uncles as well as the few non-related Reborn Jews who counted the money. There was a pretty healthy sum in the box, though it was not enough.

His father and the five remaining uncles as well as the few non-related Reborn Jews went through the possibilities: Russian helicopters were known to be cheapest, but even so the Reborn Jews had only one tenth of what a run-down Russian M117 – which at the appointed time and with two flights would fly them to the Island of the Eternal Sabbath – would cost.

The assembled company looked from one to another and without further discussion the father and mother, the five remaining uncles, their wives and children together with the widow of the sixth and the few non-related Reborn Jews promptly decided to put their apartments up for sale. They had nothing to lose; Judgement Day was nigh!

The Day of Judgement was indeed approaching. In fact, and to be absolutely precise, there were no more than twenty days remaining for this world. At any rate, that was what Simon Peter II told the Born Anew Christians and all the other South Norselanders in his speeches, which were now broadcast on the radio every morning by a sympathetic channel – to the government's great annoyance they were powerless to forbid it, since the Queendom of the South North was a well-organized democracy.

The reason why Simon Peter II announced on 3 December that there were only twenty-one days to Judgement Day and not twenty-eight, as was maintained by the other Prophets of Doom, was that ever since the Mighty One had vanished he had immersed himself in the Bible. In the Bible, Simon Peter II had found, in addition to numerous other interesting stories, a truth which everyone, including himself, had up to now overlooked: it was true the Day of Judgement would come with the change of millennium, but the actual change would naturally take place on the birthday of Jesus Christ, and not the following week.

'No!' Simon Peter II roared into the microphone. 'The Day of Judgement will come on Christmas Eve, the birthday of Jesus Christ, the Mighty One, the Lord's Son, who on his nineteen hundred and ninety-ninth birthday came back to Earth to save Our Lord's true children, the Born Anew Christians.' The Entrusted Disciple and First Apostle blinked passionately. 'With our help the Mighty One will overcome the Devil, and on the day that leads up to the night before his two thousandth birthday he will lead the Born Anew Christians dry-shod over the seabed to the Isle of Paradise and the Thousand-year reign of Peace on Earth. *For blessed and holy is he who has a part in the first Resurrection; the second death has no power over them, but they shall be the priests of God and Christ and reign as Kings with him for those thousand years.'*

The Thousand-year reign of Peace on Earth was indeed on its way – but not this year, not this Christmas. No, the Thousand-year reign of Peace on Earth would come on the day when the true Jesus Christ came down to Earth again, and that day had not yet dawned.

This was what the True Christians shouted as they marched under their angry banners through the streets of the North Norse capital. They demanded that their government should declare war immediately and without delay on the infidel and blasphemous South. Cost what it might, the false prophets must be stopped.

And the false prophets would be stopped, every man of them, the Blessed Anders Andersen had known this for a long time. So the Lambs of the Lord need have no worries over it, for when the day did dawn, the Lord himself would make short work of all the false prophets and the heathens and, aided by his shepherd, the Mighty One, he would save none but his faithful Lambs.

All the Lambs of the Lord needed do until then was to pray, smoke holy grass and burn their hair on sacred bonfires in various places around the streets of Fredenshvile as a sacrifice to Our Lord the Almighty and his son, the shepherd, the Mighty One. Then, naturally, they would carry on the battle to save, in the name of God, those few souls who were still, through their willingness to make over their worldly estates to the Lambs of the Lord and the Blessed Anders Andersen, worthy of salvation. *'For the Lamb would break the first of the seven seals, and then the second and the third and so onward until all seven seals were broken, for none but the Lamb was worthy, for it was slain, and with its blood it has bought human beings of every tribe and tongue and race and nation.'*

*

'It's all very well,' said Ambrosius the Fisherman, rubbing his chin. 'But what are we to do?'

'Name the island and all Hell breaks loose. Only one bone smith hammers shoes that can swim.' Brynhild Sigurdskær had been right: the solution was hidden in the former, the former was hidden in the latter. Captain Hans Adelstensfostre's ledgers clearly confirmed the kennings. The Captain had carried more or less the same goods to Ur Island and its southerly neighbour, apart from nails, tools, knives and other articles forged from iron. Not on a single occasion had Captain Hans Adelstensfostre transported one metal object to the island; that was what they had overlooked.

They didn't know the reason for it. Maybe the rocks were full of magnetic iron ore, which, because of the position of the rocks or on account of the wind or the humidity from the sea or something else they were naturally unaware of, made the island and the air above it into a gigantic electromagnetic field. Although they had earlier rejected the idea of magnetism – planes were built of aluminium and should therefore not be affected by this force – it was not impossible that an electromagnetic field would affect instruments or engines in such a way as to cause the planes to crash. But regardless of the cause, one thing was certain: it would be best for them to avoid taking the smallest trace of metal on their voyage to the island. Diving was out of the question, the flasks and air ventilator and probably other parts of their gear would be torn to pieces as soon as they approached the island.

They looked at the island; no one could answer Ambrosius's question. The green and orange fishing boat suddenly keeled over violently. A cup fell down, rolled over the table top and smashed when it hit the floor. The gale was so fierce that waves penetrated right into the shipyard. The Fisherman gathered up the broken pieces.

'I don't like sailing,' complained Gunnar the Head. 'I don't like sailing at all, at all.'

'None of us cares for sailing in this weather,' rumbled the Fisherman, chucking the pieces into the rubbish bin.

'Finding the solution didn't help us a lot.' Sigbrit shook her head. 'You can't go by boat because of the rocks. You can't dive because of the gear, and you can't fly...'

'Lacking the wings of thought and memory, flying will not take you far,' Odin broke in. He had recalled something Mr Bramsentorpf had said. Even if Mr Bramsentorpf had been abducted, it might well be... 'I wonder, now the regulations have been completed, if it could be that Mr Bramsentorpf's formalities are also finished, so the air connection can be established.'

'We are afraid that Mr Bramsentorpf is not able to do much about the air connection at present,' said Ambrosius. 'No, where Mr Bramsentorpf finds himself now is most likely pretty cold.'

'He who is carried by warm winds reaches further than he

who is carried by cold ones,' remarked Odin quietly, calmly twisting his beard as he shuddered at the memory of his laborious struggle over the sea to the Continent in a fearful snowstorm, which seemed a very long time ago.

Half an hour after this Sigbrit had arrived at Fredenshvile Central Library, where she borrowed everything they held on balloon flight. The safest thing would be to avoid taking anything with them they did not know for certain already existed on the island in the same form. This meant that they couldn't use helium or other gases but would have to make do with a hot air balloon.

'We can't heat up the air with modern propane or butane burners,' said Ambrosius, scratching his ear. Presumably the steel in the bottles would turn the burners into bombs as soon as the balloon moved into the magnetic field of the island.

'Maybe we could fill the balloon with hot air once and for all while it is still on board *Rikke-Marie*,' suggested Sigbrit. 'That's what they did in the earliest balloon flights.' She glanced at the book open before her on the table and leafed back a few pages. 'Listen to this: *Air expands as it is heated up, whereby the specific gravity of the air is reduced, and the hot air is carried upwards by colder layers of air,*' she read out. '*The very first air balloon, built by the Montgolfier brothers in 1783, was 17.4 metres high and 12.5 metres in diameter and had a volume of 1000m3. The balloon carried a basket which held three passengers, a sheep, a cockerel and a duck, up to a height of circa 500 metres and flew four kilometres before it landed again eight minutes later.*' Sigbrit looked up. 'You don't need much more than that, do you?'

'No,' said the Fisherman, pulling at his pipe. 'It's just that we are a bit heavier than both sheep and cockerels and ducks, and then it would probably be a good thing to have some extra time to spare when we have climbed high enough.'

'*A human passenger was on board the very next balloon,*' Sigbrit read on, when she was interrupted by the hermit.

'All that can be calculated,' the hermit cut her short, getting a pad and pencil from the shelf.

The cliffs were high, and for safety's sake they ought to leave plenty of spare height. The distance to the island from the outermost cliffs, where *Rikke-Marie* had been forced to abandon the approach, must be a couple of hundred metres, and a further seven to eight hundred metres would be needed if they were to be sure of getting to the middle of the island. There was one unknown factor in the calculation: the wind. If wind direction and strength were favourable they should not need more than ten to fifteen minutes from the moment the cable was cut until the balloon landed on the island. If not, it was impossible to say how long it might take.

'One can get nowhere without power,' Odin remarked, pulling at his beard. 'With too much power one gets past everywhere.'

'Exactly,' said Sigbrit. 'Even if you want to secure a good margin, you can't have too much surplus air if you're not to end up over on the opposite side of the cliffs.'

Ambrosius the Fisherman nodded. 'The vital thing will depend on how we steer the thing,' he said. 'Get that right and we'll probably find a way to get it down.'

A knock came from the door of the dock; Ambrosius the Fisherman went out and shortly afterwards returned with Der Fremdling. The withered old man found his corner and sat down without greeting anyone.

Sigbrit looked away. 'How are you going to steer it?' she asked.

'There's no other tiller in the air except the wind.' Ambrosius rose and walked up and down the wheelhouse. He chewed the stem of his pipe thoughtfully.

'What if the wind changes in mid-flight?' asked Sigbrit.

They looked at each other in silence for a moment. Then Odin said: 'When one horse cannot pull one must rely on the other.' The little old man pulled at his beard again, recalling how Balthazar had pulled the sledge on his own all the way to Mother Marie's stable, after Rigmarole had broken her leg in the meteor storm. 'No, in truth there is no mishap a spot of luck cannot remedy,' he added cheerfully, patting the horse-shoe in his breast pocket.

'When one horse cannot pull one must rely on the other,' repeated Ambrosius. 'Of course!' he exclaimed, laughing. 'When we can't be sure of the wind, we must make use of the other force that rules on the island.'

Sigbrit sent him an enquiring look.

'Magnetism,' laughed the Fisherman. 'We will fix a huge iron ball to the basket.' He sat down and went on with a broad grin: 'We shall be much mistaken if the magnetic forces cannot manage the rest after the wind has pushed us close enough.'

'How shall we get hold of a giant iron ball like that?'

'Gunnar the Head,' replied the Fisherman without hesitation, turning to the huge-headed man.

Gunnar the Head blushed proudly and nodded almost solemnly as he scratched his right elbow. 'I will make the largest iron football anyone has ever seen,' he said with a big grin. It was not for nothing that as well as being a superb foot-ball player he had also been an excellent blacksmith.

If they guessed aright the iron ball would be affected by the magnetism on the island as soon as the balloon passed over the inner line of cliffs, after which the ball would draw them the rest of the way to the middle of the island. That, at least, is what they believed would happen. They couldn't be sure.

Next day Harald Adelstensfostre called the South Norse Balloon Company in the guise of an eccentric Old Norseman who intended flying across the Norse countries at the millennium. And luck was with them: the South Norse Balloon Company knew that a group of members who had just bought a new balloon would be interested in selling their old one cheaply. That would cost sixty thousand, added to which would be repair and reconditioning of the balloon, and all that came to an amount of money they did not have.

'Can't we just sell the diving gear?' Sigbrit suggested.

'No, unfortunately,' said Ambrosius. 'The shop won't take it back as it was made especially for us.' He put his pipe down in the ashtray and rubbed his chin. 'No, we must find the money somewhere else.'

There was a moment's silence in the wheelhouse.

'There is no other place,' Sigbrit said at last. 'If only we could find someone who owed us something.'

Der Fremdling broke into a hoarse, braying hiccup, as if that was the most grotesque thing he had heard for a long time.

Just then Odin had an idea. He remembered Bishop Bentsen and the service Vicar Valentino had given him to understand he would make available to Odin.

*

Dear Bishop Bentsen,

The undersigned hereby begs to take the liberty of reminding Bishop Bentsen of the service he did Your Grace by taking a long and delightful holiday after Your Grace advised it, and in that connection to respectfully enquire whether it will now be possible to receive the service which Your Grace's envoy, The Reverend Valentino, gave the undersigned to understand would be available. The preferred service is to cover the sum of seventy-five thousand, to be used to establish the air connection needed by the undersigned to enable him to return to Smith's Town, whence he travelled here last year in a terrible blizzard.

Should it not be possible for Your Grace to render the service which his envoy gave the undersigned to understand would be forthcoming, the undersigned would naturally understand, and in this case will reside for the foreseeable future in the Queendom of the South Norse.

Allow me to take this opportunity to assure Your Grace of my highest esteem and respect.

Yours faithfully,
Odin

Bishop Bentsen lowered the letter and removed his reading glasses. He allowed himself a brief moment of silent cursing; a letter like this was not merely presumptuous, it was extremely inconvenient as well. The bishop's admirable generosity did not merely extend to his own means, but rather to those of the Established Church, and it was all too obvious that to meet Mr Odin's demand he would be obliged to make use of the former rather than the latter. However, Bishop Bentsen's long life and experience had taught him that the best way around a problem was not to solve it but to remove it. Although the price was high, indeed, uncomfortably high, it didn't take the bishop long to conclude that it was not too high in order to make sure of getting rid of Mr Odin Odin once and for all. The time had come to summon Vicar Valentino.

'It won't be easy,' said Vicar Valentino after Bishop Bentsen had explained to him how things stood.

'I am well aware that it will not be easy,' snapped the bishop impatiently, but went on in an ingratiating tone: 'That is precisely why I have called you here.' What Bishop Bentsen wanted Vicar Valentino to do was to comply with the instructions given in a postscript to Mr Odin Odin's letter in every particular, with the small stipulation that Vicar Valentino was to establish the exact whereabouts of the little old man. 'And then of course we must make sure there is no question of a bogus demand.'

'But the letter... no one but Signor Odin himself knows that through my humble self Your Grace advised Signor Odin to take a very long and delightful holiday...'

'Not that!' the bishop interjected. 'It is essential for us to ensure that the little old man does not just take the money and then do whatever suits him. It is one thing to pay a lot for something, but I must at least have something to show for the exorbitant amount I will have to shell out,' barked the bishop, hammering a fist on the table, so Vicar Valentino almost jumped out of his skin. The bishop lowered his voice to a whisper. 'And the something I shall have is getting Mr Odin Odin out of the Queendom of the South Norse before Christmas.'

Vicar Valentino declared himself in complete agreement on

the importance of this point. 'Trust me,' he said after a short pause for thought, 'I will not only find Signor Odino's whereabouts, I shall also see that this information is passed on to...' Vicar Valentino's laugh turned into a smirk – 'finds its way to... let us say the wrong people, in the event that Signor Odino is not out of South Norseland before midday on Christmas Eve.'

Two days later Vicar Valentino submitted to being blindfolded and led through the howling gale to the windowless goods compartment of a blue delivery van that Sigbrit Holland had hired for the purpose. To confuse Vicar Valentino Sigbrit drove around the town for a while before making for Firø Bridge. She stopped the van in front of the shipyard door, and Ambrosius the Fisherman immediately led the priest inside and on board the green and once orange fishing boat. Not until Vicar Valentino had climbed down the ladder and was sitting in the middle cabin on the Fisherman's bunk was he permitted to take the blindfold from his eyes.

Vicar Valentino blinked once or twice but very soon regained his composure. He stretched out a hand to Odin politely, then launched into a long speech about the ever generous Bishop Bentsen and his onerous task here on earth as God's specially chosen one. The speech at length came round to the statement that naturally Bishop Bentsen was delighted to return the favour as promised to Signor Odino, and in that respect naturally took it for granted that Signor Odino would leave South Norseland before midday on Christmas Eve.

As Odin's only plan was to return as soon as possible to Smith's Town and Rigmarole, he saw no difficulty in nodding his assent. 'Directly Mr Bramsentorpf's formalities have been surmounted and the air connection, with the aid of Bishop Bentsen's benefaction – which in all truth I owe more for than gratitude – has been established, I shall leave the Continent and return to Smith's Town and my unfortunate horse.' Odin took the envelope that Vicar Valentino handed him, and bowed deeply to demonstrate his gratitude and warm regard for the bishop.

Then Vicar Valentino was blindfolded again, led out to the van and driven in a detour around the town before Sigbrit delivered him back to Bishop Bentsen. All her efforts were in vain, however. For although it was impossible to say whether it was through the aid of divine providence, supernatural powers or the not inconsiderable means at the disposal of the Established Church, Vicar Valentino was in no doubt as to where he had been.

*

The next day, the second Sunday in Advent, the government of South Norseland, with the full backing of most Members of Parliament, sent its first warning to the North Norse government:

> If, before midday on Christmas Eve, the North Norse government has not released Mr Brams Bramsentorpf and withdrawn its territorial claim to Drude Estrid Island, the South Norse government will deem it necessary to close the Strait and unilaterally declare Drude Estrid Island to be South Norse territory.

'But that is as good as a declaration of war!' exclaimed Sigbrit, shocked, and switched off the radio. 'How can they go to such lengths over a tiny island?'

Ambrosius the Fisherman made no reply, but went on whittling the wooden pegs that were to replace the metal struts on the air balloon. He did not look up until the job was finished. 'We gather it is about the island and yet not about the island,' he said cryptically.

'Do you think the island is merely an excuse?' Sigbrit's fingers traced the seams of the voluminous stained canvas of the balloon and felt the holes and tears waiting to be mended.

'That may well be,' said the Fisherman, reaching for another peg. '*Name the island and all Hell will break loose.*'

'Then we just have to do something!' Sigbrit's fingers stopped in mid-seam.

'So what are we to do, Lady Fair?'

'To begin with, we can say Odin is here, so the North Norse government will let Bramsentorpf go free.'

'The only trouble with that is that we don't think it is the North Norse government who has Bramsentorpf.'

'Then why does our government say it has?'

The Fisherman kept on whittling away, deep in thought. 'It looks as if they want to go to war,' he said finally, a touch of amazement in his voice.

Sigbrit looked at him questioningly.

'Lady Fair, our government doesn't want the North Norse to comply with its demands. That's why it has made some which it knows the North Norse government has no means of meeting. The more adamantly the North Norse maintains that it has no knowledge the whereabouts of Mr Bramsentorpf, the more the South Norse people will go along with our government's view that war is essential.'

'But if we show them Odin is here, Bramsentorpf will be released by the people who hold him, and everything will look different.'

'Yes, Lady Fair, but that would be far too dangerous for Odin.' The Fisherman laid his knife on the table and rested his hands. 'If Mr Bramsentorpf is still alive he will be set free when the time is right. The only thing we can do is to put together a small package with some photos and a letter from Odin, which you will then deliver to the press after we have left.' He cut short Sigbrit's objection with a raised hand. 'That won't help anyone but Mr Bramsentorpf. For if Odin's conditions for independence give no result, you will still find the North Norsemen insisting on their demands being met.' He laughed drily. 'And while you're about it, maybe you should also get our own government to relinquish their claim.'

*

Ezra (alias Ace) hurried through town. He leaned forward, struggling against the icy wind with every muscle tensed, but still he was buffeted off course now and then. As he neared his childhood street, Ezra grabbed his shades from his pocket and pulled his cap further down on his forehead. He was there. He raised his head and looked up at the third floor. There was a notice in the window; so the advertisement had not been wrong. A shadow moved behind the window, and Ezra hurried on.

How could they have taken it so seriously, the grubby note he had thrown through the windowpane of his parents' apartment? Ezra caught hold of a lamp-post and halted. It had all gone too far. He would have to go back and tell his family everything. He turned round and began to plan his homecoming speech when he recalled his father's last words to him: '*Don't come back until you have made peace with Jahve and with the fact that Jahve and the Mighty One chose your brother and not you for the holy prophet of the new age.*'

Ezra turned around again and walked on down the street with firm steps. Despite the icy wind, a smile slowly broke over his face; it would not be long. When the Reborn Jews made a purely practical attempt to reach the island, Ezekiel's number would be up. Ezra need do nothing more than wait and see. What did it really matter if his parents sold his childhood home? Or if the five remaining uncles with the widow of the sixth sold their homes too? That would only make Ezekiel's trickery all the more serious!

A loud noise rang out further up the street, of breaking glass, shouting and feet running in his direction. Ezra slipped into a doorway and pressed close to the wall. A small group of Born Anew Christians rushed past, constantly looking over their shoulders as if they were being chased. Their pursuers soon came into view. They were twelve brown-clad men marching as rhythmically as was possible in the strong wind, apparently uncaring whether the Born Anew Christians escaped or not.

The Avengers stopped just outside the entrance where Ezra was hiding. The wind beat against their faces and made their eyes run, but the harsh weather seemed to suit them. One of them, a strong, heavy-jawed type, opened a large bag, took out a baseball bat and gave it to the man nearest him. Then he picked out another, and continued until all twelve of them held a weapon. He straightened up, folded up the bag and shoved it in his pocket, casting his gaze down the street. Ezra ducked out of sight, but too late. There was a cry, and shortly afterwards Ezra, to his own uneasy surprise, found himself smashing every shop window which had the slightest sign of being *soiled by* (as he himself had previously expressed it) the forthcoming Christmas, while listening to parts of his own speeches repeated in time to the blows of baseball bats: '*Religion is the ultimate tyranny, the ultimate tyrannical method of suppressing people by seducing their private thoughts. And Christmas is the ultimate symbol of this ultimate suppression.*'

*

In spite of the energetic efforts of the Avengers and the brutal winds that swept in from the north day and night, Christmas preparations were well under way all over the Queendom of South Norseland.

Spruce trees were felled, brought into town, sold and carried home. Ducks, pigs and geese were killed and transformed into birds and joints for the table. Vanilla biscuits, biscuit balls and spiced brown biscuits were baked in their thousands, while nougat, marzipan and chocolate were rolled into sweetmeats, and wished for and unwanted gifts were wrapped up in shiny paper and brightly coloured ribbons.

On the third Sunday in Advent the Prime Minister reiterated his warning to the North Norse government:

> *If the Norse Norse government has not freed Mr Brams Bramsentorpf before midday on Christmas Eve and withdrawn his territorial claim to Drude Estrid Island, the government of South Norseland will deem it necessary to*

close the Strait and unilaterally declare Drude Estrid Island to be South Norse territory.

Ten days before Christmas the Muslim Militia, who had been delayed because the police had discovered their first cache of weapons, raided another arms' store. The police had their suspicions but the Muslim Militia had equally strong alibis. With the arms securely stashed and Aisha confidently occupied in guarding Mr Bramsentorpf, Aisha's brother Ali made his way to the harbour – without informing his sister – and got hold of the timetable for the hovercraft to Ur Island. Now they just had to wait for the gales to abate and allow the ferries to start up again.

The last of the six apartments had been sold. Ezekiel the Righteous's eldest uncle counted the money and saw there was enough. A delegation consisting of two of the younger uncles was sent to Russia to buy the helicopter. Besides a well-used but apparently solid M117 the uncles succeeded in finding two Russian pilots who expressed themselves happy to fly it provided they were permitted to convert and join the Reborn Jews on the Island of Eternal Sabbath. Back in Fredenshvile Ezekiel the Righteous, his father and mother, the five remaining uncles, their wives and children with the widow of the sixth and the few non-related Jews merely waited for an improvement in the wind and weather conditions.

Eight days before Christmas, after fervent prayers and much speculation, it was revealed to the Entrusted Disciple that the water would divide for the Born Anew Christians at the very place where the Mighty One had first set foot on South Norse soil. Simon Peter II promptly shared this divine message with his followers and everyone else who listened to the radio that morning.

'On Christmas morning we, the Born Anew Christians, will gather on Hverv Harbour and await the sign from Jesus Christ, the Mighty One,' yelled Simon Peter II into the microphone. 'And when the sign comes, I, Simon Peter the Second, once a fisher of bodies and souls, now the Entrusted Disciple and First Apostle of the Mighty One, will lead you through the divided waters to the Isle of Paradise. The end of the world is nigh, but the Lord's Son, Jesus Christ, is come back to earth to save true believers and take them with Him into the Thousand-year reign of Peace on Earth. Salvation is ours!' The Entrusted Disciple sobbed with divine bliss.

The Born Anew Christians did not need better weather. The waters would divide regardless of the raging gale, and on their journey across the seabed they would be sheltered from the storm.

Blessed Anders Andersen, who had heard Simon Peter II's radio address, called his bank at once to find out the balance in the Lambs of the Lord account. With this eminently satisfactory sum in mind, Blessed Anders Andersen lit a pipe of especially holy grass and declared that the Lambs of the Lord were now rapidly approaching the mercy of God.

Seven days before Christmas, seven North Norse True Christians, meticulously selected for their ability to speak South Norse and holding false South Norse passports, bought tickets for the ferry across the Strait to the Queendom of South Norseland for the morning of Christmas Eve. The

assault on the Born Anew Christians had been brought to a
halt by the prohibition of entry into the South without a visa,
which was almost unobtainable for North Norse citizens.
When an anonymous voice with a marked Italian accent
swore to inform the True Christians of the precise whereabouts of the false Messiah shortly before noon on Christmas
Eve, they realized they had found a far better way of hitting at
the enemy.

The invincible Lennart Torstensson had hammered and beaten
and cut and chiselled every single detail of his peculiar dreams
into the flat stones in angular runic script. Six days before
Christmas, when he had finished the engraving, he scrubbed
the stones with sand so the text didn't look too new and perfect,
and then put them all, including the thirteenth blank stone –
'*Even if one were invincible, one should always take the unpredictable into account*' – in the bath, which he filled with water,
salt and evil-smelling seaweed. Next he went to the station and
bought a single ticket for the train that departed from the
capital of the Western Bastion on 23 December and arrived in
Fredenshvile on the morning of Christmas Eve. From there he
called at a somewhat more suspect office behind the station,
where he purchased a slightly used but perfectly valid South
Norse passport.

Five days before Christmas, the fourth and last Sunday in
Advent, the Prime Minister issued the final warning to the government of North Norseland:

> *If the North Norse government has not released Mr Brams
> Bramsentorpf and withdrawn its territorial demands on*

*Drude Estrid Island before midday on Christmas Eve, the
South Norse government will consider itself obliged to close
the Strait and unilaterally declare Drude Estrid Island to be
South Norse territory.*

The South Norse air force began to roar through the skies on
the South Norse side of the Strait, while the North Norse air
force roared through the sound barrier on the other side. The
proud South Norse warships on duty in the harbours of the
Strait laid mines in strategic places, armoured vehicles ranged
themselves along the coast, and the army engaged in exercises
day and night regardless of gales and rain. All leave was suspended even on bank holidays, and the Home Guard was put
on red alert. Air raid sirens were tested all over the country.
There were three days left before Christmas.

*

'They really mean business,' said Sigbrit almost reluctantly as
the fighter planes passed overhead, deafening them.

'Yes, we'd better get going.' Ambrosius pushed aside the
repaired balloon canvas. He took out three mugs, placed them
on the cleared table and poured coffee from the thermos. 'Once
they close the Strait, that's it. We won't get anywhere.'

Der Fremdling appeared from his corner, snatched up a mug
without a word and again vanished into the darkness. At that
moment the door opened and Odin and Harald Adelstensfostre tramped into the wheelhouse.

'I should like to announce the good news that the basket for
the air connection is completed in good order and ready for
departure,' said Odin happily, sitting down at the table.

Harald Adelstensfostre nodded. He too had finished his task.

Ambrosius the Fisherman and Harald Adelstensfostre had taken the balloon apart into all its sections and exchanged every seam and metal part for wooden pegs and cord, while Sigbrit had mended the worn-out canvas and Odin had patched up the basketwork where years of wear and damp had penetrated.

'Now all that's left is the iron ball.' The Fisherman turned his head in the direction of the rhythmic hammering coming from the end of the shipyard, where Gunnar the Head was still busy.

'Yes, and the letters from Odin.' Sigbrit took out some paper and sat down with the little old man to compose the letters she was to deliver to Bramsentorpf's captors and the South Norse and North Norse governments – with a copy for the press – as soon as the balloon had taken off.

'Promise us you'll be careful, Lady Fair,' murmured the Fisherman anxiously. 'There's probably someone or other who could get the idea that you know the way to reach the island.'

Sigbrit nodded. 'It will be all right,' she replied calmly. 'What I'm more concerned about, as you have said yourself, is that it may not work. After all, it won't solve the dispute over the island. And it's far from certain that the Prophets of Doom will believe the letters.'

'There is no telling what believing folk will believe in,' said Odin quietly, tugging his beard.

'Why take the risk at all when it doesn't help in the least?' asked Sigbrit.

'Because I have to do what I can. If nothing else the letters will at least get Bramsentorpf set free,' replied Ambrosius.

Ambrosius stood up and looked out of the window at the huge-headed man still sweating over his lump of iron. He studied the monotonous hammering for a long time. Then he slowly turned round. 'If we asked you to, would you give it up?'

Sigbrit shook her head.

'They might even decide to do away with you?'

'I don't believe that,' Sigbrit replied softly.

'War will break out anyway!' shouted Ambrosius unexpectedly. Then he lowered his voice. 'You have to see things straight, Lady Fair,' he murmured, going over to Sigbrit and gently stroking her hair. 'Neither the South nor the North Norse government is prepared to give up Odin's Island.' No, the old sailors were right: '*Name the island and all Hell will break loose.*'

Sigbrit lifted her head with a start. '*Name the island and all Hell will break loose,*' she repeated. '*An island is an island until it is no longer an island. When Kings put their names to paper, subjects keep silent.*'

Ambrosius coughed; he wasn't with her.

'Can't you see, the whole thing hangs on the agreement between the Kings?' Sigbrit exclaimed eagerly. 'Whatever the agreement was it has never been cancelled, for if it had been we should have known about the island. The agreement is still in force!' Her eyes began to shine. 'And regardless of the exact wording, there can't be much doubt that both Kings disclaim their right to the island.'

'Well, maybe,' the Fisherman nodded slowly. 'That is probably true. But you still have to find the agreement.'

'It must exist somewhere.' Sigbrit's fingers drummed on the table. Then an idea struck her and her mouth curved in a crooked smile. 'If I'm not mistaken, that place is the Queen's private library.'

'And how will you get in there?'

'I don't need to,' replied Sigbrit, laughing. 'Wasn't it you who once suggested I should just pretend I knew about the island, even though I didn't then. If the Queen gets to hear I have a copy of the agreement, then...'

Now Ambrosius laughed. 'Lady Fair, you're not at all bad for such a modern woman,' he said admiringly.

'As soon as you have left,' she went on, 'I shall request Lord Chamberlain von Egernret for an invitation to the Queen's Christmas audience. I very much doubt that the court will brush me aside if they get to know what I am in possession of...'

At that moment a cry came from the end of the shipyard. Gunnar the Head had finished and lifted up a perfectly elliptical iron ball in one hand. Everything was ready. Now all they had to do was wait for the gale to slacken enough for the balloon to take off.

*

But the gale did not slacken; instead it increased. The wind came howling from the north-west, more violent and icy than ever. The leaden clouds flew with fiendish haste across the sky without having time to drop their load. It was barely possible to walk upright and the few people who dared venture outside their cars and houses hurried close to the wall to get to the shops as quickly as possible to do the last of their Christmas shopping. Time passed on to the day before the day before, then the day before, but still the storm raged so that one could hardly hear the fighter planes swooping overhead.

Late on the twenty-third, after the felled spruce trees had been carried into South Norse homes and dressed with red and gold balls, after the Prime Minister had practised his Christmas address – which his young assistant had written for him – before the mirror, in which he would announce to the nation that they were now at war with the North Norse Kingdom, after the invincible Lennart Torstensson had stepped into the Fredenshvile train in the capital of the Western Bastion with his weighty Trojan bag clasped closely to his chest, after Simon Peter II had tried, in a final radio speech, to save those souls that could still save themselves by attending the meeting on Hverv Harbour with all the other Born Anew Christians, after Blessed Anders Andersen and the Lambs of the Lord had smoked a pipe of holy grass and lighted a gigantic sacrificial fire, after the Muslim Militia had bought two thirds of the tickets for the following day's 11 o'clock hovercraft to Ur Island, after the father and mother, the five remaining uncles, their wives and children, with the widow of the sixth, as well as the few non-related Reborn Jews, had met up in the bunker where Ezekiel the Righteous was hiding, after the Avengers had polished the cudgels and knives that would assure them of victory in the final battle against the tyranny of the church, after the seven meticulously chosen True Christians had packed their things and set the alarm clock, and after Mary's Maidens had finished their song for peace, to be sung on Christmas morning, an angry, deep rumbling came from the black Norse sky, and a moment later the clouds opened and a flood of large whirling snowflakes was let loose in the raging storm.

Ambrosius the Fisherman and Odin stood for a moment in the doorway watching Der Fremdling and Gunnar the Head disappearing into the blizzard.

'There is no mishap a spot of luck cannot remedy,' said Odin, casting a final glance at the flurry of whirling whiteness before the Fisherman closed and bolted the door.

Ambrosius nodded silently. It would take more than a spot of luck to stop a storm like this, he thought. But no matter what it was like, they could not postpone their departure any longer than noon on the following day. Not only had Odin given Bishop Bentsen his promise – and you never knew what the bishop or rather his envoy might hit upon if Odin did not keep his word – but on the dot of twelve o'clock the Prime Minister would declare Drude Estrid Island to be South Norse territory, and the closure of the Strait would begin. First the Navy would close off entry to the Strait, and before many hours had passed the area would be transformed into a vast naval exercise, and the *Rikke-Marie* would be forced to abandon any approach to the island. When the North Norsemen would launch their attack remained an unanswered question.

'I wish I could come with you,' said Sigbrit later when the Fisherman crept into the bunk to join her.

'We too,' he replied. 'But wishes won't change anything.'

'No,' Sigbrit smiled sadly. 'I know. And I know that this time it is my responsibility.' She sat up and tried to catch the Fisherman's eye in the darkness. 'The realization of freedom doesn't provide any solace,' she said softly.

Ambrosius the Fisherman kissed her brow and nodded silently. 'In a way it is true that the day you discover you have a choice, you no longer have any choice.'

*

Mr Brams Bramsentorpf was a free man.

Aisha had dropped him off, still blindfolded, in a field a long way from Fredenshvile. His hair had grown to his shoulders, his beard consisted of uneven stubble, his body was clad in a shalwar-kameez, and he had bare feet. It is a question of faith, Aisha had replied when Mr Bramsentorpf complained about his cold feet. Then she had driven off, and Mr Bramsentorpf took off the blindfold and started to stumble across the snow-covered field in the direction of a faint light in the distance. It was the morning of Christmas Eve.

In a sudden fit of mercy Aisha had decided not to kill her hostage and, as she went on repeating to herself, there really had not been any reason to do so now there would be no harm in him telling people about the Mighty One's plans. Besides, Aisha had other more important things to think about.

Aisha drove as fast as she could. Thick snow was falling, and the light of the approaching day was not yet strong enough to disperse the winter morning darkness. She switched on her radio but quickly switched it off again; she was tense and filled with a fearful presentiment. Far too soon her misgivings turned out to be well grounded. There was not a soul in the apartment where her brother, the thirty-nine other militiamen, as well as the Muslim Modernists as they were previously known, who had chosen to accompany them to the Isle of the Prophet, were to meet her. Her brother had betrayed her. On the table lay a handwritten note saying that only men were pure enough to accompany the envoy of Allah, the Mighty One, to the Isle of the Prophet, the Norse Mecca. The great Prophet Muhammad would condemn such behaviour, thought Aisha and did not doubt that the Messenger of Allah, the Mighty One, would do the same. Aisha's revenge would be sweet; an eye for an eye, a tooth for a tooth.

Aisha fetched the guidebook from the hired car and studied the map of Fredenshvile and district. There were a number of possible harbours, plenty of ferries. No, she needed something more. Her eyes roved around the mess in the empty apartment. She knew her brother well enough to be sure that somewhere here there would be...

While Aisha made a thorough search in all the nooks and crannies of the flat, Blessed Anders Andersen searched every cell of his brain. In the oddest way, the morning of Christmas Eve had arrived and with it the reality had dawned that the Lambs of the Lord were not prepared.

As always Blessed Anders Andersen laid his destiny in the hands of the Almighty Father and his Shepherd, the Mighty One, and lit a new pipe of holy grass which he sent around all the waiting Lambs of the Lord in the park. There was no need to worry, he declared as the pipe was passed round, 'Salvation will come from Our God who sits on the throne, and from the Lamb.' Before the morning was over the Lord's Shepherd, the Mighty One, would drive the Lambs of the Lord straight through the fires of Purgatory to the Island of Eternal Pastures. In the meantime, for the sake of tidiness, Blessed Anders Andersen would cast a glance at what the other – deceived – Prophets of Doom were up to; there might be an idea or two there that could be useful.

And Blessed Anders Andersen wasn't far wrong. The first thing that reached his ears was Simon Peter II's final appeal to the doubters and unbelievers.

'The end of the world has come,' the Entrusted Disciple's voice came crackling out of the transistor. 'Today Jesus Christ will save all followers of the only true faith and carry them with him into the Thousand-year reign of Peace on Earth!' The Entrusted Disciple was obliged to pause for a moment as his voice was close to cracking with emotion and the imminent arrival of the Hour of Judgement. 'Today the waters will divide, and I, Simon Peter the Second, once a fisherman of body and soul, the Mighty One's Entrusted Disciple and First Apostle, will lead the Born Anew Christians to the Isle of Paradise.' In the goodness of his heart Simon Peter II did not think it would be suitable on a Christmas Eve morning to describe the Hell that would, before nightfall, strike the rest of the world's pop-ulation.

All the same, many a soul felt the fires of Hell burning their neck – '*and the torments of the second death day and night in the eternities of eternity*' – and would have much preferred to be saved from such a horrific fate. Early in the morning, while it was still more dark than light and regardless of the ferocious blizzard, all those who were pure in faith or merely pious at heart streamed along to the beach at Hverv Harbour. Even though there was plenty of room in paradise, it was still better to be on the safe side and ensure themselves a place at the front of the queue.

Darkness gradually gave way to misty grey daylight. It was icy cold and snow whirled around like needles from every side. It took stubborn faith and a good deal of stamping around to keep the cold out.

While the Born Anew Christians stamped the snow flat on the blissful strand of departure, seven True Christians exchanged the train for the ferry plying from South to North Norseland.

The seven had to plough their way through a desperate crowd to get to the gangway. Only now had the last South Norse men in North Norseland realized that the threat of war was a reality, and at this eleventh hour they fought tooth and nail to get a place on one of the last ferries to South Norseland. The police and passport control officers were on high emergency alert, waiting for the signal to close the borders to all traffic between South and North Norseland.

On the other side of the Strait, where the border guard smiled and nodded good-humouredly to the passengers when he gave them back their passports after examining them, all seven South Norsemen were on their way home. And the seven True Christians' brand new South Norse passports were given a smile and a nod as they went on their way, and the official even winked at the two women in the group – it was Christmas, after all – as he wished the family a happy home-coming to the Queendom of South Norseland and merry Christmas, with an extra nod at the bags full of parcels. A stranger offered to help one of the women to carry her bulky bag, but she refused politely; it wasn't at all heavy. That was true, for all the bags were as light as only empty packages can be – with just one exception carried by a well-trained young man, which contained the hammer and the three hand-grenades. The True Christians were about to celebrate Christmas as well.

This Christmas would take some forgetting. For the last time Ace (alias Ezra) inspected the four groups of Avengers who were to storm the town from their appointed compass points.

'Go out and find your positions. At precisely twelve o'clock the final attack on the tyranny of the Church will begin. We shall break the enemy in Fredenshvile. From north, south, east and west we shall annihilate every single person who has anything at all to do with Christmas and its ends.' Ace clicked his tongue to give his words emphasis. 'When the town has been cleansed of all its filth, we will meet by the Town Hall.'

The taxi Ace had called for himself rolled up in front of the basement flat. He had an important task, he explained, but he would soon join one of the groups. 'Show no mercy, no pity. It is the Day of Judgement,' he cried Ace as he waved to the four groups of young shaven-headed men in brown marching away into the blizzard, each in its own direction. Then he stepped into the cab, brushed the snow from his clothes and asked to be driven to the airport.

It was high time Ezra (alias Ace) found his family again.

At Fredenshvile airport an ancient Russian helicopter waited beneath a lean-to, while two Russian pilots stood about in the staff canteen – the tower would not give the OK for any aircraft to take off as long as the blizzard raged.

Ezekiel the Righteous, his father and mother, the five remaining uncles, their wives and children, with the widow of the sixth and the few non-related Reborn Jews sat in the old air-raid shelter with their possessions and jewels in bundles of seven kilos each – what more would they need on the Island of the Eternal Sabbath – waiting for the blizzard and time to come to an end.

Although time did pass and the gale calmed down to a gentle breeze, the snow went on falling. Forty angry young Muslim Militiamen and at least a hundred former Muslim Modernists waited in the hovercraft departure lounge with a small group of Christmas passengers. The weather had cleared a little, but not enough to allow the hovercraft to set off. The eleven o'clock boat would be cancelled unless the snow stopped altogether.

Albeit with some delays, the trains kept running and at ten to eleven the train from the capital of the Western Bastion glided into Fredenshvile central station. Among the crowd of passengers swarming out to be welcomed by friends and relations was a very tall, very blond young man. The very tall, very blond young man was alone, and no one met him on the platform. In his right hand he held a heavy black bag and in the left a large suitcase; the invincible Lennart Torstensson did not know how long he would have to stay in South Norseland.

With the weighty Trojan bag held close to his chest Lennart took the escalator up to the station concourse, secured the bag in a lock-up, and still clutching the weighty Trojan bag to his chest, checked the departure times for the local trains travelling north. He was in no doubt about his destination; he had been able to pick up the South Norse radio frequencies from the capital of the Western Bastion. He had plenty of time and headed for the station caféteria at a leisurely pace. There he drank a cup of coffee and ate a good breakfast consisting of two soft-boiled eggs, three slices of toast, a bowl of porridge and milk and a Danish pastry – for nothing can be achieved on an empty stomach. Precisely a quarter of an hour after he had sat down he rose again. Cleanliness is next to heroism, to be practised in preparation for a heroic deed – it was time Lennart had a wash and brush up.

Washed and brushed up and with the weighty Trojan bag

clutched close to his chest, he went down to platform 9 and got on the train going north.

Snow was still falling, but they could wait no longer. Ezekiel the Righteous nodded to the eldest of the five remaining uncles. Snowing or not, the end was nigh. The seven-kilo bundles were picked up, and Ezekiel the Righteous, his father and mother, the five remaining uncles and their wives and children, with the widow of the sixth as well as the few non-related Reborn Jews left the bunker and walked towards the Queen's Garden.

At the airport the two Russian pilots, shaking their heads, obeyed the order they received on their mobiles, left the warm caféteria and climbed into the icy cold helicopter. The pilots watched the gently falling flakes, then looked at one another; they would never get permission to take off in this weather, and even if they were allowed to, they certainly were not inclined to fly. Nevertheless they switched on the engines, drove the helicopter on to the runway and reported to the tower. Just as the rotor blades began to rotate – like a miracle sent by Jahveh and the Mighty One the pilots had heard so much about and now would shortly meet – the snow ceased to fall, the tower gave the go-ahead to start, and the clapped-out M117 skidded once or twice on the snow-covered runway before the wheels ran free and they rose into the air.

At that moment a taxi came to a stop in front of the airport with squealing brakes. Ezra (alias Ace) pushed a few notes into the driver's hand and leapt out. He ran across to the helicopter pad and reached the gate just in time to see the ancient Russian machine disappearing into the grey sky with no one on board except the two pilots.

Ezra weighed up the situation for a moment, then turned on his heel, ran back to the car and threw himself on to the back seat. There was only one single open place in Fredenshvile large enough for a helicopter to land and take off.

The last passenger boarded the delayed hovercraft to Ur Island. The gangway was pulled up, the cables thrown off and with motors roaring the captain slowly steered the boat away from the quay and into the middle of the fairway.

The forty Muslim Militiamen and the hundred or more Muslim Modernists nodded and smiled at each other; the end of the world was nigh.

So far, though, it was only twenty to twelve. From a building site behind the bank car park, where Sigbrit Holland had worked, came a deep humming sound. The True Christians looked at the well-trained man, who pulled a mobile out of his pocket. The phone rang again and the well-trained man raised the phone to his ear.

'You will find him on board a fishing boat named *Rikke-Marie*,' the disguised voice had a marked Italian accent. 'The boat is moored in the disused shipyard on the third dock in the northernmost section of Firø. Take care, in addition to the fake Messiah you will probably find at least one woman and two men, maybe more.' The receiver was replaced before the well-trained man could reply.

The seven True Christians with Our Lord and truth in their hearts and hammer and hand-grenades in their bags walked briskly over the crisp snow along Firø Canal. When they came to the disused shipyard they did not turn the door handle but went directly around the building and with the aid of linked fingers and a little muscle power two of them lifted the other five on to the roof. The well-trained man crawled around and managed to get a hold on one of the small roof windows. He whistled quietly and carefully brushed the snow aside. There was nothing to be seen through the pane but dark water. He crawled on a little, found the next window and as soon as he had scraped the snow away he whistled an entire little tune: the green and once orange fishing boat was right beneath him.

The well-trained man waved to the others to join him. One of the True Christians took the hammer out of his bag and gave it to their leader; another passed him a hand-grenade. The well-trained man raised the hammer in one hand, holding the hand-grenade in the other while he loosened its safety catch with his teeth. Just as he smashed the hammer into the window came a hair-raising howl. The well-trained man turned his head and the movement caused him to lose his foothold. Still holding the hand-grenade, he slid down the snowy roof and tumbled over the edge to strike the ground and eternal rest with a colossal report.

Before the True Christians had recovered enough from their fright and the sudden end of their leader to be able to continue their mission, the doors of the yard opened and the green and once orange fishing boat chugged out, turned left into Firø Canal and vanished.

'I don't like sailing. I don't like sailing at all, at all,' groaned Gunnar the Head from the innermost corner of the wheelhouse, even before the *Rikke-Marie* was out in the fairway. It was twelve o'clock.

*

'I hereby declare Drude Estrid Island to be a part of the Queendom of South Norseland' came the Prime Minister's opening announcement as his speech was transmitted on radio and television on numerous frequencies and channels simultaneously. 'Until the North Norse government acknowledges this state of affairs, the government of South Norseland, the South Nordic and the Norse with Her Majesty the Queen, regard it as necessary to close the Strait to all civil traffic...'

The Queen switched off her radio. She did not need to hear the speech to the end because she had a copy of it on her desk. She rose and walked slowly up and down the carpet. She looked anxious. To the last she had believed that North Norseland would give in. Now it was too late.

Simon Peter II stepped on to a gigantic dais his followers had built of snow. Hverv Harbour was crammed with people standing so close together that neither snow nor sand was visible in between them.

'I, Simon Peter the Second,' began the Entrusted Disciple, looking out over the moving sea of humanity, his heart glowing with divine bliss, 'once a fisher of body and soul, the Mighty One's Entrusted Disciple and First Apostle, give you my pledge that the Day is upon us, the moment has come. Today is the day when the Son of the Lord, the Mighty One, will divide the waters and lead the Born Anew Christians' steps across the seabed to the Isle of Paradise.'

'To the Isle of Paradise,' rejoiced the crowd.

'Today is the day when we must uncover our hearts, for today is the day when the Lord and the Mighty One will judge each and every one as they deserve. But we, the Born Anew Christians, know that we are to be blessed. And that blessing will come as a sign from the Mighty One, who will summon us when the time has come for us to go forward.'

'A sign from the Mighty One! A sign from the Mighty One!'

'When the sign comes, we shall walk naked before the Lord,' continued the Entrusted Disciple. 'Let the Lord receive you as he created you. Dressed in the image of Adam and Eve, the garments of heaven, that skin which Our Lord created to bind heart and soul together as one. Naked shall we walk to the Isle of Paradise.'

Suddenly, from out of the dense grey sky came a distant humming, and shortly afterwards a long, dark shadow came into view amidst the snow-laden clouds about midway between Fredenshvile and the Isle of Paradise. Simon Peter II blinked passionately, but the mysterious shadow did not disappear. There was no doubt about it: it was heading straight for the Isle of Paradise.

The helicopter was full to bursting point. Ezekiel the Righteous, his father and mother, the five remaining uncles and their wives and children, with the widow of the sixth sat along the curving sides on scratched and uncomfortable plastic seats, while the seven-kilo bundles of vital belongings were piled at their feet. Ezekiel the Righteous looked out the window, and although there was nothing to be seen but grey clouds, his eyes were glued to the horizon. Then the cliffs sprang into sight and soon after that the helicopter passed the first point, the next, yet another and another before it was surrounded by dense yellowish fog. The pilots waited until they were sure of having left all the cliffs behind, then let the machine dive, and a snow-covered landscape was revealed to the eyes of the Reborn Jews.

'Ze land of heavenly blith,' lisped Ezekiel the Righteous, and his father and mother, the five remaining uncles and their wives and children, with the widow of the sixth cried out with joy and gave thanks to Jahveh and Messiah, the Mighty One.

The Reborn Jews could discern some scattered trees and further away a few small houses took shape. Then a shining silver mirror sparkled in the midst of the snowy land and soon they saw it was ice swept smooth over a frozen lake. Ezekiel the Righteous fell to his knees on the vibrating floor to thank his Creator, and just as the helicopter began to shake violently, the prophetic son shouted without the trace of a lisp, 'The Island of the Eternal Sabbath.'

The humming sound stopped abruptly and the shadow behind the clouds turned into one single sharp blue light, then there was nothing.

'The sign!' yelled Simon Peter II ecstatically and could not keep down a sob of delight. It was really true. He had never doubted, and he had been right; Jesus Christ, the Mighty One, had sent the sign. *'For I saw an angel come down from Heaven with the key to the abyss and a great chain in his hand. The angel seized the dragon and the ancient serpent, who are the Devil-and-Satan, and bound him for a thousand years, then hurled him into the abyss under lock and key, so that he shall no longer beguile the nations before the thousand years have passed.'*

'The sign!' echoed the human sea, and some of them fell, passing out in utter joy and cold. 'The sign!'

The Mighty One's sign had also been seen elsewhere.

In the Queen's Garden both related and non-related Reborn Jews fell to their knees and wept with joy. Soon it would be their turn to see the light of the eternal sabbath, which by a miracle had just shown itself to their wondering eyes.

Ezra too (no longer alias Ace) – who at this moment after a painfully slow drive through deep snow had finally caught up with the Reborn Jews in the Queen's Garden – saw the light and dropped to his knees to weep as never before. So fervent was his weeping that neither he nor the other Reborn Jews noticed the shaven-headed, brown-clad young men approaching from the east with raised cudgels and knives and incandescent with holy fire, before it was too late.

The Mighty One had also sent his sign to Ali and the thirty-nine other Muslim Militiamen on board the flying boat to Ur Island.

Ali rose to his feet and went to the toilet, where he spread out his prayer mat, kneeled down and bent forward until his forehead touched the mat. He bent forward a number of times as he whispered his prayer to Allah, the one and only. When his prayer was ended he went back to the cabin, gave a slight nod, and three of the other Muslim Militiamen followed him through a door bearing the sign 'No admittance' and up a narrow flight of stairs. At the top they waited for precisely one minute, then burst open the door to the cockpit. One pistol was aimed at the captain's temple, another at the first officer. Down below in the cabin the thirty-six remaining members of the Muslim Militia jumped to their feet and pointed their guns to left and right at the few non-Muslim Christmas passengers.

With a violence that overturned coffee cups and soft drinks and spilled their contents over seats and passengers, the flying boat swung sharply to the right and changed course, now heading straight for the line of cliffs south of Ur Island.

Meanwhile one of the Militiamen held his pistol to the terrified captain's temple, invoked Ali el Allah, the one and only, and begged him to open the gateway in the cliffs so they could sail straight in to the Isle of the Prophet.

Either Allah could not or would not hear Ali's prayer; there was a crash and, with a brutal suddenness, the flying boat ceased to move forward. Hostages and hostage-takers were hurled in all directions, and the icy cold sea-water came gushing into the hull.

Whether the dazed passengers put more strength and fervour into their prayers or whether Allah or maybe it was Our Lord that preferred the prayers now uttered – possibly helped along by an anonymous call to the police from a furious sister who had finally found the shredded timetable for the flying boat to Ur Island with the fatal line under eleven o'clock – was unknown. But one thing was certain, it did not take more than a few minutes before the coastguard reached the spot.

'The time has come!' shouted Simon Peter II, tore off his clothes and stepped down from the podium and over to the water's edge. 'Come, one and all. The moment has come.' The Entrusted Disciple waved on the Born Anew Christians and soon one pious goose-pimpled figure chafed against another as they all pushed and shoved to be first in the queue for the Isle of Paradise.

Simon Peter II stopped when the first wave rolled icily over his foot. With a solemn mien he slowly raised his right arm in the air. He stretched his hand straight to heaven, made the sign of the cross on his chest and then directed his arm over the slightly frozen restless waters. There was a moment's silence. The Born Anew Christians stood still, the waves were stilled, the wind dropped to stillness, the clouds stood still. It was as if the earth's rotation around the sun came to a halt. The only sound was the faint chattering of freezing pious teeth. The Entrusted Disciple gazed out over the horizon towards the Isle of Paradise and prayed to the Lord and his son, the Mighty One, to divide the icy waters.

Nothing happened. Seconds passed and the earth resumed its circling around the sun, the waves again rolled in on to the snow-covered beach, and the clouds flew on across the grey sky. Simon Peter II folded his hands and prayed to his God. Then he took a long stride forward directly through the frozen crust on the surface down into the cold water. Then another and another. The Entrusted Disciple gritted his teeth so that those around him should not hear his teeth chattering, and again stretched out his arm over the recalcitrant sea. At first he held it high, then a little lower, then horizontally, then higher again, as if he was searching for the particular divine angle that would make the waters obey. But the Strait was obstinate. Firmly determined to show himself worthy of the call of the Lord, Simon Peter II moved his numb feet yet another step or two, and the water reached the middle of his thighs. That didn't help either. With a flash of divine insight the Entrusted Disciple realized that Our Lord and his son, the Mighty One, wished to test not only the Entrusted Disciple himself, but all the Born Anew Christians. Simon Peter II turned his head and with stiff mouthings and dangerously blue lips he yelled at them all to follow him.

'The ocean of the Lord will purify your souls and your bodies so that you can walk cleanly through the portals of the Kingdom of Heaven. Be not afraid, come with me. Confess your sins to these salt tears, which the Lord and His son, the

Mighty One, have wept for the sake of man, and the Lord will pardon you. Walk with me until we are all cleansed, and the Lord and the Mighty One will open the portals to the Isle of Paradise.'

'The Isle of Paradise!' shouted the Born Anew Christians, as if it was a battle cry, and the first rows of naked pious turned faith into courage and threw themselves into the icy waters, while their hearts warmed at the thought of the heavenly bliss awaiting them on the other side of purgatory.

Simon Peter II had almost fallen into a frozen trance, and his voice grew weaker and weaker. 'Lift up the children in your arms and carry them with you into the sight of God. The Lord will divide the waters for the innocent. The water is cold but never fear. The Mighty One is waiting...' Simon Peter II's voice died away to a frozen whisper, and his arm waved no longer but clung tightly to his chest, not yet covered with water.

The faith of the faithful was strong, and strong also was the pressure on those in front from those further and further back, as thousands of Born Anew Christians followed the Entrusted Disciple out into the tears of the Lord.

Now the water had reached up to Simon Peter II's throat, and with a tremendous effort he succeeded in stretching his right arm up over the waves as he begged Our Lord and his son, the Mighty One, to divide the sea and allow the Reborn Christians through. But no matter how fervently the Entrusted Disciple prayed and froze, no matter how many of the Born Anew Christians followed him out into the freezing purgatorial fire, the Strait did not give way by a single centimetre. Although Simon Peter II did not doubt his Lord, he couldn't restrain a howl when a bigger wave washed right over his head and for a moment he lost his foothold.

'The Isle of Paradise,' he whispered in terror when his feet balanced firmly again. 'The Isle of Paradise.' But his spirit seemed to have deserted the Entrusted Disciple, and just then a peal of high angry laughter broke out immediately behind him.

'Ha, if the Mighty One really meant it in earnest, wouldn't he have warmed the water up a bit?' cried a bulky lady angrily as her voluminous bosom rose and sank in time to her angry snorting.

Simon Peter II tried to reply, but his purple lips and stiff jaw would not obey. 'Paradise. Paradise,' was all he succeeded in whispering.

'One thing at least is sure,' the stout lady went on. 'If the Mighty One wants me in paradise, he must see to it that the water is warmed up first!' With that the dame turned around, and a good deal faster than when she was going in, she leaped out of the water. With impressive agility and fighting spirit she found her way through the opposite moving stream of naked Pious, over to her little heap of clothes, brushed the snow off them and dragged them on without caring about right or wrong side out. Then she ran as fast as straps and clothes could stand up to the car park and let herself into the car she had bequeathed to Our Lord and the end of the world but a moment ago.

'The Mighty One would have warmed up the water if he had wanted me with him,' uttered a thin man with chattering teeth standing in the water up to his navel.

'Our Almighty Lord would have warmed up the water,' another joined in.

'Would have warmed up the water! Would have warmed up the water!' soon resounded on all sides, and as if by command the first rows of freezing Born Anew Christians turned around and began to fight their way back to the beach. Some few whose faith was stronger than their need for warmth, looked across at the Entrusted Disciple and First Apostle to find out what the Lord and the Mighty One were thinking. But Simon Peter II had no more words. His voice was frozen into silence in his icy larynx, so even the most faithful Pious stopped in bewilderment in the middle of their brave attempt to get through the fires of purgatory to the Isle of Paradise. In the course of a few minutes chaos took hold; the Born Anew Christians who were in the water tried to get back to shore, while others who had still not been immersed, pushed from behind. Pious ranged against Pious, and inevitably some of them fell over into the cold water. There was yelling and screaming and soon the water's edge had become a battleground.

This was the moment the invincible Lennart Torstensson had been waiting for. With firm long strides and still with the bulky Trojan bag held tight to his chest, he set out from his hiding place up the road across from the snow-covered sandy beach.

'Stop!' he shouted when he was within earshot. 'Stop!'

The Born Anew Christians gazed curiously at the fully dressed man climbing on to the snow platform, which Simon Peter II had left only a few minutes earlier.

'This is all wrong,' shouted Lennart in his best South Norse. 'God says you are not to go into the water...'

The few freezing, trembling and still staunch Born Anew Christians left did not need any more convincing to attach themselves to the wave of backtracking Pious already on their way out of the water. The thought of the Paradise awaiting them was pushed aside, and both the wet and the still dry, almost saved naked bodies hastened back to their piles of clothes in the snow.

'God says that the water is not the way to the Isle of Paradise,' shouted Lennart, and the Born Anew Christians crowded curiously together around the snow platform and their new leader.

However, encouraged by his immediate success, Lennart forgot himself. 'Mr Odin Odin is not Jesus Christ,' he shouted in ringing North Norse.

Curiosity turned immediately to hostility, and naked as well as fully or partly clothed pious threw themselves towards the platform where Lennart stood.

'Traitor!' screamed one. 'Come down off there immediately!'

'Come down!' Others joined in. 'It's his fault that the waters didn't divide!'

'You are wrong!' yelled Lennart. 'Mr Odin Odin is...'

'Traitor!'

With all the unbridled fury that only an abortive attempt to reach paradise can generate, several Born Anew Christians jumped up on to the snow platform and dragged Lennart, screaming loudly, down.

'I can prove it! I can prove it!' he cried, trying to get to his feet. Before he could regain his balance he was knocked down again. 'You're wrong!' he shouted, his voice weaker now, and lifted up the weighty Trojan bag with one hand, while trying to defend himself from the blows raining down on him with the other. 'Mr Odin Odin is Odin,' he whispered with his mouth full of snow and blood.

No one was prepared to listen to what Lennart had to say as long as he did so in North Norse. A bare heel dug into his ribs, another struck him in the groin, and soon his face was unrecognizable. A series of kicks rained into him from all points of the compass, then a Born Anew Christian who had been especially close to salvation leaped on to his chest and the invincible Lennart Torstensson felt no more.

While the last naked Born Anew Christians relinquished the hope of passing through purgatory and getting to the Isle of Paradise in favour of regaining the warmth of their recently deserted homes, and were on their way across the beach away from the water, a group of punch-drunk, cowled men and women were advancing from the opposite direction.

Through his divine fug, Blessed Anders Andersen dimly realized that not only had the Lambs of the Lord arrived too late for the paradisal journey to the Island of Eternal Pastures, but for unknown reasons this had gone wrong. However, this development was not completely unexpected, so Blessed Anders Andersen reached for his reserve plan and found it surprisingly quickly among his slightly clouded thoughts.

As a first step Blessed Anders Andersen pulled himself together and in an almost clear voice announced to the Lambs of the Lord the fact that the waters had not divided for the Born Anew Christians proved that the Born Anew Christians were mistaken, while the Lambs of the Lord were right. Next he encouraged all the Lambs of the Lord to find fuel for a sacrificial bonfire. And thirdly, after taking a drag or two of another pipe of holy grass, Blessed Anders Andersen fell to his knees in the snow and gazed up stiffly, as in a trance, at the grey skies. Just as he was ready to come out of his trance and – as the fourth step – tell them that the Shepherd of the Lord would certainly lead them to the Island of Eternal Pastures on his two-thousand-year birthday, but that the Lord had just revealed to him that this would not take place until the following year, since by mistake the Shepherd's birthday had been given as the year one and not the year nil, a loud shout rang out.

'A body! A body!' shouted one of the Lambs of the Lord, who had stumbled over the lifeless Lennart Torstensson as he was searching for holy firewood.

Before long, Blessed Anders Andersen was able to confirm with his own eyes that a lifeless man lay with his face in the snow-covered sand with the blood trickling from under his very blond hair and torn clothes. A large black bag lay at the man's side. He reached for the bag and tried to open it, but the lifeless man had his hand locked fast around the handle which held the bag closed.

Anders Andersen dropped the bag and turned to Lennart. He pushed the unconscious body and rolled it on to its back. A faint, almost inaudible breath came out of the swollen mouth, but the eyes were closed and Anders Andersen was in no doubt that the man was nearing his last gasp.

'May the Shepherd of the Lord have mercy on this poor lamb, and may he lift up this soul in his arms and carry it to the Island of Eternal Pastures,' prayed Blessed Anders Andersen reverently with folded hands, and he bent once more over the bag and tried to force open the lock. But Lennart's fingers seemed to be frozen fast around the black leather handle. Anders Andersen considered the situation for a moment, then folded his hands and whispered: 'May the Lord and his Shepherd forgive me.' Thereupon he resolutely broke the life-less Lennart Torstensson's fingers.

At the same moment a gigantic wave washed up on the snow-covered beach and in over Lennart's body, over Blessed Anders Andersen and the shoes and ankles of the other Lambs of the Lord and right into the weighty Trojan bag. Before Anders Andersen could grab hold of a single one of the twelve engraved and the thirteenth still unengraved stones, the wave had carried them back out to sea where they joined the millions of stones that were already in the Strait.

While the stones sank to their fate, the thirteenth and last of the peculiar dreams came to Lennart Torstensson the Prophet with his final few wheezing breaths...

GIMLA DAWN

While fire raged and all was burned
Fenris' belly shielded Odin
Fire died and flooding dwindled
Blade cut through and God looked out

Horizon empty, view of naught
Courage here, we steeds must find
brave to ride for sun to save
Courage here, Gimla Dawn come shine

But what is that which shimmers high?
'Hugin, Munin, ravens two
my mind springs green, my senses clear
Thought and Memory, welcome back here'

Perhaps these birds await us all?

'I DON'T LIKE sailing. I don't like sailing at all, at all,' moaned Gunnar the Head from the corner of the wheelhouse.

No one spoke. Sigbrit stood at the helm and urged on the green and once orange fishing boat to gain what speed she could. There was not a boat in sight and they still had not seen a sign of the Coastguard. But it must only be a question of time.

A gentle but steady wind blew from the north-east and Sigbrit steered *Rikke-Marie* towards the east side of the line of cliffs. Ambrosius drew his grandfather's yellowing chart out of its plastic pocket and compared the circles and crosses with the cliffs they passed.

'Lady Fair.' The Fisherman laid a hand on Sigbrit's arm. 'It's not going to get any better than this.'

Sigbrit nodded, slackened speed and then put the boat into neutral gear.

Ambrosius the Fisherman, Odin and Harald Adelstensfostre put on their oilskins and went out on deck. There the Fisherman lit three small gas burners they had fixed to the boat, while Harald Adelstensfostre and Odin unfolded the balloon and checked its mooring lines. Then they piped the hot air from the burners into the balloon. It took some time to get the burners to ignite, but eventually the flames began to rise. The system was working: the hot air passed quickly and smoothly through the pipes into the gigantic balloon. One side lifted slightly from the deck and at once the wind took hold. Ambrosius the Fisherman and Harald Adelstensfostre had to work hard to keep the basket lines clear of each other and at the same time make sure the balloon did not get blown into the water.

Filling the balloon took a long time, longer than expected, and inside the wheelhouse Sigbrit grew more and more nervous. It was already half past two; the coastguard could turn up at any time. Finally the door opened and Harald Adelstensfostre and Odin appeared. The hermit shook Sigbrit's hand without a word. Odin bowed so deeply that his long beard swept the floor.

'Tomorrow is another day, but yesterday goes on forever,' said the little old man.

Then both were gone. Soon the door opened again and this

time the Fisherman entered. He looked at Gunnar the Head.

'I don't like sailing,' mumbled the huge-headed man, creeping further into his corner. 'I don't like sailing at all, at all.'

'Your friend has need of you,' said Ambrosius the Fisherman gently, putting a hand on the huge-headed man's shoulder.

Hesitantly Gunnar the Head got to his feet and pulled on his jacket with clumsy haste. 'My friend mustn't worry about anything,' he said with a boldness contradicted by his ashen face.

'Everything is ready, Lady Fair,' said the Fisherman quietly when the door had closed behind the huge-headed man.

Sigbrit nodded, but she said nothing.

Ambrosius vanished down the ladder to the cabin but returned a moment later holding a fat envelope.

'Happy Christmas, Lady Fair,' he said hurriedly. 'Here are the documents for *Rikke-Marie*. She is yours now.' He handed the papers to Sigbrit, kissed her briefly on the forehead and half turned away from her.

'Thank you and happy Christmas to you too,' Sigbrit replied as calmly as she could. I have a present for you too, she thought, putting her right hand on the slight tension in her belly, but she didn't say it. 'Maybe later when everything has changed, I'll follow you,' she said instead.

The Fisherman looked at her for a moment, then he shook his head with a sad smile in his eyes.

'Maybe I'll find the fairway,' insisted Sigbrit, and suddenly tears were running down her cheeks.

The Fisherman gripped her shoulders with both hands, kissed her on the mouth and embraced her hard. He opened the door, a cold gust struck her wet cheeks, and she was on her own.

On deck Harald Adelstensfostre struggled with the balloon

that was straining to get free and up in the air. He passed the mooring line to Gunnar the Head and showed the huge-headed man how to prevent it getting entangled with the other ropes. A wave washed in over the deck, and Gunnar the Head almost lost his balance. He clutched *Rikke-Marie*'s rail hard. 'I don't like sailing,' he mumbled, his face more ashen than ever. 'I don't like sailing at all, at all.'

Harald Adelstensfostre climbed into the basket and Ambrosius the Fisherman passed him Odin's bag of presents for the people of Smith's Town and Post Office Town. Then the little old man followed and lastly the Fisherman himself. They looked at each other; everything was ready. Ambrosius made a sign to Gunnar the Head. The huge-headed man raised the kitchen knife and with four quick slashes he cut free first the balloon and then the basket.

The balloon shot into the air and snatched the basket up off the deck with a violent jerk that threw its passengers against each other. The hot air quickly pulled the balloon high up, and the wind, which on the boat had seemed light, now beat against their ears and buffeted both balloon and basket from side to side. Then the wind really took hold and the balloon moved calmly towards the cliffs, the basket following it serenely.

They could clearly make out every little outcrop and crevice in the ancient furrowed rocks like giants standing shoulder to shoulder, but there was still some distance to the outermost cliffs when suddenly the wind changed and they no longer flew westward but in quite the opposite direction, away from the island towards North Norseland. Although they knew it wouldn't help they moved around the basket trying to change the balance, and Ambrosius pulled like mad at the balloon lines, counting the lost seconds. He looked at the egg-timer;

one minute, two, three. There had also been two in the ascent and they had only fifteen in all.

'This isn't so good,' growled the Fisherman.

Odin looked up at the balloon, then touched the horseshoe in his breast pocket.

'Fortunately, there is no mishap that a morsel of luck can't remedy,' he said, pulling at his beard with his gloved hand.

And whether or not it was the horseshoe they could not tell, but at that moment the wind changed and the basket was slowly but surely driven towards the cliffs, and after just a couple of minutes they were above the first jagged points. The iron ball which up to then had dangled powerlessly on its line underneath the basket, suddenly came to life. It swung back and forth once or twice before the rope tightened with a crack to form a horizontal line that pulled the balloon towards the centre of the island, like a horse pulling a sledge.

'It works! It works!' cried Ambrosius.

The balloon accelerated and although he could no longer see them he waved to Sigbrit and Gunnar the Head on the green and once orange fishing boat far below the basket. Then the air balloon drifted into the greyish yellow mist.

Precious minutes had been lost to the caprices of the wind, and the basket had already descended so much they could have touched the nearest cliff they passed. And there was still far to go.

'We shall have to lose some weight,' shouted Ambrosius.

They had not brought any sandbags, it was more than enough for the hot air to carry the three of them, so the Fisherman took off his heavy boots, his life jacket and his wind-cheater and threw them all over the side and down into the water that seethed and crashed around the foot of the cliffs. Then Harald Adelstensfostre's oil skins went overboard. For a brief moment it seemed to help. The balloon flew smoothly a few metres above the third clifftop, but just after that they scraped the side of the next one, and ahead a high point towered up.

'I'm sorry, Odin, but now your presents will have to go too,' said the Fisherman and heaved the sack of nicely wrapped parcels over the side of the basket into the mist.

Yet even that was not enough. They struck the clifftop with a blow that grazed some of the basket side and threw Odin down on to the bottom, dangerously close to the gap.

'Here,' the hermit seized hold of Odin's hand and pulled him to his feet again.

They lumbered past the next clifftop, the basket turned around twice, then they sailed round another peak and they were through. They glided beneath the mist and the island lay before their eyes. The sun had broken through both cloud cover and mist and made the snow-covered landscape shine and glitter.

'Smith's Town!' exclaimed Odin, pointing to a huddle of small houses in the distance on the other side of a sparkling silver lake. 'To the traveller home is a place passed for the second time,' he went on, pulling happily at his beard.

The magnetic force grew stronger as they neared the middle of the island, and now the balloon put on so much speed that the air pressure made their eyes water. Ambrosius the Fisherman and the hermit were freezing in their sweaters and socks but they took no notice; they were safely over land and soon they would be inside warm village houses. The basket was only three or four metres above ground now, and if they had had a knife they would have been able to sever the line from the iron ball and sink gently down as the air from the balloon cooled. But they didn't have a knife and had to let the iron ball decide their next moves.

Exactly as Harald Adelstensfostre had calculated, the ball steered them towards the centre of the island and the silvery lake. That would have been fine if the lake had been covered with ice as expected, but it was not: in the centre of the mirror-bright surface there was a large jagged hole.

'Mayhap something has happened,' remarked Odin, uneasily winding his beard around his gloved fingers. 'For in all truth the lake did not look like this when I last was here.'

Ambrosius the Fisherman nodded. 'Hard to know what,' he said, coughing. 'Well, we can't do anything but wait and see what happens.'

What they saw was the iron ball, at full speed and with the balloon scudding along behind it, swooping over the shore towards the middle of the lake, where it suddenly came to a halt in midair just above the hole in the ice. Balloon and basket floated on a little further, then slackened speed and the basket rocked for a little while before stopping a short distance from the iron ball and the ice hole. Ambrosius took a firm hold on Odin. No one could know whether it would be only the iron ball that would disintegrate, whether the basket and balloon would also fall apart or even whether their own bodies would shatter into innumerable fragments, to atoms and wraiths, to become a part of the substance and origin of the universe once more.

The basket jerked violently, and the Fisherman, Harald Adelstensfostre and Odin fell to the floor. There followed a tremendous crack, or rather a sound so sharp that it seemed not to happen, and yet sent its waves through the air like a single all-embracing icy wind. Then all was still.

The first to get to his feet was Ambrosius the Fisherman. He gazed through the hole in the side of the basket; the iron ball had vanished and all that remained was only the ravelled end of the line dangling loose in the air. Everything else was untouched. The basket hung a few metres above the surface and had it not been for the hole in the ice they could easily have jumped down. As it was, that was out of the question. But they had to do something. The egg-timer had almost run out; they had a minute or two left before the air in the balloon cooled down so much that it would be unable to hold them above the water. The Fisherman looked around him. The edge of the ice was too far away for them to jump for it. And down here in the lee of the cliffs the wind was no more than a faint breeze that did not move the limp balloon but merely made it flutter slightly. At a loss, Ambrosius looked at the hermit, who shook his head. He had no suggestion to make either.

'Fortunately there is no mishap a morsel of luck cannot remedy,' said Odin, resolutely taking his horseshoe from his breast pocket. He pulled the ragged line into the basket and tied the end tightly to the horseshoe.

Ambrosius the Fisherman made a couple of attempts. Finally he succeeded and the horseshoe fell nicely in place around the trunk of a slim tree on the shore. The rest was easy enough. Harald Adelstensfostre and the Fisherman summoned all their strength and pulled the basket centimetre by centimetre closer to the tree and away from the dark gaping hole. They were a long way on to firm ice when the balloon gave up and the basket landed with a light bump. Although the ice was thick there was no knowing how long it could hold, and

Ambrosius jumped out at once, helped Odin and Harald Adelstensfostre out and hurried on to dry land. That was wise for they had barely set foot on shore when the ice broke and the balloon, basket and rope vanished below the dark water, where not long since, Ezekiel the Righteous, his father and mother, the five remaining uncles, their wives and children, with the widow of the sixth – and the two pilots – had met their eternal Sabbath.

Ambrosius the Fisherman, Harald Adelstensfostre and Odin tramped through the snow and up to the road where they stopped and looked around them. Odin vividly remembered the day he had first landed near Smith's Town. It had been cold, the ground was covered with snow and the sun shone through a slight mist, exactly as now. The children were not out skating but in the field opposite the lake were the three ponies rubbing against each other's thick coats to keep warm. In front of them, down the narrow road with its outlines blurred by snow, they could just glimpse a small huddle of kelp-thatched houses with smoke rising from the chimneys. Otherwise there was nothing to see but field after field, as far as the eye could reach. Then all at once the picture changed.

Shortly before the balloon had landed Ida-Anna and the other children had rushed back to Smith's Town to say they had discovered a gigantic hole in the ice when they went down to go skating. Now a delegation, consisting of everyone in Smith's Town apart from Oldmother Rikke-Marie – who still considered herself old enough that the world should come to her and not she to the world – were on their way down to the lake to take stock of the situation.

'Hmm, hmm,' went the Blacksmith and stopped. Behind him all the other villagers came to a halt too. 'Hmm, hmm.'

The Blacksmith cleared his throat again, trying to get a grip of the situation. He didn't quite know what he had expected, but he certainly did know he had not expected to find two strange men in stockinged feet.

The Blacksmith removed his fiercely smoking pipe and tried manfully to find the right words to open a conversation with. For although the question of stockinged feet was on the tip of his tongue he thought such a question would not only be ungracious, it could also reveal a touch of ignorance about customs and traditions elsewhere than in Smith's Town, as well, not forgetting Post Office Town, and so he was totally lost for words. Just as the silence was in danger of becoming painful and Mother Marie had begun to fidget, Odin stepped out from behind his fellow traveller.

'Hmm, hmm,' coughed the Blacksmith, surprised, and stuck his smoking pipe back in his mouth, only to take it out again at once. 'Hmm, hmm, it is Mr Odin, if I may be so bold.' The big man grabbed Odin's hand and shook it warmly. 'Welcome back, Mr Odin. What a great pleasure it is to bid you welcome for the second time to Smith's Town, not forgetting Post Office Town. And, not being ungracious, but I can't help noticing that you have brought the long-expected and sorely needed Veterinarius with you, hmm, hmm.'

Again the Blacksmith looked at the two men in stockinged feet and since Harald Adelstensfostre was nearest, the Blacksmith took his hand. 'The Veterinarius is most heartily welcome to Smith's Town.'

Then the Blacksmith turned to Ambrosius the Fisherman and was about to give him a welcoming hand as well, when he realized he had no idea how to place the third man in the picture. Because it was too much for the Blacksmith to get a grasp on all this at once, he decided to overlook the subject and with it the Fisherman until a more favourable moment for the time being. Ruminating, the Blacksmith chewed on his pipe stem, then turned back to Odin. 'Hmm, hmm, I don't want to seem ungracious, Mr Odin, as you know the folk in Smith's Town are very kind people, but for a short time we thought you were never coming back,' said he. 'Yes, as late as this very morning Oldmother Rikke-Marie asked after the good Mr Odin, and unfortunately I had to admit with regret that I had no news to give her.' Here the Blacksmith suddenly realized his words might be taken for a hidden reproach – which of course was in no way his intention – and he hastened to add: 'But now, now I am most exceedingly glad to be able to send a message immediately to Oldmother Rikke-Marie telling her of Mr Odin's happy return with the long-awaited and sorely needed Veterinarius.' The Blacksmith's chest swelled with pride over the elegant manner in which he had saved the situation, and he turned with serene aplomb to the children, standing in a circle with their ears primed to hear what the grown-ups were saying. 'Little Ingolf, run home and tell Oldmother Rikke-Marie that Mr Odin has returned.'

The Blacksmith stole a closer look at Ambrosius the Fisherman, but as he still had no idea how to raise the question of the third man without seeming ungracious, he chose to say nothing. He simply took Odin's arm and headed back to Smith's Town, indicating with a slight wave of the hand that everyone should follow, including not only all the villagers, the children and the Veterinarius, but indeed also the third and still unknown man.

When they came to the duck pond in the middle of the village the Blacksmith stopped abruptly and turned to Odin.

He cleared his throat nervously. 'Hmm, hmm, not to seem impolite but as one horseman to another... er... yes, Mr Odin, no doubt you are eager to see to your horses first and foremost?' The Blacksmith hesitated and chewed his pipe anxiously. There was something weighing on his mind but it was a job to come out with it. 'Hmm, hmm, Mr Odin not to be impolite but there is something I ought to tell you before you go into Mother Marie's stable.' Again the Blacksmith cleared his throat, but he could stall no longer. 'I fear I am obliged to tell you, Mr Odin, as one horseman to another, that your horse, yes the unfortunate mare with the broken leg and all that, well, to be precise, she has had a small accident.'

Odin pulled at his beard anxiously, but then took a firm grasp on the horseshoe sitting safely again in his breast pocket. 'Fortunately there is no mishap a morsel of luck can't remedy,' he said calmly.

The Blacksmith smiled gratefully. 'That's right, Mr Odin, it could not be better expressed.'

The Blacksmith and Odin and the Veterinarius with all the people of Smith's Town, as well as the third and still unknown man, now crammed into Mother Marie's stable. Rigmarole and Balthazar greeted Odin – as horses usually do – as if it was only yesterday they saw him last. Apart from the bandage on Rigmarole's unfortunate leg there seemed to be nothing wrong with her, and Odin breathed a sigh of relief. Then he caught sight of the accident the Blacksmith had referred to. Half hidden behind Rigmarole stood a foal that Odin had never before set eyes on. He was not yellow like his mother but a kind of misty orange, rather like the colour of the early morning sky just before sunrise.

'His name is Gry,' said Ida-Anna firmly, for as Santa Claus

had not been present then she felt she had a right to name the foal. And Santa Claus nodded too and did not make any objections, so Ida-Anna was just about to pluck up courage and whisper in his ear the wish she had not been able to voice to him the previous year.

Obviously this was not the right moment, for now the Blacksmith cleared his throat again and said, not to be impolite, that perhaps it was time that the long-awaited and sorely needed Veterinarius took a look at Mr Odin's horse's unfortunate leg. Harald Adelstensfostre pushed his way through the villagers. Although the leg was bound up with a thick bandage stretching from the hoof right up to the horse's flank, it was solidly planted on the ground and clearly bore as much weight as the other three legs.

Veterinarius Adelstensfostre patted the mare on the neck, squatted down and started to unwind the bandage. All the villagers watched the Veterinarius's hands intently, and those in front bent forward, while those at the back stood on tiptoe and strained their necks to see better. There was not a sound in the stable apart from the peaceful munching of the horses. The unrolling bandage revealed more and more of Rigmarole's yellow leg until the whole of it was visible. The villagers uttered a sigh of relief – it passed through the stable like a light breeze – there was neither scar nor other distortion to be seen. Veterinarius Adelstensfostre ran his hand down the leg bone, but there was nothing there but solid bone – no cartilaginous growth, no flaw, not the least unevenness. He straightened up and looked at Odin and behind him at the Blacksmith and all the villagers and children and Ambrosius the Fisherman, who had still not been introduced.

'As good as new,' he said briefly, then asked to see the mare moving to make sure there were no internal problems invisible to the eye or the hand.

Rigmarole trotted through the snow with her foal behind her, as if she had never come to grief. Her four sturdy legs all moved with obvious pleasure, and it was lucky there was no more to do for the horses, for at that moment little Ingolf came tearing across the yard.

'Oldmother Rikke-Marie has vanished!' he shouted breathlessly and stopped with a stumble in front of the Blacksmith. 'Oldmother Rikke-Marie has vanished. I have searched everywhere but she is nowhere to be found, not in her rocking chair, not on the red sofa and not in bed,' puffed Ingolf quite red in the face. 'Oldmother Rikke-Marie has vanished!'

'Oldmother Rikke-Marie has vanished!' echoed the villagers. 'Oldmother Rikke-Marie has vanished!'

The Blacksmith took his pipe out of his mouth, then put it back again and repeated the movement several times before saying anything. 'Hmm, hmm,' he went at last. 'Hmm, hmm. Not to be impolite, but little Ingolf, are you absolutely certain sure of what you have seen? I mean, maybe you didn't see Oldmother Rikke-Marie on account of the darkness indoors?'

Little Ingolf shook his head emphatically, but the Blacksmith still thought it best if he went and took a good look himself.

The Blacksmith and with him all the people of Smith's Town, children as well as grown-ups and Odin, Veterinarius Adelstensfostre and the third and still unknown man, now went out to search for Oldmother Rikke-Marie.

First they looked around the house where Oldmother Rikke-Marie had lived all her life and for as long as anyone could remember. They looked at the rocking chair in the kitchen, at the red sofa in the living room and in the alcove in the bedroom. When they were absolutely sure that Oldmother Rikke-Marie was not hiding anywhere in her own house they went from house to house, into all the rooms and crannies, and asked all the adults as well as the children and each other again and again whether anyone had seen Oldmother Rikke-Marie. No one had seen her since they had all left the village and gone down the road to see for themselves the strange happenings on the lake, where they had met their friend from the Continent and the long-awaited and sorely needed Veterinarius as well as the third and still unknown man. So when at length the procession had been through Uncle Joseph's barn, the Blacksmith's forge and Mother Marie's stable, the Blacksmith could no longer deny that it was time to call off the search.

'Hmm, hmm,' he went. 'Hmm, hmm. Not to be impolite, but at this moment, in the light of the course of events, we must be obliged to put an end to that which must of necessity be ended.' The Blacksmith spoke in a high ceremonial voice, and looked solemnly from face to face at the circle around him. 'I must thereby herewith declare, not to be impolite, but because it cannot be denied that Oldmother Rikke-Marie, my own most venerable mother, and hitherto the oldest living person in Smith's Town, not forgetting Post Office Town as well, has chosen to walk over the Cliff of this Life.'

The villagers looked at each other and then repeated the Blacksmith's words. 'Oldmother Rikke-Marie has chosen to walk over the Cliff of Life. Has chosen to walk over the Cliff of Life!'

The Blacksmith waited for a moment to make sure that the significance of his statement had been understood by all. Then he raised both hands in the air. 'Let us all wish Oldmother Rikke-Marie a good journey,' he cried and began to clap his hands enthusiastically. Almost at once the villagers joined in and Smith's Town rang out with such enthusiastic salvoes of clapping that they could be heard as far away as Post Office Town, and the far end of the island.

The salvoes went on for a long time, but at last, after all the villagers had developed red hands and warm cheeks from clapping, they died away slowly and almost reluctantly, and the Blacksmith was able to announce that when the people of Smith's Town, not forgetting the people of Post Office Town, celebrated Christmas that very evening, they would also celebrate Oldmother Rikke-Marie's journey to the next world.

After wishing Oldmother Rikke-Marie a good journey, all the villagers looked as if they would be quite happy to go back to their normal Christmas Eve afternoon occupations, except that Odin felt there was more to say.

'While I fully respect Oldmother Rikke-Marie's decision, in all truth it is more than sad that she should have taken it on this very day and not just one single day later,' said Odin, pulling his beard thoughtfully. 'For if she had walked to the Cliff of Life only one day later, or if I had come one day earlier, I should have been able to give Oldmother Rikke-Marie the answer to the question she asked me about Richard the Red-Blond, her very own father, before I left here.' Odin laid his hand on Ambrosius's arm. 'Yes, if she had only gone one day later, or if the air connection had been established just one day earlier, Oldmother Rikke-Marie would have met her father's own grandson, Ambrosius the Fisherman, who stands here beside me perfectly hale and hearty and in his own person.'

In his own person was true enough, but hale and hearty was a bit of an exaggeration because Ambrosius's stockinged feet had gradually frozen into such painful, stiff lumps he could hardly move. However the time was not yet ripe for Ambrosius to look after his feet. The Blacksmith had followed Odin's gesture, and as if he only then caught sight of the third and still unknown man, his expression changed from curiosity to amazement and finally he broke into a big grin. Without warning he went over to the Fisherman and flung his arms around him with such warmth that the air was almost squeezed out of the Fisherman's lungs.

'Cousin Ambrosius!' the Blacksmith cried when he at length let go of the Fisherman. 'Cousin Ambrosius,' he repeated, taking a step backwards to get a full view of the new member of his family. There was no doubt about the family likeness: the square face, the reddish-blond hair, the narrow grey-blue eyes, not to speak of the glowing pipe drooping from the corner of the Fisherman's mouth. 'Cousin Ambrosius,' the Blacksmith said again, and repeated it over and over as if he wanted to become familiar with the name of his new and quite unexpected relative this very moment, though in actual fact it was because he wanted to express that it was indeed the most natural thing in the world that Mr Odin had brought with him not only the long-expected and sorely needed Veterinarius from the Continent but also the Blacksmith's own Cousin Ambrosius.

It was already late afternoon and long past the time when the people of Smith's Town should have been at home preparing for Christmas Eve by taking their Christmas snooze. Naturally it was obvious that Cousin Ambrosius must stay at the

Blacksmith's house. It was arranged for Mr Odin and the sorely
needed Veterinarius to stay with Mother Marie, not only
because it was there Mr Odin had been a guest the first time he
came to Smith's Town, but also because Mother Marie had
taken a clear-sighted and quite thorough look at Veterinarius
Adelstensfostre and quite definitely liked what she saw.

*

In the meantime Sigbrit Holland's plan had proved a wash-out.

Shortly after she and Gunnar the Head had lost sight of
the balloon, the green and once orange fishing boat was inter-
cepted by the Coastguard. Sigbrit had been kept the whole
afternoon at the police station, where they had been more than
sceptical about her somewhat evasive explanations. Fortunately
she had *Rikke-Marie*'s papers to show them, and as the duty
officer was in festive mood and felt it would be a shame for the
harassed woman and the man with the huge head to have to
spend Christmas Eve at the station, in the end she was dis-
charged with a mild warning and no further questions. By then
it was already five o'clock, and the Queen's audience had long
since ended. Although it could only be a question of hours
before the North Norse responded to the South Norse's formal
occupation of the island and closure of the Strait by launching
a military attack, Sigbrit could do nothing else but go – or
rather sail – home to the Firø Canal.

Yet Sigbrit's worries were unfounded, for the Queen had
already made her decision – after much consideration and with
regard for her country, her subjects and her own history.

As soon as the Christmas audience had finished the Queen

retired to her private apartments, where she found a screwdriver, picked up her bundle of keys and hurried along the corridors and state apartments to the northernmost wall in the northernmost room. Making sure there was no one around she swiftly let herself into the private library. The Queen walked straight through the dusty oval room past generations of documents, books and dust, directly over to King Enevold IV's cupboard with the extra bottom in the lowest drawer. She worked at the drawer with the screwdriver until it gave way, and she hauled a bulky yellowed document out of the hiding place. She placed the extra bottom loosely in place, pushed the document into her handbag and let herself out of the library.

Back in her private apartments the Queen sent a message to Lord Chamberlain von Egernret, telling him that in no circumstances must she be disturbed, and sat down at her writing desk. Carefully she took the document from her bag, placed it on the table and smoothed it out gently. The Queen closed her eyes and sighed deeply, then picked up the telephone and dialled the direct line to the North Norse King.

The phone rang for a long time before it was answered, and then it was not the King himself but the Lord Chamberlain, and the Queen had a lengthy wait before the King himself came on the line.

'Your Majesty?' the King's voice was chilly. 'Such an honour.'

'Happy Christmas, Your Majesty,' said the Queen in a friendly tone. 'I wish you, your family and all the people of North Norseland a very Happy Christmas.'

'A Happy Christmas to you also, Your Majesty, to your family and the South Norse people,' replied the King without the slightest hint of warmth in his voice.

'It has been a difficult year for our nations,' began the

Queen. 'A particularly sad and difficult year, especially where relations between our two nations are concerned.'

'Yes,' said the King guardedly; in general he did not trust any South Norse person, and these days particularly not Her Majesty the Queen. 'It is not as easy these days to sort out conflicts between two countries as it was in the old days,' the Queen went on, quite unruffled. 'It was simpler when Kings and Queens could sign a peace treaty which they themselves agreed on rather than now when government, Parliament or the people have to be mixed up in the matter.'

'Well, yes, but in the old day Kings and Queens often signed up to war as well as peace,' remarked the North Norse King drily.

The Queen laughed and deliberately misunderstood the King's words. 'I am so glad Your Majesty does not share the hostile feelings that certain countrymen of yours seem to nourish for my countrymen,' she said mildly.

'Vice versa, vice versa,' said the King with a trace of friendliness in his voice.

The Queen was not slow to seize her chance. 'Yes, Christmas Eve ought not to be the time when only families and friends come together, but enemies too should meet and build bridges over their conflicts.' The Queen spoke as gently and winningly as she could. 'That's why I chose this very evening, this hour, to phone you, Your Majesty, to share with you my worries over the conflict between our two countries, and in particular to share my anxiety over the hostilities that have occurred, not to speak of those which, if something is not done, will be initiated in the coming days.' The Queen paused, and when the King said nothing, she went on: 'I am convinced that neither Your Majesty nor I want any armed conflict between the Kingdom of North Norseland and the Queendom of South Norseland?'

The King of the North Norse mumbled something that could be taken either as a 'yes' or a 'no', but the South Norse Queen was in no doubt which interpretation she should choose. 'I am really grateful that Your Majesty agrees with me,' she said easily. 'This island we are talking of, and to avoid any misunderstanding let us call it the island from which Mr Odin Odin came, is a small and inaccessible place and of no import whatsoever to the welfare of our two countries.'

'Ye-e-s...' the King replied cautiously, and the Queen continued.

'So it would be all the sadder if our two countries should damage not only our close mutual relations but also the welfare of everyone on account of this little island.'

'Then what exactly does Your Majesty propose?' asked the King, hiding his curiosity behind a tinge of sarcasm.

'I have a suggestion that will enable Your Majesty and myself to bring the conflict to a close immediately,' said the Queen, taking no notice of his sarcastic tone.

'As we both know,' said the King tolerantly, 'the conflict cannot be ended because our people do not wish it to end. Even if you, Your Majesty, and I myself were agreed on a solution, even if we were able to persuade both our governments to stop the fighting, it is no use, because we cannot win a referendum on the question.'

'True, very true.' The Queen tried her best not to imitate the King's arrogance. 'However, there would be no need to go as far as a referendum providing an old agreement existed between our two countries to relinquish the claim of right to the island. An agreement that had never been disallowed or annulled and therefore would still have to be considered valid.'

'Is Your Majesty telling me...' At last the King sounded genuinely interested.

'Yes, that is actually true. I have before me a document, an agreement signed on Christmas Eve of the year 1618 by King Enevold IV of South Norseland and and King Hermod Skjalm of North Norseland. And this is how the document reads:

> 'The island without a name, to be found behind high cliffs in the Strait, southwards of Ur Island, midway between North Norseland and South Norseland, shall henceforth be regarded as No Man's Land. According to this present document the island for the present day and forever after shall not reside in the possession of the South Norse nor the North Norse Crown, nor in that of any other Monarch or any other Kingdom on this Earth. Henceforth no alien shall be permitted to set foot on the Island, and in equal measure no person from the Island may set foot on another Land. It will be most strictly forbidden to name or in any manner refer to the existence of the Island in formal or informal speech. Any contravention of this law to be punished by hanging.'

The Queen finished reading, but the King said nothing. After a long silence he asked hoarsely: 'I suppose I can rely on the genuineness of this document?'

'Naturally. And I guarantee that if Your Majesty will make a careful search through his own and his forebears' private archives he will almost certainly find the duplicate of this agreement,' said the Queen sharply, but restrained herself and went on in her usual friendly tone: 'If Your Majesty's private archives are not complete, his experts are naturally welcome to come to Fredenshvile to confirm for themselves the authenticity of the version I have here before me.'

Another long silence followed, but the Queen knew she had won. 'I am certain that Your Majesty will agree with me that we should call our respective governments to an emergency meeting and advise them – with perhaps a very few adjustments to ensure that our two copies are identical – to acknowledge this agreement entered into by King Enevold IV and King Hermod Skjalm on the 24th December 1618 concerning Mr Odin's Island.'

*

Sigbrit opened the wheelhouse door and went out on deck with a bag of breadcrumbs in each hand. It was cold, there was a thick layer of ice on the planking which was slowly closing the water of the canal. It was eight o'clock and darkness had fallen hours ago. The streets were empty except for a pair of ducks warming themselves close to *Rikke-Marie*'s bow. Sigbrit threw them some crumbs, humming: 'They must know it's Christmas after all...'

She went in again. The wheelhouse was warm, the paraffin heater was screwed right up and a kettle boiled on the gas burner. Sigbrit made a pot of tea and sat down at the table, where a plate of biscuits waited. Then she picked up a book and began to read. But she couldn't concentrate. The letters seemed to dance, and she realized she had read several pages without taking them in. She sighed; it was strangely empty in the fishing boat without Ambrosius the Fisherman, Odin or Harald Adelstensfostre. Gunnar the Head was out celebrating with some friends, so she was quite alone. She found a pen and notebook and began to write a list of the things she had to do. First she would have to find a way to talk to the Queen, then deliver Odin's letters, with his photographs, and that was just the beginning. Even if the Queen and later the government could be convinced that the old agreement was still in force, it would not persuade the Pious to make peace. No, she would have to go out and talk to people, explain to them what in reality it was all about – but where would she start? One possibility was to go out in the *Rikke-Marie*, which was how most people had made contact with Odin, and then explain to people around the country who Odin really was.

Still, why should the Prophets of Doom believe her? How could she convince them that her version of events was more real than theirs? Indeed, how did she know that herself? She laughed aloud, there couldn't be any doubt about that, could there?

Suddenly the boat listed and nearly made her teacup slide over the edge of the table. Slow steps stumped across the deck and there was a light knock at the door. Sigbrit Holland's heart beat faster. She tried to see out through the window but it was too dark; she could barely make out a shadow. The light knocking sounded again, this time even fainter than before, and Sigbrit pulled open the door resolutely.

'What's happened?' she gasped.

Der Fremdling made no reply, merely collapsed at her feet. His face and clothes were covered with blood and his coat was in rags, with large pieces missing. Sigbrit bent down, lifted the old man up and helped him over to the bench beside the worn mahogany table. He had been badly beaten up. The right side of his face was one great bloody wound, his right eyelid so swollen that the eye was completely closed, his upper lip was gashed, and the whole of the right side of his coat was ripped up and stained with drying blood.

'I'll send for an ambulance straightaway,' said Sigbrit and prepared to run and find a telephone.

But Der Fremdling shook his head weakly. 'No longer any point,' he whispered with an oddly happy smile on his ruined mouth, and Sigbrit saw she must not insist. Instead she fetched a pillow from the cabin below and laid it under the old man's head. Then she cut off as much of his coat as she could without moving him, and carefully pulled off his boots. She poured a cup of tea and added a good dose of whisky and some honey, then tried with a spoon to get him to swallow some. After getting a mouthful or two into the old man, she laid a blanket over him and let him rest.

After a few minutes had passed Der Fremdling opened his eyes, or rather the left eye that could still open, and sat up. He waved away the tea which Sigbrit pushed in front of him. His face had turned blue, like that of a dead man, yet for the first time ever it seemed to Sigbrit to be alive; it was as if a hitherto unknown peace dwelt in each of his torn features.

She waited for some time, but as he did not speak, in the end she asked with a nod towards his wounds: 'Who did it?'

'I did it,' whispered Der Fremdling. The words came slowly and carefully through the split lips, but there was no doubt about the pride in the weak voice. 'They were about to get you all,' he went on.

Sigbrit suddenly recalled the explosion in the shipyard and the shout of warning that sounded just as they were moving off. 'So it was you who stopped them?'

'It was the only thing to do. Never forget,' whispered Der

Fremdling without answering her question, 'You must always act. Always.' He turned his head carefully and looked out of the window at the darkness and the street lights, then glanced around at the candles burning in the wheelhouse before meeting Sigbrit's eyes again. 'Christmas Eve!' he grimaced, with sudden vehemence. 'Christmas Eve. What does it mean? Perhaps nothing, perhaps everything. I don't know. But I stopped them.' Der Fremdling smiled again, happily.

'You are badly hurt,' said Sigbrit with concern, and began to talk of an ambulance again. But Der Fremdling interrupted her.

'At one time I didn't know,' he said, wheezing. 'It was only later I understood that one is always responsible. There is no choice.' His voice was growing weaker and weaker, yet he spoke coherently and with hardly a pause. 'You must fight for your principles, not for yourself. You must fight for the rights of others, not for your own.' A small trickle of blood ran from the right corner of Der Fremdling's mouth and down his chin.

Sigbrit rose and fetched a tissue to wipe off the blood. But Der Fremdling waved her hand away, and she sat down again.

'If you do not fight back, you are guilty,' he whispered, his voice suddenly sorrowful. 'That is what I did not realize in time.' He winced, as if he was overwhelmed by a terrible pain, though it clearly did not emanate from his bleeding wounds. When he started to speak again his voice was so weak Sigbrit had to lean forward to hear what he said. 'I was too taken up with my own survival, my family's survival, to realize there was something else, something greater. As it was, I lost everything anyway.' Der Fremdling stopped, his breath coming in painful jerks.

Sigbrit waited, and after a few minutes, as if Der Fremdling had been on a lonely journey through his memories, he went on: 'I ceased to exist on the day I gave up fighting.' Tears poured from his eyes, both the closed and open ones, and his whisper grew faster, as if he was afraid of having too little time. 'What have you got when you no longer have yourself? In the eyes of many that would not be so dreadful. After all, everyone did it. What they don't understand is that it is the very worst thing you can do.' The old man gave a suppressed cough. 'The worst crime of all. To do nothing.'

Sigbrit looked at the weeping man, but did not say anything. She knew no consolation would help him now. The thought suddenly struck her, that it was precisely this that people were afraid of: knowing that they had not done what they should have done, or knowing what they had done which they should not have done. It's that I must protect myself against, Sigbrit thought and laid a hand on her belly. That was what she must protect her child from. She was suddenly assailed by the absence of Ambrosius, and for a brief moment she regretted not having told him. But no, that is how it had to be.

Sigbrit rose and went over to the wall where she had hung up the small faded card with its crosses and circles. Her face lit up. Perhaps one day, when she had done what she had to do, when the change of the millennium was long gone and the Queendom was safely at peace again, she and Ambrosius's child could set sail to search for the fairway to the island.

When she turned back and looked over at Der Fremdling, who had lain down again and was smiling happily from his battered face, Sigbrit knew exactly what she had to do. She sat down at the table, picked up her pen and pulled the notebook towards her. Then she wrote in a firm hand in large letters at the top of the page:

The day Odin arrived in Smith's Town was a cold one...

*

In Smith's Town Christmas dinner was long since finished and the dancing in honour of Oldmother Rikke-Marie's journey to the next world was over too. The village was silent, everyone was asleep. Or almost everyone. Odin, who had expected Mother Marie's house to be wrapped in silence, crept out of bed, pulled on his boots and coat and tiptoed downstairs, through the hall and out of the door. He hurried across the yard to Mother Marie's stable.

Rigmarole and Balthazar whickered softly and scraped the straw impatiently.

'Yes, all right, all right, it's time,' mumbled the little old man, giving the horses a quick grooming with a whisk of straw. 'Mayhap I had better see about getting those ill tidings delivered, although in all truth I am still not quite sure what they are.' For a few moments Odin regarded the misty orange foal, tugging his beard thoughtfully. He shook his head. 'I'm sorry, little one, but I'll have to leave you here,' he said, patting the foal's back. 'To go on this journey you need to be full grown and have long strong legs.' He harnessed the horses and led them outside. Rigmarole snorted and threw a last glance at her son, who whinnied once and then started to play in the straw, pleased to have so much space for himself. Next, Odin fetched his sledge. But it was heavier than he remembered and he had to struggle and push until at last it was out in the yard and he could attach it to the harness.

Odin took hold of the reins and led the horses out of the village and a good way down the road on foot, before stopping them and climbing into his seat. He settled himself on the well-upholstered seat, pulled the sheepskin rug over his knees and was about to signal to the horses to start when he heard running feet behind him.

'Santa Claus! Santa Claus!' shouted Ida-Anna breathlessly. This was her last chance to tell Santa Claus her wish. 'Santa Claus!' she called again.

Odin held the horses back and before long Ida-Anna had caught up with the sleigh. The girl was puffing so much that at first she couldn't utter a word, but in the meantime Odin had recalled something he had not managed to say earlier and was eager to do so now. 'Mayhap you would be so kind, if it isn't too much trouble, to take a little message to your Mother Marie and to the Blacksmith and to Uncle Eskild and to the Baker and to all the other people of Smith's Town, not forgetting Long Laust and the other inhabitants of Post Office Town as well?'

Still out of breath, Ida-Anna nodded.

'Now look, in all truth I had brought the best presents from the Continent you can imagine,' Odin began apologetically. 'But before we reached Smith's Town the air connection was caught up in a turbulence and it was more than a little too heavy, so we were obliged to throw the presents overboard. So now I can only send my greatest and most sincere thanks to all and apologize for the presents that were lost on the way.'

Ida-Anna laughed aloud and winked at Odin. 'Ha, ha,' she laughed, for she knew quite well that Santa Claus was just teasing, because he had already given the best gifts anyone in Smith's Town as well as, not forgetting, Post Office Town, could imagine: Cousin Ambrosius for the Blacksmith and the long-awaited and sorely needed Veterinarius Adelstensfostre for her mother, as well as, not forgetting, the people of Smith's

Town as well. As for herself, Ida-Anna suddenly waved farewell to Santa Claus and whispered hastily: '*Never never shall I ever say a word to a soul. Never ever, or the serpent will gobble me whole!*' Then she turned on her heel and started to run back to the village, for she had just heard a young and lonely whinny from her mother's stable.

Odin waved farewell to Ida-Anna's back, took up the reins and clicked his tongue. Rigmarole and Balthazar shot forward, and their legs moved so fast that it looked as if each of them had eight instead of four. In just a few seconds both horses and sleigh were far down the road, then they took off from the ground and were soon far up in the sky. Odin turned the horses to the east and set his course straight for the North Star. Although he still couldn't remember what had happened before the meteor storm and Smith's Town, he did not doubt he had a long journey before him. He leaned back in his seat and made himself comfortable as he pondered over what he had forgotten.

Not long after that Odin's musings were disturbed. He jumped; something had moved close to his feet. Odin lifted up the rug, and out climbed Oldmother Rikke-Marie, as if it was the most natural thing in the world. She calmly sat down beside Odin.

'Sometimes when the world doesn't come to you, you have to go to the world,' she said with a smile that revealed her tooth-less gums.

Odin took the old lady's hand and pulled the sheepskin rug more closely around her. Off they flew, hand in hand up to the stars, and soon mile after mile lay behind them while the sky turned gradually to dawn light, and the mirror of the sun on the glistening coats of Rigmarole and Balthazar made Christmas Day lighter in the Norselands than it had ever been before.

It was just as the dawn light grew and lit up the path across the heavens in front of them that Odin suddenly saw something glittering on the horizon. Not one, but two, not stars, but something even more radiant. The sleigh drew nearer the two sparkling points at great speed, and Odin could soon make out what they were. And suddenly he remembered everything.

'Come, my ravens dear,' he exclaimed. 'My spirit greens, my senses clear. Thought and Memory, welcome here!'